Ron McMillan is an author and photojournalist who has been travelling since 1979. His first experience of Korea was as a part time teacher of English and full time student of Tae Kwon-do in Seoul in the mid-1980s. He began his career as a freelance writer and photographer during the run up to the 1988 Seoul Olympics.

During a decade based in Hongkong, he travelled everywhere from Afghanistan to Japan on assignment for magazines in Asia, North America and Europe, visited Mainland China nearly fifty times and made five 'tourist' visits to isolated North Korea. As well as appearing in *Time*, *Newsweek*, *L'Express* and the *New York Times Sunday Magazine*, his North Korea photographs seemingly made him quite unpopular in the Hermit Kingdom.

On his return to Scotland in 1998, Ron took on a domestic travel column for *The Herald* and wrote and photographed travel and business stories for magazines including the inflight titles of Cathay Pacific Airways, Korean Air, Thai Airways and Japan Airlines. In the Autumn of 2005, he spent five weeks in Shetland researching the first travel narrative to be written about the islands since 1869. *BETWEEN WEATHERS – Travels in 21st Century Shetland* was published in 2008 by Sandstone Press, and nominated for the 2008 Saltire Society Literary Awards.

Ron spends part of the year in Bangkok, Thailand, where a vibrant live music scene allows him to indulge his passion for playing blues harmonica rather badly.

Praise for Ron McMillan's BETWEEN WEATHERS: Travels in 21st Century Shetland

Above all, however, this is a book about people. Ron McMillan looks at Shetlanders with a sharp but affectionate eye and his style has a wit which makes reading this book a pleasure. *Aly Bain in his foreword*

There is little to find fault with in this book – apart from one or two minor editorial errors and oversights. One is almost led to believe that Ron McMillan's own personality might guarantee that he would feel welcome in Shetland (or anywhere else). Nevertheless "Between Weathers" is a well written, entertaining and informative book that will tempt readers to visit if they haven't already. Those who have, and those who reside in Shetland, will find much to enjoy – and learn besides. *Shetland News*

Ron McMillan's meticulously researched writing has a highly developed narrative style and the easy good humour often seen in the work of fellow travel writers Bill Bryson and Pete McCarthy. *The New Shetland*

A fabulous, readable book from a relaxed and entertaining writer. Full of information, witty insight and a real love of these wonderful islands, it's a must for visitors to the Shetlands and for those who want to travel there in their imaginations. *Bobbie Darbyshire (author)*

YIN YANG TATTOO

Ron McMillan

SANDSTONEPRESS
HIGHLAND | SCOTLAND

First published in Great Britain 2010
Sandstone Press Ltd
PO Box 5725
One High Street
Dingwall
Ross-shire
IV15 9WJ
Scotland

www.sandstonepress.com

Editor: Robert Davidson

The publisher acknowledges subsidy from the Scottish Arts Council
towards publication of this volume.

ISBN-13: 978-1-905207-31-2
ISBN-epub: 978-1-905207-53-4

Typeset in Linotype Sabon by Iolaire Typesetting, Newtonmore.
Printed and bound by J F Print, Yeovil, Somerset

Acknowledgements

This book has been a long time in the making. In its earliest incarnation the manuscript was constructively critiqued by members of the Paisley Writers' Group, led then by novelist and Writer-in-Residence Ajay Close. My thanks go out to the whole Group.

Advice was sought and received from many friends, home and abroad. Fellow Korea-hand Mark McTague in Baltimore, USA, provided endless encouragement, advice and input right up to the final detailed proof-read, a task also kindly undertaken by Jay Kennedy in Glasgow. Welcome commentary and counsel came from David Kosofsky in New Orleans, Charles Martin in Seattle, Roberto de Vido in Yokosuka, Japan, Anton Fielden and Iain Millar in London, England, and Dennie Tunnicliffe in Fife, Scotland. In Seoul, Michael Breen did voluntary research and fact-checking, and Douglas McTague tramped Korea's capital in the depths of mid-winter with his video camera. Another friend from my Korea days, Jim Gardner, coached me on Global Depository Receipts and the Due Diligence process. Thank you all.

Cover design input from Chris Winstanley in Auckland, New Zealand, was executed beautifully by Latte Goldstein of River Design in Edinburgh.

NOTE: This is a work of fiction from beginning to end. With obvious exceptions, characters and companies in the story neither exist, nor are based upon real ones. Where settings do exist, fictional liberties have been taken with their locations and layouts; likewise their clientele and staff are completely the product of my imagination. The K-N Group is *entirely* fictional, and is in no way whatsoever based upon any company in Korea or elsewhere, past or present.

LINGUISTIC PURISTS BEWARE: There are competing schools of thought on the Romanisation of Korean speech. I never came across one that satisfied my own views on the accurate phonetic reproduction of spoken Korean, so I took the easy route: I made up my own. Any linguistic, grammatical and factual errors are of my own making.

I welcome feedback and/or enquiries:

yinyangtattoo@live.com   www.ronmcmillan.com

Ron McMillan
Bangkok, Thailand
May 2010

This book is dedicated to Ae Shim and Shona.

Prologue

Part One: Seoul, Korea 1990

Pushing midnight and the Hill is the usual weekend war zone, music bleeding from club doorways held open by battered beer crates. Hank Williams, Wham!, AC/DC – and Stevie Wonder, who just called to say *I love you*. The street runs high on alcohol and the pressurised din of the clubs. Bar girls screech welcomes to regulars and brassy whores yell sales pitches in shameless, broken English. Syntax doesn't count for much when you are touting *'ten dalla'* blowjobs.

Darkness turns the Itaewon shopping district into a neon-tinged labyrinth of nightclubs and restaurants and bars and brothels that feed the elemental needs of thousands of American soldiers, civilians and spooks from Yongsan Military Base. None of whom I belong among, but in Itaewon at this time of night, I feel *alive*.

Polarised by race, clusters of frighteningly fit GIs cut shrapnel tracks through the throng, intent on bar or club or short-time cathouse.

Four red-eyed white boys tumble from an army base Chevrolet taxi. The tall GI from the front seat calls out for contributions towards the fare while his friends laugh and skip out of range. He pays the Korean driver, shoves his wallet into the back pocket of his Levis and raises his arms in mock ire, just as his long step is broken by a jarring collision with a small dark-haired figure.

1

'Man, why dontcha watch where – ' He swallows his anger as the little Korean with the withered leg and the tortured eyes backs away, one hand high in supplication, the other hanging low behind him. The GI shakes his head and calls out to his buddies, already climbing the steps to the King Club. 'Dyoo see that crazy gook motherfucker?'

I take a swallow of beer. 'Crazy gook just motherfucked up his night.'

'Yep,' says Bobby, 'the little guy's got balls.'

We watch him shuffle in the direction of the main drag. A familiar sight in Itaewon, he won't be on the street again tonight. For sure there is pain in those eyes, but not of any kind that the big GI would understand, and the brain behind them knows not to be around when the American discovers he no longer owns a wallet.

I nudge Bobby with one elbow, pointing with my chin. 'Cavalry's here.'

He looks at me as if I have lost my marbles, I feign indifference, and he sneaks a streetward glance. Fanned out in a line are six more soldier boys in full cavalry uniform, black felt hats clasped gently to the fronts of starched shirts in the manner of the parading Orangeman and his bowler. One of the troupe solemnly aims a white-gloved hand towards the pharmacy at the corner of the Hill. Hooker Hill is busy enough even at this time of night to support its own drug store, and as four cavalrymen join an orderly line, the other two stand easy.

I am halfway there before Bobby can put his beer down. I try to melt into the surroundings while fumbling to check the light and fit a portrait lens. Bobby sidles past, and as he strikes up a conversation with one of the cavalry, I shoot frames sparingly, salivating at the aroma from mobile food stalls that every night roll into place just as darkness falls. Edging around, I can tie the stalls into the frame. Incongruous background, delightfully confusing context, and right now it smells like heaven. Deep-fried tempura vegetables. Chestnuts roasted in a hand-spun drum of shiny black stones. Ramyun noodles with processed cheese and pungent kimchi, the staple preserved cabbage Koreans eat with everything. Pig trotters served whole on Agent Orange melamine plates. Sliced fatty pork and marinated beef cuts broiled with whole garlic cloves in shallow pans over fiery coal briquettes, and dipped in a paste of sesame oil and coarse salt grains.

On a ragged line of wooden stools sit mostly young Korean women, stuffing food into brightly-painted faces. A distracting mix of whores, waitresses and young middle-class things on the run from the rigid mainstream of Seoul society.

'We're the 7th Cavalry, man,' says the guy with the buzzcut so short I can outline the bone structure of his small head with its selection of faded scars. Evidence perhaps of a rural childhood spent tumbling from tractors and trees. 'The 7th's got history, we was once the mounted Cavalry, and go back all the way to General Custer and the Battle of the Little Bighorn – 'cept now we're a tank regiment.'

'No shit,' says Bobby, straight-faced, 'Little Big Horn, eh?'

I switch to wide-angle, and move in closer.

'Damn right. And the word is them limpdicks from Osan Air Base, goddamn chopper jockeys, they're sayin they're gonna kick some 7th ass. 'Can you believe that shit?'

'Woah,' I say. 'No way the 7th takes that from anybody.'

'Damn right. Those assholes show their faces on the Hill tonight, they're fuckin' dead meat. R'you from England?'

I nod. Close enough. A cavalryman from Potatochip, Idaho, won't be too interested in my views on Scottish nationalism.

'What's with the camera?'

I give him the friendly, can't-harm-you look. 'Just something I do. No offence, soldier.'

3

'None taken, Sir.'

Sir. He calls me *Sir*.

'Anyway, man,' says Bobby, quickly. 'Protect that heritage, right?'

We leave the cavalryman picking lint from his hat and head uphill towards the Cowboy Club.

'Got to piss,' says Bobby.

'I'll see you in there.'

I sit back on the ledge of a shop window full of baseball caps bearing trademark-infringing replica emblems of just about every American professional sports team I never heard of. A Korean beauty floats past in a cloud of perfume. She is in her mid-twenties, expensively-dressed in shiny black satin, unrestrained nipples drawing rapid, eccentric circles in the gleaming fabric of her sleeveless top. Hair in fashionable corkscrews pulled back in a thick haft, streamer-like tendrils tumbling from her temples. I spotted her in the food alley a few minutes before, slurping noisily at a steaming bowl of noodles.

She is headed for the Cowboy Club.

I judge my run to perfection so that I am just in time to pull the door wide, step back, and bow deeply like a nightclub doorman.

'Oh-so-u'ship-shi-yoh,' I say. *Welcome*. Very formal.

'Koh-muh we-yo,' she says, a familiar, almost insolent *'Thanks'*. With a smiling backward glance she enters the crowded club, where the bass-heavy sound system shakes the entire room, empty glasses shimmying condensation trails across beer-splashed table-tops. B.B. King belting out a slow croon version of the Ivory Joe Hunter classic, *Since I Met You Baby*.

Plenty of Korean women come to Itaewon for a night out, but seldom alone. I don't make her for a whore or a bargirl, so maybe she is here to meet some lucky bastard.

The Cowboy is a ramshackle hovel, one of the few low-rise hold-outs yet to be razed and replaced with multi-storey buildings coated in pink tiles. Its long history is written in multiple extensions, walls covered here in split log, there in dark green Formica sheets. Tables are of battered pine, chairs of rust-blistered chrome with herniated foam spilling from faded red fabric.

The crowd is the norm for Itaewon, half Korean women, half Western men. Few blacks, but that's more to do with the music than anything else, since this is not their scene. The Sunshine Club, only yards down a nearby alley, is almost exclusively black, jammed with loose-limbed giants wearing David Bowie suits and jewelled earrings that have to disappear before they return to Base.

As usual in Itaewon, the Cowboy Club has no Korean men – and nobody complaining about it. Put them in a situation where alcohol flows and their women don't toe the local line, and the only possible outcome is trouble. It's a cultural thing.

A small central floor is peppered with couples dragging their feet to the slow blues number. A crowd hovers nearby, impatient for something more up-tempo.

I look over to the DJ's booth, where Myong-hee sits hemmed in by three walls of tattered LP sleeves and CD cases, a huge selection of albums filed alphabetically and tended with loving care. At the counter in front of her, Bobby is flicking through the dog-eared school notepad that is the handwritten list of available albums. I catch his eye and he fires me a self-conscious wink. He has been trying to get into Myong-hee's knickers for months. He and half the Western population of Seoul.

I know that the B.B. King track is on vinyl when it jumps and squeals in pain. This happens often in the Cowboy, since the turntables are only a few feet from a misshapen toilet door whose every judder sends the needle skating across the long-playing record. It is the bane of Myong-hee's professional life, but she smoothly switches decks and we get the opening bars of The B52s' 'Rock Lobster', surely

5

a request of Bobby's; I see him smiling at her. The new track brings the crowd to life and the dance floor to heaving over-capacity, faces sparkling in tiny squares of light from a battered, old-fashioned ball of mirrors.

Miss Black Satin is now near the tall bar, still alone. She turns and casually scans the crowd, her gaze faltering as it passes over me. Promising.

My linguistic skills are near-exhausted, but I'm not about to give up on them just yet.

'An-yong hassimnika,' I bow again. 'Ne irrum-un, Alec imnida.' *Hello. My name is Alec.* Very polite.

Without a word she accepts my outstretched hand. Her grip is warm and confident, her long nails painted a lustrous charcoal grey. I try not to stare, and fail miserably.

She doesn't tell me her name, and I pretend not to notice.

'Mo joo-shi ley-oh?' I wish for *Would you like a little something from the bar*? but have to make do with a quite abrupt *What do you want*? At least it raises a hint of a smile.

'Gin-tonic, juseyo.'

At the bar I order from Miss Hwang, who looks over my shoulder and gives me a subtle smile of approval. The staff at the Cowboy are very protective of their regulars, and Miss Hwang sees no threat from the lady in black.

I hand the gin and tonic to the one with no name, and she tips her head in silent thanks. I'm playing tennis with an opponent who has no racquet, but still the bloody ball keeps coming back at me.

'Irrum-i moueyo?' *What's your name?* At least I might score marks for persistence.

Her eyes crease, and she reaches into a tiny beaded bag for a packet of *Sol* cigarettes. In a society with old-fashioned ideas about chivalry you never know when a light can come in handy, so I am in there before she finds her own lighter. In the glare of ultra-violet strip lights her dark red lipstick turns the shining black of the heroines of early talkies. Her nose has the perfection of line that comes only

6

from the cosmetic surgeon's scalpel, but the eyes are her own, elongated tear-drops rimmed with heavy black liner. She draws hard on the cigarette which, tugging at her lower lip, comes away crimped with dark red semi-circles. She stretches her head back and blows a stream of smoke straight up towards big fans that circle lazily in the toxic fog. Around her slender neck is a single fine gold chain. I am desperately trying to think of something clever to say when she leans towards me, a draught of sweet perfume cutting through the foul smoke from her *Sol*.

'It's a pleasure to meet you, Alec. You may call me Miss Kim.'

In English.

I can't hide my surprise. She tosses back her head and laughs aloud, and gleaming white teeth, a little uneven, reflect on shiny-black lips.

Part Two: A police station in central Seoul, fifteen years later.

I would be in trouble if I had to use these two goons to disprove the cliché that Orientals all look the same. Their hairlines and high cheekbones and square bony jowls are sawn from the same jig, and I can only tell them apart because one of them stands six inches taller. Big Cop exchanges nods with Small Cop. Here we go.

I back away until my arse runs hard against a table that holds the middle of the room. It doesn't move, and I glance down. The table and four chairs are bolted to the floor. The room is formed of painted metal and dusty concrete, with one tiny barred window, nearer ceiling than floor, drawing a hard-edged beam of sunshine alive with dust particles. Cobweb-strewn strip lights glare from behind paint-blistered gratings.

Big Cop moves. I retreat, like a boxer feeling for the ropes, except I am feeling for a rough wall with hands

7

cuffed in the small of my back. Big Cop lurches and I lift one shoulder and duck, but it is too little too late. Meaty hands flash high – and somewhere behind my eyes a bomb goes off. Searing pain sets tears rolling down my cheeks, and I spin and rebound off the wall. Big Cop's hands remain high, and I understand why my head is full of jet-engine roaring and my balance is in shreds. He does it again. Cupped hands slam over unprotected ears, trapped air fires white-hot pain through eardrums, legs dissolve and I crash to the floor. I don't bother trying to get up.

Eager hands clamp onto my wrists to pull them high behind me, and I scramble to my feet, shoulders on the verge of dislocation, head forced forward and so low that, through my legs, I can see Big Cop grin. Wrists flop free, my head pops up, a closed fist hooks deep into the pit of my stomach – and I am back on the floor.

Face down on the concrete, I make out the scrape of footsteps, and brace myself. Somebody unfastens one cuff and grabs my wrist in a brutally simple martial arts hold. Every muscle and nerve from thumb to shoulder screams in agony, and I join the chorus. The cries still echo around the room when the cuffs are locked again, this time in front of me, through the back of a chair. A rough shove sits me down facing the wrong way, the back legs of the chair between my knees. The door to the corridor clatters open and a uniformed officer arrives carrying thin telephone books under one arm.

The blows to my ears and solar plexus have me in tears, but I am almost certainly unmarked. The phone books can only mean more of the same.

I try to stand, but they push me down. From his pocket, Small Cop pulls long strips of double-sided Velcro. I use the stuff to rig heavy lighting equipment. It's cheap, versatile, and with enough of it, you could stick a Catholic to a Belfast Protestant. In a few seconds, my ankles are pinched painfully against the angle-iron chair legs. Small Cop tries to stand tall next to Big Cop and on cue, each rolls his telephone book in a two-handed tennis grip.

They take turns at driving them into my kidneys. The first strikes blow the wind from my lungs, cutting short my screams, and they continue with such regularity that regaining my breath is impossible, lungs receding in protection of aching organs. Spasms twist my insides and shoot down my legs, opening me up to bouts of head-spinning nausea. Before long the contents of my stomach spew over my arms. The bastards never miss a swing.

It lasts maybe a few minutes, but feels like hours, and in the end, the signal to cease only comes when my guts let go in a rasping gastric splutter.

'Aigoo,' says a voice leaden with disgust. 'Dong neo-seo.' *He's shit himself.*

Shoe heels clack on concrete, and the door to the corridor slams closed. Pain jags spark through me like short-circuits, and my legs flap uncontrollably against the restraints. Minutes later, the tremors recede enough for me to gingerly open one eye to confirm that I am alone. Vision bubbles and my head spins and my stomach convulses in a fresh onslaught of brain-swelling dry retches.

I am in a police station, thousands of miles from home. Nobody knows I am here, and the cops are holding nothing back. Bad enough, but it gets worse. They have yet to ask me even one question.

Chapter One

Nine days earlier. Islington, London, 2005.

Thursday morning, and already the day had 'brass-enamelled bastard' written all over it. Hardly in the door, I was stirring my first cup of mud when the phone rang. Naz reached for it without looking.

'Alec Brodie Photography. Hi Gerry, Al's right here. I'll put you through.' She hit the hold button and waited for me to open my eyes. 'Gerry says *'Don't even consider dicking me around, Naz, I want to speak to Brodie, and I mean right now.'* For a Brummie of Pakistani origins, she did a mean Cockney.

'So much for filtering my calls.'

'You'll have to talk to him sooner or later.'

'I'd sooner it was later.'

I snatched up the nearest phone, punched the flashing button and spoke quickly.

'Gerry, I'm glad you called, 'cos I was wanting to talk to you.'

'Oh that's good. *Real* good. You were wanting to talk to *me*. I'm calling you like three, four times a day, Naz is telling me you're out of the studio, you're in a meeting, you're on a big shoot, you're in a fucking helicopter all day long and, no, your mobile ain't switched on, and it's like *impossible* to reach you right now – and do you call me back? Do you hell. Stop messing me about. You know Johnson doesn't like me lending money to *his* clients.'

'It's just cash-flow, a temporary thing. I'm the little guy here, waiting for bean counters to approve expenses I laid out months ago, and anyway – '

'Expenses like your lab bill that's overdue by ten weeks?'

When Gerry gets like this there's no placating him, but photographers like me pay for his pension plan, and he knows it. In the new digital age there aren't many of us still shooting film, and labs like Johnson's need guys like me.

'Have I ever let you down? Tell Johnson he'll get his bloody money, and while you're at it, tell him if he doesn't need me putting three hundred rolls a month through his machines I'll go elsewhere.'

'One: you forget I know that even you, you fucking luddite, are moving to digital. Two: we both know the last time you did three hundred rolls in a month, Maggie Thatcher was still winning hearts and minds. And, Three: where are you going to take your business? Angel?'

Bluff called.

'Gerry – '

'Cos Archie Angel tells me he cut your credit line a month ago, and that you're into him for nearly a grand. Which, *Alec*, on top of the fourteen hundred you owe us, isn't sounding too fucking smart.'

A decade as a freelance photographer has taught me one thing: when your back is to the wall all you can do is lie.

'I swear I was reaching for the phone when you rang. I just opened the post, and there's a serious wedge of a cheque in there' – Naz rolled her eyes. '- You've always done the right thing by me, so if I was to settle the account this week, would Archie Angel have to know?'

Silence. Gerry smelled money getting to him before it got to Archie Angel. I pressed on, holding up my coffee mug, playing to my unimpressed audience of one. 'So listen, this cheque is from,' I squinted at the mug, which said 'Sam's

Pies – Meet the Meat, First Bite'. 'Some bloody bank in Liechtenstein, so give me a few days for it to clear, and I'll messenger your cheque right over, this time next week.'

'If you're shitting me, Johnson's going to have my nuts, then he'll have yours. Remember what happened to Conkers Russell.'

I remembered alright. When Conkers defaulted on his JB account, Johnson made a few calls, and overnight the only way suppliers would touch Russell was Cash On Delivery, a death sentence in our line of work. In a couple of months Conkers went from running one of the busiest fashion studios in the West End and driving a Jaguar convertible, to running around the city on a moped, shooting building exteriors for real estate agents.

I put the phone down and grimaced at my cold coffee. Naz stared at me, her face blank of expression.

'Something'll come up. People owe us money too, remember.'

She shook her head in silence as she filled the kettle. Even if every last penny owed to the studio was honoured – *fat chance* – it would hardly put a dent in my debts.

Loud banging at the studio door. I held a finger to my lips and pointed to my coffee mug. Naz quietly rinsed it and turned it upside down on the draining board. Not operating the sort of business that generated anything in the way of passing trade, we kept the windowless studio door on the snib. I approached it from the side, well away from the central peephole, and squinted through a second peeper that emerged on the other side amidst a confusion of Kodak and Fuji stickers. Just at that moment, the door rocked to a solid shove, and I pulled back, too late. Stop the day – I want to get off. Not yet ten o'clock, creditors lining up for a kick at me, and now I had a bloody nose. I shuffled back, dabbing at my beak with a tissue that materialised in Naz's hand. From outside came bellowing noises that were all too familiar. Billy Singh was only a little guy, but when a tenant got behind with the rent, he puffed up like a frog and generated a din that belied his stature. London-born and bred, Billy had a local accent as thick as his beard. I placed my hands on Naz's shoulders and leaned down to whisper in her ear.

'Talk to him, Naz. Tell him I'm out of town, the cheque's in the post, whatever.'

For the thousandth time I resolved to make it up to Naz – just as soon as I got my shit together. I backed quietly through the walk-in pantry door and peeked through the crack in the jamb.

Naz is a picture. She loves to be photographed, and we've spent countless hours in the studio, just the two of us, working on my lighting and her latest portrait notion. I have shot Naz in everything from Laura Ashley floral print to mud-caked rugby jerseys to barbed wire handcuffs and not a lot else.

Her Dad came to England from Pakistan in the sixties, but the last time she saw her family was ten years ago when she refused to marry a Rawalpindi haulage contractor whom she had never set eyes upon, but who came highly recommended by a Pakistani marriage broker. We had been running the studio together ever since she answered my ad in a newsagent's window for a part-time assistant, secretarial skills an advantage. That was eight years ago.

She opened the door and listened to Billy's pained entreaties, fed him calming lines, multiple soothing apologies and solemn, empty promises. If we moved from this studio, getting another lease would be impossible without a good reference from Billy's boss. Naz knew that, and skilfully avoided confrontation without giving anything away. When at last he left, still grumbling, Naz locked the door behind him.

'All we need now,' she said, as I edged from the pantry, 'is a visit from Cassie.'

That hurt, but I deserved it. Whatever way you looked at it, this was all linked, one way or another, to Cassie.

A couple of years ago Naz and I were running a busy little commercial studio, servicing steady custom that I had built up over the years since I came back from Asia. The work was varied enough, and while I never saw my name on posh gallery posters, I did assignments for big-name companies and good magazines in New York, London and Paris, and usually had no trouble meeting the rent.

When a producer called Cassie plucked my portfolio from a Soho art director's desk, I found myself with a big-budget shoot for her new High Street client.

It was the sort of fashion job they threw serious money at, mock-photojournalism in grainy monochrome, ultra-high-contrast prints with bleached whites and fathomless shadows. In the grossly self-important world of couture, this was an advertising look very much in vogue, fashion victims as war refugees in thousand-quid outfits and perfect hair and make-up. The clients were so delighted that they only took four months to pay. Cassie promised more assignments just like it, and she delivered. Soon we were living together in a big new apartment. I was a soft target, an easy sell, in love with the new work and so deeply in lust with Cassie that it was much later before I even began to worry about her taste for smack.

It was Cassie who pushed for the bigger studio, dismissing Naz's doubts, arguing that the new work it could handle would easily justify the extra cost which, for a few months at least, it did. Overheads were way up, but so were assignments that paid silly money.

Not much later, Cassie's dragon-chasing slipped the leash and overnight she became yesterday's product. Work slowed to a trickle and the bills mounted, but Cassie still had a habit to feed. She forged my scrawl on cash cheques, maxed out the shared credit card and – this really hurt – offloaded almost my entire kit of beloved Leica range-finders for a fifth of its value. When I finally moved on – alright, she dumped me for a 22-year-old with a huge trust fund and a horse habit to rival her own – I was in a debt pit that I had yet to see the bottom of.

Naz washed out her own coffee cup and took to filing slides. It was either that or talk to me. I pulled out my address book and name card file and started calling around old commercial clients and advertising and design agencies. 'Hi, it's Alec Brodie – Alec Brodie Photography, I did that shoot for you the other month? I would like to pop over and show you some of my latest work.'

Successful commercial photography has depressingly little to do with talent and a great deal to do with shameless self-promotion. Almost every shooter can do the job, but how well he does it usually matters more to the photographer than it does to the client. With nothing but familiarity separating you from the rest of the competition, the trick is to maintain your name's prominence in the thoughts of customers, actual and potential.

Two unproductive hours later I pushed the phone away, leaned back in my chair and tried to think of what to do next, anything that might keep Naz from pointing out where I was going wrong. The phone rang and this time I beat her to it.

'Hello?'

'May I speak to Mr Alec Brodie please?' In his accent it came out as 'Boorow-dee'.

I didn't know the voice, but I recognised the accent straight away.

'Alec Brodie speaking, Mr – ?'

'My name is Rhee, Y.S. Rhee. I am sorry for my English, but – '

'Don't be sorry Mr Rhee, your English is absolutely fine.' Naz looked at me, curious.

'Mr Brodie, I am the U.K. Country Manager of the K-N Group. Are you familiar with my company?'

'I am, Mr Rhee. Just last year I photographed your President Mr Chang at the new plant in Wales for Global Trade magazine's cover story on K-N's semiconductor operations.'

'The reason I am calling is I received a message from Seoul asking me to contact you about a photography assignment in Korea. President Mr Chang very much appreciated your sincere hard work on the Global Trade Magazine story.'

When a Korean compliments your sincerity *and* your work rate, you *know* you've got something he wants. Tucking the phone between ear and shoulder, I gave Naz a big thumbs-up. She squinted cautiously.

'Can I ask what kind of assignment you had in mind?'

'My company is presenting a major stock market issue and we need photography for brochures and prospectuses.'

I did a silent scream of joy. Commercial photography for companies commands a much higher day-rate than editorial work for magazines. I gave Naz an exaggerated wink, but she somehow avoided falling out of her seat with excitement.

'I see, *commercial* photography. Do you have an idea how many days of shooting might be required?'

'The fax from my headquarters indicates three weeks of photography, some in Seoul and some in other Korean cities.'

Naz at last came around to listen in. I scribbled '3 WEEKS!' on the pad next to the phone. She gave me the rolling hand motion for 'get on with it'.

'Mr Rhee, are you familiar with my commercial photography rate? I charge two thousand pounds a day.' This brought a slow-motion forehead slap from Naz. Was I out of my mind? At my end of the market twelve hundred was perfectly acceptable, and I often settled for less. However I also knew that Koreans firmly believed in the link between the price of a service and its quality.

'I see.'

I see? What did that mean?

'Will you have to ask your head office if that is acceptable?'

'No, I am sorry.'

I was about to throw the phone down in despair when he spoke again:

'I mean your rate is acceptable. No problem.'

Naz and I slipped down the fire escape and, taking a chance on one of the credit cards, celebrated with a long beery lunch of ribs and kimchi at the Seoul Palace.

Chapter Two

The next couple of days felt like I was juggling chainsaws soapy-handed.

Still drunk on beer and hot chillies, I got back on the phone to Mr Rhee, who agreed to meet for a meal the next day. Korean food two days running was fine by me. I was in training.

I asked an Anglo-Korean waitress with a face full of piercings to watch out for Rhee, and she showed him to my table. He was a heavy set guy with greying hair and a handshake that was like having a bus parked on my knuckles.

'Nice to meet you, Mr Brodie.'

'My pleasure, Mr Rhee.' He sat across from me and we talked about everything but the assignment until first the drinks and then the side dishes began to arrive. I picked my moment.

'May I ask if you managed to discuss my request with Seoul?'

'Request?'

'For an expenses advance. On an assignment like this, my costs are very heavy.'

'In my company such a request is a little difficult.'

No advance, and I wouldn't even get out of London. Rhee was still talking:

'So I did not ask Seoul about this.'

Tell me this job isn't slipping through my fingers even before the main course arrives.

Rhee reached into his pocket and brought out an envelope.

'But I managed this, from my office funds.'

'I hope it's not too much trouble for you,' I lied.

'Not at all,' he lied back.

I signed the receipt for five thousand pounds. I could use more but the line about beggars and choosers sprang to mind, and this meant the difference between being able to take the assignment and staying in London to face my creditors.

'There is another matter my managers in Seoul asked me to discuss with you.' He spoke unselfconsciously through a mouthful of kimchi. 'They tell me that you have taken many photographs of North Korea.'

'That is correct.'

He looked unsure of how to proceed.

'I cannot discuss the exact details of my company's plans, but they are connected with North Korea. The prospectuses we are preparing need good photographs from there.'

Stock photographs of the Hermit Kingdom. I sold them all the time, even to South Korean publications.

'You know that photographers sell stock photographs in this way?'

'Of course. My headquarters asked that you discuss the fees with them when you are in Seoul.'

I liked the sound of that. The more they used, the more money I made. We agreed that I would scan a couple of hundred slides of North Korean cities, infrastructure and what little I had of its industry, and that a messenger from Rhee's office would pick the DVD up the next day for immediate air-freight to Seoul.

As we ate our way through a mountain of spicy food, I tried to learn more about the assignment, but every time I broached the subject, Rhee changed it. He may have been their Country Manager, but today Rhee was a messenger at Seoul's bidding, and if Head Office chose to keep him in the dark, the loss of face involved in me knowing so was something he would want to avoid. I gave up on the questions and concentrated on the food.

At the end of the meal, we played the old sincerity game where I pretended to want to pay, but no matter how hard I pushed, Rhee resisted resolutely, which was just as well. Dipping into the envelope he had just given me would not have made a good impression.

Over the next couple of days I spread Rhee's cash around very carefully. I settled the bill with Gerry at the lab and paid part of my debt to Archie Angel, loose-mouthed git that he was; a thousand went to Naz towards wages owed and petty cash, and a token donation was paid to VISA to keep the plastic life raft afloat. The studio rent would have to wait until Rhee's bosses in Seoul came up with a proper advance that I could wire to Naz. With American Express assuming the worries of my air ticket – I refuse to concern myself over bills that have yet to arrive – I would turn up on the other side of the world with credit cards groaning, and next to no cash. I kept telling myself I would be earning by then. Earning serious money.

Checking in a mountain of luggage creates its own headaches, but the generous Business Class allowance saw off much of the excess baggage bill and the rest of the potential damage died in the face of a calm declaration that of course the heaviest of my stand bags was a set of golf clubs.

Airlines can afford to treat Economy class passengers like second-class citizens, but they fall over themselves to keep businessmen's bums out of the competition's club-class seats. With a Business class ticket, golf bags fly free if you insist, and I insisted. I may only be an average photographer, but when it comes to lying to people in uniform, I *know* I am world-class.

I was flying Korean Air because to my hosts, ardent patriots to the last, my arrival on the national flag carrier could only generate points in my favour. In Asia, little things go a long way towards setting things off on the right foot.

There was another reason for flying Korean Air. Like mobile foreign embassies, airliners are patches of mother soil arranged in an ever-moving diaspora, never mind that the livery and the fittings all hail from Seattle. The moment I stepped aboard that Korean Air jet at Heathrow I was already in a little fragment of Korea, and that was fine by me.

I settled into my upper deck lounge bed of a seat. I had done it, mission accomplished, and I was buckled up and Seoul-bound. *Pre-flight orange juice or champagne, Sir*? Just leave the bottle, will you. The champagne bottle.

The public address system burbled with the soft tones of the Captain welcoming everyone aboard, wishing us all a pleasant flight, and taking a moment to remind us to switch off all mobile phones before the aircraft left the terminal. My hand reached instinctively towards my pocket, but stopped half-way as my mind's eye drew an instant picture of my mobile exactly where I had left it, plugged into the charger at home.

Right now the only other cloud on my horizon hung over the seat next to me, enough perfume to wrinkle noses downstairs in Economy. I have a theory that the power of a woman's scent is directly proportionate to her ugliness and here was a case in point. She was an ageing Filipina, hair of the monotone dulled black that comes only from a bottle, heavily-painted face pulled surgically taut across razor cheekbones, a reptilian neck ringed by oversized pearls.

At least she was on the window side, as I was in the aisle seat that I had been so careful to reserve. Window seats are fine for tourists, but the frequent flier knows an aisle seat is all about freedom. Freedom to walk off the threat of deep-vein thrombosis, freedom to have drinks and whatever delivered as you like, freedom to hit on the stewardesses in their tight primary-coloured dresses and immaculate make-up, lustrous black hair pulled back in pony tails that accentuated almond eyes and broad, honest foreheads.

Once we reached cruising altitude I gave Miss Lee the flight attendant my warmest smile and, speaking Korean, asked for a Bloody Mary, a double in a tall glass, plenty of pepper and Worcester and three big drops of Tabasco. Two minutes later, with the drink and a bowl of smoked almonds in front of me, I ran through some mental check-lists. I had every intention of drinking far too much during the flight, but first, there was thinking to be done.

I was surprised when Rhee vetoed my request to take an assistant to Korea. This kind of work almost invariably involved one or more paid assistants, but Seoul insisted that local help would be provided, and I reluctantly conceded the point. More of a worry was the expenses situation. Standard practice is for half of the entire fee to be paid upfront. I had settled for a fraction of that from Rhee, and now I hoped that had not been a mistake.

I caught Miss Lee's attention and raised an eyebrow towards my empty glass. As she carefully set another double down on a fresh paper coaster, she murmured, 'Cho-shim-haseyo, chui-halgoyo.' *Take care, you're going to get drunk.*

'Kenchun-ah, chui ha'goshipeo.' *It's alright, I want to get drunk.*

I pecked ineffectually at the food when it arrived and drank my way through an action movie that struck me as having a few too many exploding aircraft to qualify as ideal in-flight entertainment.

When the credits rolled I switched the audio channel to jazz and pulled on my eye mask.

I awoke hours later, neck painfully stiff and mouth parched. My ears popped as the 747 shed altitude. Daylight streamed through the windows, we were nearing Seoul, and I had slept undisturbed through a couple of meals and a staff shift change. I knew this because the hostess politely waiting for my eyes to adjust was taller and slimmer than Miss Lee. Her badge identified her as Miss Seo, and she was as welcome a sight as I had woken up to in a long time, not least for the tall glass of iced water and the three painkillers she placed on the tray in front of me. Thank you, Miss Seo. Bless *you*, Miss Lee.

I squinted through the window on the far side of the snoring Filipina. We came in on an easterly approach and, spread out below us in bright late-summer evening light, Seoul stretched to the horizon and beyond. Above the homes of ten million people a grey-brown smog blanket drew a horizontal line so distinct that it was like looking at the scene through a photographic filter.

Winding its way through the city from east to west was the huge track of the Han River, its broad curves skirted on both sides by crowded multi-laned highways. Over a dozen long bridges laden with traffic linked the heart of the city to sprawling southern suburbs of geometrically-arranged apartment towns and walled-in luxury villas. Terrifyingly expensive real estate stood on acreage where, thirty-five years before, only rice paddies occupied land that farmers could hardly give away.

To the south I saw the old Kimpo Airport, and thought of the first time I landed at what was then Kimpo International, in 1989. I was seated next to a family of Canadian missionaries, four freckled kids listening to their parents reminisce about landing at Kimpo in the 1960s and watching their baggage proceed from airliner to tiny terminal by ox-drawn cart. By the late 80s, it was one of the world's most modern airports, but that didn't stop the government pushing on with the construction of a newer, even bigger international hub at Incheon, twenty miles to the west. Say what you like about the Koreans as a business force, but don't dare accuse them of lacking long-term vision.

Final approach seemed to take forever, and I just caught sight of the ocean before the pilot executed a textbook landing at Incheon International.

I cruised through Immigration without delay and moved on to Customs.

Hauling cases full of expensive equipment that could fetch double its cost on the local market, I was prepared for clearing Customs to take a while, but when I steered my overloaded trolley through the 'nothing to declare' lane, the fat man in the black uniform only did a double take at the photo in my passport before he smiled and waved me through. I never did like that photo.

Automatic doors slid open and spat me out to face an expectant crowd held back by a sturdy stainless steel barrier. I caught myself looking out for faces I knew, a ridiculous notion that I choked back almost as soon as it surfaced. Instead, I scanned the crowd for the K-N Group logo. There, on a handwritten sign held up by a young Korean man wearing what looked like an Armani suit: 'Welcome to Korea, Mr. Alec'. I was working for one of the richest, most sophisticated corporations in the country – and the man meeting me didn't understand Western names. This works both ways. I once laughed my way through a best-selling novel whose Korean characters suffered Western-reader-friendly names about as realistic as Jones Brown, Smith Anderson and Bronstein Murphy.

I waved and pointed a forefinger at the tip of my nose. The young man with the sign looked pleased to see me.

I was back.

Chapter Three

Armani suit shook my hand.

'Welcome to Korea. My family name is Lee but you can call me John.'

He barked into a mobile phone while we zig-zagged along crowded pavement. In the No Parking zone outside, a tangle of cars, taxis and minivans sat at crazy angles, hurriedly loading up with luggage and grey-faced jet lag victims. Kids asleep on their feet or in their parents' arms, heedless of the piercing whistles of blue-uniformed security men who tried to enforce some order but only added to the chaos.

Screeching tyres drew my eye to a large black Hyundai that squealed to a halt outside two taxis. The driver leapt out, the boot lid popped up, and from its underside flapped damp cloths looped over bungee cords and a polishing device like a Chihuahua with a baton up its backside – essentials of the Korean chauffeur's trade.

He was a burly guy with a crew cut and a badly-set nose, but his blue suit was immaculately pressed, red tie clipped neatly to white shirt by a company pin. Pushing through two tired families, he plucked the trolley from my grasp and started to load the boot, hefting leaden cases as though they weighed nothing. Lee ignored him completely. Classless, Korea is not. When one of the taxi drivers cursed the chauffeur for blocking his exit, our man drew him an opaque glance and the taxi driver clammed up. The big city chauffeur suffers all manner of shit in the course of his working day, but occasionally he gets to pass some down the line. Right now the taxi driver was wearing it.

As we butted our way onto the expressway for Seoul, Lee tried to make small talk, but I was more interested in what was going on outside the car.

'You are very tired from the flight.'

'I'm sorry, John. Yes, I am a little tired.'

The driver slotted into the outside lane and I went back to watching the city unfold around us. Soon we hustled along a riverside expressway, eight lanes of compressed motorised anarchy. To the north, the Han River and the twinkle of the city centre. To the south, massive new apartment towns that to the first-time European visitor are something of an enigma. We are used to high-rise inner-city ghettos, dilapidated low-rent pigeon lofts for the flight-less poor who live with peeling paint, boarded-up windows and overlapping graffiti, the installation art of the terminally bored. Seoul apartment blocks stood tall and proud, modern and clean and fully-occupied by middle-class citizens who paid huge sums for a three-bedroom high-rise box, and who couldn't pick their next door neighbours out of an identity parade.

Coming out of a spaghetti plate intersection we found Youido, a mid-river island that forty years ago was a military airfield. Now, as well as being home to the National Assembly, it was covered in apartment and office towers, many of them new to me. In the middle of the island, a massive paved Plaza swarmed with rental bikes and all around it, tall office towers glowed fluorescent green. The Korean white-collar worker doesn't even think about leaving his desk until the boss heads for the elevator, and a rigid behavioural code means Korean bosses work late every night.

Crossing the northern branch of the river we hit ageing tracts of low-rise housing punctured by eruptions of yet more shiny office and apartment towers. Between the gleaming monoliths, long-time city residents clung to life as they had known it for generations. Small businesses carved a sliver of the wealth created by decades of spectacular economic growth. Fashion retailers, beauty shops, hardware stores, coffee shops, restaurants, Internet cafes and beer-and-fried-chicken joints jostled for space with one-room churches, after-school study institutes and neon-lit Tae Kwon-do *dojang*, their windows flung wide to let in cool air heavy with the fumes of traffic jams that never really cleared.

I scoured the streets for locations that sparked memories. A *bulgogi* beef restaurant where I first encountered *soju*, Korea's take-no-prisoners staple liquor. A side street coffee shop where I met a doctor's wife for weekly English conversation lessons that soon adjourned to a cosy back alley *yogwan*, or inn, where the lonely Mrs Choi cheerfully took over the role of teacher to her diligent and grateful student.

The padded luxury of the big Hyundai must have won out, because the next thing I knew Lee was watching two men in overcoats and top hats load my luggage onto a tall brass trolley. As I climbed from the back seat, a vision of beauty in a burgundy uniform stepped forward and bowed deeply.

'Welcome to the Grand Hyatt, Mr Brodie. I hope you had a pleasant flight. My name is Miss Kim.'

Miss Kim. Three-quarters of Koreans share three surnames, one of them Kim, yet ever since this trip was mooted, *my* Miss Kim had been tramping regularly through my thoughts.

One of the top hats held open the door, and I followed today's Miss Kim into the hotel.

Although I had been to the Hyatt many times, this was my first visit as a guest. The check-in experience was of the programmed efficiency and fawning courtesy you would expect of an ancient Eastern culture polished and shaped by exacting American training standards.

When Miss Kim asked me for my credit card I hesitated and looked to Lee. He stepped forward.

'Is something wrong?'

'I wonder if your office mentioned the hotel bill.'

'No.'

'I expected your company to want to take care of it.' My eye was on the full-priced 'rack rate' printed on the form, US$275 per night. A company with K-N's clout could easily secure a heavy discount on that figure. Lee looked embarrassed and Miss Kim looked away. This was better side-stepped than confronted.

'Perhaps I can leave my credit card details for now, and you could talk to your office about this?'

Lee looked relieved and Miss Kim's smile was as fixed as a flash photograph.

She tried to make some amends by taking my VISA card with two hands, palms up and thumbs pressing gently down on the card, implying formality and respect. I tried to look unconcerned. That card was nearly maxed out, and I already had no idea how Naz was going to make the next bill.

Eight p.m. local time and I was ready for a long soak in a hot tub, a couple of drinks, followed by about nine hours adrift in a bed the size of a tennis court. I asked Lee about the plan for the morning.

'President Chang has invited you to dinner.'

'Tonight?'

'He will pick you up at nine o'clock.' *Will*. Client's privilege.

Scratch the hot tub. I had time for a quick shower and a shave and maybe a restorative hit of caffeine.

Five minutes before nine saw me back among the top-hatted doormen.

Precisely on the hour a big black Mercedes purred to a halt and John Lee jumped from the front passenger seat to open the rear door. Inside, President Chang carelessly folded an Asian Wall Street Journal. He wore a dark grey suit with the faintest of pin stripes. The suit jacket was double-breasted, unusual in Korea, and he wore it open to show off a tie so unforgivably ugly that it could only be Versace. His jet black hair was on the long side, yet looked as if he had only just risen from the barber's chair. He had the ageless features of the healthy Korean; in his mid-fifties, to the Western eye, he could pass for twenty years younger. He stretched out a pale hand with shining, freshly-manicured nails. As we shook hands, I managed to bow and made sure the fingertips of my left hand, palm up, touched my right fore-arm. Maximum respect to a person of superior standing.

'It is so nice to see you again, Mr Brodie.' He spoke with a plummy English Public School accent that was so much at odds with his handsome Oriental appearance.

'Thank you for inviting me to dinner.' *And for the assignment from heaven.*

Chang looked up to the rear-view mirror and nodded. The Mercedes bolted from the kerb, folding me back in my seat.

'I do hope you like Japanese food.'

'Very much.' I tried to hide my surprise. For many Koreans an invite to the table of their former Imperial ruler might imply that their country's cuisine was inferior to that of its arch-enemy. The car slid to a gentle halt in a narrow lane running between the high, broken glass-topped walls that surrounded homes of the seriously rich. We had travelled no more than a quarter of a mile from the hotel, and now the same driver who met me at the airport held the door for Chang. John Lee stepped up to the other door. A rubbish collector in plastic sandals and filthy hand-me-downs manoeuvred a hand-cart around the Mercedes, still clanging oversized shears, crying out for newspapers, card-board boxes and other recyclables. The gap between rich and poor in Korea is like a continental divide.

A tall wooden gate slipped sideways, and an elderly lady in full Japanese Kimono clacked forward on wooden san-dals to welcome Chang like an old family friend. Over the gate, CCTV cameras watched us from three different an-gles, doubtless letting the mama-san know who she was welcoming before he even got out of the car. Chang and I strode in to ringing choruses of 'welcome' in Japanese and Korean.

The courtyard was groomed to perfection and beyond. A clear rock-lined fish pond wove between white-painted boulders and teemed with gold and white carp, their hungry maws yawning among floating lilies and orchids that I couldn't begin to name. Over the pond stretched a tiny arched wooden bridge, painted bright red, and beyond that sat a house straight out of a Kurosawa movie.

'Isn't it something?'

'It's beautiful.'

'It used to belong to a businessman who was a great admirer of Japanese art and design.' He led me over the little bridge and towards the entrance where half a dozen figures in kimonos performed synchronised jack-knife bows.

I didn't tell him that I had been here before, or that I knew it used to belong to a business magnate who founded his giant empire by collaborating with the Japanese Im-perial Army's occupying forces in the 'thirties and 'forties. For nearly fifty years its owner had watched his fortune grow until he fell foul of the military regime of the early eighties. Facing doubtful but genuinely threatening espio-nage charges, he bolted to Japan and died in exile in Kyoto, leaving his home and much of his wealth to be divided up by the Generals and their hangers-on. It was a very Korean story, and I wondered who ended up owning this place. For all I knew it could be Chang.

Inside, young women clad in exquisite silk competed to remove our shoes and replace them with open-backed slippers embroidered with cranes in flight. They ushered us along a broad hallway decorated with Japanese watercolours of bamboo stalks and more birdlife. A dark-stained wood-and-paper door slid back, and Chang stepped aside to wave me in. The room was small and classically minimalist, with square cushions around a low, lacquered wooden table set in the middle of the *tatami* mat floor. The whole of the far wall consisted of glass that looked out upon a private courtyard of potted *bonsai* trees, miniature bubbling streams and precision-manicured gravel. Standing to greet us were two Korean women in their twenties, fashionably dressed in Western outfits that hugged impressive figures. The room smelled of fresh make-up and the lingering rasp of hurriedly-extinguished cigarettes. They bowed demurely, eyes down, hands clasped, and I looked the other way to hide my smile.

Chapter Four

Chang drew the hostesses a blatant look of appraisal before settling himself down beside the taller of the two. She had shining black hair whose thick wavy tresses flowed forward as she reached for a hot hand-towel which she unwrapped and offered to Chang. I took to the cushion opposite them and the second hostess settled beside me. She was very trim, with small breasts pushed skywards beneath a lacy top. Gently hennaed hair was parted dead centre and razor-cropped just below her ears, framing a face immaculately highlighted with expensive make-up in a purplish theme. It had to be *the* current look in the Korean fashion magazines, and though it didn't quite work with her slender facial features, it was still a face that could bring London's rush hour to a screeching halt.

Addressing them with the casual familiarity of an aristocrat talking down to his serving staff, Chang asked their names. Each bobbed her head as she responded, and Chang did the honours.

'This is Miss Hong.' His fingertips brushed oh-so-casually against her breast. She shone a white-toothed welcome, first to Chang, and next to me.

'And beside you is Miss Pang.' He switched to Korean. 'This is Mr Brodie.' Miss Pang, reaching for a hot towel, dipped her eyes as she and her friend chorused,

'Anyong-hassimnika.' *How do you do?*

This kind of personal attention from Chang was a

surprise, but the situation was nothing new to me. Fifteen years before, my friend Mr Cho used to take me to his 'room salons', plush, hideously expensive night clubs where every party occupied a private room. Orders were placed by intercom telephone, and professional hostesses of every stripe might as well have been listed on the menu, so central was their role in proceedings.

It was a role built on fawning obsequiousness, shameless flattery and braying laughter. For some it never went any further, but many were available for a price. I remember the first time Mr Cho took me to a room salon. After a few drinks while we picked at a mountainous fruit salad and struggled for conversation, he reached for the telephone and issued precise instructions. Soon a man in waiter costume arrived with a wiry, tired-looking young woman in garish clothes and carrying a hotel room key, which she put on the table in front of Mr Cho. Pushing the key and a wedge of cash back across the table to my new partner, Mr Cho wished me a cheerful goodnight.

As I sneaked a glance at Miss Hong, something intruded in my peripheral vision. A piece of pineapple on a cocktail stick, held by Miss Pang, her other hand cupped protectively below. I opened my mouth and smiled with my eyes.

As she fed me, the painted nails of her left hand came gently to rest, high on my inner thigh. Things hadn't changed much. Across the table Miss Hong was making clucking noises in Chang's ear while kimono-clad waitresses shuffled in bearing trays stacked with unbelievable quantities of food and drink.

Miss Hong and Miss Pang competed to give us maximum face by pouring the Chivas Regal. Chang played gentleman patriarch by politely pouring shorter whiskies for them.

'Welcome to Korea, Mr Brodie.' He raised his glass in two hands, implying unwarranted respect that I nonetheless appreciated. I was slipping effortlessly into the Korean routine of vital courtesies displayed at all times.

'Thank you Mr Chang. Please call me Alec.' He nodded, and I pretended not to notice that he failed to return the compliment. In the foreign media he was Peter Chang, but in present company, it was *Mr.*

'Mr Rhee mentioned publications for a stock market flotation?'

Chang's eyes narrowed like a bad poker player's. I glanced at Miss Hong and Miss Pang, who nuzzled and grinned, on high alert for cues to join the conversation.

'Is this a bad time – '

'Not at all. I was just enjoying a moment free of company pressures.' As you might expect of a veteran of countless hi-pressure negotiations, he lied without effort. Billionaire Asian industrialist takes time out to kick back with near-stranger Scottish photographer. *Give me a break.*

'I understand.' Lying was my only option, too.

'Mr Rhee was right, of course. K-N Group is about to undergo a major series of stock market issues in New York and Tokyo. They will be the first of their kind for a Korean *Chaebol.*' He paused. 'You are of course familiar with the *Chaebol*?'

Anyone with even a passing interest in Korea knows about the *Chaebol*. Vast, family-controlled conglomerates that make everything from silicon chips to the world's largest container vessels and cruise liners, a handful of *Chaebol* dominate the Korean economy. I nodded and he went on.

'Since this is the first issue of its kind for K-N Group, its confidentiality is absolutely imperative. So forgive me if I don't go into any greater detail.'

Time to change the subject. Before I could think of anything Chang did it for me and addressed the women.

'Yong-au-rul haeyo?' *Can you speak English?*

Miss Hong raised forefinger and thumb, half an inch apart, universal sign-language, Lesson One.

'Jekkum-man.'

Miss Pang nodded an earnest 'me too'.

Chang pointed to the growing spread of dishes laid out across the scorched teak table top. 'These are a big favourite in Korea. Do you know why?'

I thought I knew, but this was a time to play along.

'Is it because they're spicy?' The last thing they would be was spicy, but I could role-play, too.

'Noooooh,' he laughed. 'It's because in Japan they are called 'kai seki'.' The women's hands shot in front of their faces, shielding their amusement in the modest manner of the well-brought-up Korean female.

'Ah-haah – you mean like kae-seki?' More explosions of suppressed laughter at my pronunciation of the most common yet most passionate of Korean swear-words.

'Han-guk-mal charrashinae,' cried Miss Pang. I too had to laugh, imagining a Korean guest at an English dinner party shouting out 'fucking arsehole', to gleeful declarations of 'he speaks English!'

'Que yang-ban-ee, hanguk-mal nomu charrashinae,' said Chang to two pairs of raised, pencilled eyebrows. 'Yet-nal-ae, Seoul-ae sarrasoyo.' Murmurs of understanding came from our hired partners.

What was this? Last year when I photographed Chang I gave him my standard line of having 'spent some time' in Korea, but I never said that I used to live in Seoul. Or that I spoke any Korean. Now, Chang spoke to me in English.

'When did you first come to Korea, Alec?'

'In 1989. Why do you ask?' Too late, I wished I could swallow the insolence implicit in those last four words.

'Did you originally come here to teach English?'

Who said anything about teaching English?

'Or was it Tae Kwon-do that really brought you here?'

'Tae Kwon-do?' said Miss Pang, picking up something she understood. Chang answered her in Korean.

'This gentleman knows Tae Kwon-do. He studied it while he was living in Seoul for more than five years.'

As if he could read the confusion on my face, he fed me a wry glance. Miss Pang said something and the three of them laughed. Chang explained:

'She says she envies you.'

'Really?'

'Your hair.' He translated, and the two hostesses giggled.

Miss Pang took her hand from where it rested on my forearm and casually ran her fingers through ringlets that got curlier the longer they grew. In a nation whose entire population has straight black hair, my curly, collar-length blond hair was often a source of fascination. Miss Pang's fingernails played gently with my scalp.

We turned our attentions to a table full of food. It was authentic Japanese cuisine at its best, a subtle feast presented artistically, innumerable small dishes laid out like elements in a landscape painting. Miss Pang poured soya sauce into a tiny round dish and nodded at the lime-green *wasabe* paste.

'Do you like?'

Using metal chopsticks, she nipped a bud of green *wasabe* mustard paste and mixed it carefully into the soya sauce, pinching the broken pieces until they dissolved, turning the sauce a lighter brown that I knew would now pack a wicked bite. *Wasabe* is an absolute delight so long as you remember not to breathe in through your nose while you chew. Instant tears.

Chang made small talk in English and Korean, drawing happy laughs from the women and occasional polite involvement from me. My thoughts kept turning to what he had said earlier. Why would he be so interested in what I did fifteen years ago? How could Chang know about the English teaching, the Tae Kwon-do – and what else did he know?

'Do you remember Ben?'

'Ben?' *Oh no.*

'Last year when you photographed me. Don't you remember Ben Schwartz, my PR man?'

Clunk. Pieces falling into place. Ben Schwartz was a New Yorker who had lived in Seoul for nearly twenty years. When I first came to Korea he was a low-level hack at a local business monthly, but last year I heard from Chang that Schwartz had his own Public Relations outfit and was calling himself a 'Consultant'.

Chang was waiting for a response.

'How is Ben? Is he still in Korea?'

I hoped not. The bastard's interference made that portrait assignment a nightmare.

'Ben's been here for so long that he's almost a Korean. He has a Korean wife and he speaks Korean like a native. You and he will be working together very closely.'

No.

'He's in charge of all the printed materials that will use your photographs.'

My heart sank. 'It'll be nice to see him again.' Some lies are harder to utter than others.

'He'll meet you for breakfast at the hotel at eight o'clock.'

I could hardly wait.

The rest of the meal passed in a depressive blur, the combined powers of creeping jet-lag, Chivas Regal and the thought of working with Schwartz doing their best to spoil my homecoming. I thought of poor Naz sitting in London, fielding ugly calls from my creditors. The whole point of this was to generate the bucks to put an end to those phone calls and, if that meant dealing with Ben Schwartz, I had to make it work.

The dinner concluded with characteristic abruptness. One minute it's all 'dipshida' (*cheers*) and wrestling with the bottle for the privilege of pouring the other guy a drink, and the next, without announcement, on go the jackets.

The women had slipped out earlier, to the ladies room I thought, but now there was no sign of them. They were paid help, their job was done, and I missed them already.

We departed to loud, grateful Korean and Japanese cries that implored us to come again soon.

Chang's Mercedes waited outside the gate, and two minutes later he left me at the door of the Hyatt. I thanked him and wished him goodnight. Fat tyres clawed asphalt as the limousine sped into the darkness.

The cathedral-sized lobby buzzed with midnight chit-chat and restrained music from a string quartet in starched dinner suits. Reluctantly discounting the notion of another drink, I headed for the elevators.

I stepped out on the nineteenth floor and padded the thickly-carpeted corridor to my room. When I reached into my jacket pocket for the key card, it wasn't there. Nor was it in any other pocket, no matter how often I looked. I kicked at the door in anger.

The door swung open and there, side-lit by a warm tungsten glow from the open bathroom, stood Miss Hong. Her hair was newly brushed, she smelt of soap, and was wrapped in a heavy towelling bathrobe tied lightly around her narrow waist. She was barefoot, and her painted toe-nails glistened a suggestive pink. In one hand she cupped two crystal glasses. Between the fingers of the other, miniatures of whisky rattled as she waved them at me.

'Oh-so-u-seyo.' *Welcome.*

Chapter Five

The hotel coffee shop at the height of the breakfast trade was just about more than I could handle. Artificial lights glowed weakly from recessed reflectors rendered all but redundant by the morning sun blazing through a double-height glass wall like the flash hell of a nuclear blast. Beyond the blue swimming pool, the grey-brown expanse that was the Han River swept westwards, its southern bank a uniform concrete horizon.

The coffee shop diners were the usual mix of fresh-faced locals and weary foreign business travellers, jaded from long flights or late nights or both, complexions paled by lives spent in airports and fluorescent-lit factories and conference rooms. The existence of the international business traveller owed more to routine tedium than the outsider could imagine. A half century before him, the travelling salesman trudged the length and breadth of Britain by rail, lugging a cardboard suitcase of samples from station to boarding house to prospective client. Today, 'Marketing Vice Presidents' crossed continents from airport to deluxe hotel to airport, Samsonite Oysters and eel skin briefcases heavy with laptop computers and multimedia presentation kits. Like the factory workers back home who thought their lives so exotic, an awful percentage of these latter-day Tupperware men would expire face-down in middle-age, heart disease or alcoholism snuffing pipedreams of happy retirements on sunlit golf courses.

Florid faces picked listlessly at greasy food and sucked at iced water or coffee or orange juice, their jet-lag, hangovers and the day's work worries writ clear on furrowed brows.

I knew exactly how they felt.

I had emerged very tentatively from my whisky-sodden slumber at six o'clock, a little surprised to find myself alone. Miss Hong had slipped away sometime before dawn without waking me, but the Rolling Stones could have held a sound-check at the foot of my bed without disturbing me. I made straight for the mini-bar, shuddering at the sight of empty miniatures lining the shelf above it. I pulled long and hard on a bottle of tooth-achingly cold mineral water. The stuffy room was still heavy with Miss Hong's scent and I had to laugh at the exhausted face that stared back from the mirror. My head felt like I had out-drunk a pub full of football fans on Cup Final night, but my loins had that delicious spent feeling that comes only from a good night's romp.

Miss Hong was a wild and welcome addition to a long succession of Korean memories linking heavy drinking to hearty, uninhibited sex. When I finished showering, she led me by the hand to the huge bed, lay me down on my back and, after gently exploring my navel with a manicured fingernail, carefully filled it with whisky. She batted mascaraed eyelashes mischievously before lowering the tip of her tongue and licking me dry. A gentle kiss left a perfect lipstick print high on my inner thigh before she lay back and handed me the bottle. My turn.

Only then did I notice the Korean flag tattooed around her navel, a fetching yin-yang roundel in blue and red, complete with black trigrams clean and rigid on her pale flat stomach.

Before long she laughingly pointed out an obvious disparity in belly-button capacities, and soon I was supping three to her one. After every few rounds, she would pick a different part of the room, jiggle into position and, with the merest hesitation while she made sure I was still wearing protection, let me slide inside her. After who knows how many tattooed navels full of Scotch, I was a wreck.

I came downstairs early, hoping to get some food and coffee down my neck before I had to face Schwartz, but as the waiter in butler-grey turned to scan for a suitable table, up popped Schwartz from a horse-shoe alcove against the right-hand wall. He waved imperiously to catch the waiter's attention, and pointed at me with one finger. It was about as rude as you could get in Korea, and he knew it.

'Your friend?'

'Mi-guk kongdaeng-ee.'

He stifled a grin and led me to where the 'Yankee asshole' stood with his hand outstretched. Ben Schwartz was a trim five-eight, olive-skinned, with thick black hair brushed back from a widow's peak. Eyes the colour of burnished mahogany stared from expensively fashionable metal-framed spectacles. He forced me a beaming expression of welcome. I had forgotten how disarmingly, disgustingly handsome he was.

'Nice to see you again. Please, take a seat.' As if I was planning to stand and watch him eat.

With a practised flick the waiter unrolled a starched napkin across my lap, and turned over my cup. I asked him for a large pot of coffee and a jug of iced water. With a shake of his head, Schwartz sent him on his way.

'You look tired. Rough trip?'

'Not rough, long. After that, I was out late with Mr Chang.' The best lies are built on a kernel of truth, and I doubted that he spent many nights dining alone with the President. With a guy like Schwartz you scored points every chance you could.

Schwartz laughed. 'The man likes to tie it on, doesn't he?'

I said nothing, and he leaned forward as if to share a secret.

'You smell like a brewery. Or maybe a distillery.'

And you smell like the peel-and-sniff aftershave adverts in a tits and ass magazine.

'Like I said, a long night.' A long night sucking whisky from a whore's brightly tattooed belly button.

'Care to share the joke?'

I had been smiling into space. 'It is nice to be back. So what does the shooting schedule look like?'

'Let's get some food first.'

He dropped his napkin on the table and headed for the buffet.

I could have put money on what this New Yorker would choose from the vast spread. Sliced fresh fruit, muesli, low-fat yoghurt and tomato juice. My hangover demanded something else entirely. I filled a plate with fried rice, crispy bacon, two poached eggs and three fat sausages.

I tucked in with much more vigour than I felt. 'Do you have a shot list for me?'

'I'm in charge of the production.'

Like a schoolkid asserting supremacy in the playground.

'What sort of shooting schedule do you have lined up?'

'One or two things have to be sorted out. You'll be kept informed.'

At the money they were paying, I should be hitting the ground running.

'When do I get to see some of the sites, scope out the locations?'

'John Lee will be here later.'

This was getting me nowhere.

'Who do I talk to about money?'

'That's not my department. K-N has hired you directly on this one.' No wonder he looked pissed off. As a go-between, he would have been able to charge K-N a standard PR mark-up of nearly twenty percent on top of my fee.

'I was a bit surprised to hear from K-N's London office.'

'Surprised?'

'Apart from the Global Trade assignment last year I have had nothing to do with K-N Group.'

'You know what the Koreans are like. They know you from one successful job, and when they take a shine to someone, nobody else will do.'

He reached down to a briefcase at his feet, pulled out a fat envelope and threw it down next to my coffee cup. Hot coffee swilled into the saucer.

'Some background material for you to read up on. Company profiles, descriptions of Group activities, plants, factories, key projects, all possible areas that you might be photographing.'

'Possible areas?'

'Is that too complicated?'

I suppressed the urge to slap him with a handful of his own muesli.

'I expected to get started on a shot list right away.'

'Until the tentative shot list gets approved by the right people, nothing gets done.'

'I don't even get to see this *tentative* list?'

'Correct.' Looking smug, he stood up and strode towards the buffet.

I endured another half hour of evasions and small talk. Schwartz wasn't going to get pinned down on anything to do with the assignment, and when I asked who else in the Group I would be dealing with, he stone-walled me. I already knew my two contacts, he said, himself and John Lee. Great. One an arsehole, the other unable to find his arse with both hands. He stood up, brushing imaginary crumbs from his lap, and a waiter came running with his jacket.

'John Lee will be here soon. Great to be working with you again.'

He left me to sign for two expensive breakfasts.

I drained the coffee pot and sucked ice cubes while I scanned the Herald. Despite tiny English readership numbers, Korea had two competing English dailies, each as bad as the other. When I first got to Korea, they kissed government arse incessantly, reserving the top left-hand corner of the front page for a photo of the latest ex-army General President. Every other day he would be presenting the Kangwha Medal for Diplomatic Merit to a visiting third-world Deputy Under-Secretary for Torture.

I cut through the lobby, wondering how John Lee was meant to locate me. I didn't have to wait long to find out.

I hadn't seen Bobby Purves in over two years, but as he passed through a tall door held open by a statuesque bellboy, I was reminded that he hadn't changed much from the Bobby who helped me drink my way through many a sunrise. Back then he was doing nine hours a day teaching conversational English in a hovel of a downtown language institute, a regime he suffered for years. I often chuckled at the notion of thousands of middle-aged Koreans with the slowed, flattened vowels of Yorkshire hill-country. His was an accent that the southern English often confused with dullness, but in the ten years since he took a job as a copy writer for a busy Seoul securities house, Bobby acquired an insider's understanding of the murky world of Korean big business. He now held a senior managerial position with a leading Korean brokerage.

I had called Bobby not long after I finished breakfast, when I was paged to a lobby telephone for the surprise news from John Lee that I had most of the day off.

His hair was a little greyer and the waistline a touch more rounded, but he was still the friend I valued so much.

We settled into padded armchairs in the lobby and ordered large draft beers from the dark-suited waiter, who tried his best not to look disgusted. The Hyatt's sumptuous lobby lounge and draft beer went together like a tiara and dungarees.

'What brings you here? It must be something plum if it's

paying for this.' He waved a huge hand at the lobby. All around us, the heads of serving staff popped to attention.

While he slurped hungrily at his beer, I explained about K-N Group needing photography to support upcoming share issues, details of which were a mystery to me. I told him the story of my evening with President Chang, by the end of which my beer was almost untouched and Bobby's was near-empty. I signalled for one more.

'Sounds odd to me.' He held his glass an inch from his lips.

'What do you mean?'

'How come they bring you all the way from London? There must be decent enough photographers here, or Tokyo or Hong Kong – or are you in a class of your own?'

Hardly. Asia was crawling with shooters easily capable of performing this assignment, many of them charging fees considerably lower than the inflated day-rate that Rhee accepted without blinking. All of which threw up questions that had been gnawing at me.

'You know how Koreans are. They take a shine to someone and no-one else will do.' I regurgitated Schwartz's line. 'And their London guy told me President Chang loved Global Trade magazine's K-N cover story I shot last year.'

Bobby didn't look convinced.

'Do you have any idea what kind of trouble K-N Group is in?'

'Don't tell me.'

'This cocktail reception they're holding tonight.'

'I have to be there, to take pictures.' That was the other thing John Lee called to tell me earlier.

'It's been brought forward a few days at zero notice.'

'So?'

'So, when an outfit as big as K-N Group re-schedules important events in a hurry, tiny alarm bells go off all around the markets.'

'I was told that tonight is about something called a GDR.'

'Right, a Global Depository Receipt. It has been whispered about for months, and now it's being rushed into place.'

'OK, but what is it?'

'A mechanism set up to attract huge amounts of inward investment that the group badly needs to service a debt situation that's been out of hand for years.'

He downed the rest of his beer and waved the empty glass in the air until a waiter cantered off towards the bar. This was a quiet lunch by Bobby's standards.

'You know that none of the *Chaebol* could have survived until now without successive governments bailing them out time after time? For decades, so long as exports and turnover continued to rise, they were allowed to expand into whatever businesses took their fancy.'

'K-N Group being a case in point.'

'Of course it is. And like all the other *Chaebol*, for decades K-N Group funded its growth with huge loans that the government forced Korean banks to extend, never mind that the groups routinely defaulted.'

'I've got a hangover, Bobby.'

'Bottom line. The Group's near broke. There are tales of K-N managers flying in from London and Lagos and all points in between with suitcases full of US dollars and Euros, off-the-books cash being used in desperation, not even to repay loans, but to see off part of the outstanding interest. Otherwise the banks will start foreclosing, and that could start a run on K-N liquidity that would sink the entire group. Even if the Korean banks don't close them down, K-N Group owes *billions* to banks in Europe, Japan and America. Chang and his boys bet the farm on a list of overseas projects that tanked. Car plants in Central Asia, oil exploration in Africa, power stations in former states of the old Soviet Union – and they're only the fuck-ups that the Press know about. Their debts are so out of hand that rumour has it even the government was ready to let them go down, as an example to the other *Chaebol*.'

'So what's with the GDR? Why would anyone invest in K-N with all these rumours that they are about to go belly up? And hold on. Back up a bit. What do you mean the government **was** ready to let them go down? What has changed?'

'In two words? North Korea.'

The northern half of the peninsula was still technically at war with the South, and for over half a century had been completely cut off from its brother neighbour. North and South remained separated by the world's most heavily fortified frontier, one that nobody – bar a handful of very senior politicians and a few big noises in UN colours – had passed through for more than fifty years.

North Korea would be ridiculous if it was not so bloody ruthless. Communism the world over is dead or dying, with even China soaking up investment from any capitalist quarter, South Korea included. This made the Korean Peninsula the only place on the planet still divided by the Cold War, which was a source of undying shame to the forty-odd million South Koreans, because they knew enough to understand. Their poor cousins in the North wouldn't know what day it was if their government didn't tell them.

For the first time in decades, and despite the Northern half of the peninsula being tagged in Washington as an 'axis of evil', recent political moves in Seoul and Pyongyang had created a faint possibility of detente.

'So this is all to do with the South being open to anything that will bring the two halves of the peninsula a bit closer?'

'Correct. K-N Group aims to be the first South Korean *Chaebol* to get a proper manufacturing foothold in the North.'

'What about the manufacturing zone up there that's all over the Press?'

'The one in Kaesong. That is completely cut off from the rest of the country, and the scuttlebutt says propaganda from both sides is grossly exaggerating its success, because neither of them can be seen to fail. K-N wants to go one giant step further, to be the first South Korean company to set up factories in North Korea proper.'

I was beginning to get it. 'Hefty investment in the *real* North by a *Chaebol* means South Korea scores points all-round. It could be the biggest PR coup in decades.'

'And?' Bobby smiled his thanks as the waiter delivered yet another litre of foamy draft beer.

I thought about it. 'And it'll give jobs to lots of North Korean cousins and aunties and uncles?'

'Exactly. In the process, forcing a complete about-face by the Seoul government so far as K-N goes. The Group instantly becomes the benevolent face of all-powerful Southern capitalism, the visible proof that the way of the South is the righteous one – and safe from any threats of being closed down.'

'All of which begs a question.'

'You mean, 'What the hell are they doing bringing you all the way from London if they're so broke?''

That was exactly what I meant, and there was no answer to it. I reached for my beer and Bobby did the same.

Chapter Six

Deep sleep peeled away in layers by the insistent trilling of a strange telephone. I fumbled for the handset, guided by the green light blinking bright in the near darkness of a hotel room with the drapes pulled closed.

'Good afternoon, Mr Brodie, this is your wake up call.' A young man's voice dripped with fake warmth.

I was instantly filled with dread that I should be else-where. I had an idea I was in Seoul but no clue what day it was, nor even what time of day. Long seconds passed before I noticed the afternoon glare leaking through the crack in the heavy curtains. It wasn't morning, and I hadn't screwed up. Not yet, anyway. A guilty conscience is a terrible thing.

Ten minutes in the shower and a routine check of the camera bag later, I was in the taxi line in front of the hotel, ignoring attempts by Deluxe Taxi drivers to draw me their way. At the regular taxi rank I waited while the short line was whittled away by arrivals of 'normal' cabs. When I managed to prise some expenses money out of Lee I would happily leave the regular cabs behind, but right now the costly privilege of overstuffed seat covers and sickly air fresheners could wait.

In light traffic the Shilla Hotel was only ten minutes away, but Seoul's hellish three-hour rush hour was well under way, and my taxi driver edged impatiently through a rolling nose-to-tail jam. Threading through this were motorcycles laden with gigantic cargos, some of them terrifying, like three large household LPG tanks held cross-wise on the rear seat with springy cables made from strips of car tyre. Even with loads so heavy they made the bikes' front wheels skim the tarmac, they wove embroidery trails through the traffic fabric, drawing horn blasts and verbal outbursts as they progressed. Compared to Seoul traffic, the manic motorists of Rome are positively meek.

The road skirted south of Nam San, two thousand feet of rock and flora that leaned over downtown Seoul, its dash of natural greens and browns a welcome relief from the city's man made landscape of concrete and glaring glass.

I hardly put money in the taxi driver's hand before John Lee locked onto my forearm and hauled me towards the hotel.

'Hurry – the reception is starting.'

I squinted through the lobby crowds at the bank of clocks above the front desk. New York, London, New Delhi, Singapore – Seoul.

'You said 6:30. It's only 6:15.'

'Mr Schwartz is looking for you.' It was delivered thick with reproach. Typical. I arrive fifteen minutes early, and because the PR flunky has his knickers in a knot, it's my fault.

While we weaved through a moving forest of dark suits, red ties and highly-polished slip-ons, I slung one camera around my neck and another on my shoulder, zoom lenses already attached. Ahead of us burnished steel doors swept open almost on cue, and along with half-a-dozen business-men we swept into the elevator. It was decked out in the standard deluxe hotel interior of stainless steel and badly-lit photographs of Mr and Mrs Stylish suffused with joy at the delights laid on by various hotel outlets. I had just enough room to attach flashguns to cameras. At least I didn't have the worry of what film to use. On a job like this, shooting digital was the only sensible option.

The doors slid open and Lee bowed his apologies to the six silent Koreans as we pushed on towards the function suite.

A herd of Press photographers and television cameramen stood to one side of the wide entranceway, corralled behind thick red ornamental ropes. Some of them trained cameras towards the guest arrivals, impatience all over their faces. Lee led me straight past them, and twenty pissed-off stares followed me.

Eyes still on the media pack, I ran chest-first into a brick wall. A Korean brick wall in a cheap blue suit, who didn't move a millimetre when I hit his outstretched hand at full chat. Built like a rhino and twice as ugly, he wore the miniature radio earpiece beloved of security forces and pub door hardmen the world over.

'*Where's the Yankee bastard going?*' he growled in Korean, painting grins on every last face in the Press corral.

A flash of embarrassment darkened Lee's face before he pulled out a security pass and looped it around my neck, where it immediately became entangled with my cameras. A new wave of Press Corps grumbling followed us into a function suite bigger and considerably more crowded than a football field.

Ben Schwartz materialised from nowhere and as he fired off instructions without preamble, his appraising gaze swept back and forth across the room. He nodded respectfully towards Asian guests and flashed an outstretched hand, politician-style, in acknowledgement to Westerners. My job description for the evening held no surprises. I was to photograph the more obviously important people as they sipped cocktails, then make sure I got good shots of the speakers at the official announcement. Schwartz and Lee would help me identify the key faces, and I knew what that meant: every few minutes I would be dragged across the hall to catch another crucial spontaneous grip-and-grin. Photographing cloudless skies would be more interesting and a lot less demeaning.

The mostly male crowd worked hard at small talk and the giving of face. About one-fifth of them were Western businessmen and diplomats high on the social circuit, ever on the lookout for new friends on the inside track of Korea, Inc. The targets of their earnest gazes were all Korean, middle-aged or older, most of them trim, neat figures who contrasted sharply with their counterparts, many of whom looked damaged by life on the cocktail circuit.

I split from Schwartz and Lee and did my rounds. It was easy to identify the more important guests by the cut of their suits and the density of sycophants hovering in their proximity. The mere hint of a camera pointing in their direction had the also-rans jostling for positions closer to VIPs.

Bobby Purves arrived with a Westerner whom he intro-duced as Eric Bridgewater of the British Embassy. As I did my best not to recoil from Bridgewater's dead-fish hand-shake, Bobby gave me a lop-sided grin.

'You ever find yourself in trouble over here, any trouble at all, pick up the phone, Alec, and whatever you do, don't bother calling Eric.' Bridgewater laughed politely, but made no effort to protest.

'Nice to meet you.' He turned his back and addressed a couple of rotund Europeans in what sounded like native German. I grabbed Bobby by the elbow and took him a few paces into the crowd.

'What do you know about K-N Group factories in Cholla-do?'

'You're kidding, right?'

'Tomorrow morning I have to go to Cholla Province to photograph a factory.'

'You do know what 'K-N' stands for?'

I didn't know. He helped me: 'Kyongsang-namdo. K-N.'

The southern end of the Korean peninsula had a cultural

divide going back centuries, and the rivalry between the Kyongsang provinces in the East and the Cholla provinces in the West was almost as fevered as the one between North and South Korea.

'K-N is a Kyongsang company, and always has been. It has offices and businesses and factories all over the country, but there are *no* K-N factories in Cholla.' Shaking his head, he pushed through the crowd towards where Bridgewater held two wine glasses high.

The rumble of hurried foot traffic announced the opening of official events to the impatient hordes of Press photographers and cameramen. Company juniors herded them to a platform set up behind ranks of seats. On a raised podium facing the seats was a long table in front of a brightly-lit partition emblazoned with the K-N Group logo.

The formalities were blessedly brief. Schwartz played master of ceremonies, switching effortlessly from English to Korean and back again, welcoming all distinguished guests, many of whom he drew attention to by name.

Next up, a government Minister delivered a ten-minute address in a Korean monotone that made even the locals squirm with boredom. Schwartz made no attempt to translate, an apparent oversight that was only explained when the Minister repeated the monologue in stilted, uneasy English.

When Chang's turn came he spoke English, breaking his speech into short paragraphs, followed by pauses while Schwartz translated into flowing Korean. As an icebreaker it was inspired, drawing murmurs of appreciation all round. The speech itself was a stream of platitudes, and soon he wrapped up with the hope that his esteemed guests might remain and enjoy a celebration of cocktails and other delicacies. Cue enthusiastic applause and clinking of glasses which the security men took as their signal to move in and herd the still-grumbling Press pack towards the exits.

After another hour I needed a break. I intercepted a waiter and relieved him of two champagne goblets, which I downed in quick succession before tackling the cold meats and cheeses. When I had my fill I moved on. Cameras held to the fore in fake professional zeal, I zig-zagged to the exit and along the corridor to the toilets where I idled in a cubicle for ten minutes and wished I still smoked. I hadn't had a cigarette in years, but occasionally I would give almost anything for a smoke. This was one of those moments.

Back in the crowded reception I stayed well away from Lee, who stood next to the buffet with a fat European man who plucked relentlessly at the spread of food while talking non-stop.

Schwartz popped into view on the far side of the room, talking to a well-dressed woman with her back to me. Her immaculately coiffed black hair, perfectly straight and severely cut to hang just below her ears, showed signs of greying. Even Korean men dye their hair at the first hint of grey so I assumed she was foreign and even from this far across the room, I could tell she was an attractive thing. I plotted a course that might give me a better look.

The ever-shifting crowd forced me to change direction and move in closer. I was curious, but not curious enough to cop a fresh set of instructions from Schwartz, whose radar at that moment locked onto me. As he gently took the woman by the arm I looked in the other direction, listening to him call my name. Maybe he wanted me to photograph them, which would suit my current curiosity. With a camera in front of your face, a long rude stare becomes a badge of professionalism. I turned casually towards them with my camera held to my eye. Schwartz leered at me.

'I think you know Miss Kim – Jung to her friends.'

He whispered an apology in her ear before retreating into the crowd.

'Hi Alec.'

The pause stretched forever. I stood numbed, my ears filled with a rushing sound that drowned the conversational hum of the cocktail party. Standing maybe five foot four in low Italian heels and a shimmering grey two-piece suit, she displayed the effortless sense of style that I knew so well. As ever, her make-up was immaculate, and if it weren't for the grey in her hair, she could easily pass for ten years younger. I hadn't seen her in ten years. I realised I was still looking through the viewfinder of the camera. I let go and it bounced harmlessly on its strap. If it had broken into pieces on the polished floor I might not have noticed.

'Jung-hwa.' It came out almost as a whisper. 'What a surprise, I mean what a nice surprise. I – '

'Didn't expect to see me?'

'No, I didn't. How do you know Ben Schwartz?'

'Very well.'

Cryptic. I raised my eyebrows in an unspoken request for more information. She obliged, and I instantly wished she had not.

'We've been married for nine years.'

Schwartz chose this moment to return.

'Darling, there's someone you really must meet.'

She took his hand and didn't look back. My Miss Kim.

'You're as white as a ghost, Brodie.' Bobby Purves looked at me, curious, as Schwartz and Jung-hwa slipped through the throng. 'You didn't know?'

'*You* knew Jung-hwa was married to Schwartz?'

'Of course I bloody did. Everybody here knows. I assumed you did too, and that's why you never mentioned it.' He started to say more, but swallowed his words. The look on his face was one of pity that made me feel very small.

I escaped a few minutes later. I hadn't been able to have another word with Jung-hwa, but after the way she had looked right through me, I wasn't even sure I wanted to try. At the hotel entrance there was a line of waiting taxis.

Thanks to the quieter evening traffic, a few minutes later the cab set me down at a corner shop near the Hyatt, where I stocked up on cheap beer.

Back at the room I walked around in a near-daze, sucking from a bottle of OB. What a first twenty-four hours back in Korea it had been. I'm wined and dined by the K-N Group President and treated to a high class whore who entertains me with a night of sex and whisky. I find out I have to work with Ben bloody Schwartz, that my client company is nearly bankrupt – and that tomorrow I have to photograph a factory in a part of the country where K-N Group has never manufactured anything. On top of all this, from nowhere, my very own Miss Kim pops up wearing Schwartz's wedding ring and freezes me with a chill glance that belies the years we spent joined at the hip. It surely could not get worse than this. I looked at my watch. John Lee was picking me up in less than five hours.

Chapter Seven

Picture a major highway leading out of any capital city on a holiday Saturday. Hopelessly overcrowded, multiple lanes saturated with nose-to-tail traffic that alternates between dead stop and a fifteen miles per hour crawl. On Korean highways rolling jams hurtle along at eighty miles per hour, nothing but blind faith and two yards of Tarmac separating one car or van or truck or express bus from the vehicle in front, the one behind – and the ones on either side.

Koreans are proud of their country's many achievements and quick to boast of their inclusion in world rankings of all stripes, but one top placement they don't go out of their way to publicise is Korea's regular inclusion among the world's top five most dangerous nations for drivers.

Two terrifying hours into the trip and the sun was almost up, the pre-dawn light on the road signs telling us we were nearly half-way to Kwangju. We were barely moving, which could only mean one thing. In traffic this dense travelling this close together, accidents were as catastrophic as they were commonplace. Closing my eyes and reclining the seat I tried to get some sleep, my thoughts crowded by a sense of dread at what lay along the highway, and other worries that refused to go away. Maybe it would only be a breakdown; and maybe I was not involved in what might be an assignment from hell.

I woke to the realisation that traffic was beginning to pick up pace. I tried hard to keep my eyes closed but morbid curiosity won out just in time for me to see a yellow taxi concertinaed to half its length between the back of a 20-ton truck and the front of an express bus. Six feet from me a young man's dead eyes stared from the front passenger seat. Behind him a slender arm, a woman's watch on the wrist, hung limp from the crumpled window frame, blood dripping from carefully-tended fingernails to pool on the ground below. As we passed, a fireman casually threw a blanket over them. I didn't want to think about what that guy saw in his nightmares.

Lee drove on without comment. He had hardly said a word since Seoul, and now conversation seemed almost out of place. Soon the flow regained its normal mad momentum and, as there was no slow lane, nowhere to seek safer passage, we had no option but to join in the fray.

We were still about twenty miles short of Kwangju when Lee pulled off the highway and soon afterwards we swung under a shiny metal archway so new that it was absent of signage. A freshly-paved two lane road flew arrow-straight to a building the size of an aircraft hangar, an isolated man-made island in a sea of rice paddies. In its car park sat six K-N Group buses angled nose-first together in sets of three, like giant sergeant's stripes.

As Lee led me towards an entrance I noticed there were no markings anywhere on the new building. Inside it was another large, industrial-looking structure, single-storeyed with a sloping, corrugated roof, and on the far side, cut in half like a full-sized architect's model. Behind it the hangar's vast walls were one giant, soft-focus mural backdrop of brown rice fields and jagged Korean mountains, almost completely bare of trees. I couldn't remember mountains like that anywhere near the hangar, and South Korea's peaks were all thickly clad from decades of reafforestation since the Korean War.

I turned to Lee. 'What's going on?'

'Let's get your equipment.'

He walked out past two men in K-N uniforms handing out simple denim jackets, red neckerchiefs and what looked like small, gold-and-red badges, to a grinning line of men and women with the round, sun-burnished faces of country farm folk.

Chapter Eight

Whether they realise it or not, tourists to the Democratic Peoples' Republic of Korea experience a bewildering array of citizen actors playing out bizarre roles in a social experiment of Orwellian bleakness.

Swallow the propaganda and North Korea is a land of great joy, of uniform, unshakeable faith in the doctrine of *Juche*, or 'self-reliance', of deep national pride in their stance as resolute isolationists, dependent lackeys to no-one. It is a complete crock of shit.

The abject misery of the Northerner is as plain as the eyes on the actors' faces. The eyes of ordinary people forced to role-play as happy citizens, coerced into feigning blissful contentedness in a land portrayed, however implausibly, as a workers' paradise.

I once watched 'real' actors on a film set at a North Korean movie studio, their unchanging wooden expressions, even in front of a rolling camera, giving the game away. One look at the expensive film camera explained why. Since only the take-up spool was moving, the tool at the centre of the charade obviously had no film in it.

On another visit to the North I witnessed the resigned look of a department store 'shopper' as she surrendered to the store assistant a gaudy sweater that she had just seemingly bought in front of me, her role as a contented consumer suspended until the next foreign visitor ventured onto the painstakingly-directed stage that was Pyongyang Number One Department Store.

The same numbed pain afflicted the eyes of the middle-aged student in the vast Peoples' Library. Open on his desk was an arid tome on the effects of global weather patterns on the rainforests of Brazil. Referring to the text with painstaking attention, he printed in his notebook with a blunt pencil in a childish hand: *Where are you going yesterday? I go to the movies with my good friend Mr Park.*

Three hundred miles to the south, unselfconscious tanned faces laughed loud while they compared badges and, with fat fingers callused from years of farming the land, struggled to fit them to lapels. No matter how blurred they were by decades of prosperity and freedom, the roots these people shared with their northern cousins were instantly recognisable. Where a Northerner's gaunt face would be clouded by a mix of reticence, resignation and fear, these plump-featured southern farm folks bubbled with the humour and curiosity that marked them as a parallel family strand a half-century distinct from their benighted brothers and cousins in the North.

I wondered what story was spun to explain their presence here, dressed as North Koreans and sporting lapel badges bearing the face of the dead Great Leader, instigator of the fratricidal Korean War, and sworn enemy of the South. It would not be too difficult. Tell them they are extras in a documentary film, slip them a few readies and the promise of a decent group meal and *soju* by the crate. It was the 'why' that really bothered me. Why would K-N Group have me here, in provincial South Korea, photographing a mock-up of a North Korean textile factory, phoney North Koreans and all?

I had a tripod and two lights set up when Schwartz arrived swinging an attaché case, cabin luggage tag flickering from its handle. I had suffered a pre-dawn death race on the highway to hell while Schwartz flew down, thirty minutes in the air, the biggest threat to his wellbeing presented by the in-flight coffee.

'What's the story here, Schwartz?'

'Are you ready to get to work?'

'Photographing a fake factory filled with phoney North Koreans wearing Kim Il-sung badges?'

'Do what you have been hired to do, and maybe you'll get to pick up that cheque.'

Maybe?

'My job fee's got nothing to do with you – '

'I don't give a shit what you're making here because I could buy and sell you twice over, Brodie, but if you don't do the job right do you really think Chang's office will sign off on your fee?'

He turned his back on me and I fished out my colour meter and toured the hangar. For the moment, dealing with a nightmarish blend of artificial light sources was a welcome diversion only interrupted by the scream of high-performance engines that shook the entire building. Through an open door I saw a low-flying jet fighter, delta wings reflecting in the water-filled rice fields.

From then, relief from the din of the fighters was fleeting and momentary. Every few minutes one and sometimes two jets screamed overhead, closing down conversation and jangling nerves. The warehouse had to be directly in line with the final approach path of a military airfield.

For four hours I struggled to get giggly sturdy South Korean farm folk to look like downtrodden under-fed North Korean factory workers, an impossible task that called upon every professional trick I could muster. I populated foregrounds with the skinniest people in the building. I made compositions and camera angles draw the onlooker to one or two sharp faces, and used a restricted depth of field to push other subjects out of focus. A critical viewer might commend artful use of focal planes to accentuate my subjects, when in reality I was burying giveaway details in the background blur.

In a business where making the most of every given situation is the norm, I was in new territory, and didn't like it one bit. Tuning my equipment to show an ugly portrait subject in the best possible light, or letting dense shadow hide the run-down machinery in the background of a factory shot was one thing, but save for the contrived con that was advertising, in my line of photography, portraying a completely fictitious environment as reality was unexplored territory.

I worked against rising unease that threatened to push me over the edge into full-blown panic. These photographs had to be part of a scam of proportions I could only guess at. I was thousands of miles from home, up to my ears in debt – and the job that I had hoped would save me now threatened to sink me for good.

'Everything OK?' It was Schwartz, standing right beside me.

'Exactly what am I doing here?'

'Your job.'

'Since when was major-league fraud in the job description? I don't need this.'

'We both know exactly how badly you need the money.'

What did he know about my finances?

'I've still got a return ticket to London, and right now I'm inclined to use it.'

The electronic trill of a mobile phone made him turn away and dip into his jacket pocket.

'Yoboseyo.' Pause. 'Yessir, everything's going fine, on schedule and we just finished the last shot.' *'We'.* I liked that. He looked at me and turned his back again, moving away a few paces, lowering his voice. It had to be Chang on the other end. He must have spoken to Schwartz in English, making replying in Korean an unthinkable insult. I caught snippets of Schwartz describing in impressive detail each of the shots I had set up. Like every PR person I ever worked with, he shamelessly implied that everything achieved so far was only thanks to his personal creativity and deep understanding of the job at hand. He raised his voice to counter the din of yet another passing jet.

'Hello? Hello? Can you hear me? Yes, the Due Diligence team arrives on Friday. They'll be too late to go to the office, and we have their weekend pretty much covered.

'Yessir, the shots from here will be ready in plenty of time. We'll have prints and digital files made for distribution, and leak a few to the newspapers before the London guys land.' After a few more 'yessirs', he rang off, and turned back to me.

'A Due Diligence team arrives in a few days, so if you even *think* about messing us around, you'll never see a dollar of your money. I'll make sure of that.'

He walked away, punching a number into his mobile as he went.

Between fitful snoozes on the long drive back to Seoul I saw only one inter-city bus in a rice field, tyres in the air, windows blown out, completely ignored by passing traffic. An everyday episode of carnage already a few hours old, it might merit a column inch and a postage-stamp photograph buried on an inside page of tomorrow's newspapers.

As traffic flowed through the notch in the line of hills that marked the beginning of the Seoul plain, a curtain of brown smog rose up against the grey-blue sky.

Lee left me at the hotel with instructions to be ready at eight o'clock the next morning. If he knew what or where we were to be shooting, he saw no need to share that information with me, and I wasn't about to ask.

By the time I walked into JJ's, I was freshly showered and fed, and feeling at least the physical benefits of forty-five minutes in the hotel gym.

The bar in the Hyatt basement heaved with singles of all ages. Groups of Korean men hunkered around tables shrouded in blue smoke. Lone Western businessmen sipped selfconsciously at bottles of Bud or Heineken and warily scanned the abundant supply of overdressed women. Scoring in a joint like JJ's was easy. The real challenge was scoring sex that didn't break the expense account budget, as the bar attracted some of the most expensive whores in Korea.

On a small stage of chrome and mirrors a four-piece Filipino band, fronted by a curvaceous Filipina, belted out cover versions of Top-20 hits through the ages. Like every Filipino cover band I ever heard – and they pop up in hotel bars and lobbies all over Asia – they were tightly rehearsed, note-perfect, and with the exception of the singer's curves, eminently forgettable.

Bobby Purves stood alone, tie loosened, one polished brogue on the brass rail, a half-empty litre of draft on the bar in front of him. I saw him make a signal for two more of what might be the most expensive beers in all of Korea.

'I can't afford this place, Bobby. I'm tight for cash until K-N comes up with an advance.'

He shook his head even as he slurped at the fresh glass. 'We'll grab a couple here, then move someplace where the eye-candy's better.'

'Remember I wanted to ask you something?'

'Cutting straight to business?'

'Tell me about Due Diligence.'

'Back to K-N again?'

I nodded and he thought about it for a moment.

'Due Diligence is mostly a formality, but it has to be done before every major company merger or stock flotation or bond issue – like the Global Depository Receipt that K-N is planning now. It's usually carried out by a team of young accountants and investment bankers working out of the big financial centres – London or New York or Tokyo.'

'I hear a team comes here later in the week.'

'That would be about right. They have to pore over the accounts, inspect plants, and check that everything is the way the company says it is, in case there are any surprises.'

'Like?'

'A few years ago one of the big Korean car makers ended up with egg all over its face. Inspectors worked out that actual corporate debt was something like ten times what the company had on the books and a planned take-over by an American car giant was called off like THAT.' He snapped his fingers loudly enough to jolt two barmen to attention. Bobby didn't notice until they both arrived, seeking instructions. He waggled a meaty finger at our glasses.

I thought about what he just said. 'So K-N might be shitting themselves?'

'That depends on how many lies they've been telling. Same as anywhere else in the world, no set of corporate accounts here tells the complete truth.' He lifted his glass halfway to his mouth and stopped. 'Have you heard something I should know about?'

'Schwartz talking about Due Diligence today. I wanted to understand it.'

'Remember who you're talking to here.'

'I'm not hiding anything.' Apart from a fake North Korean manufacturing plant in the rice fields of Cholla province. Bobby had already surprised me by not bringing up the Cholla factory that only last night he had been adamant could not exist. Maybe at the reception he was more plastered than I thought.

I steered the subject away from K-N Group and for a while resisted any notion of drawing it back there. Bobby kept hosing himself down with beer, and I did my best to keep him company.

We decided to move on and when I came back from a visit to the Gents, I found Bobby in earnest discussion with a tall Westerner I had seen before. His was an easy face to remember and at the GDR reception, I noticed him hanging around close to Chang and Schwartz. In his late forties, he had the big build of a sportsman gone to seed – and he wore the worst hairpiece I ever saw, a monstrosity of an avian crash-landing. He was prodding Bobby in the chest with a meaty finger, their faces only inches apart. Bobby pitched further forward until their noses almost touched, and I didn't have to be a lip reader to understand what he said next. *Fuck you.* Bobby pushed past him and joined me at the exit.

'What was that about?'

'Typical Geoff Martinmass. He's a Brit, a banker – you'll get to know him in the next few days, since he is up to his idiotic rug in the GDR.'

'What was he so pissed off about?'

'Me talking to you. If you and I are up to no good, he says, he'll see me ruined. Whatever that's supposed to mean.'

When this job came out of nowhere, I worried that it seemed too good to be true, and now it looked like I might be right. Ignoring Bobby's pleas to accompany him out of the hotel for more drinks, I pled exhaustion, saw him into a taxi, and headed for my room.

I was half-way across the lobby when a small hand slipped under my arm. Even before I looked sideways I recognised the perfume. Miss Hong.

'Hello Alec.'

She played it as if bumping into me at midnight in my hotel was an everyday occurrence. Maybe she was in the neighbourhood. She nuzzled closer and spoke in Korean:

'Would you like me come to your room?'

Did I want to spend another night in bed with the delectable young woman with the tattooed midriff? I led her to the elevators.

In my room she slipped off to shower, modestly pulling

the bathroom door closed behind her. Perfect. I flicked back the latches on one of my equipment cases, peeled back a foam insert and took out a small video camera. If I was quick, I would have time. The tired face that looked back at me from the desk mirror broadened in the first smile of a long day.

Chapter Nine

When John Lee hurried into the Hyatt lobby at eight o'clock sharp I was rooted to an armchair, trying and no doubt failing to look better than I felt. Another night cavorting with Miss Hong had been fun, but right now I would trade some of that frivolity for a little more in the way of sleep.

I levered my way out of the chair and he changed course, the soles of his gleaming shoes mouse-squeaking across the polished lobby floor. I flipped one of the trolleys onto its wheels, stuck it in his outstretched hand and let him follow me to the door.

Lee stood aside and watched as I stripped the two trolleys and filled first the boot, followed by the front seat of his small grey Hyundai. Treating him like a chauffeur was just too tempting a response to the way he lorded over me during the last couple of days, so I stretched out across the back seat and watched him settle, grim-faced, behind the wheel.

While he jousted with the traffic I tried to work out what the hell I was going to do. The implications of photographing a fake factory central to a stock issue worth hundreds of millions of dollars had me spooked. A big part of me argued that I should walk away right now, but the immediate price of doing that was bankruptcy. *We both know exactly how badly you need the money*, Schwartz told me with obvious relish, and the bastard was right.

I could write the whole job off and head towards a queue

of creditors in London, or stick it out to see if I could score as much as possible of the promised fee and somehow steer clear of any fall-out over the GDR. It wasn't much of a choice, and in any case, my threat to leave town had been nothing more than that, since if I went home without the assignment money I was ruined.

We reached Youido in a little under thirty minutes. As the car skirted the broad plaza, Lee pointed across the traffic at the newest of the skyscrapers.

'K-N Towers.' Despite the name, Group HQ was made up of only one building. Sixty floors of oval-sectioned pink curtain wall with a rounded glass-domed atrium, it was unbelievably phallic. Ugly and extravagant and visually gauche, every feature contrived with an unerring eye for bad taste, it was a true slice of corporate conceit. In the 1980s a pre-Olympics ordinance decreed that all new tower buildings must come complete with statuary, and Seoul's broad avenues quickly transformed into open-air art displays. Some were truly inspired, while others exhibited varying degrees of awfulness. In front of K-N Towers stood what looked like dozens of fifty-gallon drums welded together, blown open by explosives, and dipped in chrome.

The appearance of the Hyundai rolling down the steep ramp made a man in uniform leap out of his glass cabin to salute as we careened beneath a rising barrier, spiralled into a dimly-lit underground car park, and took up a free space in a corner filled with a mini-forest of metal piping.

Lee helped unload the car, and after I spread the equipment between the two trolleys he took control of one and led me to a freight elevator. Its battered doors rattled open to reveal inner walls protected by splintered plywood and a worn-out old man in a uniform shiny from long use. His unhealthy pallor and stooped frame made me wonder what came first, the job or the infirmity. The musty interior reeked of cigarette smoke and garlic. The lift operator asked Lee where we were going and Lee told him, very abruptly. The sworn ethic central to Korea's Confucian value system dictates eternal respect for one's elders, except when you can pull rank on strangers, in which case you treat them like shit.

The elevator disgorged us in an unfinished corridor with cigarette ends half-buried in cement dust along its grimy edges, but where one set of fire doors was all that separated us from the ostentatious designer chic of an upper management suite. The abruptness of the change made me think of deluxe hotels, of the instant shift from the grease and grunge of inner-warren worker trails to the glowing luxury that is 'front of house'. Lee looked uncomfortable hauling my heavy trolley past colleagues bearing box files and attaché cases and he stepped up the pace, turning through a set of double doors. I followed him into a swank boardroom, parked my trolley, and leaned one hand on the end of the vast central table. Designed to impress but built down to a cost, it sagged under my weight.

'Mr Schwartz wants to photograph Mr Chang and Mr Martinmass in here, with this,' he waved an open hand at a huge piece of calligraphy, 'as a background.'

Goody for Schwartz. It was a typical PR hack's portrait location, selected without any practical consideration for composition, lighting, or any of another half-dozen of my immediate concerns. The setting was too crowded, the table oversized and too close to the calligraphy – which was covered in reflective glass – and the low ceiling seriously cramped my lighting options. I turned to Lee.

'I will have to take a look around, to see if I can find a better place.'

'Mr Schwartz said – '

'If I have to I'll do the shot here. But first I am going to see if there is anywhere better.'

I was wasting my time and I knew it, since even at his most co-operative, Lee would never second-guess his superiors, but a last vestige of professional pride made me go through the motions.

In ten minutes we were back in the boardroom, Lee looking pleased with himself. His smirk faded when I produced a roll of tools and attacked the underside of the table. When he leaned down to see what I was doing, I handed him a screwdriver.

'I need space to work so we have to get rid of at least half of this table.' Instead of joining me he walked out of the room, and I stifled a stream of curses, some of them addressed at my own folly. Butting heads with Lee was only going to give me a headache and after too much to drink and next to no sleep, I already had one of those.

A few minutes later I was still wrestling with the first oversized screw when Lee returned with two men in boiler suits and tool belts who good-naturedly shooed me from under the table and set about tearing it apart. In the time it took me to ready a tripod and a couple of strobe lights they had two-thirds of the table broken down to component pieces and spirited from the room. At last I could get on with the bit I was good at.

I positioned chairs where Chang and Martinmass would sit and took a good look at them through the camera lens; eye to viewfinder, I moved the tripod around to improve the framing. Of the picture I planned only the bare bones were on view, so in my mind's eye I put meat to them. The task was to set up my strobes in such a way that, in a synchronised flash lasting less than one thousandth of a second, they painted the entire scene with sculpted light that contrived to look natural. There is an industry obsession with the 'art' of commercial photography, but what I do is more about craft. Lights, cameras and everything else I drag to a shoot are no more than tools, and if I can lay any claim to craftsmanship it is only because I am so familiar with the contents of my toolbox.

I felt almost relaxed until Ben Schwartz appeared. He

glanced at me standing behind my camera and loitered in front of the tripod while he surveyed the set-up. At length he turned around.

'Mr Chang and Mr Martinmass will be here in five minutes. You will have ten minutes to take the shot, and after that they have an important meeting to attend.' He swept back out the door, leaving me to do forty-five minutes' work in a tenth of that time. Added to this, today I was using medium format film cameras in search of a crisp, corporate look to the images; working with film required far greater care and more time than digital, and now time was short. I reached for the Polaroid camera and waved at the two guys in boiler suits.

Chang and Martinmass arrived, hands in pockets, chatting like old friends. If the English banker remembered me from the night before he gave no sign. I got straight to work. Chang chose the chair on the camera's left and I showed him the latest Polaroid. He looked at it closely while Martinmass peered over his shoulder.

In the Polaroid, two boiler-suited men, eyes glinting, sat in stiff parody of executives in two-thousand-dollar business suits. Chang handed the print back to me, leaving Martinmass pawing at thin air.

'I'll just shoot one or maybe two more test shots to fine-tune the lighting.'

'Do you have to?' Martinmass looked uncomfortable already. He was probably camera shy, which was hardly surprising. If I wore what looked like a dead bird on my head, I too would avoid cameras. Without replying, I floated around the set with my flash meter checking exposures before I moved to behind the tripod.

'OK, since I am shooting transparency film, the first thing I do is take another Polaroid.' The flashes fired in sync. 'One more.' Again. One eye on the clock, I switched to the working camera and double-checked its settings. Peeling the back off the first Polaroid, I stood under one of my lights to view it through a magnifying loupe that lived on a string around my neck.

'That looks fine.' At this point, if there was time, I usually showed the Polaroid to the subjects, but today I was in a hurry.

'Let me see.' It was Martinmass again. Schwartz was already looking at his watch. I passed the Polaroid to Chang, who looked at it, nodded, and handed it on as I peeled the backing from the second preview shot. Martinmass waved at me like I was a waiter who had brought him the wrong order.

'Give me that magnifying thing.'

Since you asked so nicely.

'What's that?' He poked a chewed fingernail at his head in the Polaroid.

He meant a faint shadow on the calligraphy frame behind him, and that I had already spotted.

'I'll take that out by lengthening the exposure. The Polaroid camera doesn't let me do that,' I lied. I had set it wrongly, but it was an easy mistake to rectify.

'I'm not sure that I like the look of it.'

Schwartz turned to me, pointing at his watch. 'You have to get a move on. The meeting – '

'The meeting will not start without them. Now, to real film.' They sat up in their chairs. 'I'm going to take a couple of rolls of film, so we'll be here for a few more minutes. That way we get a selection of good shots where nobody is blinking, and the second roll is in case anything happens to the first one at the lab.' This was standard spiel, designed to let me feel for the limits of my subjects' patience.

'Do you *really* need two rolls?'

No surprise that it was Martinmass, the limits on his patience there for all to see.

I spoke to Chang:

'The sooner we get started, the sooner you can be off to your meeting.'

'This shouldn't take long Geoff.' Geoff scowled, and I fired the camera. He looked at me angrily. I fired again. Two-nil.

'That's the way. Nice and cheery.' Bobby Purves was right, he was an arsehole, but on top of that, unless I was wrong, something more than an aversion to cameras was making him very uptight, and whatever it was involved me.

As soon as I finished the second roll of film, Martinmass made a show of stomping from the room. Chang beckoned to Lee. Young Koreans, when under pressure to give maximum face to a senior of far superior standing, sometimes adopt a strange gait, a flat-footed scuttle with arms locked at the sides, palms facing downwards. It always makes me think of stray penguins desperately trying to catch up with the colony. Lee did that now, crossing the room in an ungainly flash, and Chang spoke quietly to him. Lee looked over at me, nodding as he spoke, acknowledging an instruction. At the door, Chang turned back:

'Mr Lee will bring you to my office.' He left the room without waiting for a response. People like Chang get to speak when they want and listen to the rest of us only when they feel like it.

Twenty-five minutes later Lee left me with a trim, middle-aged secretary who hovered like an insect beside a strategically placed desk that controlled access to an executive suite. After giving me an unashamed look of appraisal, she pulled a freeze-dried expression that might have been a smile.

'This way, please.' Prim efficiency, not a hint of an accent. I walked in the wash of an expensive scent that failed to override the foul undertones of Marlboro Red. She led me along a broad carpeted corridor hung with original oil paintings until we stopped at a heavy wooden door. Placing herself between me and a wall-mounted security pad, she dialled a six-figure entry code, waited for a low buzzing followed by the clunk of powerful dead-bolts, and palmed the perfectly balanced door inwards.

'Mr Chang will be with you in a moment.' The big doors closed quietly, leaving me alone in an ante room slightly smaller than the Centre Court at Wimbledon. There were ornate Asian rugs, dozens of examples of Korean celadon pottery, several huge pieces of overstuffed furniture, and along the far wall, floor-to-ceiling windows that looked down over Youido Plaza.

The Plaza was speckled with walkers and joggers and weaving, wobbling bicycles from hire stalls that lined one edge of the giant square. A long time ago I saw it loosely filled with a several hundred thousand-strong rent-a-crowd, bussed in from the suburbs to cheer for a Presidential candidate. He did the politician's JFK waving routine, posed arms aloft for the phalanx of scuffling photographers and dutifully promised his delirious supporters a prosperous Korea free of poverty and corruption. The same man went on to win the election and rule the nation for a term marred by precisely the same kind of corruption that cursed all his ex-military predecessors. Astonishing degrees of change had arrived in Korea over the last quarter-century but some things, tragically, were too deeply engrained in the cultural fabric to disappear overnight.

I had enjoyed my photography back then. Jostling for position with the Korean Press Pack might have been brutal at times, but it was good clean honest work, far removed from the shitfest I found myself in now.

'It is a wonderful view.'

Chang looked amused to have startled me. He had come through a set of doors that led to a private office. Right on cue came a soft knock at the corridor entrance and in came a short woman in company uniform, who somehow managed to bow repeatedly while porting a full tray. Chang pointed dismissively at a low table with soft chairs on two sides. She quickly poured two steaming cups of coffee, gestured theatrically at the dishes of sugar and powdered cream, and retreated backwards through the doors, still bowing.

'Sit down, Brodie.'

Any hint of warmth in Chang's manner was gone.

Chapter Ten

Chang fingered his coffee cup as the door from the corridor opened and Schwartz slipped into the room as if he belonged. He let the door close behind him, and stood leaning against the wall. Chang's eyes flitted towards him before coming back to stare into mine.

'You have an idea how important the Global Depository Receipt is to my company?'

'I think I do.'

'Its success depends very much on the quality of its marketing and presentation. Which is where you come in.'

'Normally I would have no problem with that.' Emphasis on *normally*.

'But?'

'The fake factory shoot.'

'Ben said that troubled you.'

'It involves me in something that could put me in jail, and I want no part of it.'

There, I had said it. Chang shook his head and looked to Schwartz, who remained mute. Chang turned back to me.

'We have a business arrangement – '

'To take photographs. Nothing more.'

'At a day-rate far in excess of what you usually command in London.'

Fuck, was there anything he didn't know?

'Rates vary from one project to the next.' I sounded lame and I knew it.

'Yesterday in Cholla province was a very small part of the assignment, one forced upon us by political realities. A *representation* of factories that exist already but which we have no way to photograph due to political sensitivities in the North. My company requires those photographs to make the GDR launch a success.'

He made it sound almost plausible. Maybe the factories were in place on the other side of the border, and maybe I was making a big deal out of something that might, for all I knew, be a level of subterfuge common in such big share market deals.

I stood up. 'I'll think about it.'

'You should also think about whether you need to be paid for this job.'

The condescending smile on his face said he knew he had me.

'Needing money is one thing, Chang,' I said, the insult implicit in addressing him by his surname. 'But agreeing to this is another thing altogether.'

Chang shook his head and turned to Schwartz, who looked back at him, eyebrows raised in question. Chang nodded sharply. An unspoken instruction. Schwartz opened the door and left the room. I shivered involuntarily and headed for the same door. As I reached for it, Chang spoke again.

'John Lee will pick you up in the morning, as usual.'

He sounded very sure of himself.

Chapter Eleven

Long and thin and laced to a single main street like a rural village set amidst an urban sprawl of ten million, Seoul's inner suburb of Itaewon always did have a split personality. By day it was an innocent shopping magnet, by night a seedy pit of after-dark entertainment.

Nightfall had already drawn the curtain down on a day's shopping, but I didn't want to buy jeans or sneakers or a ski suit.

I was after the darker side of the Ville and my priorities were plain. I was going to get hammered, and if even a hint of Itaewon's seedier side remained, I might go there too. For it is in his cups that the reckless male finds his focus, making perfect sense of even the most casual back alley flophouse jump.

First I had to eat, and for that I wanted to go truly local. Yong San Kalbi has traded from an Itaewon side alley since long before I first set foot in the country. Nearly every Korean neighbourhood has a *kalbi jib*, or 'rib house', a dining delight evolved from the village with refreshingly few concessions to the big city. Abject poverty sits vivid in the memories of Koreans who can recall the period immediately after the war, three years that tore the peninsula in two. In the first decades following the 1953 armistice – a 'temporary' peace agreement remains in place, more than fifty years later – millions of Koreans lived with poverty and hunger while farmlands were brought back to pre-war outputs, and from a flattened nation grew the beginnings of an export-driven economy. In a country where meat on the table was once a luxury, it is no surprise that restaurants overloaded with meat options are so popular today.

The typical *kalbi jib* has basic sturdy furnishings and glowing charcoal fires in mini braziers that are wedged into holes in the middle of scarred and scorched tables. On offer is a selection of raw, marinated meats roasted above the coals to carbonized perfection and surrounded by spicy side dishes of chopped and pickled vegetables, sticky white rice in shiny stainless-steel bowls and tall bottles of chilled beer on demand.

The squeal of an ill-fitting aluminium door drew an automatic staff chorus of welcomes. The restaurant was one large room with an uneven concrete floor and maybe fifteen heavy tables, six of which were busy with locals, mostly men doing the after-office male bonding thing, drinking hard and loud and unabashed in their enjoyment. I made my way to a corner table next to an open window, not that it would make much difference. Going home smelling like a barbecued garlic clove was fundamental to the *kalbi jib* experience.

A short waitress in her thirties with chunky legs, flat shoes and a glaring squint plonked a heavy glass of barley tea in front of me and waved at a menu framed on a concrete pillar.

A few seconds later she scurried off to deal with an order for a double portion of pork ribs, one bowl of steamed rice, the full array of side dishes and the coldest tall beer she could find.

I picked at the side dishes while a charcoal brazier was summoned and carried in at arm's length by a wiry young man in sooty t-shirt and blackened jeans.

The waitress returned carrying an alloy platter draped with pork ribs beautifully filleted to leave a long tress of transparent marinated meat clinging to each short bone.

Using metal chopsticks she painstakingly arranged ribs on a silver grille that sat above the glowing coals. As the meat readied I got the standard demonstration of how best to enjoy it. She palmed a lettuce leaf, smeared spicy bean paste across it with the back of a spoon, swept a piece of sizzling meat through the mix of coarse salt and sesame oil, and added it to the leaf with some diced spring onion. Next, she carefully folded the leaf until it was a tightly-packed bite size and placed it, loose ends down, on my rice. I picked up the package in my chopsticks, popped it in my mouth, and met her enquiring look with enthusiastic nods. It had my approval, and she was visibly pleased.

When she got over the initial surprise that I could converse in Korean she chatted incessantly, telling me she was single and that all her free time was spent at a nearby church where the minister was a very great man. She loved her church which was like a second family to her. She repeated this several times in slightly different language, as if unsure that I could grasp its importance.

I was glad when at last she left me alone. I felt for the lonely soul, her peasant roots and sad looks condemning her to a lowly job and a solitary life in a society where women who failed to marry and to breed barely merited inclusion on the social register.

My thoughts turned to Jung-hwa. She would be nearly forty now. I wondered if she had children, and what life was like with a bastard like Schwartz for a husband. Better than anything I ever offered her, was the obvious answer. When I picked up the beer bottle it came off the table too quickly; I had already drained it. Shameless drunken escapism screamed loud, and I was in Itaewon to wash away fears old and new. I called for the bill, tipped the waitress generously, and hurried out in search of a glimpse of my past.

On that first night in the Cowboy Club, the sexy Miss Kim surprised me. We danced and drank and talked and laughed and danced some more. I remembered the tease and the seeming promise of the slow numbers, 'Careless Whisper' and 'Midnight Train to Georgia', songs that today still take me back to that dingy club all those years ago, still inspire a memory-driven stirring of the loins.

The surprise was in her refusal to come home with me. She took no offence at the request, but no matter how hard I pushed the point, she held her ground. At three in the morning, I walked her to a cab. She lived with her family so I couldn't have her phone number, but she did take mine after a little persuasion and promised to call. As she waved at me through the back window of the taxi, I almost believed her. Then she was gone, without so much as a goodnight kiss. Bobby and I eventually rounded off the night at the infamous Flower Shop. Not many flowers, but a great deal of money changed hands in the Flower Shop's back rooms. We each took a shop girl through the back for a *short time*. How short was immaterial, since I was so drunk that when I awoke the next morning I would never have recalled even being there if not for the wilted carnation pinned to my shirt pocket. I couldn't remember a single thing about the whore I had been with, but clear and sharp was the memory of Miss Kim's amused expression when I forced my telephone number on her as she clambered into the back of the taxi.

One morning a few days later, the phone woke me early. On the telephone her English became even more self-assured, and we talked and laughed like old friends. She agreed to meet me that Friday night.

The NFL was an Itaewon institution, one of the earliest American-run discos with decent music, cold beer and hot and cold running local women. Local men who made the mistake of trying to climb the club steps were politely turned away by the ever-smiling Amerasian bodybuilder who reigned supreme at the door.

The club belonged to a football-mad American soldier-turned-civilian whose Korean wife handled the minefield that was licensing and local government and police corruption. She did such a good job that prosperity grew unimpeded for years until she caught her husband with another woman. Divorce negotiations started out nasty but soon fell away, and within days the club was closed down by police for a long list of 'violations'. It was an act of contrived vengeance, Korean style. If the American thought he was going to keep the place to himself, then she had ways of showing him how far off the mark he was. It re-opened a few days later after a deal had been struck, one that reportedly cost the American a lot more than he had ever anticipated.

Miss Kim arrived late, setting a precedent that she kept up for all the years we were together. She wore black again, another revealing low-cut number with strings for shoulder straps and a tight, fifties-style skirt that hugged her thighs and restricted her steps but didn't stop her dancing sinuously for long spells.

As closing time loomed I couldn't decide. Go for broke and take the chance of spoiling a great night, or settle once more for the uncertainty of another phone call? Then she stood up, slipped one arm through the long strap of her shoulder bag, and looked at me, rising amusement parting her painted lips.

'Taxi?' I said.

'How about your place.' She said it with a smile that made me weak at the knees.

I had tidied my room especially, and left the heating on to warm the freshly laundered Korean bedding that lay on the hot papered floor. Not a lot of sleep was had that night, but we did stay warm.

After that we met at least once a week, almost always in Itaewon, usually ending up on my warm floor. In bed just as out of it, she had a strength and confidence that belied the blinkered stereotype of the demure Asian woman. We

85

explored endlessly, experimented tirelessly, and often exploded together in spontaneous laughter.

Sometimes we met during her lunch break near the import/export company where she worked. These were quick hot hours of passionate surrender in a small inn on a back street in the thick of Dongdaemun Market, leaving us no time for lunch before she repaired her make-up and hurried to her office and I went back to spend the rest of the day teaching English, deliciously conscious that I smelled of her sex.

I wandered from club to bar, led by discarded pockets of memory fogged by alcohol and years of separation from Itaewon's singular brand of hedonism. Two hours later I sat next to the window in the top-floor Starship Bar and looked out over the lights of the city and down on the glow of the clubs and the action on the streets.

I checked my watch. Nearly eleven o'clock, time for a change of scenery, and the Nashville was only a couple of hundred yards away, but in a separate world. Another Itaewon survivor story, the Nashville was a cluttered bar that served mostly middle-aged Westerners, civilian beer guzzlers whose personal sporting efforts stretched no further than the bar's pool table and darts boards.

Bobby Purves sat at a round table bent under the strain of chunky glass mugs full of foamy draft lager. When he weaved over to meet me I knew he had had a few.

'Hey-up, Jock, you look like you've already sunk some piss.'

I looked around the room. 'Then I'll fit right in.'

I waved through the smoke to the Korean barman, an old face I recognised from days gone by when I used to be here several nights a week. I held my palms horizontal, one far above the other, and waggled two fingers. He got straight to work. Drunks love a professional.

'I was wondering if you'd drop in.'

'Didn't mean to. Got tired of my own company.'

'How's the job going?'

'Alright.' Beyond Bobby I recognised a face I knew. 'I see our pal Martinmass is here.' The grimace Bobby pulled was answer enough.

'I had to photograph him today along with Chang. You're right. He is a bad-tempered arsehole.'

'He'll be in a better mood tonight. See the guy trying to sit on his knee?'

Beside Martinmass, a smooth-faced Korean in his early twenties and wearing a blue suit jacket buttoned up tight had his chair pulled close. He was hanging on the big guy's every utterance.

'Martinmass is gay?'

'He thinks nobody knows.'

'The same guy who thinks wearing a dead crow on his head will make him one of the lads.' I remembered him tugging nervously at his ring finger whenever the camera was pointing his way. 'He's married, right?'

'You almost never see him and his missus in the same room. She's a pillar of the Chamber of Commerce wives' scene, does endless conspicuous charity work. She has recently been lobbying for a memorial to Diana in the garden of the Embassy.'

I had enough of this place already.

'Let's go somewhere else, get ourselves one for the road, eh?'

Famous last words. Two hours later, I poured myself from a taxi outside the Hyatt and did my best to negotiate the still-crowded hotel lobby with minimum collateral damage to civilians or hotel furnishings. Just another night in Korea. When I lived in Seoul it was like this, too. Dangerously high levels of alcoholic intake on multiple nights of the week. No wonder I loved every minute of it.

I got myself to my room and, switching on the shower full-blast, stripped off clothes that reeked of sweat and stale tobacco smoke. I was drying off when the doorbell rang.

Twice in the last three nights, the lovely Miss Hong had surprised me. Could this be her again? I pulled on a towelling dressing gown and pulled open the door.

A Korean man in a dark suit and a baseball cap pulled low stood in the murk of the corridor.

'Mr Brodie?'

'Yes?'

'For you.'

He thrust a small package in my hand and was gone. No signature required. It was a box about the size of a paperback book with wrapping around it, and it felt chilled, as if recently taken from a refrigerator. I tore at the paper, and immediately recognised a Fuji instant film box like the ones I used. Inside that, something was wrapped in greaseproof paper, smaller and more dense than a sandwich. I carefully unfolded it, and screamed loud enough to shake the curtains.

Vile and glistening and almost alive, the bloody contents fell to the desk blotter with a sickening wet thunk. Miss Hong's belly button, yin yang tattoo and all.

Chapter Twelve

'Good morning Mr Brodie, how may I help you? Mr Brodie?'

'Never mind.'

'Yessir. Have a nice day.'

It was too late for that. I couldn't remember picking up the phone, and the programmed chirpiness of the hotel receptionist had slapped me from an awful nightmare into a reality no less dire. The base unit of the telephone was splashed with droplets of dark red that drew fattening trails to the flap of flesh that sat screaming at me from the centre of the desk blotter.

Miss Hong was a beautiful thing. A little heavy on the make-up, but despite their natural beauty, Korean women see no irony in being the world's biggest consumers of cosmetics. Her expensive clothes were on the showy side, but nothing on the everyday surface of Miss Hong hinted at her profession. She was a stunning young woman. Determined, hard-working, making a success of her talents – and very, very good at her job.

Only when the clothes came off did she shed some of her patina of professional class respectability. Not being a pop star or a gang member, the two tattoos she sported marked Miss Hong indelibly as a sex-industry pawn. One was a tiny flower on her left breast, exaggerated pink and dark reds glowing from flawless olive skin. The other was the Korean flag around her belly button.

The *'Taegukki'* is bright and cheery and as overused on the streets of Seoul as the Union Jack is in tourist-trodden London. In its centre is a circular yin yang in red/blue on a pure white background, with four black trigrams representing seasons, points of the compass and other worldly elements I could not recall. Koreans love their flag and take every opportunity to fly it or, better still, to wave it. Miss Hong wore it, in a three-colour yin yang tattoo around her belly button. Now it lay on the desk, shrivelled and discoloured, yet unmistakeable in all its hellish detail.

I fished a name card from my wallet and picked up the phone again. After three rings someone answered awkwardly, followed by a thud as the phone at the other end bounced off a hard surface.

'Yoboseyo.'

'John Lee? It's Alec Brodie.'

'Mr Brodie.' Long pause. 'It is two o'clock in the morning. What is wrong?'

I thought about telling him exactly what was wrong, and decided against it.

'I need you to come to my hotel room.'

'Can I see you in the mor – '

'Mr Chang will be very angry if you don't come immediately.'

'Mr Chang? I'm sorry, I do not underst – '

'Shikurrup. Pally-waa.' *Shut it. Come quickly.*

I put the phone down. He would come. The mention of Chang was enough to guarantee that. I gently placed a sheet of writing paper on top of Miss Hong's *Taegukki* and sought solace from the mini bar.

I had polished off the whisky miniatures and was making a dent in the vodka stocks when I heard a quiet knock at the door. I checked the spyhole before opening up. Lee's face was of the luminescent red that suffuses many Asians when they drink. In London a face so red would make you call the paramedics, but in Seoul at this time of night he didn't warrant a second glance. Before he spoke I silenced him with a raised hand and let him follow me into the room. I stood by the desk, and with the tips of forefinger and thumb raised the writing paper by its edge. His face blanched instantly.

'Aigoo jingeruh.' *Disgusting.* 'What is it?'

I raised my tee shirt and with finger and thumb drew a rectangle around my navel. His gaze flicked from my stomach to the desktop and back. I watched realisation dawn, his expression widening in growing horror. His mouth hung open, and he drew a glistening tongue across dry lips.

'You remember the two business girls from the Japanese restaurant?'

He nodded.

'When I came back to my room that night, one of them was waiting for me. This,' I waved the paper at the desk blotter, 'was hers.' Lee, hand hard against his face, pivoted and rushed towards the bathroom. I opened another vodka miniature, sat down on the bed, and tried not to listen. Just as I realised that nausea had yet to even affect me, saliva flooded my mouth. I fled in Lee's footsteps and found him staring blankly at the mirror, hands hard on the edge of the wash hand basin, taps running at full power. I sank with my knees astride the toilet bowl and heaved explosively.

When I returned to the room Lee was reaching for the telephone.

'Not that line. Use your mobile.'

I had watched the cop shows, and calling Chang from the room phone was not the smart move. Lee nodded, reached into his inside jacket pocket for a late-model Samsung, and hit a speed-dial number. While it connected, he took himself back to the bathroom, and from there I heard him talking urgently in a low voice laden with honorifics.

An hour later when Chang arrived, not a hair out of place, I was leaning back on a mountain of soft pillows, alternating sips of vodka with swallows of icy mineral water. A beer can sat in a pool of condensation on the cabinet beside me. It popped open with an angry hiss that startled Chang and Lee into momentary silence. They looked at me with contempt before going back to their conversation, voices low and speech so fast that I barely caught a word.

I closed my eyes and tried to answer two questions. Who could have done this to Miss Hong and, forchrissakes, why? I thought back to Lee's face when he realised what lay on the desk, a genuine look of spontaneous horror. Chang seemed much less affected but he was older, more experienced, and from the phone summons, had known what to expect. More importantly, his place in the chain of command dictated the cool exterior. I pried open eyes heavy with the blunt force of alcohol working its way through my system. It was nearly four o'clock in the morning and Lee and Chang were still deep in dialogue. I dozed off to the twin soundtracks of voices murmuring in the room beside me, and others shrieking at me from within my own head.

I awoke to set eyes upon a small video camera that nestled high in the upper folds of the heavy curtain. It had completely slipped my mind. I buried a look of horror in a bout of fake coughing and covered my face with my hands. Lee sat impassively in a chair at the end of the bed while three men in dark suits and latex gloves tore the room apart. Chang was gone. I sat up and fingered a mystery bruise over my ribs that I had first spotted early the previous morning. Maybe Miss Hong had played rougher than I remembered. I made sure it was covered by my shirt before I sat up. That made two things I hoped would escape their notice.

'What's going on?'

Lee rubbed life into his tired face and pointed to one of the three dark suits.

'This is Detective Kwok. He and I went to high school together; we are old friends.'

Kwok was tall, painfully thin and for a man in his thirties conspicuously bald, with what little that remained of his hair cropped close, a fat black stripe above each pointed ear. His features were angular to the point of jaggedness, and from a dark mole on the edge of his jaw a half-dozen wiry black hairs trailed long.

'Are you ready to talk?' He spoke in casual, American-accented English.

I hesitated. He looked impatient.

'Should I have a lawyer here?' My tongue had trouble getting around the words.

Kwok pointed at the bloody mess, now ziplocked in a clear evidence bag. 'Tell me what you know about this.'

My mouth felt like it was coated with animal fur. I raised my hands in a 'wait a minute' sign, and went to the bathroom to brush my teeth, but everything I owned, toothbrush included, had been bagged and tagged. I rinsed my mouth and drank metallic cold water straight from the tap before returning to where Kwok had set out a seat for me. He leaned against the desk, forcing me to look up at him. Basic interrogation techniques, paragraph one. A notebook and pen appeared in his hands.

'Three nights ago, on Sunday night, I met two women at dinner with Mr – '

'Detective Kwok already knows about that.'

Kwok silenced Lee with an angry glance and waved at me to continue.

'When I came back to my room, one of the women was waiting for me. Her name was Miss Hong. She had taken the room key from my jacket pocket and let herself in.'

'So you arrived back at the hotel alone?'

'Yes. I came in the front entrance at about eleven-thirty. I remember looking at the clocks above the Reception desk.'

'Did anyone see you with her?'

'No, I don't think – wait a minute, yes. There was a security guard.'

I plucked at a memory of Miss Hong opening my room door from inside, wearing only a towelling bathrobe. She waved the whisky miniatures and expressed her breathy welcome just as a deep voice from behind made me jump with fright. A hotel security guard on corridor patrol, smiling indulgently. I related all of this to Kwok.

'And after you came into the room, what did you do?'

'What do you think?'

He frowned at the thought. 'Tell me about the tattoo.'

I explained how Miss Hong liked drinking games, how we ended up licking whisky from each other's belly button and, since hers was tattooed so distinctly, I wasn't about to forget it in a hurry.

'Was there any dispute between you and Miss Hong?'

'Definitely not. We stayed up most of the night drinking and having sex.'

Kwok seemed to believe at least this much. He doubtless had already talked to the hotel's housekeeping department. If what happened to Miss Hong had taken place here, no room maid could have failed to notice.

'When did Miss Hong leave?'

'When I woke up, she was already gone. I was really drunk, so she could have left anytime.' I finally grasped what he was getting at. 'But nothing happened to her that night.'

'Why not?'

'Because she was here again on Tuesday, the night before last.'

'You asked her to come here again?'

'No, she just appeared. I bumped into her in the lobby and she invited herself up.'

'For more sex?' He was taking notes as he spoke.

'When I woke up she was gone again. Same as the first time.'

'How much did you pay her for the two nights?'

'What?'

'She was surely a prostitute. When did you pay her, and how much?'

I knew before I even spoke how stupid I sounded.

'She didn't ask for money.'

'How about the first time?' He looked at his notepad. 'Sunday night.'

'I thought Mr Chang sent her.'

'You're a photographer.'

'Yes.'

'A professional photographer.'

'Yes.'

'How often do you spend days taking photographs for other people, free of charge?'

I shook my head.

'Is there something so special about you that a prostitute would spend two nights in your bed without cash changing hands?'

'I never paid her.'

Kwok looked sceptical, and asked about the delivery of the package. I explained that it was very dim in the hotel corridor, and that I didn't get a good look at the delivery man. I could only remember was that he was Korean and that he wore a dark suit, not a hotel uniform, with a baseball cap pulled low. Kwok spoke softly to one of his colleagues, who stepped out into the corridor. A few seconds later he was back, murmuring in Kwok's ear. He glanced at me.

'What?'

'Light bulbs outside your door have been removed.' He changed tack:

'Can you remember anything else about what happened between you and Miss Hong that might help us?'

'Not really. The obvious thing is right there in the bag.'

'Aren't you forgetting something?'

My stomach lurched. Maybe he knew.

'I don't understand.'

Kwok picked up the clear plastic bag that held the green Fuji instant film box that the package had arrived in.

'The serial number on this matches the boxes in your camera case.'

Without looking away, he plucked yet more evidence bags from a folder and laid them out in front of me. Ten of them. Ten instant photographs of Miss Hong and a visibly pissed Alec Brodie, naked and in a variety of pornographic poses. One of them showed me holding a whisky miniature and pointing gleefully at her tattooed stomach. We were sitting at the bottom of the bed and she took the photograph by pointing the camera at the mirror. In bedrooms the world over, digital cameras were used to the same ends, but I liked the tactile experience of shooting Polaroids and sharing the wait for the results. We had shot all ten and laughed together at the blurry square frames. Our fingerprints had to be all over the pictures in the evidence bags.

'Are you aware, Mr Brodie, that in my country the penalty for murder is death?'

I leaned down, hand on forehead, hiding my face and trying to keep their attention on me. I prayed that they didn't look up.

Chapter Thirteen

When Kwok and his colleagues left I gave them twenty minutes to be sure they were not going to return and, after checking the deserted corridor, slipped back into the room and double-locked the door behind me. From the chairs that flanked the small coffee table it was impossible to credit how lucky I had been when Kwok and his boys failed to spot the little video camera clamped amidst the ruffles at the top edge of the heavy curtain. I had watched, frozen with panic, while one of the juniors pulled back both curtains, gave a cursory glance at the empty window ledge, and roughly tugged the drapes back into place, the overlap almost entirely concealing the camera from view. For two solid hours, I lived in fear of them spotting its lens peeking from within the curtain fabric. Now, it took me twenty seconds to unfasten the little bracket and bring it back down.

I slipped back out to the corridor carrying only a package wrapped in a laundry sack. Two scary minutes of jiggling at a time-worn lock got me into a chambermaid's store-room. I leaned back on the door and lit up the bare bulb suspended by a cord from the ceiling. Metal shelving covered three walls, the fourth taken up by a long stainless counter and double sink. High in one corner looked good, a pile of linen tied in neat bundles, still in fine condition, but in the pampered world of the deluxe hotel, already too well-used for a spoiled clientele. I worked my package deep within the folds of towels coated in dust that looked undisturbed in months.

Pre-dawn in a five-star hotel lobby is a setting I have often enjoyed, whether sitting half-pissed and sucking on an ill-advised nightcap, or ahead of an early morning flight, perking up my senses with caffeine.

I lounged close to horizontal in the plush armchair, cup and saucer on my chest. Six o'clock in the morning and sleep was the last thing on my mind. A low table supported my feet and beside them sat a large pot of strong coffee. Enough of that and I might out-run the cloud of fatigue that threatened to smother me like a heavy blanket.

The cathedral-sized lobby hummed with the muted din from an electric floor polisher swung around by a cleaner in a dark green boiler suit ironed so lovingly it had knife-edge creases down the sides of the arms and legs. Waxy dough-nuts passed in sweeping arcs from polishing pad to marble floor, bringing it to a sparkling state worthy of the big-bucks customers upstairs. Guests whose heads had yet to stir from over-sized feather pillows.

Down below them, my head was a mess. Arriving in Seoul four nights ago felt like a homecoming, but right now, I never felt further from home.

Being allowed to sit here was confusing enough. A short while ago, when I thought I could be facing months behind bars while Korean justice sat locked in the mire of bureau-cracy, Detective Kwok only advised me to 'stay close to the hotel'. They took my passport, but they didn't even finger-print me, and I couldn't work out why I was getting the kid-gloves treatment. Maybe it was all down to the power of Chang's money. With K-N Group on the verge of an investment drive that might pluck the entire corporation out of the debt fire, the last thing Chang needed was bad publicity. Dining out with a whore who wound up mutilated after spending a couple of nights screwing his contractor would not be great PR. If so, I hoped he could keep this under wraps until the real murderer was found. Wrapped up in that thought was the assumption that Chang already knew I didn't kill Miss Hong. This in turn might mean something else: that he knew who did.

I drained the coffee cup, signed the tab and walked out into the pre-dawn cool.

With over ten million inhabitants, a million-plus vehicles, hundreds of thousands of oil and coal-fired heating systems and a ring of factories around its perimeter, the city of Seoul never sees too much in the way of fresh air. Before the sun rose and the traffic revved up and the factory chimneys cleared their throats, there was an illusion of clarity about the city skies.

I used to live not far from here in a flat that backed onto a high school music room that students invaded before dawn, throwing open the windows next to their pianos and hammering out scales and arpeggios with robotic precision. It took me a long time to realise that I was the only person in the neighbourhood who took offence at this, and after that I used the thundering pianos as my alarm clock. It was around this time that I developed a liking for early morning walks.

At the exit of the Hyatt car park I stood on what for me was once a well-trodden path. Turning right, I crossed the near-empty road and headed west towards a gateway to the inner-city parklands of Nam San. Pedestrian traffic was already beginning to pick up, sociable clusters of elderly men and middle-aged women chatting happily, brightly-polished hiking boots clumping in near-unison.

Many carried empty plastic containers tied together in bunches. Decades before them, their parents or grandparents had hiked the same trails up Nam San's flanks, water containers slung from wooden yokes balanced across their shoulders. Now, their descendants made the same daily pilgrimage to the same hillside springs to replenish their stocks of '*yak su*' – literally, 'medicine water'. Many of them hailed me with a cheery *good mawning*. I returned the greetings, minus the good cheer.

Jung-hwa and I often took morning walks together hand in hand, conduct rebellious enough in conservative Korea to turn heads in disbelief or distaste or a combination of the two. I loved those early mornings when we would stroll slowly side-by-side, either in relaxed silence or talking at length about anything that came to mind, frequently making each other laugh until tears coursed our cheeks. Only now did I recognise those times for what they represented. I was in love.

Near the peak of the small mountain, we usually left the trail and perched on a favourite rocky overhang and watched the sunshine bleed its way through the murk that shrouded the eastern horizon.

I sat on that rock now as the changing sky announced the imminent arrival of the morning sun, polluted air softening and filtering the light in the warm orange glow that looks so good on film. I took my old rangefinder camera from the belt pouch where it lived and fired off a couple of frames. Somewhere in a dusty file cabinet in London I knew I could find shots that would differ only in the number of high rise buildings growing into the skyline of a city that was evolving more rapidly than strangers to Korea could possibly conceive.

The deep rumble of the early rush hour gathered tenor as I departed the rocky perch and headed for the east end of the city. After the better part of an hour I left behind the rocks and trees and found my way down into a part of town that has been a marketplace for centuries. Named for the giant vaulted gate that once provided access to the city from the east and which now sat necklaced by incessant road traffic, Dongdaemun – East Gate – Market took up entire city blocks, hundreds of choked alleyways and narrow back streets overflowing with everything you might ever need, and a lot more besides.

Before I reached the market, Seoul's ever-changing face delivered one of its little surprises. I knew this area well, and the thoroughfare that was Chongyechun inspired dark memories of overcrowding and pollution. When I was last here it was one of the most vivid visions of urban hell I ever enjoyed exploring, and I was a regular in this part of town, camera forever at the ready. At street level, pavements overflowed with everything from coat hangers to caged animals, and bristled with pedestrian shoppers, men pushing wheelbarrows overloaded with cargo and motorcyclists carrying more of the same. This went on in a fog of smoke from coal briquette burners that street-level shopkeepers and stallholders huddled over, and petrol and diesel fumes from noisesome vehicles clogged on two levels. Between the pavements were at least six lanes of traffic stuck in the permanent gloom of another four roaring lanes of overhead highway supported by giant concrete pillars and beams. To cross the street on foot meant negotiating the steep, uneven steps of steel pedestrian bridges that squeezed under the dirt-clogged expressway, and picking a track through an ad hoc arrangement of vendors who claimed a share of the bridge to spread their pathetic wares on tarpaulins and old blankets.

The transformation between that hellish, decade-old vision and what spread out before me now was the sort of thing that can only be achieved in places like Korea, where the combination of all-powerful officialdom and infinitely flexible rules and regulations allow stark transition to happen almost overnight. A few years earlier, a city mayor with sights set on higher political office declared his intention to revive Chongyechun by tearing down the expressway and ripping up the road that for decades had hidden a tributary of the Han River. I had read of the plan, but was completely unprepared for the transformation.

The overhead expressway was gone save for a couple of concrete supports that towered like giant, grey capital 'T' symbols of darker days. The supports plunged beneath road level into the reclaimed stream that more than a century ago gave the street its name. I used to watch men with overloaded bicycles dice with fume-belching traffic in the permanent shadow of an overhead highway. Now, couples walked hand in hand and took photographs of each other next to a smooth-running stream.

Some things are thankfully more resistant to change, and beyond the all-new Chongyechun, Dongdaemun Market was exactly as I remembered it. Seoul street markets are strictly departmental, each alley or roadside presenting a parade of near-identical wares. In turn, strips of tightly packed stores peddled camping equipment, hill-walking boots, sportswear, army surplus uniforms, light bulbs and lampshades, false limbs, herbal medicines, plastic piping, tools and ball bearings from microscopic to cannonball-sized. Even at this early hour, the market hummed with life.

Tourist brochures paid minimal lip service to Dongdaemun, and in the middle of the day the occasional foreigner paced its main roads, mouth agape at fly-encrusted open-air meat stalls or grotesquely crowded pet shops, tiny wire cages full of dogs piled high on pavements.

At this early hour it was in the back streets, sheltered and protected from Seoul's incessant road traffic, that the real Dongdaemun thrived. Wiry unshaven men struggled under wooden A-frame backpacks loaded impossibly high with stock, and jostled for space with hand pulled carts packed with building materials or boxed shoes or multi-coloured rolls of fabric. I slowly padded the narrow alleys, all senses wide open to a part of the big modern city that somehow maintained its spiritual links with the Korea of old. This was a land whose communications stretched back through the ancient Manchurian trade routes to the pan-

Asian Silk Road that for centuries connected the Korean peninsula to China and beyond. Never mind that now, nearly everything on sale in Dongdaemun was made in Korea for, on the outside at least, Koreans were immensely proud of their manufacturing prowess. Foreign-made goods were there if you knew where to look – and in sufficient demand that they fetched a significant premium on the ever-booming black market.

Rounding a corner I came to an alley stuffed with *pojang-macha*, mobile restaurant stalls set up around elaborate hand-powered carts. I was hit by the smell of food broiling over coal flames, the peculiar Korean aroma that is a potent mix of garlic, sesame oil and any three or four of a dozen preparations of fiery red chilli peppers. I hadn't eaten since the previous afternoon, and the women stall-holders, ever on the lookout for fresh custom, called out to me good-naturedly, so I sat down at one tiny stall. My new hostess's friends yelled out at her, ribald remarks about the foreigner choosing her because she was the youngest and prettiest, for she was strikingly attractive in an undeniably street-hardened way. Her body language welcomed me.

'Pego-payo ajoshi?' *Are you hungry, Uncle?*

'Pego-pa chukke-seo.' *I'm dying of starvation.* She laughed, hand over her mouth, and I heard unabashed giggles following my response as it passed along the alley.

I ordered a bowl of spicy fish soup and savoury rice cake in a hot red sauce, and sat nursing a glass of barley tea and enjoying the attention of the stall-holders. Among the blue-collar classes, even in the big city, there was still a refreshingly innocent curiosity about outsiders, a native hospitality free of the sometimes poisonous preconceptions of the more educated, self-assured city types. I was a foreign guest, able to communicate with them in their language, and so they worked hard to make me feel welcome.

'Ody-seo-o'sheosoyo? Miguk saram imnika?' The slow

voice came from a small man across the stall. *Where do you come from? Are you American?*

'Anniyo. Yong-gook saram imnida' *No, I'm from England.* In Korean, England and Britain are the same word, *Yong-gook.* The little man leaned heavily on one elbow, the remains of a cheap meal scattered in front of him. He wore a soiled white undershirt with ragged holes under the arms, an old army webbing belt bunching filthy khaki trousers several sizes too large for him.

He explained he was a rubbish collector, and that his work was already done for the day. The stall-holder told him to stop pestering me, but I silenced her with a wave of one hand that told her he was no bother. He responded by barking out an order in a voice that could be heard at the other end of the market:

'Woman. Another *soju* glass over here.'

Even at breakfast time it would be rude not to share his *soju*, Korea's potent rice wine that is made from potatoes and tastes like vodka. I took the glass with two hands and held it the same way as he poured me a shot, smiling at my understanding of the niceties of giving face.

By the time the third shot glass-full had warmed my throat I felt just fine.

'Yong-guk shinsa. Dipshida,' shouted my host, whom I now realised was seriously drunk. *English gentleman. Cheers.*

English gentleman. At least it had a better ring to it than Scottish murder suspect. As I looked around, my gaze fell upon a baleful stare untouched by curiosity. A man in a rumpled blue suit. A couple of hours ago I bumped into him on the Nam San pathway when I clambered back from the rocky perch. The blue office suit was totally out of place on a mountainside at dawn, but at the time I thought nothing of it, and plodded into town without once looking back. Now he sat ten yards away watching me.

I bought another bottle for my new friend and settled my

bill and, after much shaking of hands and passing of grand compliments, tore myself away from the attentions of the stall-holder who cheerfully waved me off. I walked straight past Blue Suit, and out of the corner of my eye saw him slap a banknote on the counter top and jump to his feet. Five minutes of zig-zagging through tight alleys later, he was still on my tail. He was not one of the cops who had accompanied Kwok last night, but that meant nothing. I felt the *soju* kick in, and decided to lose him.

I knew these streets as well as any I had ever been in. Years ago, Jung-hwa and I spent afternoons in a nearby *yogwan*, a back street inn that rented rooms by the night or by the hour. It took me only two minutes to get there, and as I paused suddenly outside its low entrance-way, I looked back to see my pursuer pretend to admire a window full of laboratory glassware. Two steps into the traditional courtyard, and I was delighted to recognise the same matronly *ajumoni* who had owned the inn all those years ago. She threw up her hands in genuine delight, and I was overcome with guilt that I was not here to rent a room. When I quickly told her I had a problem and I had to slip out the back way she sought no explanation but shepherded me towards the gate with a maternal pat and a conspiratorial whisper.

'To-oshipshiyo.' *Come again.*

The tiny back lane was deserted. I jogged to the nearest main road and shouted down a taxi.

Chapter Fourteen

The taxi pulled up outside the Hyatt and the moment I put foot to pavement my radar locked onto a shadowy threat. There was nothing clever about this. Spend enough time on the streets of faraway cities where you might as well wear a neon hat that screams 'Foreigner – Soft Target!,' and before long you develop a security instinct that triggers the moment any person's track alters to intersect your own.

I was still smarting from failing to pick up on the bastard who followed me all the way from the hotel to Dongdaemun, so when the dark shape appeared in my peripheral vision, I spun and bolted – straight into a uniformed doorman. I cannoned off his hip in an ungainly pirouette, went over on my ankle, and to a chorus of bystander oohs and aahs, head-butted the taxi door on my way to the pavement. No points to Brodie for dignity.

The dark suit was quicker than the doorman. Even before I looked up he leaned over me, big hands reaching, callused knuckles speaking of long hours spent in the martial arts *dojang*. I braced myself for the vice grip, the arrival of uniformed reinforcements and the public humiliation of handcuffs. I screwed my eyes closed in anticipation of pain, but all I got was a fraternal hand on one shoulder. I opened my eyes again.

'Are you OK?' I could have slapped myself. It was Chang's chauffeur, the big guy who met me at the airport and later drove us to dinner the night I met Miss Hong.

Onlookers broke out in relieved chatter as he helped me to my feet and growled a few words in Korean at the hovering taxi driver, who quickly thought better of complaining about what my forehead might have done to his car door. The big man spoke to me again.

'Mr Chang says please come to my office.' It sounded like he was reading it from a phrasebook. Only as I brushed myself down and followed him to the Mercedes did I realise that he had said nothing about bringing my equipment. When I slid into the front passenger seat, he looked bemused. Koreans don't sit up front with the chauffeur. Koreans don't bother much with seat belts either, but I reeled mine out and clicked it into place as the driver woke up the big V-12, fired us out of the car park and punched a Mercedes-sized slot in the frantic morning traffic.

He drove with the practised ease of a professional who spent much of a long working day in dense traffic. Smoothness and confident arrogance in equal measure are the true assets of the big city chauffeur; this guy never missed a gap, however small – and where there was no gap he made one. When a battered taxi cut across our bows to make an insane late exit from the expressway, my man hardly let off the gas and kept his hand away from the horn. As a dozen other car horns raged, I took my foot from the footwell where it had lunged involuntarily for the brakes, and said in Korean, 'Crazy sonofabitch.'

Chang's driver nodded in silent agreement, eyes sparkling and shiny skin tightening across high Mongolian cheekbones, accentuating his badly-set nose.

At K-N Towers the sight of the Chairman's Mercedes nosing onto the narrow rampway scared a rushed salute from the security man in the glass cabin as we accelerated beneath the barrier, spiralled downwards, rubber screeching, and pulled into a reserved space. Before I even reached for my seat belt another uniformed figure held open my door and pointed me towards a private elevator. Inside it, the guard used a key to access the only floor available before he stepped backwards and saluted the doors closed.

The lift rushed skywards fast enough to make my ears pop, and I hardly heard the muted ping as the doors opened into a private hallway, where the same middle-aged PA who dealt with me yesterday bowed a forced welcome.

'This way.'

At the heavy wooden entrance I watched her do the trick with the security pad and swing the big door inwards.

Chang was sitting in the same seat he had occupied when I walked out on him the day before, and he showed no signs of having spent much of the night dealing with the police. Schwartz sat in the other seat next to Martinmass the banker, who had divined a third matching armchair from somewhere. The man seemed incapable of hiding his feelings, and right now he looked on the verge of blowing a gasket.

Chang waved me to a straight-backed wooden chair that towered over the low coffee table, which bore only three cups. The pretence of politeness was gone.

'We spoke yesterday about the importance of the GDR to my company.' It was not a question, but a statement.

My plan was to stay calm. 'I am facing a murder charge, and you want to talk business?' So much for the plan. Schwartz looked at me with undisguised contempt.

'Shut up and listen.' He was enjoying this. Martinmass cracked his knuckles. Chang spoke again: 'I am in a very difficult position now.'

Not as difficult as mine. Or Miss Hong's.

'I had nothing to do with – '

'Korea does not have the tradition of tabloid journalism that exists in your country, but things are changing here, and any connection to this nasty business of yours could have very damaging consequences.'

My nasty business.

'Do you really think I killed her?'

'Some say I have already done more for you than you deserve.' Schwartz and Martinmass nodded in unison. Chang went on:

'I convinced Detective Kwok not to put you under arrest – '

'I appreciate that, but – '

'Let me finish. I am trying to protect the K-N name, but if you are found guilty – '

'I didn't do a thing to Miss Hong.' I was shouting. He waited to be sure my outburst was over.

'If you are *found* guilty, it will not only damage my company, but it will cast a bad light upon me personally.'

'What about me? I am innocent.'

'Your guilt or innocence is of no interest to me. My only concern is K-N Group, and at the moment that means the successful implementation of the GDR.'

He sat back as if there was nothing more to add, leaving me still in the dark.

'So what's your point?'

Chang looked to Martinmass, who lifted a heavy handful of printed materials from his lap and let them fall to the table. With an involuntary start I jumped in time with the coffee cups. Prospectuses for the GDR. They had been busy.

It was your typical four-colour corporate hard-on. I have worked on hundreds of them, commercial profiles that opened with the requisite cliché-ridden corporate portrait, before jumping quickly into sales mode, touting the company's latest venture in page after page of upbeat prose and glossy illustrations, many of them blatantly diversionary.

Much of the gloss and almost all of the photographs were down to me. A sweet twilight view of K-N Towers faced the introductory passage watched over by a tight headshot of Chang. I speed-read it. Unbridled optimism over the GDR and the future of South-North economic cooperation that hinged on the success of K-N's visionary investment in the North Korean manufacturing sector.

I never tire of looking at my own photographs when they are well laid-out, but as I flicked from page to page, fears confirmed sent beads of sweat running down my spine. For days I had known I was in the shit, but now I had an idea how deep. I was up to my neck in the stuff.

It was what came after the introductory pages that scared me. A pictorial feature, ostensibly on K-N's business activities in the North, most of the pictures selected from the stock I supplied Mr Rhee in London. The camera may not lie, but wrapped up cleverly in the right text, it *can* tell a story far removed from the truth.

The text told of clothing industry start-ups in the North, factories already in production and exceeding targets, much of the output destined for high-demand export markets in China, Russia and the old Eastern Bloc. It explained that textiles were no more than a modest beginning to a multi-billion-dollar master plan; supposedly in place were planned K-N sister plants for consumer electronics, heavy engineering, shipbuilding and car production aimed at next door's booming Chinese market. Splashed throughout were my shots from the fake factory in Cholla province, their credence shored up by genuine North Korean street scenes drawn willingly from my London files. To my fast-growing list of grievances I could add the fact that we had not agreed on a fee for the usage of those stock pictures, but maybe now was not the time to bring that up.

To pull off this sort of illusion the pictures were everything, and the photographs enjoyed a cohesion and unity of quality and film stock and photographer's angles and vision that came together seamlessly. As a package it presented credibility that money could not buy, except that the mere promise of money had brought me running all the way from London.

Just in case I was still kidding myself, there, staring out from the inside back page, was my portrait taken from my own portfolio. Below it were two paragraphs that inflated my role as corporate advisor and researcher for documentation backing K-N's Global Depository Receipt. Alec Brodie, editorial and corporate photographer of international repute, whose client list included some of the world's best-known news and business publications, and *'whose recent work in North Korea on behalf of K-N Group so ably illustrates the visionary potential of the Group's investment in the North.'* Talk about being caught between a rock and two hard places. Major-league corporate fraud, bankruptcy – or a murder charge. Or all three.

Chapter Fifteen

Chang plucked a tiny mobile from his shirt pocket and pressed a soft pink fingertip to one button. I thought I heard the answering chirp of a phone nearby before the door from the corridor blew open and three men, Chang's driver one of them, came straight for me. Before I could react the driver had me in a headlock. His friends took hold of one wrist each and twisted hard enough to make me squeal, which the driver put a stop to by moving the headlock up to cover my mouth with the crook of an arm that felt like it was made of mahogany and reeked of stale cigarette smoke. As I fell from the chair I kicked out, sending cups flying but doing nothing to put off my attackers, one of whom responded by leaning a heavy knee across my thighs. I was helpless.

No-one appeared in the least surprised. Schwartz looked smug and Martinmass clearly enjoyed the show, eyes flicking excitedly from me to Chang and back again. Chang spoke:

'Geoff doesn't trust you. Ben agrees with Geoff, and I see no point in questioning their judgements, do you?'

My face buried in the chauffeur's jacket sleeve, I took that for a rhetorical question.

Chang nodded to Schwartz. While my captors man-handled me into position Schwartz unbuttoned my shirt down to the waist, ran his hands across my chest and around my back, then loosened my trousers to check inside my beltline, and patted down my pockets and both sides of my legs. He winked at me then he pulled off my shoes and squeezed my socks before shaking his head at Chang who, with a raise of his chin, signalled that I be released. My three attackers brushed their hands over their suits and backed out the door as Chang spoke to me.

'What we have to discuss here goes no further. We have to be sure you are not wearing any kind of recording device.' While I tried and failed to regain some sort of composure, Chang continued.

'Do you have any idea how far Korea has come in recent decades? Forty years ago we were the poor boys of Asia, lower down the economic ranks than even the Philippines and Burma. In the sixties the West laughed at our pleas for investment but today, every EU member state is on its knees at our door, begging us to build new factories to shore up *their* run-down economies. Korea is now the twelfth-largest trading power in the world.'

I waited for him to get to the point.

'You know Koreans are driven. We are committed. We put everything we have into anything we do, whether it is business, sport, politics or religion. Look at the spectacular success of the Korean Olympics or the World Cup we shared with Japan. Outsiders poured doubt and scorn on us until we showed them how to run major international events without so much as a hiccup.

'K-N Group is no different. I started out on my own, travelling the world from one trade fair to the next, nothing to show but a suitcase full of textile samples and a list of Korean suppliers desperate to work on any order I sent them, never mind how small it might be. One telex from anywhere in the world set production lines rolling.

'Today, over fifty thousand Koreans work for K-N Group. Fifty thousand families are dependent on the company. But now the Group is in trouble, and if I don't sort out the problems, every one of those jobs is in danger.

So now we,' he waved at himself and Schwartz and Martinmass, 'We have a way to turn it around, to get the Group started on the road back to profitability, to safeguard those jobs.'

'And this is it?' I slapped a hand on a prospectus. 'A huge shell game built on a non-existent North Korean investment plan?'

'The plan exists, though perhaps not quite on the scale presented here. This is about much more than investment in North Korea. It is the new beginning for the Group, something that will draw investment from all over the financial world.'

'Driving up your share prices in the process.'

Chang drew me a look of pure contempt. 'You Westerners take *such* a short-term view of things.'

It was Schwartz's turn to butt in:

'This guy is a nobody who came running at the first sniff of money – '

'Money I've seen not a penny of.'

'You could still see your money,' said Chang.

'Could?' I shook my head in disbelief. 'Could?'

'It is simple enough. If you want the fee, all you have to do is your job.'

'I came here to take photographs.'

'That remains a major part of your job.'

'What's the rest? Helping pull the wool over the eyes of investigators who can't get near North Korea to see these non-existent factories for themselves?'

Schwartz was furious: 'I get it now, asshole – you're just angling for a bigger share for yourself.'

'You forget that I haven't seen a dollar of my fee.'

Chang looked at me over the rim of his coffee cup. 'If you don't start showing some interest in what we propose, you never will.'

There it was, on the table at last. Blackmail.

No wonder they were so cagey about security that they

114

insisted on the heavyweight frisking before the real agenda emerged. Chang spoke again:

'You seem to forget that it is only thanks to me that you are not facing a murder charge. That is, not *yet*.'

Martinmass and Schwartz exchanged knowing looks. Chang continued:

'Finish your assignment, do as you are told and go back to London with a handsome fee. We know you need the money. You get paid well for your role, and nobody gets hurt.'

What about Miss Hong?

'Do I have a choice?'

'There is the option of a very public trial whose verdict will be a foregone conclusion. Followed by maybe a year or two in jail while you await the death penalty. A process that I will do nothing to obstruct.'

I tried to suppress a shiver.

'I still don't get it. This is worth hundreds of millions to K-N, right?'

Chang's face gave nothing away.

'So why do you need me? Schwartz got it right. I'm a nobody here.'

Chang went on as if I had said nothing. 'I want an answer. Will you cooperate with us and do what is re-quired? We – ' A telephone rang next to his elbow. He put up one palm, picked up the phone, and listened carefully before responding.

'Ee boon.' *Two minutes.* He turned back to me.

'Detective Kwok is here, and wishes to speak to you immediately.'

He looked to Schwartz and Martinmass, who were visibly angered by the interruption. They picked up their coffee cups and papers and left by way of Chang's office. There was a tap at the corridor door and the detective and his two sidekicks came straight in. Kwok pulled a plastic evidence bag from his pocket and held it in front of me. Inside were the wrappings from a video tape.

'This was found behind the curtain in your hotel room. We are going to search the room and your equipment cases again.'

If they had just found the wrappings, that meant they had already been back at the room, where they had found the equipment cases securely locked. Breaking into the cases might render evidence obtained inadmissible.

Kwok waved a hand at me. 'Come with us, please.'

'We will see you again tomorrow,' said Chang. Like it was a done deal.

Half an hour later I sat on my hotel room bed as the two detectives rummaged through my equipment cases while Kwok and I looked on. Kwok pulled out the evidence bag with the video wrappings.

'What can you tell me about this?'

'Nothing.'

One of the policemen called out.

'And this?' said Kwok, chin pointing at his colleague, who held up a layer of cut foam from one of the cases. Beneath the layer, lying across a wide slot was an unused video tape still in its cardboard wrapping, identical to the wrappings Kwok held in an evidence bag. Next to the tape, a neatly cut cavity in the foam lay empty.

'I sometimes carry a video camera on assignment.'

'Where is it now?'

'London.'

'I can have you arrested at any time.'

'I sometimes carry the video camera to make records of locations and lighting set-ups in case we have to re-create the same lighting at another time or in another location. But on this trip I was travelling alone, and my luggage was overweight, so I left some things behind in London. The camera was one of them. I must have missed the tape when I re-packed in a hurry.'

'So how did this get to your room?' He waved the evidence bag of tape wrappings.

'It may have been in one of my bags, from an earlier shoot before I came to Korea; it could have fallen out when I was checking my equipment.' Hypothetical situations can work both ways. So far, they had no evidence to disprove this possibility, and if I had anything to do with it, that would continue to be the case.

The detectives had finished their search, and had nothing new to crow about. Kwok looked pissed off, his suspicions alone not enough to act upon.

'When this camera turns up,' *When*. 'It will be further evidence against you. Hiding it from us will only make things worse.'

They walked out, and I buried my face in my hands. For the first time in days, maybe I just did something right.

Chapter Sixteen

I savoured the quiet of the room for a moment. Apart from an alcohol-soaked nap in the small hours of the morning I had not slept in thirty-six hours, but right now, sleep was the last thing I could afford. The brushes with Chang and Kwok had been fortunate for me in their brevity only. The morning was not yet over and, so far as I knew, my clients would not be requiring my services today. Tough luck if they did.

Two minutes under the shower freshened me up and gave me the chance to change out of the beige trousers and off-white shirt that Kwok and his boys had last seen me wearing. I pulled on a pair of dark chinos and zipped a black cotton bomber jacket over the top of a grey polo shirt. I checked the peephole in the door. Nothing. I opened the door in one smooth move and stepped confidently into the corridor. If Kwok had anyone watching for me I would go looking for the chambermaid and ask for some toiletries to replace the ones his detectives had confiscated. The corridor was empty, except for the chambermaid's trolley sitting outside a room fully thirty yards away.

Credit card at the ready I turned towards the store-room. I hoped to repeat my earlier easy victory over the lock, but it refused to budge, the door rattling in its frame as I jiggled the card and pushed and pulled at the handle. From the corner of my eye I caught movement at the end of the corridor. I tried to shrink into the shallow recess, one cheek flat against the door. The chambermaid came out of a room with her arms full of soiled linen which went into a bin on the trolley. Only when she retreated back to the room with fresh sheets under one arm could I return my attentions to the lock. This time it gave way, and I was in the store-room, door pushed gently closed behind me. Five seconds to regain my package from high on the shelving, twenty seconds with my ear to the door, and I was back in the corridor and straight across to my room. I transferred the package to a waist bag that I clipped into place beneath the folds of the bomber jacket. I picked up a small backpack and slipped it over one shoulder. Now came the hard part.

I took the lift directly to the basement and walked quickly into JJ's. Five paces inside the bar I spun around and looked straight into the gaze of a blue suit following in my tracks. He immediately cut left through a swing door marked 'Staff Only'. Either he was very good or he actually did work here. From an exit onto the hotel patio I looked towards the pool deck where the only figures visible were uniformed hotel staff and an elderly Japanese couple in matching Burberry bathing suits and sun hats. I hugged the building all the way around to the edge of the car park on the other side, senses alert for any signs of urgency. Just when I was about to relax, Blue Suit cut out of the main entrance and ran towards the pool deck. I nicked around the end of a dividing wall and was gone before he looked my way.

I kept well apart from the traffic headed for the main entrance, and when the driveway was clear, slid around the gate pillar and slipped into the nearest alley. Fifty yards on, I looked back along the deserted lane as I emerged onto a busy suburban street to find a deluxe taxi parked, driver smoking, the car's polished nose pointing uphill towards the hotel. Just as I spotted him, the driver picked up on a potential fare. One twitch of my eyebrows and his cigarette was rolling in the gutter. I slipped into the back seat.

'Where you go?' He looked at me in the rear-view mirror.

'City Hall.' Ten minutes away – and in the opposite direction to where I was headed. I checked my watch. It was tight, but I should make it.

He set off back towards the hotel and I sat low in the seat, peering around the door-frame. As we passed the main gate Blue Suit came running up the driveway, chest heaving, head sweeping from side to side. I ducked lower in the seat. In the mirror, the driver fired me a glance heavy with unasked questions. I pretended to doze off, questions ignored, and he said nothing. He was a taxi driver. Being treated like he didn't exist went with the job.

At City Hall I waited until the taxi disappeared around a corner before dipping downstairs into the subway system. Three minutes later I was aboard a train heading south. Instinct sent my hands to check that the video camera fixed to my waist was safe. It was. The subway journey would take about twenty minutes. I scanned the faces of my fellow passengers, but recognised no-one.

The video business was yet another worry, and with Kwok suspicious about the tape wrappings and the empty space in my equipment case, leaving it in the maid's storeroom for much longer was not a sensible option. All it took was for someone to stumble across them and Kwok would think he had even more evidence of a guilty conscience. Mine.

Not that there was anything untoward about the videotape itself. I don't see anything wrong with enjoying tapes of me having sex. It's a personal thing, consenting adults doing something that gives them pleasure, an innocent turn-on that hurts nobody and breaks no laws. So what if Miss Hong didn't know about the small camera that I fixed high on a curtain rail while she showered. The way she went along with the Polaroids two nights earlier, I am sure it would not have bothered her. I had known a few women who had participated willingly, even encouraged it, and shared the turn-on of snuggling up to view the resulting show.

Jung-hwa introduced me to this pleasure source. She arrived at my flat one night with a box in a carrier bag, a clunky video camera that belonged to a family member who was unable to get it to work – or so she said. It took me a couple of minutes to seat the battery and find the correct switch. A little red light blinked above the lens, a grainy black-and-white viewfinder came to life, and I pointed the camera at Jung-hwa, who stuck out her tongue and crossed her eyes. Still looking through the camera I followed her to a cassette tape player that sat on top of the television. She hit the play button and tinny speakers filled the room with the sound of canned sex: Sade's *Smooth Operator*. Jung-hwa danced a sinuous weave, palms painting the contours of her tight top and even tighter jeans. I yelled encouragement and painted nails moved teasingly to the buttons of her blouse. She started to strip slowly, playing to a rapt audience of one, carelessly flipping clothing over her shoulder, where it came to rest on the TV, on a lampshade, on the floor. When all she wore was a pair of flimsy white underpants, I carefully set the camera down on a coffee table. I walked into shot and was welcomed into Jung-hwa's arms for a long, hungry kiss. Without breaking away she lowered her hands between us and started to undress me. With a wriggle, she pulled free of my embrace and sank to her knees.

Fourteen years later, I could replay every last frame of that video in my mind.

An announcement crackling from muffled subway train speakers jolted me back to reality. I pushed through the crowd to the carriage doors, joined the busy station platform, and began to work my way back above ground.

Bright sunlight washed over the southern suburb of Seogyo dong. From the station exit I imagined that I followed my own well-worn tracks from years ago to a three-storey concrete building in a crowded lane parallel to the main road. On the second floor, whitened window frames were filled by bold red Korean lettering. Tae Kwon Do.

The old man at the local store by the building's entrance did a double-take as I nodded to him and skipped up the stairs. I was excited in that way when you are about to be reunited with a dear friend after a long absence. He was a creature of habit and, six days a week, this was morning work-out time. Later would be time for a sauna and perhaps a massage followed by a rich lunch of *bulgogi*, but at noon, I was certain he would be in the *dojang* working out. As I tripped up the stairs, the sounds exploding from the gym told me my guess was correct. I slipped quietly along the corridor and put my head around the door jamb.

Mr Cho wore a fresh *tobok* held in place by a black belt worn grey from years of use and thousands of washes. He was practising a three-kick attacking combination. A right front snap-kick, followed by a left front side-kick feint that morphed into an airborne spinning right back kick, a deadly *tui-dollyo-chagi* that folded the heavy leather bag in half, rattling the sturdy chains that attached it to the ceiling. Even before the bag began to unfold itself Mr Cho was back in the ready stance, gauging the bag's movement, preparing for the next explosion of strikes.

I stepped into the doorway and my reflection in the full-length mirror on the far wall immediately caught his attention. He stopped in mid-kick and walked over, hand outstretched. Pushing fifty, he had the body and feline grace of a young Jackie Chan. His face was unlined and he still wore his jet-black hair long. He shook my hand hard and pointed to the backpack hanging from my shoulder.

'Your *tobok*?'

'Yes.'

He welcomed me to his gym. I paused in the doorway

and, from etiquette engrained by years of training, bowed deeply to the *Taegukki*. I tried not to dwell on the last couple of times I had looked closely at that flag. While I stretched and warmed up, Mr Cho continued to beat lumps out of the bag, talking to me calmly between strikes.

'When did you arrive in Korea?'

'A couple of days ago. I'm here on a photography job, and I didn't call because I wasn't sure when I would have time to visit.'

We caught up on what he had been doing since I last saw him during a trip to London three years before. He told me of his son and daughter, now both in middle school – I was living in Seoul when they were born – and of his wife, recently taken to classical flower-arranging lessons. He rolled his eyes at that one. Mrs Cho was a lovely woman, but given to immersing herself in one expensive pastime after another, none of which lasted more than a month or two. Not that Mr Cho couldn't afford it. He assured me his three bars and two nightclubs were doing just fine.

I was too ashamed to admit that for the past couple of years my Tae Kwon-do work-outs had been sporadic at best. Technically I was mostly all there, but in terms of fitness and speed I was far from my peak. We worked out together, going through a solid ninety-minute routine, with me taking increasingly frequent breaks to regain my composure. Kicks, punches, combinations, patterns, bag-work and sparring, we did the lot. My lungs screamed and muscles complained at every leap and lunge, and only pride prevented me from folding to the floor in defeat. Mr Cho shook his head knowingly as we donned protective gear for a sparring session that I fervently hoped would be brief.

I have more chance of punching a rainbow than I have of laying a foot on Mr Cho. He, however, picked me off at random, every touch from foot or hand a gentle hint at the enormous power that resided in his slender frame.

He barely broke sweat, and at no time did even a hint of exertion disturb the grace and precision of his every move.

From the *dojang* we went directly to the local bath-house for a soak, and on to Mr Cho's favourite *bulgogi-jib* for a high-protein lunch of marinated beef broiled on a burner mid-table.

There, I asked if he could look after something for me, and handed over the video camera and tape, bundled up in the plastic laundry bag. He looked in the bag and raised an eyebrow.

'I have a problem, and I don't want anyone to find that.'

'Is it serious?'

'It could be very serious.'

'It will be safe with me.'

'Thanks, Mr Cho.' *Thanks for asking no questions.*

He smiled in a way that I always interpreted to be fraternal. Fifteen years ago, when I was the eager student taken under the Tae Kwon-do Master's wing, he used to jokingly introduce me to other Koreans as his 'little brother from Scotland'. Back then I found it embarrassing, but in present circumstances, the protectiveness of an adopted older sibling felt good. I hadn't shared with him the true extent of my worries but if I did, I was sure he would be there for me.

When I walked into the hotel in the late evening, it was hardly a surprise when at least three different pairs of eyes locked onto me. They already knew I had gone out. Where I had gone and whom I had met was what they couldn't know. In one hand I held a plastic bag full of cold beers. I waved to my onlookers with the other, but none of them waved back. At the front desk I picked up a message from John Lee, confirmation that photography was to re-commence tomorrow and that he would pick me up at 08:30. I needed to relax and try to get my mind around what was going on, and one of the luxuries I associated with five-star hotels was nursing a couple of cold beers while I took a long, hot-as-I-could-bear soak in a bubble bath. Soon I was near-submerged in scalding bubbly water watching rivulets of condensation run down mirrors and tiled walls and beer bottles that nestled in a full ice bucket positioned within easy reach.

I awoke spitting bubbles, dizzy from the heat. My watch and the scorching water confirmed I had only dozed off for a few seconds. I heard a knocking sound from the room door, the noise that had, fortunately for me, disturbed my sleep. I shouted:

'Who's there?'

No response. I shouted again, this time in Korean. Still no answer. Who could this be? If it was Kwok, he would announce himself, as would anyone on the hotel staff. If it was another body part delivery, it was time for a change of hotel.

I drew myself from the slippery tub, torn ribbons of weightless foam floating behind me as I plucked the heavy robe from the hanger behind the bathroom door. Foamy puddles formed around my bare feet as I put one eye to the peep-hole. Nothing. Even if the corridor lights were still out, I should be able to see something. More knocking, this time louder, a heel-of-hand hammering that shook the heavy door.

'Who's there?'

Silence. This was starting to piss me off. More knocking, incessant now, a regular pulsating enraging thump thump thump. I thought of calling down to reception. *'A naughty man's knocking on my door, and he won't tell me what he wants.'* Yeah, right.

I plucked the security chain from its resting place on the jamb, and slotted it into the metal channel on the door face. Turning the handle very slowly, I eased the door back while I squinted through the growing gap at the door's edge. The security chain tore loose as the door exploded inwards and clocked me a crunching blow above the right eyebrow. I half-spun and hit the carpet face first.

The door rang like a gong as it hammered against the stopper. I couldn't look back in case I turned straight into a kick, and in any case my eyes were still full of soap. Footfalls drummed on the carpet and the door slammed shut. Before I could move, every last fragment of breath blew out of me as knees landed full-force in the middle of my back. A wiry hand gripped my shoulder, turning me over into the attack. Another hand reached into the bath robe and took a firm grasp of my balls. Still gasping for breath I brought an arm up to protect my face, but it was too late. Lungs already empty and air sources cut off, I began to suffocate.

The hand on my shoulder had moved to cover my mouth and nose, while the other hand tugged at me aggressively. Only when a tongue flicked against my teeth and I finally awoke to the taste of lipstick did I even begin to understand. Abruptly, the smothering sensation stopped and I heaved for breath as two warm hands cupped my face, thumbs gently clearing bubbles with a tenderness that instantly took me back to childhood bathtimes. At last I was able to open one eye, and it looked straight into one of my attacker's.

'Oreh-gon mannee hamnida, neh?' *Long time since we did this, eh?*

Chapter Seventeen

Like foreground detail in an oil painting, two hundred feet below us the swimming pool glistened, a tungsten-cyan rectangle that shone from the shapeless black of the hotel grounds. In the distance, traffic pinballed along riverside expressways, its muted drone interrupted only by sofa and shoulder blades playing a rhythmic beat-squeak on the hotel window.

Jung-hwa perched on the sofa's seat back. I stood ankle-deep in velour, fingertips splayed across the glass. Her legs were clamped tight around my hips and her shoulders drew twin channels in condensation that beaded the cool pane. Long fingernails gouged parallel stripes down my back, and widescreen chaos was reflected in the window behind her.

From a cut on my brow, blood snail-trailed across an eye that was already swelling to a close, fresh blued bruising under stretched skin, a schoolyard shiner in the making. Behind me the hotel room looked like a tornado had passed through it.

Heavy curtains hung askew, one of them partly dislodged from its runners. The entire contents of the writing desk – telephone, notepads, menus, blotter and more – spread across the floor. A chair lay overturned, its seat pad dislodged and propped against the brass limb of a standard lamp held at a crazy angle by the short cord that drew a treacherous line to the wall socket.

The door to the mini bar hung ajar, a triangle of light bleaching scattered ice cubes, shadows pooling into the carpet pile. The whole room flickered to the images of a television pay-channel, hardcore porn playing silently to an audience of none. The huge bed in the centre of the room looked like the eye of the storm had passed over it. Blankets, sheets and feather bolsters tumbled in chaotic disarray. The bathroom was out of view, but I knew that it held more of the same. I would have to remember to tip the chambermaid, I thought, as Jung-hwa threw herself giggling onto the sofa.

I was smiling, not from amusement, but in welcome recognition of something very special. Everything, even Jung-hwa's entrance, was just like things used to be. Unpredictable, impulsive, and as uninhibitedly sexual as ever.

What we had going here wasn't exactly a meeting of great minds, but a long time ago we had something pretty wild going for nearly five years. After a decade away, I had a fresh taste of everything I missed.

I didn't know it at the time but fifteen years ago, when Jung-hwa led me home from the NFL Club to a wild night thrashing around my flat, we were etching out a pattern. A pattern that survived, never mind the confusion it wrought in those around us, and one that suited us equally.

Once or sometimes twice a week Jung-hwa would pop into my life, as often as not unannounced. It was never difficult to hunt me down, to intersect a track that was predictable yet somehow never felt monotonous. Friday nights I would be sucking gassy draft lager with friends at a window table in the Bavaria Bar. I always found a seat with a view downhill towards the human chaos of the main Itaewon drag, where I would watch Jung-hwa turn heads the moment she emerged from a taxi. Men nudged one another as they tracked her, eyes narrowed, lips pursed. Streetwalkers made no attempt to hide long looks of envious appraisal.

She would make a dramatic entrance into the seedy Bavaria, cut a track straight to the table where I stood waiting, and kiss me. Koreans don't kiss in public, and this was never a modest peck but a lusty full-on-the-lips, arms-round-my-neck cinematic clinch that brought near-silence to the noisy bar. Impervious to stares radiating from all corners, she would slowly break the embrace and almost reluctantly join us.

Strictly territorial, the males around the table displayed little curiosity. I was one of the boys and I was seeing her regularly, and that was enough. Their Korean girlfriends, despite natural inquisitiveness, knew little more. Jung-hwa never brooked much casual chatter, and the other women eventually gave up trying. After a couple of drinks and to no obvious dismay we would beg off. We went drinking and dancing, always at a venue of her choice. Sometimes it was the mainstream joints like the NFL or the King Club, but on other nights she would be of a different inclination, one that I could never predict, and which forced me to cast off self-consciousness like an extra layer of clothing. As the only white man weaving through a forest of enormous blacks (the term 'African-American' had yet to be embraced) in the Sunshine Club, the only Scotsman with no cowboy hat in the Dixie Bar, or just the only man not bending genders in the transvestite Love Dash, I learned to go with the flow.

After a couple of hours of drinks and sweaty dance floors, we would reach an unspoken decision, two minds on one track. Time to go.

In bad weather we joined the scramble for taxis, but whenever possible we walked the mile-and-a-half to my place. This was a teasing thing, prolonging the wait until the privacy of my flat set us loose. Heightened anticipation never failed to add flush to the moment, even if it was prone to the occasional backfire. Like the time we were disturbed by a fresh-faced kid of a beat cop, baton drawn, unsure how to deal with the couple apparently wrestling, partially undressed in a doorway not far from his darkened police box. While I tried to re-gain some composure, Jung-hwa engaged the young cop in conversation like he was an old friend who should have known better than to disturb us. Soon we were on our way, gently admonished, shoulders rigid until we turned the corner and collapsed in fits of giggles. For months afterwards we made a point of walking past the police box, never failing to elicit a comical salute and a beaming grin from our uniformed friend, who gladly accepted our gifts of hot coffee, cold Coke or steaming-hot *dok-bo-gi* rice cakes.

Back home we'd go through my flat in a frenzy that knew few taboos. She was mesmerising in action, and I thought I saw in her a determination to satisfy not only the two of us but some imagined observer, like an actress playing to her audience. It was a recurring impression that never dulled my passion, for if she was acting out a script in her head, it was surely not *Breakfast at Tiffany's*.

I emerged from the bathroom to find Jung-hwa propped up in bed, sheets and blankets strewn around her. The television was switched off, and she rummaged in her handbag for cigarettes and lighter. She offered the open pack to me.

'I gave up.'

'Do you miss it?'

'Only after sex.'

She fired the lighter and drew hungrily at the smoke. 'Aah, luxury.' She blew smoke at the ceiling.

'Luxury?'

'I don't smoke much now. Ben hates it.' She drew again on the cigarette, her silence heavy with unstated resentment. An electronic squeal of complaint came from the phone that lay upside-down on the floor. I picked it up, returned the receiver to its hook, placed the telephone on the desk, and pointed to what was left of the mini bar.

'Thirsty?'

She nodded and I stopped to pick up the ringing telephone. As I put the receiver to my ear, I signalled to her to keep quiet, but I might as well have asked her to make love in silence.

'What's going on?' *Ben Schwartz*. 'Who's there with you?' I shook a frantic hand across the bed.

'Ben?'

Eyes round as a cartoon cat's and shining with mischief, Jung-hwa held a hand over her mouth.

'Who's there with you?'

'If there was anyone it would be none of your fucking business. It's the television.'

'Didn't sound like the TV. Why has your phone been off the hook?'

'None of your fucking business.'

Jung-hwa started to lose control, her mouth covered now with two hands. I pushed the button to disconnect the call, placed the handset in its cradle and padded, barefoot, into the bathroom. Even before the door closed behind me, the phones began to ring. I examined my battered face in the bathroom mirror for five rings before I picked up the receiver and held it six inches from my ear.

'You hung up on me.' He was nearly screaming. I stuck my tongue out at the mirror.

'Tell me what you want, or I hang up again.'

'Did anyone ever tell you you're an asshole?'

'The pleasure has been entirely yours. I'll be seeing you –'

'Wait. Did you get the message from reception?'

'The message that John Lee is picking me up in the morning?'

'Yes.'

'I got the message. Anything else?' An electronic tone buzzed in my ear. He had hung up. That would teach me to show more respect.

Back in the bedroom, Jung-hwa looked unfazed by her husband's call. Her arrival had been so unexpected, so violent even, that I hadn't given it any thought – and

Schwartz was suspicious that I might not be alone. Did he have any reason to suspect Jung-hwa was here? Had he told her anything about the GDR, did her husband have anything to do with whatever happened to Miss Hong? If he did, what about Jung-hwa?

The object of my thoughts lay naked on my bed only partly covered by a crumpled sheet – and I had never felt more alone in my life. I wanted to confide in her, but there was a torrent of shit bearing down on me, and maybe she knew more about it than I did.

'What's wrong?'

I walked to the bed and leaned forward to kiss her. The sheet that hung lightly on her body peeled back to reveal the ice cube that she was absently applying to an erect nipple. One kiss became an embrace, and before another word was said we were making love again, this time gently, conciliation after the borderline violence of before. Afterwards, we stretched out together, her head resting in the crook of my neck like it always used to.

When I awoke, I walked around the room and checked the bathroom before I would admit to myself that she was gone. On the bedside cabinet, a handwritten note sat propped against the lamp:

Maybe I will call you soon. Jung

Maybe. As she used to do so often, she left more questions unanswered than resolved – and left me to a confused mix of joy and regret.

Considering the way I let the curtain fall on our relationship, her re-appearance, never mind that it was the stuff of recurring dreams, was more shock than pleasant surprise. Maybe it was my turn to be left to dangle.

There was something inevitable about how we fell apart back then. Inevitable considering my own abject fear of commitment and Jung-hwa's sociologically driven dread of abandonment. In the end her source of terror became self-fulfilling.

In our last year together she began to cast a jealous eye on other Westerners willing to follow their hearts and marry their Korean girlfriends. A transition from sparkly-eyed cultural maverick to a figure overtaken by mawkish broo-diness presented itself with a finality that shocked and frightened me. My prevarication became a personal insult and a festering sore of anger. If my friends were able to marry women younger than Jung-hwa, what was she to do with a man unable to consider any sort of commitment? When plain talk failed, she reached for the sensuality card and tried to fuck me into submission. She never knew how close that came to working. The sex was out of this world and I revelled in the erotic attention until she pulled the plug and delivered a stern ultimatum. Marry me or lose me.

A week later I gave the entire contents of my flat to a family of *yon-tan* coal briquette vendors who lived in a dust-engrained shack, and slipped out of town. I said no goodbyes and took with me only regrets that continued to fester even now.

Chapter Eighteen

John Lee walked into the lobby at exactly 08:30 and, as he gave my black eye a look of curiosity, handed over a sheet of K-N notepaper with one line of computer printing. 'Photography at K-N Towers,' it said. Lee took one trolley, and I followed him out the door with the other. In the car to headquarters he evaded all efforts at initiating a conversation, except to tell me that I would be photographing managers.

That is what I did, photograph managers, with another mini-production line in the boardroom, the lighting arranged to match the portraits I had shot in the same setting.

At least these guys had a saving grace for me to grasp at. They were yet to cross the vanity threshold that comes with promotion to the ranks of upper management. The more senior the subjects, the greater the self-importance and the more predictable their my-time-is-too-precious-for-this bluster. In front of my camera sat people who were still looking *up* the promotion ladder, and who were happy to go along with anything that might give them a boost. Amiable subjects make portraiture a pleasure.

Predictably, every person paraded through my production line was male. In corporate Korea a woman's responsibilities are routinely restricted to delivering hot drinks at a moment's notice and fluttering mascara-laden eyelashes for hours on end. Even this she can only get away with until a woman's *true* duty calls and she resigns to take care of her 'salary man' husband and to gird herself for the earliest possible production of male offspring, males born to look down on female colleagues in the Korean offices of the future.

I introduced Lee to the alien concept that K-N's brochures could look a little more first-world if they included one or two females on their pages. After initial confusion he presented me with a trio of pretty women, two executive secretaries and a Human Resources manager. I readily killed a couple of hours photographing them in three different settings. All the while I failed miserably to block out thoughts of Miss Hong, of the impossibility of the situation Chang and his cohorts had put me in – and of Jung-hwa's surprise re-appearance.

My thoughts moved on to Ben Schwartz and the look of delight on his face when he, Chang and Martinmass presented me with the printed prospectus. With that task already taken care of, why was I being kept around? The corollary to that mystery scared the shit out of me. What would happen when I became surplus to their needs?

I asked Lee if Schwartz and Chang were likely to be around today, but he told me they were 'busy'.

By the time I wrapped up the last portrait of the women, Lee had seen enough.

'We are finished.'

I tried to hide my relief.

'The dinner is at seven o'clock.'

'Dinner?'

'To welcome the Due Diligence team from London. Mr Chang wants you to attend.' *A partial answer to one of my questions*, I thought. *Maybe Chang still needed me.*

'Why? Does he want photographs?' I hoped not.

'No photographs.' He told me the name of the restaurant, a famously expensive establishment in parkland near the presidential palace.

'I will arrange a car to take you to your hotel.' He walked

from the room. If I had anything to say on the matter, he didn't want to hear it. The transition from honour-bound respect to barely-concealed contempt was complete.

The taxi pulled up by the formidable front gate of the Dae Ji Restaurant complex at a few minutes before seven. I kept telling myself that I had to find some way to stand up to these bastards yet here I was, not just on time but early. Maybe I could confuse them with my unflinching courtesy and respect.

The Dae Ji was in Samchong dong and only a few hundred metres from the Blue House, the Presidential palace on the north edge of downtown. For decades after the end of the Second World War a succession of dictators had to ring the Blue House with a high-profile security cordon to protect themselves, not only from North Korean hit squads (in 1968 one guerrilla unit made it to within a few hundred metres of the palace), but also from their own citizens and ambitious junior army officers with their eyes on power. A half-century after the end of their own fratricidal war, the continued existence of machine-gun nests and plain clothes patrolmen and the near-impossibility of planning permission for Samchong dong made it a peaceful green dot on the downtown fringe of the big grey city.

Long before it became one of Seoul's best restaurants, Dae Ji was a *Gisaeng* house, Korea's spin on the Japanese *Geisha* establishment. Like its Japanese cousin the *Gisaeng* house was an upmarket recreational club for society's elite males, one that hid behind a smokescreen of cultural gentility. Despite the placid woodland setting and grand sculpted grounds, it amounted to little more than a whorehouse for the super-rich.

By the time I first knew it in the late eighties, Dae Ji had already transformed itself into a restaurant styled as a nineteenth century rural village and, in the decade or so since I last visited, it had clung to its charms. Heavily wooded grounds were ribboned with footpaths that ran between traditional Korean cottage buildings so cute they had the whiff of Disney about them, private dining rooms where guests sat cross-legged on heated floors and dined from low lacquered tables overflowing with expensive dishes. Some buildings were spacious enough to host full wedding banquets, while others could turn a dinner for two into something very intimate.

As I walked through the grounds, I spotted movement in a cottage doorway. Ben Schwartz waving impatiently. I altered course and followed him into the small building. Sitting on the floor were Chang and Martinmass, tall earthenware mugs of steaming barley tea on the table in front of them.

'Aah, Brodie,' said Chang. *No more 'Alec',* I thought.

'Good afternoon.' It hurt to be so civil. I spoke to Schwartz:

'I thought we were meeting your London visitors?'

'That's right.'

I looked around the small room, and Schwartz answered the unspoken enquiry.

'Dinner is at seven-thirty. John Lee is bringing the guests, and we will be dining in one of the larger suites.'

'And?'

'Mr Chang wants to talk to you.'

'What makes you think we owe you any explanations?' It was Martinmass. 'How about you just sit your Scotch arse down and listen.'

Tie loosened and jacket rumpled, he looked like he had been drinking, so I made a point of ignoring him. With one stockinged toe I dragged a flat cushion from a pile in the corner. As I sat down, there was a soft knock and the paper door slid sideways to reveal a young waitress in traditional attire, long hair gathered high in a tight bun and held in place with a lacquered wooden post like a fat chopstick. She asked me if I would like a drink. Schwartz answered for me.

'Just barley tea.'

I spoke up. 'Jam-kan-man.' *Just a moment.* After I changed the order the waitress bowed and scuttled off backwards. Shouting up a beer when my hosts were drinking tea was offensively rude, but where I stood, the odd insult was not going to make a lot of difference. Anyway, I needed that beer.

Barely a minute later, another gentle knock announced the waitress's return. She gathered up her bulky dress and kneeled to pour my drink from a tall bottle that dripped with condensation and that Martinmass eyed with visible longing. I raised the glass to him in mock salute and took a long swallow at the chilled lager. There was nothing mock about the intense chemical joy of the hit from the first drink of the day. I took another pull at it before I put the glass down. The waitress darted forward to re-fill it but Schwartz told her to leave us. Eyes down, she bowed her way out the room and Chang spoke:

'I'm sure I don't have to tell you that this meeting with the Due Diligence people is very important.'

Important. Always 'important'.

'Why am I here if it is so important?'

Martinmass slammed his mug down; tea flew from it, splashing the front of his shirt.

'If you'd shut your mouth for one fucking minute – '

A sidelong look from Chang silenced him in mid-sentence.

'The situation is this. Hosting the Due Diligence team is our opportunity to make a sales pitch upon which the future success of the Group depends. We must get this right.'

'We?'

'However reluctant you may be, we are a team. For now the team's goal is to sell the North Korean project to the investigators. However, *we*' – he indicated himself, Schwartz and Martinmass – 'We have never been there, and the Due Diligence investigators cannot go there. You, on the other hand, have been to North Korea on several occasions and have more than enough photographic evidence to lend yourself and the Group's plans vital credibility.'

Now I understood. Due Diligence was the final hurdle that stood before the successful launch of the GDR, and my near-imaginary role in the sales pitch to the visitors from London remained significant. Schwartz interrupted my thoughts:

'What Mr Chang is saying is that if you play your part here you will get your job fee – '

'What about the murder investigation?'

Schwartz looked to Chang.

'It is in our best interests that the investigation is brought to a close as quietly as possible. I have powerful friends who will listen to me, but only *if* you play your part to our satisfaction.'

However much it pained me, playing along was the only option that made any sense. Whatever fraud was involved in the GDR was not of my doing, nor was I to blame for what had surely happened to Miss Hong. If the success of the flotation meant I got my money and Chang saw to it that the Miss Hong thing went away, what did I have to lose? More importantly, what choice did I have?

Three faces, three entirely different smiles. Chang's was seemingly benign, that of a consummate businessman savouring the pleasure of negotiations that were going his way. Martinmass's cat-like grin reeked of pure greed. Only the knowing sneer on Schwartz's face smacked of greater complexity, of deeper satisfaction whose roots continued to confuse me.

Chapter Nineteen

They thought they were the cat's pyjamas, but with preppy arses fidgeting on the lacquered floor and knees pointing at the ceiling, they looked more like fish out of water or kids cross-legged in a splintery Boy Scout hall; angled caps, cloying camaraderie, left-hand handshakes and *Bingo Was His Name-Oh*.

Six thousand miles out of London they might as well be on a different planet. They had just arrived from the city I called home, but here in the middle of Korea, the Due Diligence team were the foreigners.

Leader of the pack was a tall Londoner, slightly older than his colleagues, lean and knotted and tanned like a cricketer, with thick blond hair that lapped at the tops of his ears. At regular intervals, a runaway fringe crept down over his eyeline, to be met by a reflexive sweep of his right hand, the long nail of his little finger slipping under the hair, flicking it upward with polished flamboyance that surely spoke of years in the making.

There were six of them, all but the leader in their twenties, all in pressed chinos and polo shirts embroidered with the insignia of stockbroker-belt sports clubs, and at least half of them boasted the one-handed tan of the regular golfer. A variety of regional accents pointed to roots in different parts of England, but the job and its prestige and money and the clubbiness of their outfits brought them together.

The odd one out was a quiet Irishman they called Paddy, who spent a lot of time looking around him as if committing the contents of the room to memory. He examined at length the crockery and cutlery and took bird-like pecks at the appetisers with chopsticks gripped tight between pink office-dweller's fingers. At least he made the effort. His colleagues tittered with relief when serving staff, hiding their amusement at the clumsy attempts to engage chopsticks, offered up heavy silver-plated cutlery, fresh from the box.

Their team leader introduced himself with a beat-you-to-it handshake that ground sinew between my knuckles, and a pewter-plated sincerity stare straight from an MBA training manual.

'Nethers. Nethers Hollands. Team leader. Birt, Matthews and Lumberg, Merchant Bankers. London.'

Nethers?

'Alec. Alec Brodie. Proprietor. Alec Brodie. And Associate. Photography. Islington.'

A glint of what might have been anger flashed across the blue eyes. Schwartz's glare warmed the side of my neck.

'Saw the prospectus,' said Hollands. Thumb and forefingers grouped, he tap-tapped at a manila folder like an auctioneer punctuating a sales pitch. 'Very impressive. You and me have to sit down. Have a long talk.'

'I look forward to it, *Nethers*.'

'Nickname. Had it for years. Real name's Bernard.' Emphasis on the second syllable. Bern*ahrd*.

'Really?'

'Actually it's rather clever. Hollands, Netherlands – Nethers. Nowadays even Father calls me Nethers.' He spoke as if I ought to know Father, never mind that I obviously went to the wrong schools.

'*Very* clever.'

The condescending look suggested that bosom buddy status was out of the question.

There were a dozen of us around the long low table that held the middle of a room lined with classical watercolours of sparsely-wooded rocky mountaintops. Chang presided over one end of the table, and I sat around the corner from him with the Irishman by my side and Nethers facing me. The rest of the Due Diligence team were broken up by Korean directors and Schwartz and Martinmass. A gregarious Korean called Yu helped Paddy with his chopstick technique. Schwartz chatted with a couple of wide-eyed boys, hinting broadly at how much they were going to *enjoy* their first taste of Korea and, no, he wasn't just talking about the meal. Knowing grins were exchanged.

Martinmass sat next to a heavyset man called Joss who matched him beer for beer. They talked in a rude private murmur punctuated with explosive cackles.

Schwartz rang a metal chopstick on the side of a beer glass. Conversation dwindled, and after a few more seconds even Joss and Martinmass put a stop to their murmuring.

'Gentlemen,' said Schwartz, 'Don't worry, I am not going to bore you with a speech – '

'Because that's my job,' said Chang, earning a round of laughter. The timing was so perfect that I wondered if it was a regular gag of theirs. Schwartz smiled while he waited for silence.

'As ever, Mr Chang is ahead of us. I would like to wish you all a warm welcome to Korea before I hand you over to Mr Peter Chang, President of K-N Group. I am sure that Mr Chang's reputation in the commercial world means he requires no introduction – '

'But you won't let *that* stop you,' said Martinmass. More laughter, this time polite and a little hesitant. Schwartz shot Martinmass a cold glare before re-attaching his smile and taking up where he left off.

'Mr Chang is not only the President of K-N Group; without him, there would *be* no K-N Group. Nearly forty years ago, armed with only a small inheritance and a duty to help support four younger brothers and sisters, Mr Chang founded the company. He started out trading textiles at a time when the economy here was only just beginning to recover from the Korean War.

'Today, as I am sure you know, K-N group is one of the most progressively-expanding *Chaebol*, or conglomerates, in Korea, with dozens of member companies employing tens of thousands of workers here in the domestic economy and in multiple overseas markets. Group turnover for the last financial year exceeded twenty-seven *billion* pounds Sterling.'

Schwartz knew his audience. If you wanted to impress a bean counter, you showed him a hill of beans almost too huge to contemplate. Twenty-seven billion pounds Sterling set off a Mexican wave of approving nods and respectful headshakes. The bank's involvement in a Global Depository Receipt of the size planned would generate many millions in fees, and in the merchant banking world, happy employers gave out Bentley-sized performance bonuses.

Job done, Schwartz handed us over to Chang, who said very little of substance but heaped it high with charm and sincerity. Anything the visitors required, anything whatsoever, all they need do was ask. As their hosts, K-N Group were proud and pleased to serve their every need. Emphasis on *every*. But enough talk of business, because tonight was about introducing his guests to hospitality, Korean style. Sadly, due to a previous engagement Chang had to leave the guests in the good hands of his colleagues, who would do their best to make this a night to remember.

After a flurry of handshakes and unblinking eye-contact sessions, he left the room to drawn-out applause.

The Due Diligence team had hardly hit the ground, and already they were putty in Chang's hands.

The door was barely closed behind him when Mr Yu bellowed in the Irishman's ear:

'Yoboseyo.'

Paddy nearly jumped out of his chinos as a waiter scuttled in from the corridor.

'*Soju*,' shouted Yu.

The waiter waited.

'Yol byong.'

I shook my head. Paddy watched me.

'What was that about?'

'He's just ordered ten bottles of *soju*. Rice wine, they call it, except it's made from potatoes. The national tipple, used to be dirt cheap because of government price controls going back decades. One dictatorship after another figured if they let half the population stay pissed, that was half they needn't worry about rising up against them.'

'And that's why you're shaking your head, is it?'

'Eh?'

'The shame of supping the poor man's balm?'

This guy was off the wall. I liked him already.

'I was thinking about the hangover you've all got coming to you. In recent years they've dressed it up in fancy glassware and polished away a few rough edges, but *soju's* still fiery stuff, a bit like vodka, and just as bad for you. The locals love it with a passion, Paddy.'

'The name's Conor.'

'Yet they call you Paddy?'

'That's these eedjits for you,' he said, softly. 'Been gettin' it every day for three years, and they still think it's a feckin' scream.'

He turned when Mr Yu thrust a shot glass at him. Conor took it in his left hand and raised it to meet the bottle. I said:

'Use two hands, the way he's holding the bottle.'

Conor was quick. He switched the glass to his right hand, and rested his left fingertips against its side. Yu grinned in response.

'Very well done,' he shouted, filling the glass to the rim.

144

'You know Korean customs.' He sat, still clutching the bottle, watching Conor.

Conor looked to me.

'You'll be good at the next bit. Slug it back in one go, then hand him the glass and pour him a shot. Two hands at all times.'

'The same glass? After me just drinkin' out of it?'

I remembered the first time I encountered this Korean notion of comradeship, beer and *soju* glasses swapping hands in a centuries-old ritual that declared mutual respect. Hygiene issues apart, it was a custom that soon grew on anyone who enjoyed a drink.

'Trust me, you'll get used to it.'

I needn't have worried. All around the table glasses soon passed back and forth with metronomic regularity. Sublimely ignorant of the deadly brew, the Due Diligence team were soaking up *soju* with the abandonment of youth. I had been there many times, so I was determined to stick to beer. Then Conor pushed his glass in my face, and my resolve went out the window.

I threw back the shot glass and a shiver wracked me from head to toe, then the liquor lit tiny warming fires all the way through my system.

Joss, the heavy-set Londoner sitting next to Martinmass, surprised me by putting an oversized elbow among the side dishes and shouting across the table.

'So you're the North Korea expert?'

Before Martinmass could open his mouth, Schwartz answered quickly:

'Alec has a great deal of experience in both halves of the peninsula, which is why K-N hired him to document the North Korean operations. Isn't that right, Alec?'

'Something like that.' *That and the small matter of a hanging offence.*

Joss had something on his mind, and the drink was lubricating its way to the surface.

'What I don't understand is why we're not going to the factories in North Korea. We've been brought half-way across the world to perform the Due Diligence – and we can't go a couple of hundred miles up the road to do it right? Something funny about that, isn't there?'

'Funny? It's fucking hilarious, so long as you get a giggle out of having your country cut in half, ten million families permanently split up by the Superpowers, then Cold War politics keeping the two halves totally divided, not so much as a postcard getting over the border for the next fifty-odd years.'

'You're shitting me.'

'No pal, *you've* got to be shitting *me*. Your job is to fly across the world to Korea and check out a deal worth hundreds of millions, and you don't know the first thing about – ' Martinmass leaned forward to interrupt:

'You have to *remember*, – '

'Geoff is right, Alec. Joss and his colleagues just got here,' said Schwartz. 'The team will need time to get up to speed.'

Like the relative at a family gathering who just asked after the host's pregnant thirteen-year-old, Joss nodded in thoughtful agreement as he unwittingly bit a curling green chilli pepper right down to the stalk and chomped happily into it, violently hot seeds and all. I watched his face turn red and tears cloud his eyes before he reached hungrily for a beer glass and drained its entire contents in one swallow.

Two hours later we were sitting on the floor again, in a different part of town, and in an establishment where a lot more than food and drink were on offer. This northern suburb was quietly famous throughout Korea for its high-end brothels. Night-time entertainment in this part of town had always been too rich for my blood, but tonight K-N was pushing the boat out for the visitors, and for some reason I was expected to tag along, even if I wasn't exactly kicking and screaming.

Traditional wood-and-tiled single-storey buildings with inner courtyards still survive in older parts of Seoul, and here they ran in crooked lines forming narrow residential alleyways. These lanes easily pre-dated the 1980s explosion of car ownership, meaning many of the homes in them were accessible only by foot. On both sides of the alleys, ornate doorways painted with colourful yin yang roundels lay invitingly ajar. I concentrated on what might lie behind them, setting aside all thoughts about a yin yang tattoo and an almost-certainly dead Miss Hong.

Flanking the gates stood wiry young men in well-pressed black trousers, white shirts and dark ties. Touts-cum-bouncers. Through the gateways, flashes of brightly-dressed beauties teased window shoppers with hints of what went on behind the paper doors that masked elevated wooden walkways lining inner courtyards.

When five black Hyundais unloaded our well-oiled crew at the mouth of one alley, the touts stepped quickly forward, competing welcome cries on their lips. Without a glance at them, Mr Yu and Ben Schwartz led us into the alley and through one of the bigger gateways into a courtyard where a mama-san with a bee's nest hairdo was already flapping around, banging door posts with the palm of a meaty hand, calling staff to muster.

Soon we swayed in front of more than twenty young women lined up in the courtyard in full *Han-bok* costume, long hair pinned back in precise tight buns, hands clasped in front of wide flowing dresses in garish clashing colours, broad, heavily made-up faces beaming professional welcomes.

Mr Yu, unsteady on his feet, swept a hand at the line of women and spoke to the guests, who stood in an uncertain cluster. Red in the face from drink, he had lost some of his earlier capacity for flowing, unblemished English.

'Gentlemen, whatchoo like?'

The visitors just looked at him, so with a laugh he led by

example, taking the youngest of the women by the elbow and leading her towards a room that the mama-san indicated with a series of mechanical toy bows. Soon a line of freshly-formed couples followed Yu into the room. I rescued a shy-looking lass from the fast-diminishing selection and joined them.

'So this is just another day in the life of the ex-pat abroad?' Conor sat next to me. A gorgeous Korean woman fed him fruit salad with one hand while with the other she casually teased his inner thigh.

'Koreans are big on hospitality, and Chang wants you people on his side.'

'Ah hell, an ulterior motive. Now you've spoiled the illusion that the life of the foreigner is always like this.'

I thought of my past few days. Aside from the odd interruption for photography and blackmail, it had been a constant trek from bar to restaurant to nightclub to bed. No wonder I was so tired.

'Much of the ex-pat's working life is about smoothing relationships with Korean clients over evenings like this. It's not a game for the weak-livered.'

Conor drew his fingertips around his partner's slender waistline, making her wriggle. 'How about weak marriages?'

'Asia's been the death of a lot of them – and a few of the strong ones too.' Across the room Schwartz, face slack from too much drink, was trying to get his hands down the front of his girl's dress. That only made two of us being unfaithful to his wife.

'Was it too much drink that got you the keeker?'

I had forgotten about the black eye, and not one other person today had mentioned it.

'Exactly. Got up in the night after a few too many beers, thought I could find my way in the dark – and took a dive in the hotel bathroom.'

A couple of young bankers were being led from the room

like tame elephants under the control of diminutive hostesses. Nethers had acquired two girls all to himself, and showed signs of leaving with them at any minute. Conor turned away from a grape on a stick that his girl was trying to feed him. 'What do the locals think of all this? Don't they resent it?'

'Half the guys in here are Korean.' I brushed a piece of imaginary lint from the breast of my new friend, who nuzzled closer. I stood up, and like an expectant puppy springing to heel, she followed.

'If you'll excuse us, we have stereotypes to explore.'

Chapter Twenty

I popped out of deep sleep like a day-old chick ejected from the nest, dazed and bruised and featherless on the forest floor. Except I was butt naked and clinging to the underside of a rectangular rug, scant protection from the relentless blast of hotel air-conditioning. My mouth felt like it had been turned inside-out and freeze-dried on a desert floor, my breath so foul I could smell it with my mouth closed.

I stood up slowly. Only my quarter of the huge bed was a mess, the rest of it undisturbed, so apparently I had made it back to the hotel alone and to my own bed, albeit temporarily. Scratching at balls hanging satisfied and loose, I remembered why, thinking of the slim young *agashi* I had plucked from the courtyard line at the suburban whorehouse. She was surprised by my request for 'only' a good massage, but when I said she could tell the Mama-san to bill K-N for the whole package, she entered into the conspiracy with visible glee. One randy foreigner she didn't have to service, yet still get paid. It was her lucky day.

Her strong hands skilfully kneaded me all over without once crossing the pain threshold that forever lurks at the edges of a quality massage. When her fingertips strayed across my shorts and found me aroused, she furrowed her brow in mock rebuke and reached for a lotion jar.

A few hours later, and my hotel room might as well have been filled with dense fog, so complete was my *soju* hangover. I scrambled my way to the mini-bar and leaned down to pluck a bottle of water from the shelf low on the fridge door. A lancing pain knitted my temples, blurring my vision with tears; my stomach did a back-flip, and my mouth filled instantly. I let the bottle slip from my fingers and bolted for the bathroom, where I jack-knifed before the pedestal. Between after-shocks I hugged the bowl-rim, rested my head in my arms, and swore I would never touch the stuff again. Even in the most bare-faced lie there is a sliver of hope, which might explain why drinkers are such terrible liars.

I woke again when my head hit the wall and the stench of disinfectant cut through me like smelling salts. Throwing the toilet brush to one side, I put hands to wall and levered myself onto numbed legs, palmed my way around three right-angles to the wash-hand basin and squinted at the all-too familiar horror in the mirror. Eyes like nailholes in a rotten board, crusted at the corners, the swelling around the right one receding now, angry purple tending towards jaundiced orange. Grey-pale face wrinkled and lined, lips faded and near bloodless. On my forehead, a crescent weal where I had slept on my watch before sliding from the toilet bowl and waking with a head-flick to the bathroom wall. I put one shaky hand to a ridge above my left ear and winced: a cartoon-egg bruise, growing beneath my finger-tips.

From the wall phone I called down for a large pot of coffee, two litres of still mineral water, a jug of freshly-squeezed orange juice, three bananas and a bucket of ice. Shuffling from the bathroom, I opened the door to the corridor, flicked over the security bolt to leave it unlocked for room service and lay down again, on the bed for a change. A few minutes later – it may have been seconds – a ringing door bell broke into my erotic reverie. Arranging the heavy towelling robe as best I could (what is it with hangovers and hard-ons?), I yelled to come in. A disgust-ingly cheerful young man bounded across the room, heavy silver tray floating easily on one hand. I waved at the coffee table and with his free hand he cleared newspapers, dirty socks, and a pile of coins. Avoiding eye contact I signed the bill, thanked him and turned away. Apart from those coins I had no Korean money left to tip him. Something had to be done about that.

Nearly eleven o'clock. At least it was Saturday and, unless my memory was playing tricks, Schwartz had said I wouldn't be needed again until Monday. I had one hour before Bobby joined me for brunch. I switched the TV to CNN, volume low, and attacked the water and orange juice, rehydrating and raising blood sugar levels before settling down to coffee and bananas. The coffee wouldn't help the dehydration, but I needed that caffeine jolt in a hurry, and the bananas would further help the sugar levels. Bobby never goes anywhere without a beer thirst, and if I was going to join him for a hair of the dog I had to get myself into better shape quickly. Certain times are entirely wrong for stopping drinking. Right now, even a momentary pause was out of the question.

I got to the coffee shop five minutes late. Bobby was sitting in an alcove attacking a tall draught beer while he flicked through the local papers, his big honest face lined with worry. I sat down opposite him and asked the waitress for a beer. Bobby gave her the Winston Churchill fingers, signalling to make it two. When he turned to face me his expression was grim.

'I got a phone call at six o'clock this morning.'

For all I knew it could have been me. 'Who was it?'

'A Korean speaking English, but slow and near-perfect, like he was reading from notes.' Bobby sucked at his beer. When he raised his eyes over the edge of the glass I thought I saw tears form.

'The bastard threatened my family, said he knew where we lived.'

'What do you mean 'threatened'?' I dreaded the answer.

I could guess what this was about. The beers arrived, and I took them from the tray and shook my head at the waitress. She left us.

'He said something like, 'You should be careful. It is better for you if you stay away from some people. Certain things are none of your business'.' He raised the beer glass, his hand shaking. 'I asked him what he was talking about, and he said 'Stop talking with the wrong people about things that don't concern you, or your wife and little Min-hong and Min-tae will be in danger'.'

Whoever it was knew Bobby had two boys, and even knew their names. *Our business*.My drink was in my hand, close to my lips as if awaiting instructions. I put the glass down hard, beer splashing over my hand onto the table.

'Jesus, I'm – '

'You've been messing me about ever since you – '

'Wait – '

'You've been using me, pumping me for information about K-N and the GDR – '

'Bobby I'm in a fu – '

'I told you everything I knew, and when you kept me in the dark, I told myself it was no big deal. My old mate Alec always did like to play his cards close to his chest.'

Sometimes it's better to say nothing. I licked beer from the back of my hand. It tasted acrid.

Bobby stared unblinking. I tried to look back at him.

'Bobby, I never for a moment thought anything like this would happen.'

'Just tell me what the fuck is going on. You've fed me nothing but shit since the day you arrived.'

I dabbed at the spillage with a napkin so heavy with starch that beer ran off it like beads of golden glass.

'For what it's worth, I told you mostly the truth.'

'Right. Mostly.'

'I didn't think the bits I kept to myself could hurt you – because I thought they were my problems, nothing to worry you about.' I had an awful thought. 'Hang on, where are Myong-hee and the boys? Tell me they're not at home alone.'

'They're spending the day at her sister's. I took them there in a taxi.'

'Did you look out for anyone following you?'

'We're talking about my wife and kids. What do you think?'

The waitress arrived with fresh beers. I hadn't noticed Bobby ordering them, but his glass was almost empty again. Bobby drinks hard enough when he is happy, but when he is under pressure, he *really* goes for it.

'Anytime you are ready. I've got all day.'

'Listen, I'm not making excuses.' I held up one hand. He settled for another hit at his beer. I went on.

'No excuses, but if this sounds bad, wait until I tell you the rest of it. Maybe then you'll see why I kept it to myself.'

'Are you going to tell me, or just talk about telling me?'

I sat up and looked around us. The only adjacent alcove was empty, and at the nearest table three Africans in finely cut pinstripe suits were talking French. Still, I lowered my voice.

'I'm being blackmailed by Chang, Schwartz and Martinmass into helping them with the GDR and the Due Diligence investigation.'

Bobby gave me a look of pure disbelief. 'You're a fucking *photographer* – how does a London snapper fit into a GDR issue worth several hundred million?'

'That bit confused me, too. I must have been set up by Schwartz, who knew I'd been to North Korea. The pictures from those trips ran all over the bloody place.' Bobby watched me closely, showing no sign of any effect from the beers. I took another deep breath. 'K-N's North Korean factories are completely out of reach of the Due Diligence investigation. So they need someone who has been to North Korea to back up K-N's assurances about the factories they are supposed to have built.' I stopped for a drink.

'Don't tell me. Last time you were up there, you just happened to get pictures of these factories?'

'The idea is I took the pictures because I was working for K-N up there, too.'

'Only one thing wrong with that.'

'I know. I wasn't working for them in the North, and I didn't photograph any modern factories – no journalist gets to see that kind of thing up there. But Chang and Schwartz had thought of that.'

'And?'

'And I photographed the factories this week.'

'Eh?'

'In Cholla-do.'

Bobby's face went slack. 'The other night, at the reception, you asked about K-N factories in Cholla province.'

'You told me there were none, and you were right.'

He looked incredulous. 'They've got you faking evidence?'

'Exactly.'

'Why?'

'Why? You're the Stock Market whiz, Bobby, you told *me* the Group was in trouble – '

'I know why *they* would do it, but why the fuck would you cooperate with them? We're talking fraud on a scale that could get you put away for years – '

'I already told you why. I'm being blackmailed.' I let out a long sigh. There was no point in keeping it to myself any longer.

'They've got me framed for murder, Bobby. Murder. No matter what way I turn here, I'm fucked.'

Bobby called for more beer, but I declined. Despite my best efforts and six aspirin and two large beers, the hangover was making a come-back.

I told him the whole story. Dinner with Chang, the nights

with Miss Hong, my resistance to going along with the GDR scam and the late night delivery of her belly-button. Detective Kwok and the Polaroids, the confrontation with Schwartz and Martinmass in Chang's office. The stock photographs of North Korea, the phoney North Korean factory in a warehouse in Cholla province, and the ultimatum from Chang: cooperate or we feed you to the police for the murder of Miss Hong. I only kept quiet about Junghwa – and the video camera and tape I had sneaked off to Mr Cho.

He sat with two big hands around his beer mug and stared towards the brightly-lit windows. Now he looked confused.

'They already have you in a corner, but still they're leaning on me and my family?' He took another pull at his beer. 'They've seen you and me talking more than once. I work in the Market, so if I heard even a whisper of Due Diligence fraud, K-N would likely end up under investigation, and the three of them could get locked up. They can't get any more leverage over you than they have already, so they play safe and put the shits up me with the early morning call threatening my wife and kids.'

'Sounds about right.'

'Ironic, isn't it?'

'What?'

'They're worried about what you're leaking to me, while the whole time it's me who's filling *you* in.'

I sat with my hands open but idle, wishing I had ordered that last beer.

'All of which makes sitting here a very dumb move.' He looked worried again.

'Christ, here we go.'

Nethers Hollands, Geoff Martinmass and Joss, the banker's big pal from last night, were being led through the tables by a waitress. They stopped next to us, and Hollands spoke first.

'Afternoon, Brodie. Heck of a night that. Good one. Overdid the old pop, though. Bit of a head. Sore. Very sore.'

Joss nodded sagely, and Martinmass angled a wafer-thin smile at Bobby.

'How's things?'

'OK.'

'Family fine?'

'Perfectly fine.' Bobby's stare never left Martinmass's face.

'Great. If you'll excuse us, we better go put on the nosebags. I promised the lads a briefing over lunch.'

They crossed the restaurant to a reserved table next to the window. Bobby's gaze threw daggers at Martinmass's back.

'You did the right thing, Bobby. Playing it cool was the only thing you could do.'

The look he drew me said he was not convinced.

A phone rang quietly. Bobby patted the pockets of the jacket that lay crumpled on the seat beside him, pulled out a mobile phone and thumbed the tiny green button. A high-pitched unbroken stream of words leaked from the ear-piece. Bobby held it close, cutting off the sound. His face grew dark.

'Calm down, and tell me exactly what happened.' He listened. 'Where are you now?'

'Get people to look in all the friends' houses and play areas and shops. I'll be home in half an hour.'

Standing up, he plucked at his jacket, thought about it for a second, put it back down, and walked away. Nethers, Joss and Martinmass looked up as he approached their table. The smirk on Martinmass's face evaporated as Bobby reached down, grabbed him by the lapels and wrenched him from his seat. The banker's nose exploded like rotten fruit on Bobby's forehead, and his bulky frame went limp. Bobby let him fall face-down on the table, and when Joss made to jump to his feet, took him out with a short right, the entire weight of his upper body behind it. Joss hit the seat back, arms flailing, blood spraying from his mouth. Nethers sat in shocked disbelief between two unconscious dining partners, his palms out in surrender. Bobby walked quickly back to me, wiping blood from his forehead with the back of one hand.

'Fuck playing it cool. That was Myong-hee on the phone. There was a change of plan at her sister's, so they went home earlier than expected. Now Min-tae is missing. Another kid saw two men leading him to a car that drove off.'

Min-tae was the younger of Bobby's two sons. Seven years old and unfailingly good natured, he had learning difficulties that made him seem younger. Across the restaurant, a waiter splashed cold water on Martinmass's face. I called out to Bobby to wait for me.

Chapter Twenty-one

The taxi driver launched his cab into traffic like somebody's life depended on it. Maybe it did. Bobby slouched low in the back seat, strain written all over his face. He sucked distractedly at weeping gashes that sliced through the first two knuckles of his right hand, wounds so deep they would need stitches to close them. If Joss still had two front teeth to call his own I would be surprised. I dipped into my pocket for a clean handkerchief, and Bobby wrapped it around his fist without comment.

We sat captive to our own thoughts, the car filled by a fizzing silence. Bobby's expression told of an explosive mix of anger and despair. I was angry too, but mostly I felt paralysed with guilt. Being a screw-up was something I had long since accepted, but now I was taking it to new heights. If Min-tae was harmed, it would be down to me. Somewhere in the middle of all this stood Ben Schwartz. Right now, fooling around with his wife didn't seem like such a smart move. I was screwing up on multiple fronts.

Fifteen-storey apartment towers stood at neat angles like hotels on a high-stakes monopoly board, rigid lines defined by crowded car parks, primary colour play areas and grey-green rectangles of worn turf and stubborn shrubbery. The entrance to the block was marked by a tight group of mothers, some still in aprons and kitchen slippers, talking behind their hands, faces lined with a mixture of concern and that thinly disguised look of schadenfreude humans wear when the unthinkable bypasses them to befall others. They turned together to watch two kids dragged towards the elevators by a mother terrified that whatever happened to Min-tae might be contagious. This was no time for rational thought.

Bobby jumped out of the taxi in a slick movement that belied his bulk, and a little security guard in crumpled navy uniform shuffled forward to meet him. I stood a few feet away as they talked in Korean that most of the time was too fast for me to catch, even if I was trying my hardest. Nor was I alone. Without a hint of shame the local wives edged closer, necks and ears straining, like extras in a pantomime. Bobby left the security man and walked over. The women looked galled when he spoke in a low voice, in English.

'Myong-hee is still out looking. I didn't tell her about the phone call this morning because I didn't want her to panic. One of her sister's kids was unwell so they came home early. Min-hong always looks out for Min-tae, but he got wrapped up in some game with his mates, took his eye off the little guy for a couple of minutes and lost him. Another kid says he saw Min-tae going with two men to a 'big' car that drove off.'

The security man was at Bobby's elbow. He broke in with a question, something about the police. Bobby thought for a moment, then nodded his assent.

'Nae. Chon-wa-haechuseyo.' *Yes. Call them please.* I wondered how he could still be so outwardly calm, so polite.

Just as he said it the chatter from the local women rose sharply, hands pointing. Bobby and I looked along the path that ran between the car park and the front of the building to where Myong-hee reeled towards us under the weight of a heavily-built child who squirmed in her grasp. Even from a distance the boy bore a striking resemblance to Bobby. Myong-hee was of child-like build, but nothing short of her arms falling off was going to make her release Min-tae. She held his face to hers and as she cried uncontrollably, their cheeks ran with streaked mascara. Bobby lurched forward, swept them both off the ground in a giant, gentle bear-hug, and moved off along the path before softly putting them back down. He crouched and held Min-tae's face between his hands and kissed him on the forehead. They huddled like a basketball team, Bobby talking in a persistent murmur. At last, Myong-hee nodded and released Min-tae from her clutches. Bobby signalled to a young woman who hovered nearby, who took Myong-hee firmly by the arm and led her into the apartment building. He waited until they were gone before he lifted Min-tae and, with a flick of his head, motioned me to follow.

The three of us sat on a bench beside a deserted play area out of sight and earshot of the building entrance. Min-tae sat in the middle, looking very small.

'I'm sorry, Daddy.' His head was bowed.

'You don't have to be sorry, kid-oh.' Bobby thumbed tears from his son's cheekbones.

'But Daddy told me.'

'Told you what?'

'Don't go with strangers.'

'Listen, son, I'm not angry. You are alright, aren't you?' Min-tae nodded, uncertain.

'But you have to tell me, did the men make you get in a car?'

'2005 Hyundai Santa Fe five-door, black, alloy wheels and silver roof-rack and a factory ladder up the back door beside the spare wheel with a custom cover.'

Bobby looked at me.

'He's absolutely obsessed with cars. Can name every model from a hundred yards.' His son was speaking again.

'They said Daddy's buying ice cream, quick, Min-tae, get in the car. They said they would take me to Daddy.'

'Korean men? Speaking Korean?'

'Korean men,' he nodded again, gaze fixed somewhere between his swinging legs. So he was bilingual, too, learning difficulties or no learning difficulties. Where I came from, most kids made a pig's arse of one language.

'So what happened next?' Bobby spoke softly, one hand resting gently on his son's shoulder.

'We went to a shop for ice cream, but you weren't there.' Indignation overtook the little guy's innocent expression. 'I told the men I wanted to come home, but we went for a drive – I saw a Mercedes, a CLK convertible with the roof down. When they stopped I got out and Mummy found me.'

I could read Bobby's mind. This didn't add up. The little guy had been missing for nearly two hours, so he had lost track of time. But without a threat or a message, what was the point? Bobby tried one more tack.

'Did the men talk to you?'

'They said stop crying Min-tae, we will take you home soon. But I didn't stop crying.'

'Did they tell you to say anything to Daddy or Mummy?'

'No.' He fingered the neck of his polo shirt. I put a hand on Bobby's forearm.

'I think there's something under his shirt.' A look of horror crossed Bobby's face before he took a hold of the shirt tails and smoothly turned it inside-out as he hauled it up and over Min-tae's head, the practised move of a Dad well-used to tending to his kids.

Two blood-red lines of flowing Korean script crossed Min-tae's shiny-smooth chest. Bobby put a fingertip to the script then turned his hand. Dry. It was marker pen. Behind me, the local wives had come searching for us, shameless in a quest for threads on which to hang their gossip. Bobby flipped the shirt back over his son's head and hugged him tight. I tried to keep my voice low, but still it sounded like a scream.

'What does it say?'

Bobby stared blankly through welling tears. He ran a big soothing palm slowly back and forth over the short-cropped hair on the crown of his son's head.

'It says, 'Next time he doesn't come back'.' Bobby lifted Min-tae from the bench and walked towards the entrance to the apartment building. I hurried after them.

'Bobby.'

'I don't want to deal with you right now.'

'I understand, but there's another small problem.' Bobby turned around, still moving backwards, forcing me to follow.

'What now?'

I felt like a drug addict with the shakes cornering commuters. 'We left the hotel so fast I came out with no cash. Could you sub me a taxi fare?'

Bobby gave me a look of pure contempt. Hitching Min-tae onto one hip, he dipped into his trouser pocket.

'I'll *lend* you your *bus fare*.' A handful of coins bounced on my outstretched palm as he spun on one heel and strode away, murmuring gently in his son's ear.

I asked around until I located a bus stop, ascertained the correct bus number from a couple of rebel teenagers with tea-coloured hair and nose rings, and eventually got myself on an express bus. The last thing I needed right now was a stop-start torture session hanging from a handrail in an overcrowded city bus.

I got stuck with the unpopular seat above the rear wheel arch and sat with my knees at my chin. Every thought I had shouted 'disaster' in my ear, but still I saw no other option than to do my job, take every photograph as instructed, ask no questions, rock no boats, and tell only the lies that I was expected to tell. I might even stop bedding Jung-hwa if it would help me get out of Seoul with my money.

Back at the hotel I nearly made it past Reception before I heard my name being called. I looked over to see Miss Kim, the receptionist, edging her slender frame through a narrow gap in the counter.

'My front desk manager would like to talk to you.'

'Not right now thanks. I am very tired, and must go lie down – '

'It will only take a few moments.' She pushed at a featureless section of marble wall, which surprised me by sliding smoothly back to reveal a short corridor of neat windowless offices, where she stopped and pointed at a doorway. I went into the room, and the man behind the small desk cut short a phone call and rose to shake my hand.

'My name is Park,' he said. I knew that. A gold perspex badge on his lapel said it in big letters. 'How are you enjoying your stay with us?'

I flopped into a well-worn swivel chair in front of his small desk.

'What is the problem?'

'It is a matter of your bill. It is hotel policy to seek an *arrangement* whenever a bill reaches a certain level.' He paused. My turn. I let the pause go on for a few seconds before responding.

'What level is that?'

He looked at a sheaf of computer print-outs that topped a pile on his desk.

'At the moment, the amount outstanding is a little more than two thousand US dollars.' *Chicken feed for a five star hotel. Doubtless Schwartz or Chang were behind this; they were doing anything they could to keep me reeling. Not that any such plea would impress Park.*

'That is based on a ridiculous full-priced rack rate. K-N Group will take care of this, almost certainly on a corporate account at their normal rate of discount.'

'But I am afraid we have heard from nobody at K-N – '

'In any case, you have my credit card details.'

He frowned some more and picked up a fax from his desktop.

'It appears the VISA Corporation will authorise no further expenditure on this account.'

'There must be a mistake.' I knew there was not.

'Perhaps you can leave us the details of another credit card.' He was doing this strictly by the numbers.

'Tomorrow I will talk to K-N and get this sorted.' I surprised him by standing up. Instinct and years of training and cultural conditioning made his hand shoot from his cuff to meet mine.

'Thank you Mr Park for your help and for being so understanding. Goodbye, Miss Kim.' They nodded, professional faces fixed in place. As I peeled around the door jamb I stopped.

'Could you please do one more thing for me?'

'Of course.'

'Ask Room Service to send up a bottle of Stolichnaya and everything else I need to make Bloody Marys, will you?' He knew how to make me squirm, but there were ways for me to return the compliment. Treating him like a room service waiter while I racked up my tab on imported liquor was one of them.

'Certainly.'

I left him reaching for the phone, his face an emotionless mask, only the eyes flickering with fury.

I took the elevator up and walked the corridor towards my room, fishing for the keycard, ready to call room service and tell them to get a move on with the Stolichnaya. Vital supplies. Tonight I had my sights set on a familiar sanctuary. Oblivion. Again. So what if I had a hangover tomorrow. The bastard of a hangover I had today turned out to be the least of my worries.

I was still looking for the keycard when I got to my room door. It lay ajar. I looked for a chambermaid's trolley, but the corridor was deserted. I pushed the door wide with my foot and Detective Kwok looked at me from the seat in front of my desk. A cigarette burned in a saucer full of butts. Spread around the saucer were papers and documents that I had left locked in my room safe. One hand moved to his belt. Behind him the muted television flickered with *Ssirum*, Korean traditional wrestling, Sumo without the decorum or the beer-bellies. Kwok's two side-kicks looked up from their work, and one of them pushed past me to block my exit. The room was trashed again. I looked at my watch. Three o'clock. Another nine hours until the day was over. Surely to Christ it couldn't get any worse than this.

Something gleamed in Kwok's hand. 'Alec Brodie, I arrest you on suspicion of murder.' The handcuffs were open and waiting.

Chapter Twenty-two

I nodded to nice Mr Park as we passed Reception in tight formation. He responded with a cold professional glance which transformed into a glowing smile the moment he saw the handcuffs behind my back. Maybe he wouldn't beam so broadly when he remembered my unpaid bill.

Seoul's traffic was uncharacteristically light, and in minutes we were at the north end of the Namsan road tunnel that, day and night, floods the city centre with traffic. A few hundred yards downhill stood the capital's most ritzy department stores and upmarket boutiques, but here we faced a two-storey 1970s eyesore painted a uniform flat grey. Windows thick with filth hid behind sturdy iron grilles fixed in place by chunky countersunk bolts that might have come straight from a shipyard.

Two uniformed cops stood guard over an entranceway of battered aluminium double doors that rattled as Kwok's men shouldered them wide, pulling me behind. Inside the plain grey hallway another cop sat behind a scarred desk with a wide plastic-bound logbook in front of him. Like the guards outside he snapped to attention and saluted Kwok as we walked past. He stared at me with unabashed curiosity, and it wasn't lost on me that the logbook remained closed, his pen capped. I was never here.

The two flunkies pushed and prodded me down a side corridor. A wrench at my hair pulled us up at a rusty blue door with a covered peephole. They threw back a deadbolt and launched me into the room so hard I stumbled and fell to the concrete floor. I pivoted on one knee and stood up to face the two men who a few minutes earlier had been rooting through my belongings for the second time in under a week. The door rang shut behind them.

Next came the cupped hands to my ears and the blows to my solar plexus and the double-sided Velcro straps around my ankles and the telephone books to the kidneys.

I awoke face down in my own vomit for the second time in a few hours. While out cold I had been moved from the chair to a recovery position on the floor, where I made the next in a long line of mistakes. I tried to get up. Having my wrists cuffed to a table leg and one ankle Velcroed to a chair proved troublesome, but the real problems lay everywhere else. Shooting pains dug their claws deep within my back and ripped through my abdomen and chest, spiralling around my innards until I emptied my lungs in one long, throat-searing scream that only set the pain sensors jangling some more.

I lay still in the vain hope of refuge from blinding aftershocks, my breathing reduced to irregular, fit-like hiccups that fired yet more waves of pain.

'Having fun?'

I spoke without opening my eyes. 'Sure, Chang. I enjoy a good beating.'

The toe of a shoe probed gently into my right kidney. It might as well have been a stiletto blade. My eyes were screwed shut, but still tears found their way down my cheeks.

'Kwok-Susa.' *Detective Kwok.*

'Nae.' *Yes.*

Chang spoke a few rapid words of Korean. The sound of footsteps retreating towards the door was drowned out by the rasp of Velcro torn apart, and my leg flopped to the floor. Rubber-gloved hands took my wrists and a rattle of keys released the cuffs. I was lifted so high my toes dragged along the floor. My whole body shrieked in protest and I sang along until a rubber glove that smelled of fake strawberries fixed itself over my mouth. Only then did I manage to open one eye. Bright corridor lighting, doorways receding like parked cars in a slow-motion film clip, a clumsy scramble down two flights of stairs to an open door and an agonisingly-bright, white-tiled room. A deserted basement bath-house, rows of sinks and showers, deep plunge pools and steam and sauna rooms attached.

The two cops threw me to the floor. I sat up gingerly, conscious of the stink that rose in waves from my body and clothes – and looked into the brass nozzles of two thick hoses. Icy jets tore the buttons from my shirt sending two halves flapping behind me, pausing only while a uniformed cop forcefully stripped me of what remained of my clothing. He backed away and the powerful blasts pummelled every square inch of my battered body. After the telephone books, the hoses might as well have been spitting bricks.

They stopped when Kwok threw a tired-looking towel and a pair of faded boxer shorts to the wet floor in front of me.

'Cover yourself up.' Another cop appeared with two wooden chairs, which he set down, facing each other, in the middle of the bath-house floor. Kwok sat in one, and nodded to me to take the other. A pair of men in uniform stood guard over the only exit. It took me several agonising minutes to pull on the shorts. I sat down and gently explored my abdomen with the rough towel. Big Cop and Small Cop stood breathing down my damp neck.

'Did you bring me here just to pound the shit out of me, or did you have something else in mind?'

'You know exactly why we have you here.'

'Even if *you* don't.'

He didn't take the bait.

'I am in the course of a murder investigation and I strongly suspect that you may have the answers I require.'

'Shouldn't that be the answers you were told to get?'

Kwok's head flickered to my right, Big Cop latched onto my shoulders – and little brother stepped forwards to repeat his right-hook-to-the-guts trick.

I doubled over and retched, taking as long as I could to recover, and when I finally looked up, Kwok stared at me, his face devoid of emotion.

'Start again?'

I nodded.

'What happened in your hotel room on the two nights you spent with the prostitute?'

'There's nothing to tell. On the first night I got back to the room and she was waiting for me. Chang must have sent her. We spent a few hours doing what she was paid to do. We drank a lot of whisky, and she left while I was asleep. A couple of nights later she surprised me in the lobby, and we went up to my room again. I didn't plan for her to be in the hotel, she just turned up. When I woke up in the morning the second time, she was gone again. I never saw her – '

'Until an unidentifiable caller just happened to deliver her navel to your room.'

'Exactly. Can I go now?'

'Let's talk about cameras.'

Here we go.

'You took Polaroid photographs together, didn't you?'

'You know we did. You have the photographs. Souvenirs, nothing more.'

'So tell me about the missing video camera.'

'I have explained that a half-dozen times already. I left it in London because my baggage was overweight.'

'And the video tape wrappings in your hotel room?'

'Left over from a shoot I did in London last week.'

Kwok shook his head like a schoolteacher disappointed at his student's transparent fibs.

'It's the truth.'

As I spoke, the brother cops moved in, expertly hand-cuffed my hands behind my back, and pulled me to my feet until I faced a broad plunge pool that came up to my waist. They lofted my wrists, forced my head forward and down, and two strong hands on the nape of my neck finished the move. Face-down underwater in two seconds flat. No time to snatch even a token breath.

Resistance was not an option. My feet were off the floor, thighs locked between the cops' legs and the sharp, tiled edge of the tub. My hands, cuffed behind me, pointed to the ceiling, and two big mitts on the back of my neck held me firmly in place. Blue water bubbled with what little breath my lungs still held. Within seconds I was in trouble and forgot that resistance was futile. I tried kicking, tried to twist my shoulders and tried to wriggle my neck free from their grasp. Useless.

The blue receded and I was on my knees by the tub and heaving desperately for air, Kwok standing over me. He stepped back and his boys wrenched me to my feet. It occurred to me that this was time to pay attention. No problem, I was ready to listen. I was ready to talk, too. I could tell them things, maybe not what they wanted to hear, but right now I could talk for Scotland. Kwok stood in silence, took a breath as if to speak, and flicked his head towards the tub. An instant later I was swallowing water.

This time they held me down for longer. I tried to relax, to burn as little air as possible. I forced my thoughts elsewhere, away from the water and the questions and the video camera and the tape, but from there they jumped straight to Mr Cho. The trail that Kwok was following led directly to Mr Cho.

I could not let that happen. Korean courts take an under-standably dim view of foreigners accused of murdering their women, and any evidence that Miss Hong and I had been together would surely be twisted to imply guilt.

Slipping the camera and tape out of the hotel had been an act of pure self-preservation, but passing it to Mr Cho had been thoughtlessly selfish. Now, the buck had to stop with me, and not with Mr Cho. Not after everything he had done for me. Hands heaved me clear of the water and I sucked air into complaining lungs just in time to be plunged back beneath the chilled surface.

Korea in the late eighties was a very different place, one ruled by lightly polished military dictatorships who maintained illegitimate authority with a network of security forces as much set up to control the locals as anyone else. Favourite of all the bogeys regularly dragged out to keep South Koreans controlled by fear was the threat of infiltration from Communist North Korea, or its agents. However exaggerated it might have been, the propaganda was so pervasive that it coated an entire society with suspicion of the next man on the street. Any person who stuck out from the crowd stood the chance of being reported as a spy. Twenty-four-hour telephone hotlines made doing so as easy as picking up the phone and dialling 113. Reports could be anonymous and dialled in from any public telephone, making it a favourite revenge move among enemies settling personal scores unrelated to North Korea.

The powerful military department that dealt with such reports went by a variety of names over the decades, but was commonly referred to as the Korean CIA. The KCIA were the SS, the Stasi, the Ton Ton Macoute and the KGB rolled into one. Since the government had grown from the military, and since the KCIA's activities were regulated only by the military, they operated virtually free of restriction. With unfettered powers and immunity from legal process, the KCIA was a force with a bad name that was completely deserved.

The last thing *any* Korean wanted was the KCIA casting a shadow on his door, and back then Mr Cho dealt with just that on my account. I was living in his family's apartment for a few weeks while I trained at his *dojang*, the only foreigner in the entire middle-class neighbourhood. Since I went everywhere with a camera on my shoulder, it was perhaps inevitable that some would-be patriot fingered me for a spy.

Years passed before Mr Cho's wife told me about the gruff men in bad suits flashing dreaded ID cards at their apartment door, demanding to know everything about the suspicious foreigner who enjoyed sanctuary in their home. Only then did I hear that Mr Cho laughed them out of his home – and never once mentioned their visit to me.

I owed Mr Cho. He didn't need a billionaire on his back, and if I could help it, I wasn't going to give him one.

Three, maybe four slaps bounced my face from side to side until finally I cleared the airways in one instinctual explosion and retched the watery contents of my innards all over Big Cop. I sucked greedily at the air, still coughing, vision blurred. Kwok allowed me a few seconds.

'Unless you cooperate this will get even more unpleasant. I ask you one more time: Where are the video camera and tape?'

I shook my head. Kwok shook his, and the grip on the back of my neck tightened once more.

Chapter Twenty-three

'London. The video camera is in London. The video camera is in London.'

I said it over and over to myself when my upper body was pushed hard underwater and, between ever-lengthening submersions, out loud, time and again. I had to outlast them, give them nothing but the one answer they didn't want to hear, and do it for long enough to plant the merest embryonic doubt in their minds. Never mind that I wasn't telling the truth. A good liar knows it is not about the lies you tell – it is how convincingly you tell them.

I might have been the one wearing handcuffs and close to death by drowning, but I still held a trump card. Kwok had messed up. The thrashing with the telephone books meant that I would be pissing blood for a week, but after the switch to the water treatment they gave away more than they learned and put me back in control. The flash of panic that crossed Kwok's face when his boys pulled me back from near-drowning was all I needed to know. I knew how far he was prepared to go, and that wasn't far enough. At least for now, the prisoner dying in custody was not an option, so I didn't have to endure anything worse than they had already done, and even that for just long enough to convince them that they might be barking up the wrong tree.

Not that I had any alternatives. I was boxed into a corner of my own devising. In the week since I got here, with

every last move I had lost or thrown away almost everything that mattered. Being charged with Miss Hong's
murder would be the end. The end of the assignment.
The end of any hope of ever seeing a job fee that would
delay the inevitable bankruptcy. Now that I had brought
his family into the firing line, almost certainly the end of a
valued friendship with Bobby; and the end of any tantalis-
ing hope that Jung-hwa and I might somehow survive this
mess in one piece. Murder was a capital offence, so even if I
struck lucky I could have life in Korean prisons to look
forward to. Right now, not one thing I could tell Kwok
would make the slightest bit of difference.

Face down in an oversized bathtub, ears roaring, arms
contorted upwards, lungs folded in on themselves, I
struggled to convince myself that the screw-ups had gone
far enough. From now on I had to think of Mr Cho, and
how I couldn't, I *wouldn't* bring any of this shit to bear on
his family.

London. The video camera never left London.

I awoke to the concerned scrutiny of uniformed paramedics and the antiseptic coolness of bottled oxygen, and I
knew that for now I had won the battle, if not the war. I lay
on a hard vinyl sofa in the office of a senior cop whose
photographs covered three walls. A saline drip fed a
catheter buried deep in the crook of my left arm and a
wire ran from a clothes-peg-like clip on my index finger to a
digital read-out that beeped reassuringly in time to my
pulse. The electronic life signal was steady, if slow.

When I opened my eyes again I was alone, and wondered for a moment if it had all been a nightmare, but a tiny
disc of band aid inside my left elbow and a fading ridge on
my forefinger confirmed the vision of paramedics. Bolts of
pain arcing around my midriff told me the rest was real
enough. As if he had been keeping a remote eye on me,
Kwok came into the room. Chang followed, hands in
pockets, grave expression on his face. He spoke first.

'Detective Kwok still thinks you are involved in the murder of the prostitute.'

'So?' I didn't sit up. I wasn't sure I could.

'But he is prepared to let you go for the time being.'

'That's big of him.'

'I beg your pardon?'

'Apart from a free admission on my part that I slept with Miss Hong on two occasions there is nothing to connect me to anything that might have happened to her. Despite the torture he doesn't have a single reason for keeping me here.'

'I think he might disagree,' said Chang.

'Won't he speak unless you tell him to? Why don't you push his buttons and see if they still work?'

Kwok remained blank, but I knew that he must be raging. Chang gave him a tiny shake of the head.

'Due to the importance of the situation affecting K-N Group, Detective Kwok will release you into my care. You would do well to remember that we hired you to do a job. One that remains of the utmost importance to my company, if not to the entire Korean economy. John Lee will pick you up at your hotel tomorrow at eight.' He started for the door.

'Hold on a minute.'

Chang gave me a 'what now' look.

'I need money.'

'Detective Kwok will see you back to the hotel.'

'I don't mean a fucking taxi fare, I mean *real* cash money. I've been spending my own ever since I got this assignment, and now I've run out of petty cash to pay *your* costs. If this job is so important, how come you won't even meet my day-to-day expenses? The hotel is pushing me to settle a bill that *you* should have taken care of by now.'

Chang looked at me as if playing for time before he reached into his jacket pocket and pulled out a Chanel wallet that was fat, not with cash, but with bankers' cheques, or *supyo*, just as good as the real thing but not nearly so grubby. He flicked through the cheques until he found what he wanted. Brandishing it between fingertips like he was thinking about tipping a ma?tre d', he let it fall to my chest.

'John Lee will have a receipt for you to sign.' He turned on his heel again and left me holding the *supyo* for one million Korean *won*. Whoopy-doo. Just over five hundred pounds Sterling – and the bastard had again side-stepped the unpaid hotel bill.

Small Cop drew the short straw and had to drive me back to the Hyatt. I hobbled and winced my way out of the police station and into the back seat of the same beat-up Hyundai. We made the trip in silence, and at the other end I climbed out, leaving the car door wide, forcing him to get out and walk around to close it. That would teach the little bastard not to beat up on me with a telephone book.

At the front desk, after checking that Manager Mr Park was nowhere in sight, I changed the *supyo* for cash, ignored the stunned stares at my torn shirt and water-damaged trousers, and at the front desk picked up a telephone message, which simply read, *'Call me. J.'*

I exchanged a note for coins and called Jung-hwa's mobile from a public phone that nestled in a cleft between two potted palms, and hung up when the call was re-routed to a voicemail box. Anyone can listen in on voice-mail messages and I was running out of friends to drop in the shit. That assumed Jung *was* a friend, but right now I was hanging onto every friendship I had, real or imaginary.

Getting back to a room that was not only empty but tidy came as a double surprise. Notch up one more gigantic debt to deluxe hotel housekeeping. For the first time in days, I had some money in my pocket, and since I wanted to keep it there, I called down to Room Service for French onion soup, a Korean omelette and fried rice, plus three litres of still mineral water and a bottle of painkillers.

I ordered the water and the painkillers immediately, the rest to be brought up in an hour. Moving slowly around the room I disconnected three telephones, emptied the entire selection of bath salts and bubble mixture into the tub, jammed a hand towel in the overflow drainhole and ran the hot water full blast. A few minutes later the first of the Room Service orders arrived. Two bottles of water went into the mini-bar fridge and the last came with me into the bathroom, where I swallowed six painkillers, twice the recommended maximum dosage, and one more for good luck. If six or seven wasn't perfectly safe, no way the pharmaceutical giant's lawyers would dare advise you to take three.

I stripped in front of the bathroom mirrors, gingerly picking at my ragged shirt and slowly peeling still-damp trousers over bruised hips. The whole of my abdomen was angry and hot to the touch, skin taut with tissue damage, the first dark inflections of bruising working their way to the surface. I fingered every inch of ribcage that I could reach, breathing in as deeply as possible, holding the breaths until I could contain them no longer and exhaling in single explosive bursts of air. If any ribs were cracked I would be writhing on the floor, but as it was, I only felt as if I had been run over by a herd of cattle. My throat smarted from all the throwing up and my lungs were as bruised as the rest of me, but so long as the kidneys weren't too badly affected I would get over it before too long. I had come out of full-contact Tae Kwon-do tournaments feeling worse than this and recovered soon enough. Never mind that I was fifteen years younger and much fitter.

I checked the foaming bath water. Almost too hot to bear. Perfect. It took several slow-motion minutes to lower myself into its scalding aromatic embrace. Shiny reflective bubbles popped, releasing sickly pockets of artificial sweetness. Beads of condensation ran down every wall. Steaming froth overflowed and coursed down the outside of the tub, across the tiled floor and out of sight down the corner drain. All very civilised, no danger of flooding the downstairs neighbours. As if I gave a shit about the neighbours.

With the hot tap drip-replenishing the bath's therapeutic powers, I lay back, head on a towel, sucked on mineral water and let the scorching bath and the painkillers do their best for me.

Ninety minutes later, I still felt like I had spent a week hanging from the ceiling of a kick-boxing gym, but the hot bath and food had done me good. I could now move around without wincing. I plugged the phones back in and checked for messages, but there were none. I tried Jung-hwa's mobile again, and once more hung up on her voicemail service. Whatever she had in mind when she called earlier, it wasn't important enough to keep her phone switched on, and somehow that made me feel better. Right now, I would take reassurance from anywhere I might imagine it.

It was still only ten o'clock, and since sleep was out of the question, I carefully pulled on a fresh pair of trousers and a loose shirt and headed for JJs, where at least I could still sign for the beers. Now that I was resigned to a hotel bill that I would never pay, the thought of adding a few zeros to it held no new fears.

Liberated by the notion that the more I drank, the more money I saved, I sucked on one frosty overpriced Heineken after another. All around me the nightly procession of life in JJ's fast lane buzzed. Middle-aged business execs with corned beef complexions sweated into ugly shirts and uglier ties as they tried their damnedest to look cool and failed. All around them high class, glossy-painted whores with ice in their veins did their best to look hot and succeeded. I did my best to become invisible, enjoying the feeling of being an uninvolved fly on the wall, until a waiter tapped me gently on the shoulder.

'Telephone call for you sir, this way please.' He led me

to an extension stretched out from behind one end of the bar.

'Hello?'

'Alec?'

'Jung-hwa? How did you find me?'

'There was no answer in your room, so I called around. I didn't even have to tell the waiter your name.' In the background, an electric Chicago blues version of 'Key to the Highway' interfered with the microphone on her mobile.

'Where are you now?'

'Can you come down to Itaewon? I'm in the Blues Room. Do you know it? Near the *Seo-bang-so*.' The fire station. I could find it.

Outside the hotel I clambered aboard the first Deluxe taxi in the line and told the man to get me to Itaewon. We were still in the hotel car park when I knew which Hyundai was following us, two different-sized shadows in the front seats. I took my driver through the centre of Itaewon, got him to hang an abrupt left at the lights in front of the Hamilton Hotel, and another quick left into a narrowing alleyway. Here, twisted lanes picked their way through a thicket of churches that occupied the upper floors of ordinary concrete buildings marked with red neon crosses on their roofs. Korea has the fastest-growing Christian population in the world, and its cities blaze with gaudy red crucifixes.

Very soon we were less than two hundred yards from the fire station, but separated from it by a maze of footpaths too narrow for anything wider than a bicycle. I overpaid generously and high-tailed it from my cab even before it came to rest. Ignoring my groaning innards, I took ten seconds to put half-a-dozen right-angle turns between me and whoever was following. From there, I could be headed for any one of a hundred clubs and bars and cathouses.

Two minutes later, and satisfied that I was alone, I climbed the dusty stairs towards the welcoming sounds of The Blues Room. The live band's extended version of Key to the Highway was still playing. This sounded like my kind of bar, and waiting for me was my kind of woman. Maybe, just maybe, things were looking not so bad.

Chapter Twenty-four

The Blues Room was a long rectangle with a tall bar at one end and a low performance area at the other. High-mounted floods blasted the stage with harsh cinematic light and shade, and at the opposite end of the room the bar was backlit by mini spots set into the undersides of shelves groaning with bottles. Floating candles bobbed in heavy glass jars set on steel tables watched over by a slim Korean who inhabited a dark shadow by the door like The World's Most Low-Key Bouncer. Customers sat in deep aluminium chairs, faces flickering in the candlelight, heads nodding in time to the music.

Alcoves lined the far wall under blacked-out windows that allowed liberties to be taken with whatever this month's licensing restrictions might be, and from one alcove Jung-hwa signalled, not to me, but to a waitress, who headed directly for the bar. Before I negotiated the shadowy aluminium maze, the waitress was already there, small round tray held lightly, tall bottle opened, beer glass fresh from the freezer and starred with a patina of ice.

Jung-hwa stood up to meet me, a vision in black silk that stripped away the years taking me back to the night I first saw her, no more than fifty yards away from where we stood now. Tonight's black two-piece was more modest than the one she wore then, but all the more alluring for it. The top had a high mandarin collar and a sweeping diagonal line of fabric loops and knotted textile buttons that clutched it tight to her lean figure. The skirt, a continuation of the same, clung fast to her hips and ended abruptly half-way between knee and ankle. Her greying hair was butterfly-clipped high at the crown, and her make-up bright and immaculate as ever.

I kissed her gently on the cheek and she spoke in my ear.

'Ore-gon mannae pohmnida.' *Long time no see.*

A whole forty-eight hours had slipped by since we spent the night creating nightmares for the Hyatt chambermaid. She sat down and I gently lowered myself onto the padded bench beside her.

'Did they hurt you?'

'You heard?' Maybe I shouldn't be surprised.

'Ben said you had been arrested for questioning. What is going on?'

'He didn't tell you?' I could not imagine Schwartz missing the opportunity to gloat.

'Tell me what?'

'About a prostitute called Miss Hong who is missing, and probably dead.' My eyes never left her face, but all I saw was confusion.

'I was one of the last people to see her alive.' I explained about the two nights spent with Miss Hong, and her later disappearance. Pangs of guilt over the admission that I had shared the same bed with a whore only the night before Jung-hwa visited my room were short-lived. For all her seeming enthusiasm, Miss Hong was a professional who insisted on condoms at all times and, in any case, Jung-hwa seemed unconcerned by such niceties.

'What has it got to do with you?'

I told her about the gruesome late-night delivery, and how Detective Kwok and his boys were brought in but kept at arm's length by Chang until today, when they dragged me in for questioning, probably at Chang's instigation. She looked puzzled.

'Why today?'

'They wanted to ask me about a video camera.'

Her expression betrayed just a hint of wry amusement. It was a knowing glance that in the past would have us making a beeline for the nearest horizontal surface, discarded clothes forming an untidy trail behind us.

'You video-taped yourself and Miss Hong?'

I was ready for the question and met it with a shake of the head. Alec Brodie, practised liar. Shameless.

'No. I left the camera in London. But Kwok found the empty spaces in my case, and some old tape wrappings.'

'He wanted the truth about the video camera?'

'Do *you* think I'm lying too? I already told you, it's in London.'

'I was only asking.' She straight-fingered me playfully just above the beltline, expression flashing from amusement to near-panic in the instant before I pitched forward, elbow to the table, head on forearm. As I sucked deeply and tried not to scream she wrapped her arms around my shoulders and leaned her head next to mine. Deep breaths picked up the mixed scent of make-up and soap and expensive shampoo. I raised my head to find Jung-hwa's eyes full of fear and concern. She took my face between her soft, cool hands.

'I'm sorry.' Like a mother kissing away her child's pain, she pressed her lips to my forehead. It worked for me.

I told her about the telephone books and the near-drownings, and she kissed me some more and I kissed her back. Stares bristled at us from nearby tables, but they couldn't hurt me, and I learned years ago that they did not bother Jung-hwa in the least. Onstage, the band's rendition of Jimmy Rogers' *Blue Bird* never missed a beat.

The next hour passed slowly. We drank and talked and enjoyed the band, four long-haired Korean misfits whose enthusiasm for the blues was not only palpable but contagious. Star of the show was the lead guitarist and singer who, Jung-hwa told me, owned the bar and called himself Junior Kim.

He waved to a pasty Westerner loitering expectantly at the edge of the stage.

'Ladies and gentlemen, Harmonica Luke.' The introduction scared up a sparse round of applause.

The big Westerner seemed nervous. In his twenties, he stood about six foot three in grey snakeskin cowboy boots that leered from beneath faded, threadbare Levis. A washed-out Monterey Bay Blues Festival t-shirt hugged a muscular frame. He stuck his acne-scarred face next to Junior Kim's ear. Kim nodded and passed the word to the rest of the band. I was not optimistic.

'*Since I Met You Baby*,' said Kim into the microphone, as he led them off with a wailing guitar intro that made the hairs on the back of my neck stand on end. When Kim nodded, Harmonica Luke bowed to the mike and surprised me with a soulful baritone, his diction clear, perfectly inflected, rhythmically precise. I raised my head towards the tiny dance area that was already beginning to fill, but Jung-hwa looked uncertain, so I tugged at her hand and she followed me. Before we even got to dance, the big man brought the first verse to a close and broke seamlessly into twenty-four bars of blues harp, if not straight from the heavens, then at least straight from the South Side of Chicago, as near to heaven as mattered in the modern blues world.

Jung-hwa folded herself into my arms like she belonged there. This was one of 'our' songs, the one that shook the long-gone Cowboy Club as I did my jokey Korean doorman routine for Jung-hwa the night we met.

Junior Kim led the band through a good six minutes of the song before thrashing it to a close, only to open immediately with the Elmore James classic, *The Sky is Crying*. It was a song that defined blues irony for me ever since, a few years after he made it his own, Stevie Ray Vaughan died in a helicopter crash. Harmonica Luke stepped back to let Junior take over on vocals, filling every momentary silence, cued or otherwise, with dead-on harp riffs. The man was a natural.

Back at our alcove, Jung-hwa summoned up fresh drinks.

'Cheers.' I raised my glass to meet hers. She looked tense.

'We have to talk.'

Here we go.

'I have been worried about things I hear from Ben.'

'Things to do with K-N?'

'Yes.'

'I'm not surprised. You're married to one of the guys at the centre of it.' She looked hurt. I laid my hand on top of hers. 'Sorry. Go on.'

'Just Ben is so busy with this new business, the GD-something – '

'GDR. It's a stock market thing, a big deal.'

'Ben is so busy with it, and I keep hearing your name, and what he is saying sounds scary.'

'It is scary.' The words came out before I had time to think. I still didn't have a clue how much I could trust Jung-hwa, but there was one thing she should know.

'You remember Bobby Purves, married to Myong-hee who used to work in the Cowboy Club?'

Of course she did. There was a time when the four of us shared a table at the Bavaria Bar almost every Friday night.

'I had lunch with Bobby today. I have seen him a few times already this week, and you know he works for a Korean stockbroker? I've been asking him about the GDR, trying to learn more about it. Bobby gave me some background information – nothing secret or anything, just things that nobody at K-N would tell me.'

'So?' I was evading the issue, and she knew it.

'Early this morning Bobby got a phone call warning him to stop hanging around with me, then later his little boy Min-tae went missing, taken away in a car by strangers for a couple of hours.' I explained about the message written on his chest.

'Poor Myong-hee.' She looked genuinely shaken, and I felt guilty for doubting her. I remembered something she said earlier.

'What did you mean when you said things about Ben were 'scary'?'

She thought about that for a moment. Despite myself I was suspicious again.

'I don't know exactly.' She sounded evasive. 'But it seemed like you were in trouble, and Ben sounded happy about it, like it pleased him.'

She had that much right, at least.

'I'm just trying to see the assignment through. I don't give a shit about K-N Group. I came here to do a job, and I just want to do that, shoot the photographs I get paid to shoot, and get out of here in one piece, get back to London with my money.'

A look of deep hurt clouded her eyes, and I cursed my clumsiness.

'I don't know if you *can* finish the job and get your money. Ben told me something today. He said, 'We've got plans for your ex-boyfriend, darling. If he thinks this is trouble, by the time we're finished with him he's going to be well and truly screwed.''

It scared the hell out of me, too – and I didn't like the reference to her 'ex-boyfriend' one little bit.

Chapter Twenty-five

Eight-fifteen, and as I cut through the lobby it buzzed with worker bees pre-occupied with their morning's tasks and goals. Dark-suited Koreans oozed intent and confidence, determined to turn difficult meetings in their company's favour. Westerners, lightweight suits marked by the long-haul, slurped hot java in search of a kickstart to the day. Bright-eyed uniformed staff, hours into their shifts, quietly fielded each mundane request as if it were the bidding of a visiting Head of State. Nobody paid me the slightest bit of attention as I slipped through the scene, intent on one thing alone. Disappearing.

Last night's terse voicemail message from John Lee was surely calculated to insult.

'Tomorrow you will do photography of products in my company's display centre at K-N Towers. Arrive before nine o'clock.'

No more car and driver at your beck and call, Brodie. It's you and the rest of Seoul in the morning scramble for a cab. A petty insult designed to put me in my place, it did me a big favour.

I had only one trolley creaking under the weight of four bags. A pill-box-hatted youngster pulled the door wide to the fleeting pleasures of morning sunshine and a warm breeze. Such basic joys are denied within the cocoon of the air-conditioned hotel, windows built never to open and doors designed to spring hastily to a close lest anything from outside sully its antiseptic atmosphere.

The line for regular cabs was long and agitated. Distressed heads peered towards the distant gate, perhaps hoping for a cavalry charge of empty cabs to crest the horizon and save the day.

I waved to the man leaning on the front car of a short line of deluxe cabs. He jumped happily to attention. Together we stripped the trolley and transferred its load to the car's boot.

I told him to take me to K-N Towers and as we left the car park, Big Cop and Small Cop, making no attempt to hide, followed close behind in the beat-up Hyundai. A few minutes into the journey I broke the silence and, speaking Korean, asked the driver if he saw them. He glanced momentarily at the rear-view mirror.

'Nae.' *Yes.* Curious.

Talking to the mirror, I spun a tale about how my Korean girlfriend's father hired *gang-pae*, or street thugs, to beat me up, and now they followed me everywhere, waiting for their opportunity.

Never mind that the story was plausible enough, it could easily backfire, since a lot of Korean men resented a foreigner having any sort of relationship with a local woman. I was also depending on this particular taxi driver being unable to recognise an unmarked cop car stuck to his rear bumper. I got lucky and the noises he made were an encouraging mix of sympathy and outrage. I explained what I wanted to do, and he responded with a series of conspiratorial nods. The hefty tip that I promised probably helped.

I thought of last night. My body was battered and sore, but three hours of gentle love-making with Jung-hwa in an Itaewon inn had put some of my aches and pains in the shade. Her strong fingers had kneaded and probed and tended to tired and abused muscles in long periods of therapeutic massage that worked wonders. What came next didn't do any harm, either.

Afterwards we lay entangled, our breathing synchronised, and Jung-hwa was the first to speak.

'You didn't get married?'

'No.'

'So no children?'

'None, thank goodness. Why?'

She lay in silence for what felt like a long time.

'Never mind.' She turned away and I lay watching until at last her back rose and fell in time to the rhythmic susurrus of sleep.

Lingering memories were interrupted by the driver speaking out over the traffic noise.

At K-N Towers, we ignored the crescent of tarmac that kissed the busy main entrance, and took the side lane towards the underground car park.

I hung out of the window, delighted to spot the same guard I had seen in recent days pop his head out of the security shack. I was betting that John Lee would have informed security that the big nose foreigner with the camera bags would be arriving by taxi before nine a.m., and my bet proved right. The barrier rose, and the taxi's tyres grumbled downwards over corrugated concrete.

We pulled up deep inside the basement car park, and while three long minutes slid by, I rolled myself in a ball behind the driver's seat, hard against the offside door. When we drew off, the taxi kept tight against the kerb that ran past the security man's window, meaning the only way the guard could spot me was if he levered himself from his chair and looked straight downwards. I held my breath as we paused at the brow of the ramp, and accelerated away. Heavy traffic closed around us for several minutes, until at last the driver spoke:

'OK. Where to?'

The cops would surely have noted his license number, so I directed him to a hotel south of the river, where I made a show of pushing through the main entrance while he drove away, his happy wave making me feel guilty. Today at the taxi drivers' lunch stop, he would have a good story to share with his mates. Tomorrow, after Kwok's boys put him under the spotlight, he would have a different story to tell.

I was soon back on the street. At the next big intersection I flagged a cab and took it to a high-rise apartment complex in the southern suburbs. There I picked up another taxi, this time downtown to a back street behind a gigantic office building. Five minutes on foot got me inside Seoul's main railway station, and two more minutes saw most of my gear safely stowed at the station's left luggage counter. The huge digital clock above the archway that led to the platforms said 9:58 a.m. Not bad. With only one heavy camera bag on my shoulder and a hold-all I had pulled from the stand bag, I trotted downstairs into the subway system.

When I first came to Seoul, its downtown flophouses crawled with cocky young Europeans and Americans, in town for one night only before flying off on the next leg of multi-city smuggling runs operated by moneyed cynics in Hong Kong and Taipei. For free air travel and a laughably small amount of hard cash, these naive fools criss-crossed Asia for a week, consumed with self-importance at the novelty of 'free' travel around the region – albeit at a price. With them went suitcases they had never seen before, into countries whose restricted markets meant there was money to be made on everything from hair dryers to ladies lingerie to jewelled watches to dried mushrooms – and where being caught with a suitcase-handle filled with miniature gold bars could land them in jail for years.

A common cargo for the Seoul-bound petty smuggler was the brand-name foreign camera, top of the range stuff that satisfied local demand for a standard of equipment

191

that was off-limits to importers rendered near-powerless by the same protectionism that helped make their capitalist customers rich. Even now, when import regulations were supposedly loosened, many of the high-end foreign cameras in Seoul shops were black market goods.

When I popped up from the subway maze on the north side of Chong-ro I knew exactly where I was going, even if I was unsure that it was still there. To my relief the little foreign camera enclave was much as I remembered it, a half-dozen stores side by side, small windows crammed with the big names in Japanese and European photography.

The shop I wanted was last in the line, and I pushed the door open to find the same fat little owner, cigarette burning in his mouth, one eye part-closed to the smoke running up his face. Since I saw him last, his hair had turned white, except for a boyish cow's lick of a fringe, stained nicotine brown. He sat wedged behind a glass counter brimming with camera gear, some of it older than I was. In case he remembered me, I wore a baseball cap pulled low over dark glasses, but from the moment I walked through the door he paid me no attention. His greedy little eyes were glued to my large Domke camera bag.

In the 1970s, American newspaper photographer Jim Domke despaired of the padded amateur-oriented monsters that dominated the camera bag market. At home in his Philadelphia kitchen he set about designing a lightweight bag that combined ease of access with premier-class durability. The resultant creation, crafted from heavy-grade canvas and military-style webbing, very soon had fellow-professionals clamouring for copies, and before long Domke was in the bag business. Thirty years later, working professionals the world over depended on Domkes, and decades-old bags with frayed flaps and colours long-ago washed out were touted like badges of respectability.

Mr Nicotine-Fringe certainly knew this and, at the sight of my heavy bag, immediately perked up.

Fifteen minutes of hard bargaining later I browsed the store's shelves, my back to the owner while his assistant ran out to gather cash from who knows where. When I left I was no longer the owner of two expensive cameras and three lenses, and with a pocketful of hard cash in large bills, more than I had paid for the equipment in London two years before. The rest of my gear was safe at Seoul station, where the left luggage counter would hold it for up to fourteen days. If I could not pick it up within two weeks I would not be needing it. The thought made me pine for a stiff drink that would have to wait.

A jam-packed city bus got me back across the river to the inter-city bus terminal, where I scanned the departure boards and bought a one-way ticket to Taejon, a regional capital about a hundred miles to the south.

They may be fraught with danger, but Korea's inter-city buses run with astonishing frequency. Less than ten minutes after reaching the bus terminal, I sat near the back of a luxurious single-decker as it crabbed around a sweeping cloverleaf onto the main highway south.

A video began to play on a television screen suspended from the cabin roof. The TV series *Friends* was never a favourite of mine, and badly dubbed into Korean and broadcast at distortion levels through cheap ceiling speakers, it soon had me wishing for earplugs. I was thankful that in the last ten years some sort of regulation had forced the screen well aft of the driver's seat; in the bad old days the lone TV screen was usually just above the driver's head, meaning passengers had to make do with watching him divide his concentration between the road ahead and painfully long spells spent peering upwards at the monitor, chuckling along with those of us not frozen to our seats in terror.

A half-hour of cross-cultural torture later there was a

long hiss of air brakes and a rattle as the doors clanged open. I looked up front to see a uniformed policeman mount the steps, salute the passengers, and proceed slowly down the centre aisle. The checkpoint by the roadside looked permanent, but that meant nothing. I saw fellow passengers produce their citizens' identity cards, which the policeman scanned as he walked the aisle. Maybe this was just a routine search for potential North Korean spies, but since Kwok had my passport, I had zero proof of identity. As the blue uniform got closer, matte-black revolver dangling from a shiny holster high on one hip, I pretended to search my holdall for papers. Head low over my bag, I watched his gleaming boots approach and pause directly in front of me for long seconds before he spun on one heel and walked the other way. After another formal salute he was gone. I pulled my hat low and waited for the trembling to stop. It took a long time.

Taejon is a forgettable provincial town with the trademark Korean architecture of bland, poured-concrete buildings with blue and red plastic signage lining its main streets. In its favour it was big enough and close enough to US military bases for me to slip through town without drawing a second glance. The oil and diesel-stained bus terminal was only a short walk from the railway station, and I stopped along the way only once, to buy a half-dozen cans of beer and some snacks. Pusan was still more than four hours away. From now on I needed to avoid drawing attention to myself, which meant no foraging from the train's snack trolley.

Boarding the correct carriage near the middle of the train, I sat in the assigned window seat and placed my bag next to me to discourage other passengers from sitting too close. The carriage never filled up so I sat alone, stiff and bruised but undisturbed, facing the window. Outside, the country scenery rolled past at speed, saw-tooth rocky mountain ridges, lower slopes lined with well-managed forestry, the fruits of a national campaign to re-clothe the naked land-scape that was the southern half of the peninsula at the end of the Korean War. In the impoverished North, where electricity remained scarce, every spare scrap of timber still ended up in the fireplace, its mountains as denuded of basic vegetation as its people were deprived of much else that their southern cousins took for granted.

Agriculture swept over every square inch of the odd-shaped plains that ran between mountain ranges. Painstak-ingly-maintained irrigation systems flooded rice paddy fields and watered swaying thickets of sweet corn. Giant complexes of makeshift greenhouses shaped like shrunken quonset huts enclosed large pockets of fecund ground. Thanks to these 'be-neel' (*vinyl*) houses formed from miles of piping and plastic sheeting, the supermarkets of South Korea stocked fresh-cut flowers and strawberries and grapes and fresh water melons, even in the depths of a long Siberian winter, when the daytime high regularly lingered well below freezing.

I tried to keep my mind cluttered with thoughts of the land I was crossing and the route I still had to take, but inevitably the mess that I was fleeing crept up on me. Running away made no sense, but neither did staying in the capital to play a role of my very own in a massive financial fraud. The reward for that would be a one-way trip back to Kwok's place of work, followed by prosecution for murder in a court system not noted for its objectivity in cases involving the death-by-mutilation of beautiful Korean women at the hands of foreigners. I needed time to re-group, to think things through and get on the tele-phone to anyone who might be able to help. Jung-hwa had tipped me off on the need to get out of town, yet I still didn't know how much I could trust her. Running to the country could buy me some time and, more importantly, would protect Mr Cho and his family, at least for so long as I could elude the authorities.

A loud Korean voice shouted in my face and two hands gripped my shoulders, dragging me up from the depths of beer-heavy sleep. I looked up at a dark uniform, coiled braid, polished badges and silver buttons. Palms to his chest, I surged to my feet and threw him across the aisle where he fell floundering on the opposite seat. The seat was empty. The whole carriage was empty. The train was at rest. I glanced out the window at the surging chaos of a mainline train station. Grabbing my bag I leapt towards the doors, but stopped before I took two steps. Putting the bag down, I turned to the shocked ticket collector and, offering my hand, spoke to him in Korean.

'I'm so sorry. You gave me a fright.'

He shook off the terrified expression, gripped my hand and pulled himself to his feet, apparently more embarrassed than offended.

'This is Pusan Station. Please disembark now.'

I backed out the train door still apologising profusely, cursing inwardly. So much for keeping a low profile.

Pusan is a sprawling port city of nearly four million, and I emerged from the station straight into what seemed like half of them stuck in traffic. The ferry terminal I wanted was about a mile away, so I opted to walk along the waterfront, where foreigners from visiting ships commonly wandered. Even in the fading light of early evening, I felt as if the whole city was watching me, the weirdo hiding behind the baseball cap and sunglasses.

I was three hundred yards shy of the terminal when the Angel Ferry slipped away from the dockside. I trudged onwards to discover that I had only just missed the last boat of the day. I bought a ticket for the next day's nine-thirty boat to Tongyeong, and headed back out into the heaving city.

Thinking safety in numbers, I ate at a crowded noodle bar before hitting the back streets, and quickly found a *yogwan* at the quiet end of a dead-end alley. Before settling in for the night I walked the streets for half an hour. Forever looking over my shoulder for I-didn't-know-what, I bought stored-value public telephone cards from three different small shops.

At the corner shop nearest the *yogwan* I picked up four bottles of chilled beer, two packs of biscuits and an apple and a pear. Nightcap and breakfast taken care of, I went back to my room and American Forces television. Sucking beer and munching on biscuits, I watched an entire American football game without properly understanding a single moment of it.

I awoke the next morning to the vague feeling that something was out of place, and it took a while to guess what it was. This was my first morning in ten days without a hangover, and it occurred to me that maybe I should try it more often.

I breakfasted on fruit and biscuits and, looking forward to a coffee on the way to the ferry terminal, took a long hot shower.

Refreshed and almost cheerful I set off to walk to the terminal, with one welcome detour into a crowded McDonalds. Big styrofoam cup of steaming coffee in hand, I headed for the stairs in search of a window seat overlooking the harbour. At the foot of the steps stood a newspaper rack, six or more titles suspended from unwieldy alloy bars clipped to their spines. Without pausing I plucked the Korea Herald from the rack with my free hand, and made it up three steps before stopping dead. I clutched the styro cup so tightly that the lid prised itself open, spilling hot coffee all down my front, but still I didn't move.

Call Girl Murder: Nationwide Manhunt screamed the headline. Right there, above the fold, smiling calmly at the world, was me.

Chapter Twenty-six

The next few hours played themselves out like the nightmare that refuses to go away, the one where the bogey man is closing down on you while your legs churn ever-decreasing circles in air thick as melted chocolate.

Double toilet doors dampened the paper rustles and distressed plastic noises of a crowded McDonalds dealing up the usual fare of fats and sugars. Locked in a narrow cubicle I dabbed paper towels at blood-spatter coffee swooshes that covered my trouser legs. I sat on the pedestal and enjoyed a fleeting sense of sanctuary and a powerful temptation to surrender to the cubicle, to curl up in a ball and never leave, but I could think of better places to curl up, and to get there I first had to catch a ferry. Ear to the door, I checked the bathroom was empty before sliding back the lock.

I had one immediate problem, and it stared at me from the mirror over the washbasins.

The photo in the Herald and by now doubtless on every newspaper and television screen in the country, was the smiling portrait from my own portfolio. A three-quarter profile head-and-shoulders, it was beautifully lit and tack-sharp. As it should be, since I set it up and Naz shot it, a world away in our London studio. In the mirror, distinctive curly blond hair, a bit on the unkempt side, surrounded a face with pale-pink Celtic complexion and bright blue eyes. In a country of forty-four million people, every one of them with olive skin, arrow-straight jet black hair and dark brown eyes, I might as well have a flashing light and siren attached.

I stuck my head under the tap and hurriedly combed out the wet curls, sweeping the hair directly back, using an elastic band from my wallet to fix it tight in the shortest of pony tails at the nape of my neck. With collar set high and baseball cap pulled low, the majority of one distinguishing feature nearly disappeared. After a last sceptical glance at the mirror, I picked up my bag and toed open the door.

Head down and nerves bristling, I hustled along the busy pavement, and almost immediately I spotted a parallel movement, another person's pace exactly matching my own. Before I could snatch a better look, I slammed into the rear end of a bus queue, knocking an elderly woman to her knees.

'Mian-eyo,' I said, offering my hand in apology, scared to look sideways in case the other guy was moving in.

'Michin-nom,' she hissed, waving my hand away. *Crazy bastard.*

I apologised again, stepped aside – and chanced the quickest of glimpses at my pursuer who, like me, wore a baseball cap pulled low over his eyes. I was running from my own reflection in a shop window.

Framed by a display of baby clothes, my body language radiated fear and tension. I turned away to face the wide street, which was congested with traffic, packed buses, chauffeur-driven cars and taxis with front seat passengers reading newspapers I wanted to rip from their hands. My own face stared confidently from behind the windows of at least a dozen gridlocked Hyundais and Kias.

I forced myself to take deep breaths, rolled my shoulders, and raised the skip of my hat. No longer hunched over, no longer with my eyes glued to the ground at my feet like a wanted man, I moved on, desperately trying to emit a carefree confidence that had nothing to do with reality.

I made it all the way to the ferry terminal without being arrested even once, but I got there with a half hour to kill. Half an hour to stay away from the television that blared from a tall stand in the waiting area, and to steer clear of every shop and stall that sold newspapers, and anyone who might be reading one.

I ran my gaze around the busy terminal as confidently as possible, drawing slow deep breaths of air thick with sea salt, tobacco smoke, diesel fumes and my own nervous perspiration. Mental checklists of everything I hoped to get done in the next few hours ran in my head like looped video previews. One of my more pressing worries was communications, a concern compounded by my mobile telephone sitting plugged into the charger at home in London.

Public telephone cards were fine for calling anyone who posed no threat – Naz in London, or Mr Cho in Seoul – but for everyone else, they were not only useless but a liability. Caller ID was common in technology-savvy Korea, so any call I made could be used to trace my location. Purchasing a new mobile was out since I had no idea if a pay-as-you-go service was available and, even if it was, how much ID was required to make the purchase. Now that my face was all over the news there was no way to find out; if it took only five minutes to buy myself a mobile, that was five minutes too long.

The answer presented itself a few minutes later, a mobile telephone peeking from the side pocket of a hold-all on a bench, its owner, a middle-aged Korean man, dozing, chin on chest. I sat down gently and placed my bag beside his. As I pretended to rummage through the outer pockets of my bag, I quickly palmed the phone – just as he shouted out. Caught red-handed, clutching another man's property. Except he was talking in his sleep. His chin lowered back to his gently moving chest.

The terminal's public toilet was a stinking nightmare, but

at least it had a cubicle door that locked. The display on the shiny new Samsung telephone was blank, so I pressed the power button and got the one thing I didn't want to see. Korean script, surely a request for a security code. I wiped the phone with paper tissue and left it on the cistern.

My ferry was beginning to board before another chance cropped up. A trio of well-off young females, expensively dressed in new brand-name leisurewear. I watched one of them talk excitedly into a mobile, then slip it into a neat pouch clipped to a shiny new rucksack. The group huddled around a vending machine well apart from their luggage, which sat piled on a bench. Sometimes it's just too easy to be a bastard.

On the way to the boat, I put coins in a box and picked out copies of two English dailies, the Times and the Herald.

Squeezed into a front-row window seat I checked the phone. The battery indicator showed it was fully charged. I pressed the power switch to close it down, then fired it up again, and to my relief it came alive without the need for a security code. OK, the damn thing was a garish purple and covered in cutey-pie stickers, but it worked. I switched it off to save the battery and because I didn't need incoming calls from a tearful teenager.

For the duration of the sea journey I stayed in the seat, my back to the other passengers. Sensational accounts in the two newspapers were predictably, depressingly alike, and contained only one piece of real news, something that I had known would come, yet hoped I would never hear. Miss Hong's mutilated naked body had been found tangled in rusted junk in shallow waters by the banks of the Han River, less than a mile from the Hyatt. Now the police and the media were all over the case. So much for Chang's ability to keep it under wraps, I thought. I read on. The foreigner suspected of killing Miss Hong was on the run, somewhere in Korea. Police were posted at all international departure points, and citizens were asked to watch out for the man in the photograph, who had a Scottish accent and spoke some Korean. A substantial cash reward was offered. Nowhere was there a single mention of Chang or K-N Group. Maybe Schwartz's PR efforts were reaping dividends.

As I watched scenery peel past the salt-smeared window my thoughts drifted to Jung-hwa. It was thanks to her that I had escaped from Seoul, and not a moment too soon. I yearned for the woman's gentle touch and mischievous smile.

Powerful diesels pushed us south-west across calm seas that glinted in the morning sun as we followed a low-lying coastal plain speckled with factory stacks and fishing villages that barely registered on my consciousness.

I brooded until the ferry pulled into the southern port of Tongyeong. Dense housing, no two homes the same, clung to steep slopes that looked down from three sides over a harbour basin packed tightly with fishing boats, ferries, and rusty coastal puffers, all function and no form.

I prowled the aisles of a modern supermarket and filled a hand basket with a variety of lightweight snacks while I scanned the ceilings and shelf-tops for security devices. I saw only one small CCTV camera covering the check-outs and a mirrored office window that would allow staff to monitor parts of the store. When one corner display put me momentarily out of sight, I slipped a bottle of men's hair dye and a pair of scissors into an inside jacket pocket, then joined the short line at the check-out counter.

My journey resumed on a creaky old bus that had seen better days, and soon crossed the short bridge linking the south coast of the mainland to Geoje Island. Tower cranes and a blanket of rust marked a massive shipyard on our left, and shortly after that I changed to another bus that continued south. It laboured through hilly countryside that shrugged off all signs of modern architecture or industry, and terminated at the tiny fishing-and-seafood resort of Haekumgang. A picture-postcard bay and spectacular off-shore rock features gave the place its name – *diamond mountain of the sea*. On the hill overlooking the bay stood the village's one modern *yogwan*. Walking from the bus stop I heard steps behind me, and at a corner I sneaked a backward glance at a Western woman, casually-dressed and toting a small backpack. At the reception desk of the inn, she hung back, politely giving me space while I checked in and made my next mistake. The middle-aged lady behind the counter complimented me on my Korean as she pointed the way to my room, through the door directly behind the Westerner, who stepped forward to the desk. As we passed she nodded, and I mumbled a quick 'hello' in English from under my hat, cursing my stupidity. Being unable to speak Korean was part of my new identity, and already I had fucked up.

The room's red-tiled bathroom had a small mirror blotched by fungus that seemed to grow in the light of a tired fluorescent tube that dangled from rusted chains of unequal lengths. I stripped to the waist, pulled a battery-operated beard trimmer from my toilet bag, and set to work. The trimmer made heavy weather of cropping my hair, tugging and tearing painful slow sweeps across my scalp, and it took the better part of an hour to achieve what I wanted: every last curl flushed down the toilet and only the shortest of hairstyles remaining in place.

Stage two was complicated by Korean-only instructions on the bottle of dye. Products like this were the only reason so few Korean men have grey hair. The stuff had to be straightforward to apply, but the instructions taught me next to nothing. I understood something about 'three minutes', which was how long I left the first mucky application before rinsing it out. The mirror over the desk in the bedroom showed me the results. The hair was uneven in length and in colour, whole patches showing flashes of dirty blond – and half the lines on my forehead had taken to the dye best of all.

I went back to the sink and this time worked the dye into every short hair on my head, ruining a soft shaving brush in the process. After another three-minute spell of growing panic I took a long hot shower, scrubbing hard at hair and scalp and forehead.

Back to the room mirror, where things looked much better, if shockingly black. Another couple of minutes of probing scrutiny passed before it finally dawned on me what was wrong. I returned to the bathroom, this time to take a toothbrush to my eyebrows. I spent another hour tweaking and trimming with the scissors, trying to get rid of that home-made look.

I propped myself against a pile of pillows at the head of the bed and thought about the stranger in the mirror. Maybe if I saw him often enough he would start to look natural. Natural was important, but what I needed most of all was to be different. So different from my photograph that I could walk the streets without the constant fear of a strong hand landing on my shoulder. I would find out soon enough.

Less than thirty-six hours had passed since I fled Seoul. Yet today's newspapers, proud bearers of yesterday's news, were full of me, which meant that Chang or the police, or both, had gone public as soon as I went missing. I knew I had to speak out and make my case, which was where the purple telephone came in.

The phone at the other end rang eight or nine times before being picked up. To my relief I got a real human being to talk to, not an automated answering service to negotiate.

'British Embassy, how may I help you?' A Korean woman, complete with near-perfect Home Counties accent.

'Eric Bridgewater, please.'

'I am sorry, but consular hours are from – '

'Believe me, he will want to take this call. My name is Brodie.'

A long pause.

'Can you tell me your name again?'

'Brodie, Alec Brodie.'

Another pause.

'Please hold the line, Mr Brodie, and I will see if Mr Bridgewater is available to take your call.'

A few seconds later:

'Eric Bridgewater.'

'We met at the K-N reception in the Shilla Hotel, when Bobby Purves introduced us and told me never to call you if I was in trouble.'

'I remember. Where are you calling from?'

'Do you want the address of the nearest police station while I'm at it?'

'You have caused the Embassy a great deal of trouble, not to mention embarrassment.'

'If I had just foreseen being falsely accused of a hideous murder, maybe I could have saved you the ordeal of a few awkward phone calls.'

'Witnesses put you with the dead prostitu – '

'Her name was Miss Hong. And yes, I knew her, but I didn't kill her.'

'So why did you run? Our advice in such cases is always the same. If you are innocent, surrender yourself and let the authorities take care of it. You are only making things worse.'

'Worse than WHAT?' In the mirror above the small dressing table, my face was bright red, a forehead pulse point throbbing so hard that one eyelid flickered out of control. 'Do you know how I spent the other day? Let me tell you – five hours in a Seoul police station, getting my kidneys pounded with phone books and my head held underwater for so long paramedics had to bring me back from the dead. The police wanted a confession. To a murder I know nothing about. Now there is a nationwide manhunt under way with my mugshot on the front of every newspaper in the country. Tell me, wise counsel, just how much fucking worse can it get?'

He let that one sit for a few seconds.

'If you are arrested and charged while still on the run it will make things worse. Anything that hints at guilt can only work against you.'

He had a point.

'But I'm being set up.'

'You will have to do better than that. This is Seoul, not Hollywood.'

'I assume you're taping this.' I said, 'Just for the benefit of anyone with a brain who might listen later, I did not kill Miss Hong. The last time I saw her, she was alive and well, and pouring whisky into my belly button – not the typical behaviour of anyone under threat from a murdering maniac.

'Next. I don't know who killed her, but I have a fair idea why they did it. To blackmail me into participating in the massive con game that K-N Group are pulling off with their GDR issue – '

'Blackmail, too. What are you going to claim next, that – '

'Shut up and listen. The GDR issue is a complete fraud. K-N is facing bankruptcy, and the GDR is their last chance. K-N needed my photographs from recent visits to North Korea, along with credibility they could borrow from my trips to the North to help convince the Due Diligence team of the GDR's viability. They also had me fake photographs of what was supposed to be an existing K-N plant in the North, photographs I took last week in a warehouse in Cholla province. The fake photographs are right there in the brochure K-N Group is using to promote the GDR.'

'Apart from hearing you admit to participating in this supposed act of fraud, I fail to see how your finger-pointing might in any way provide you with any defence – '

'Precisely. You get the point, at last. If I turn myself in just now, K-N's powerful mates and Chang's money bury any hint of trouble with the GDR. And at the same time, they bury me.'

He mulled that one over.

'And what are you suggesting the Embassy might do?'

'Begin by looking into the GDR. The Due Diligence team that's being suckered is British, as are the banks and many of the investment funds behind the issue. The chief banker involved in the scam is British – Martinmass – who works for a British bank. Bobby Purves' son was abducted for two hours on Sunday and his family were threatened with violence – most of them are British, too. And then there is me. British. As in citizen of Her Majesty's United Kingdom. As in what the fuck happened to British Diplomatic Service responsibilities to its overseas citizens.'

'OK, OK.'

'OK? I'm warning you ahead of time about a threat to British citizens and companies, and the open criminal involvement of a Briton who is a regular guest at British Embassy functions. So get this: letters telling everything, including the fact that you are already aware of this, are on their way to the Press in London and Seoul as we speak. Another copy is addressed to your bosses at Whitehall. So if you have any desire to hang onto your job, you might want to start doing it, and now.'

'Now hold on right there – '

'Get to work, you useless prick.'

I switched off the phone and set it aside. It was time to get started on those letters.

Chapter Twenty-seven

Night had long since fallen when at last I descended into the village in search of the first proper food of the day, and if the meal was overdue, the darkness could not have suited me more. Bare-headed for the first time since I left Seoul, I was testing public reaction to my new look, and even the prospect of a near-deserted fishing village on an island off the south coast scared me.

Narrow twisted lanes were dark but free of threat, an occasional curious face peering out from corner store or tidy courtyard. The flickering blue of televisions lit households from within; a pro-baseball match was under way and, by the sounds of it, much of Haekumgang was following the action.

Nearer the harbour a wider lane took on the green cast of fluorescent strip lights suspended at odd angles along the outsides of seafood restaurants, most of which sat deserted. In the lower halves of windows, murky glass tanks teemed with live fish, eel and squid. Five minutes after watching their choice swing from tank to kitchen in a dripping net, customers would be putting chopsticks to dinner – cooked or raw. Freshness re-defined.

Selecting a place to eat out of a dozen lookalike establishments was never easy, but tonight the decision was made for me. A cheery middle-aged woman stepped onto the street and ushered me indoors, not about to take no for an answer. The restaurant was exactly as I would have pictured it. Concrete floor, powder blue walls with vertical lines of dark red Korean script advertising its menu, and a small wooden counter by the door for diners to lean on while they argued over who would pay the bill. About ten customers dotted the dozen or so tables, and I was pleased to see that the obligatory television screen was blank.

I could have done without the small group at a corner table where the Western woman from the *yogwan* sat with two European men. Walking straight back out would only draw more unwanted attention, so I took a window seat in the opposite corner as far from them as I could get. Earlier, I was too busy hiding my face to notice how attractive the woman was. Her lightly-freckled cheeks were aglow with alcohol, and she wore wavy brown hair in a long pony tail that she fingered absent-mindedly as she talked. She was somehow familiar, yet only in the vaguest of senses, as if we might have crossed paths recently in a taxi line or subway car.

The cheery *ajimah* stood patiently by my table, battered red worker's hands flat on the hips of her apron, talking non-stop at me, unconcerned that I had yet to utter a single word in response. From now on unlike that guy in the newspapers, this foreigner spoke no Korean. I pointed to the menu painted on the wall, shoulders shrugged and palms raised in a pantomime apology. She shuffled off, plastic slippers grating on concrete, and plucked something from between the two men at the table in the other corner. The foreigner's menu, a small album of laminated photographs labelled with prices.

I knew exactly what I wanted but pored over the photographs for a minute before pointing at the blurry image of *hwae top-bap*. Almost as an afterthought, I did the sign-language for drinking.

'Beer?'

'*Maek-ju*' said the *ajimah*.

'Yes, *maek-ju*. One bottle of *maek-ju*, please.' This was a lot easier in Korean.

Visibly pleased with herself, my helper headed for the kitchen, and emerged a few seconds later with a tall bottle and a glass.

'*Kam-sa-hamnida.*' I made my speech clumsy and uncertain.

She bowed her head politely and left smiling broadly at the foreigner who could almost say 'beer' and 'thank you'.

I drank my beer and tried not to stare at the trio in the corner. I wanted to avoid attention, to project the impression of a tourist without a care in the world, not the terrified look of the hunted man I had seen in the shop window that morning.

The three spoke English, small talk about the food and the beer and prices of things and places they had visited. I made her for about thirty years old, and American. Her companions sounded French and German, and looked five or six years her junior. They called her Rose. She looked like an office professional on holiday, while the other two had the air of budget travellers, hair unkempt, clothes faded, tired footwear fraying at the seams. The German called out, a brusque demand for more *soju*, and I saw a flicker of concern in the face of the *ajimah*. At the end of their table stood five empty bottles, more than enough to sink three *soju* novices without trace. The German grabbed the new bottle and made a production out of re-filling the Frenchman's shot glass. Rose covered hers with one hand in a firm gesture that said 'no'.

'Cheers, stück dreck.' The German toasted the Frenchman.

'Santé.' The cheerful Frenchman was oblivious to being called a piece of shit. They hectored Rose into picking up her glass and, while they threw the liquor back with theatrical gusto, she took a token sip. The lady wasn't having much fun, but her boyish suitors were too far gone to notice.

My food arrived. I scooped sticky red chili paste, or

kochujang from a plastic dish into the middle of the ball of white rice that lay almost obscured by long thin slivers of translucent raw fish and finely-chopped raw vegetables.

One autumn weekend on the east coast years before, I was the attentive pupil as Jung-hwa taught me the joys of raw fish, Korean style. The trick with *hwae top-bap*, I learned, was to get the chili paste mixed uniformly through, to soak its spicy garlic-heavy flavour into the entire dish. Fresh, unseasoned raw fish falls apart, invading the mouth with the taste of the ocean. Soak the fish in *kochujang* and its effect enters a whole new dimension. Surround it with crunchy fresh vegetables and a hint of sesame oil, and you get a meal you will never forget, and that no fast-food afficionado will ever come close to understanding.

I spooned the first mouthful home just as the *ajimah* pointed a remote control at the television suspended over the kitchen doorway. The screen came to life at the top of a news bulletin, and it was all I could do to resist the temptation to run for cover.

I was demoted down the news order, but only as far as third story, after a pitched battle between opposing factions of Seoul pacifist monks and striking shipyard workers in Ulsan. Next, the manhunt story led with a full-screen shot of *that* photograph. The one with the confident gaze and the curly blond hair. I leaned back in my chair and feigned casual interest. The bulletin went on forever while citizens were assured that everything possible was being done to bring an evil foreigner to justice. My stomach lurched with fear as I watched interviews with an extravagantly uniformed police chief and detectives in ill-fitting suits, and at one point Detective Kwok hurried away from a chasing camera, palm outwards signalling 'no comment'. More uniformed cops knocked on doors and handed out two-colour flyers bearing my photograph. There were reports from Immigration counters at Incheon airport, and footage of passengers queuing for the daily ferry from Pusan to Japan. After an age I peeled my gaze from the screen, and only when I was rescued by the latest action from the big baseball match did it occur to me: not one person in the room had paid me so much as a glance. The new hairstyle had done its job. I picked up the empty beer bottle and waved it to the *ajimah*.

Half of my meal had disappeared unnoticed. The television picture dissolved leaving a silence broken only by the quiet murmur of conversation and the odd explosion of drunken laughter from the two Europeans. Their companion looked increasingly uncomfortable. She tried to get up and leave, only to be loudly persuaded, almost bullied, to stay 'for just one more drink'. I pulled a dog-eared Robert B. Parker novel from my pocket and read it one-handed while spooning the last of red-tinged rice and raw fish with the other. It stretched my multi-tasking skills to their limits.

I was struggling to maintain concentration on a showdown between the Boston private eye and two knife-wielding Chicanos when the Frenchman got to his feet, let a couple of banknotes flutter to the table and staggered out into the street. I almost felt sorry for him. I knew all about that deathly moment of realisation when the hitherto limitless joy of inebriation was snuffed out by the raging power of the drink.

A few minutes later, I closed my book and walked to the counter beside the door to settle my tab.

Rose was hemmed in by the German. She signalled to the *ajimah*, calling in Korean for the bill. The German gave her some money and disappeared towards the toilet as I shouldered the door wide and headed out into the cool night air.

I made it about half way to the *yogwan* when the sound of hurried footsteps made me turn. The American woman held the middle of the trail as if frightened by its shadowy flanks. She looked up from the path and straight at me.

'Hi.'

'Where's the fire?'

'Pardon me?'

'You look like you're in a hurry.'

'Just heading back to my room.' She pointed up the hill. 'We came in on the same bus.'

'I remember.' I was hoping she hadn't remembered the blond curls hiding under the baseball cap.

She fell into step beside me.

'Where are you from?'

'Ireland.' I had anticipated the question coming up at some point, and a lot of people, Americans and Koreans included, can't usually tell Scottish from Irish.

'I thought I heard an accent.'

'You mean an un-American accent?'

'I'm Canadian, but I suppose that's exactly what I meant.'

'Where's your friend?'

'Stefan? I don't really know him. I just met him and Jean-Marc on the way to the restaurant.'

'And got roped into more than you bargained for?'

'They are new to *soju*, and wouldn't listen when I said they had to be careful with the stuff. After a while, the macho posturing wore a bit thin.'

Rounding a corner in the steep trail, we stopped to catch our breath and take in the unbroken view over the village and beyond, to a horizon ablaze with fishing boats. Powerful floodlights shone downwards to attract schools of fish and squid, and sent rippling rays like outstretched glowing fingers that fanned across inky black sea to the rocky shoreline.

'It's beautiful,' she said.

'One of my favourite places on the planet.'

'You've been here before?'

'A long time ago.'

'And now?'

'On holiday. You?'

'The same. I live in Seoul.'

I had not enjoyed an innocent conversation in a very long time. Before I could respond, Stefan appeared from around the corner and stopped abruptly, chest heaving. He swayed like bamboo in a typhoon. Very thickset bamboo.

'Ach sooo, now I find you.'

He wasn't talking to me.

'Why did you run away?'

Rose looked tired. 'I wanted to get back.'

'We were going to walk together, you said so.' As if picking up on my presence for the first time, he switched his wavering look to me. 'And who are you?'

'No-one.'

'OK, so fuck off Mr No-one, and give me and my friend peace.'

He waved his big right hand directly at my face. The last thing he wanted me to do was leave while he put on a show in front of his dinner companion. He prodded at my chest with a fat finger, catching me square on the nipple. It hurt like hell. He did it again. I didn't move.

'You maybe have some problems to understand English?'

I knew exactly where this was going. I also knew I should walk away right now, but I had taken more than enough shit for one day. I gently slid my left foot back and stood, weight evenly distributed, hands clear of my body.

'You're drunk.'

'You think you are good enough, Mr No-one? Something special, eh?' His whole body off-synch from the *soju*, he wavered forward to stare me down. He reeked of alcohol and garlic. I edged back slightly and made one last weak attempt to side-step an inevitability, the prospect of which I was beginning to relish.

'We were only talking while we walked up the hill.'

I was still speaking when he swung a looping right hook at my chin. If nothing else, he was predictable.

I dipped back, and as his fist whistled past my face, I hammered it along its wayward track with a forearm block and made for a low kick with my left that instantly drew broad forearms crossed over his groin, but my kick was a feint. I planted the foot, spun, and drove my right heel deep into his solar plexus.

Movie heroes prefer the more cinematic spinning back kick to the head, but in the real world, a shorter strike at a bigger target is the only way to go. His lungs emptied with a *whoosh* and he went down like he was there to stay. Face purple, he fought for oxygen and when it came he threw up, spasms shaking his entire frame.

Rose looked shocked.

'You didn't need to do that for me.'

'I didn't. It was me he was trying to knock me into next week.'

'So you just *had to* put him down?' She shook her head, and her expression changed. This was getting us nowhere, and she knew it. 'I could do with a drink.'

'What about him?' I pointed a toe. Stefan flinched reflexively, and I pointed the toe again, prompting another flinch. I could get to enjoy this.

'He and the other guy are sharing a room at the *yogwan*.'

'I hope they have the sense to sleep with a window open.'

At last her look softened, and she turned towards the village lights.

'Come on.' I followed in her footsteps, wondering why a woman so wary of one set of drunks was apparently without fear of spending time with a guy who, for all she knew was another one; and wasn't I supposed to be keeping a low profile? I followed her along the track towards the village.

In a narrow back street, she knocked on the sliding doors of a corner shop, spoke to an old man in Korean, and came away with two soft plastic bottles of milky *makkali*, a beery, unrefined rice wine.

'Home-made.'

'Fine by me.' I loved the stuff. 'Where will we go to drink it?'

'Back to the *yogwan*, I guess. So long as you behave.' She wasn't joking.

At the front entrance to the inn, she pulled up.

'Your place or mine?' There was a hint of humour in her tone, but nothing else, I was sure.

'Yours. Mine is a mess.' Blond hair all over the bathroom.

Her room had a traditional *ondol* heated floor, brightly-coloured fold-up bedding piled neatly against one wall. While she rinsed two plastic toothbrush mugs I peeled the top from a *makkali* bottle.

Shoes off, we sat cross-legged on the warm floor and clinked mugs.

'Cheers, Rose.'

The look she drew me was dusted with suspicion. 'I'm at a disadvantage here.'

'Sorry, it's John.' My brother's name.

So much for keeping a low profile I thought again, as we worked our way through both bottles of the beery wine. I shouldn't even be here but, right then, the draw of innocent chit-chat, totally divorced from all the shit in my real world, was impossible to resist.

We stuck to small talk. My brother John ran a bar in Hong Kong, and since I know a thing or two about bars, I told her that was what I did. She had never been to Hong Kong, so I ran off a few ten-year-old impressions and vague generalisations before changing the topic.

'What about you. Where did you learn to speak Korean so well?'

'I grew up here.' It came out in a way that flagged the subject as a no-go area, so I left it.

I was alone with an attractive woman in her bedroom,

yet the air remained flat and uncharged, completely devoid of sexual intrigue. She sat tugging distractedly at her pony tail, clearly pre-occupied. I remembered the unlikely group she made with the two Europeans at the restaurant. Perhaps she chose my company for the same reasons she opted to sit with them – an unwillingness to be alone. Innocent escapist companionship, strings neither attached nor desired. Maybe we had more in common than I would have guessed.

I drew back the sleeve of my sweatshirt to look at my watch, then quickly pulled it down again. Even if sex had been in the air, I thought, unless it took place in pitch darkness I was off-limits, arms and chest covered as they were in downy fair hair.

'What are you smiling at?'

'Nothing. Just thinking. I better go. I've had a long couple of days.'

Of course she didn't object. At the doorway, while I struggled with my shoes, I said:

'I might take a walk along the coast in the morning. Not too early. Want to come?'

'I don't know. Maybe I'll see you around.'

Then I did something I hadn't done with a woman in years. *I shook her hand*.

Chapter Twenty-eight

The eastern sky signalled the emergent dawn, a dark blue horizon tinged with gold and smudged by the distant rolling of powerful currents.

When the ringing tone came, it brought with it the comforting familiarity of a number called a thousand times before. I held my breath.

'Hello – '

'Naz! It's me. I'm – '

'You know what to do. Wait for the l-o-n-g beep, then leave a message.'

I waited. She was right. The bloody beep went on forever.

'Naz, it's me, are you there? Pick up the phone, this is important. Naz? Come on, talk to me Naz, talk to me.'

Nothing. I stood shivering until the machine cut the connection.

The card slid silently from the public telephone. I pushed it back and dialled the studio. Same thing. Except this time I listened to myself tell me to please leave me a message and I would get back to me. Since I hoped Naz would be there some time soon, I did.

'Naz, it's Alec. Sorry I haven't called for a few days but, well, I'm in trouble, a lot of trouble. The assignment's gone to hell and now the police are looking for me. You've probably heard about it already, but I didn't do what they're saying. I'm still in Korea, because the police have my passport. I'm pretty safe now, just trying to work out what to do next. When I've got a better idea what's happening, I'll call again. Bye.'

I clattered the receiver into place, spun outwards and pressed my face against the cold glass of the booth. Choking sobs slowly died away, tears, salty and full of shame, ran down my cheeks and into the corners of my mouth. Lights in the village flared and merged into watery starbursts.

I flopped onto a dew-soaked bench and fought the urge to lean back and wail at the sky. I had put off talking to Naz out of dread at the thought of her voice, normally so full of spirit and mischief, reduced to a one-dimensional squawk by the transcontinental phone line and the news I had for her. Dread at the image of her, wide-eyed and wordless at the latest shit I was dragging my feet through.

Not that she would stay wordless for long – and that was where the tears came from. I ached for her friendly voice, even if it did rail at me for being a fuck-up.

I dug the purple phone from my pocket, thumbed the power button and dialled the number for Jung-hwa's mobile. After a few seconds of electronic limbo, the connection came through.

'Yoboseyo.' *Hello.* Jung-hwa's voice. Sleepy and irritable.

'It's me. Can you talk?'

'Wrong number, *asshole*.' In Korean. Convincingly angry, playing to the audience I had hoped might not be there.

'Call me back,' I said, just before the line went dead.

I walked down to the village as the rising sun shot fiery stripes into the sky. Cockerels wandered narrow lanes, their discordant wake-up calls echoing off flinty stone walls.

Five wooden fishing boats with boxy cockpits sat motionless in the fuel-rainbowed water of the miniature harbour, decks cluttered with the gear of their trade. Spiders' webs of ropes and pulleys secured batons of tungsten lamps in giant stainless reflectors the size of umbrellas.

On one boat deck, a man in patched overalls sat deep in concentration. The nub of a cigarette smouldered in the corner of his mouth while, from gnarled hands, fluid blue stitches flowed across a sun-bleached net.

Another fisherman stood on the stone jetty and wielded a sturdy bamboo pole with a heavy loop of thick rope fixed to one end. With each downward swing he drove the rope onto a fishing net spread out across the pier. Plumes of dust and salt rose with each strike. Enshrouded by a particle cloud and backlit by the rising sun, the man became part of the landscape, a vision of ancestors who had worked this coastline for thousands of years before him. Deep-rooted instincts of my own took over, and while I perched un-noticed on a rope-wrapped bollard I calmly shot frames with the rangefinder from my belt pouch, freezing a dark sinewy silhouette against the dawn sky. The old camera was near-silent, and if he picked up on my presence, the man paid no heed, until the tinny wailing din of a Korean pop song from the purple phone in my pocket destroyed the moment for us both. Pole in the air, he stopped in mid-swing and looked at me, expressionless.

Thumb on the green button, I read the number flashing on the small display. Jung-hwa's mobile.

'Jung-hwa? Are you OK? Has he gone?'

'Let's take your questions in order, shall we? No, it's not Jung-hwa. Yes, she's fine, thank you, sound asleep, in fact. And no, you prick, *I* am right here.'

Schwartz.

'What's wrong? Don't tell me that for the first time in your miserable existence you're stuck for words?'

'Any misery going around is of your making.'

'Good for you. The slightest little thing goes wrong, and somebody else has to get the blame. You got yourself into this mess, remember.'

'Slightest little thing? Like cutting a young woman to bits?'

'Life goes on, man. Can't turn the clock back.'

'Screw you, Schwartz. I've heard enough.'

'No. Wait. Where are you now? My guess is you're still in Seoul.'

He was fishing.

'Does it matter where I am?'

'We could meet and talk.'

'Give me a break.'

'I'll come alone. We can help each other, trade.'

'Trade punches, maybe.'

'What about the video tape?'

'Christ, you too? You just don't get it, there *is* no video tape.'

'Now who's taking who for a fool. Meet me. Maybe we can help each other out.'

I let the silence stretch for a few seconds:

'My location, my terms.'

'No problem.'

'I see one face in the crowd I don't like, I'm out of there.'

'You have my word.'

Like I could take that to the bank.

'Han Il Kwan restaurant,' I said.

'Myoung dong, right? Between Midopa department store and the Cathedral?'

'Twelve-thirty.' I hung up and switched off the mobile. Along the pier, the fisherman resumed his attack on the net, muscles gleaming with sweat and speckled with salty dust rendered warm-earth brown by the rising sun.

From a tight curve of rocks and discarded scallop shells in the lee of the harbour wall I picked up a handful of pebbles and launched them, one at a time, at a soft drink carton that bobbed in the tide. Once or twice I came close, but with every miss I became ever more exasperated, my efforts increasingly erratic. I threw and threw until the sinews in my shoulder began to complain.

Schwartz was still after a video tape that he could not be sure existed, and the only satisfaction I could derive was from sending him on a wild goose chase through one of the country's busiest restaurants in the grips of the lunchtime rush.

I watched one last stone rip through the water's surface three feet from the unaffected target and turned to find Rose so close she could have reached out and touched me. Twenty feet of rocks and shells stood between us and the nearest pathway.

'How the hell did you manage that? I didn't hear a thing.'

'Grow up with three older brothers, you develop any number of survival skills. You were so far gone, a herd of elk could have snuck up on you. I thought I'd take you up on that offer.'

'Offer?'

'Last night, you mentioned a walk.'

'Last night you didn't seem very keen.'

'I had a lot on my mind.'

You and me both.

'When do you want to start?'

'Meet you in an hour at the *yogwan*?' She spoke over her shoulder as she glided towards the footpath, creating barely a rustle.

'I'll see you there,' I shouted at her back.

At the village's cramped little supermarket I bought mineral water, bread rolls, cheese, fruit and biscuits. Back at my room I loaded them into a daypack and slipped the purple mobile into the belt pouch beside my camera.

I stepped outside to find Rose relaxing on the same bench that I had collapsed onto a couple of hours before.

'This way.' I pointed to a path that left the south end of the car park.

I did this walk a couple of times with Jung-hwa. A few

minutes of steep pathway wound a tight line through a stand of pine trees until we broke out onto a miniature patch of open farmland clinging to the hillside. On a muddy ridge that enclosed a terraced plot half the size of a basketball court, an infant sat on his heels, five thousand years of ancestral impassiveness already writ plain on his stoic young features. He watched a grizzled little man work a wooden plough pulled by an ox, man and beast struggling across deeply rutted soil. We stopped beside the boy and sat on our heels. The child leapt to his feet and treated us to a deep, respectful bow. He nervously tongued a gritty stripe of dried snot that occupied his upper lip.

We waved to the farmer who waved back, seemingly unsurprised by two foreigners popping up at his remote workplace.

Rose dipped into her backpack and came out with a gleaming slice of water melon. She had to coax the boy to take it, but when he did, his face shone with pleasure, and soon shone with water melon juice as he attacked the bright red fruit. The man left his ox in mid-field and walked towards us, and the boy came over all shy again until Rose once more did the backpack trick and presented the man with a melon slice. His weathered face broke into an even white smile as perfect as anything you ever saw on a toothpaste box.

I listened to Rose converse easily with the kid and his father until the Dad went back to his ox and we walked on. We turned inland onto a narrow wooded path that quickly became little more than a goat trail through dense vegetation. Tiny gaps in the foliage teased us with glimpses of startling coastal views, until at last we crested a mini-summit and shed our packs.

The rocky perch gave us 360-degree views that stretched for miles. Inland to the north, thick foliage held off ever-spreading tendrils of agriculture. To the west and east, pitted stony coastlines surged and dived from sheer precipice to rock-peppered shoreline. To the south, a hillside draped in a hundred shades of green tumbled over an invisible cliff-edge into a blue-white seascape dotted with rocky outposts too tiny to be called islands, large enough to support a few hardy trees and little else.

Pooled candle wax and spent matches and names scratched in stone marked a flat rock as the obvious picnic spot. I set my backpack down.

'Ready for something to eat?'

'Thirsty.'

'I brought mineral water.' I opened my bag.

Droplets splashed in the dust at my feet and I looked up to see a six-pack of beer dangling from Rose's hand.

'Freshly cut fruit *and* cold beer? You can join me on walks anytime you like. Got anything else I could really use?'

'Just the one more thing, Alec.'

Alec. My stomach folded in on itself. She put the six-pack on the rock and dipped two fingers into the breast pocket of her cotton blouse. They re-appeared holding something pen-like, slender and black, silver lettering along its side.

'You could use this.'

She placed it in my hand. The lettering was in Korean, a brand name that meant nothing to me, and towards one end was a pen-like cap. I pulled, and it came away – long, thin, inky and brush-like. Mascara.

'You forgot about the eyelashes.' She pushed a cold beer into the crook of my arm. I popped the seal, drained half the can, edged sideways until my legs hit the flat rock, and sat, waiting. Rose took her cue:

'Yesterday, when I saw you at the *yogwan* and later at the restaurant, I was certain I knew you from somewhere.'

I recalled that she had vaguely reminded me of someone, too. Perhaps we did see each other in a Seoul taxi line.

'And then there was the bullshit about your accent.'

I looked away.

'My brother married a Glasgow woman, and if your home town is more than a few miles from hers, I'll be surprised. But you told me you were Irish. And after you left me in my room last night I took my first good look at yesterday's Herald.'

I was rumbled.

'At first I was scared witless, until I realised none of this explained where I knew you from. But when I read the story, I called my parents, and the penny dropped.'

This made no sense. After she discovered I was a murder suspect, she spoke to her folks *then* volunteered to accompany me on a stroll up a lonely hillside?

I sucked the last of the beer from the can. 'What do you mean the penny dropped?'

'Yesterday, I was Rose, right?'

'Don't tell me you were lying, too?'

'I never did tell you my full name. It's Rosemary Daly.'

Rosemary Daly. Korea. Canadian. At last, pennies of my own began to fall into place. When I flew into Korea for the first time in 1989, I sat next to a family of Canadian missionaries. At first I mistook them for Americans, but they soon put me right. Mum and Dad and four kids. Three boys and a girl. *Grow up with three older brothers, you develop any number of survival skills.*

The Dalys, the Christian Dalys, as I always thought of them. I was the newcomer to Korea and they were the experts, fluent in Korean, completely at one with a culture that I had yet to experience. Rose's father Vincent and I shared a passion for photography, and like all photographers we also shared a love of the equipment involved. He proudly showed me his latest acquisition, a sturdy Canon SLR in its stiff leather 'never ready' case, and pulled out a pocket album of family portraits taken during their period of leave in Canada; three generations of loving extended family beautifully photographed at ease in an Ontario suburb. They were about as far as they could get from the few remaining blurry Instamatic shots of my dysfunctional childhood in Central Scotland.

Over the following months and years I saw Vincent and Jemma regularly, usually with the family in tow, other times alone. They were always delighted to see me and never showed a moment's discomfort over the chasm that separated their evangelical Christianity and my unspoken but avowed atheism. We always managed to keep in touch, and though I hadn't seen them in over ten years, they still sent me Christmas cards. Sometimes I even sent one back, usually around the middle of January. I looked around me at the beauty of Haekumgang, and another element fell into place: about a year after we met on final approach to Kimpo Airport, they recommended a quiet get-away holiday spot on the south coast. Geoje Island, Haekumgang fishing village. That was the start of several visits in the company of Jung-hwa to the very place where we stood now.

I had a vision of their youngest that day in an airliner on final approach for Seoul, a freckled pre-teen, squirming restlessly in her seat, shy and giggly and with tooth braces and long tight braids that she twirled endlessly between her fingers.

'You're Rosemary Daly?'

Chapter Twenty-nine

OK, so we hardly knew each other, but at least we had *some* history, which is more than your average two strangers perched above a rocky shoreline on the southern edge of Korea could say. Until now, in the absence of lust, a natural state of reserve had chilled our curiosity, a reserve now shed like an unwanted layer of clothing.

Soon the makings of a picnic covered the middle of the flat rock, which was big enough for us to sit cross-legged, looking over the food at the coastline and the sun swept ocean.

'Don't want these to go warm on us.' I reached for a fresh beer.

'Not much chance.' She popped the ringpull on one of her own. 'Mum and Dad told me all about it when I called, so are you going to explain what is going on?'

'Do you mean 'Did I do it'? If you really needed an answer to that one, you wouldn't be sitting here.'

'I might be trusting my instincts.'

'Dad would love that.'

'His instincts, too. He is certain you've got on the wrong side of someone powerful, and now you're a convenient scapegoat. Add to that the crush I've had on you ever since I was eleven years old, and yes, I'm betting you didn't do it.'

I turned away as casually as I could. My eyes glazed over with the threat of tears, blurring the scenery for the second time that day. Until now I had been carrying all this around in my own head, sharing it with no-one.

That she had a crush on me all those years ago was news to me, too.

'The whole shitty tale?'

'If you want to tell it.'

'It'll take a while.'

'I'm not running to any kind of a timetable here.'

So I poured it all out, from being in debt in London to being on the run in Korea, and everything in between. Miss Hong. Chang, Martinmass and Schwartz. And Jung-hwa. Fuck. *Jung-hwa.* Here I was paralysed with self-pity because I had been keeping all of this to myself but, only a couple of days before, Jung-hwa had already played Rose's role, hearing me out, concern and alarm written all over her lovely face. Alright, so she only got an edited version – but I had managed to forget telling her even that much. Jung-hwa hadn't appeared in my thoughts in hours, despite the abortive phone call this morning. What that told me, I didn't want to know.

I told Rose about the interrogation and beating I had undergone in the police station. I showed her the still-angry bruises, yellowed rainbow streaks wrapping my abdomen. I even told her about the video camera and the tape I had stashed with Mr Cho, and about Schwartz's continued interest in the tape, never mind that he could not be sure it existed. She frowned.

'What's the story there?'

'Schwartz and the tape? I wish I knew. Maybe, same as the police, he is desperate for something that ties me in with Miss Hong.'

'And he expects you to give it up?'

'Doesn't make a lot of sense, I know.'

I explained how Jung-hwa warned me that Schwartz had told her I was never going to get out of this one, never going to be paid for the assignment, and explained how I had slipped away from the police tail, sold some equipment and fled town.

I picked up the last of the beers.

'Are you sorry you asked?'

'You couldn't have made it up if you tried.'

'I wish I had.'

'But at least you know what you're up against. So do you have a plan?'

'A plan?'

She lowered her chin, compressed her neck into her shoulders and spoke in a comical deep voice: 'A man with no plan, is a man going nowhere.'

I got it right away. She was mimicking Vincent, a bear of a man with a window-rattler of a laugh and a bottomless store of homespun aphorisms.

'I haven't got that far yet. I just got out of Seoul to find some breathing space.'

'I know that feeling,' said Rose, her face falling. I remembered she had said something similar last night. She had things on her mind, too, but after my days of weary solitude I wasn't quite ready to give up the spotlight.

'I know I'll have to go back sooner or later, but first I want to try and get some things working in my favour – instead of Alec Brodie versus the whole bloody country. Yesterday I telephoned an idiot at the British Embassy and told him about the GDR scam. He is pretty tight with Martinmass, but he will still have to do something, because I told him I have written it all down and sent it to the Press and to his bosses in London.' Which reminded me. I had not yet posted the letters that I had sat up half the night writing.

'That's a start.'

'But?'

'But it's not enough. In the meantime, Chang and the rest of them will continue to manipulate things to suit themselves, and will do anything to safeguard the GDR. You have to get back at them directly.'

'Without ending up in jail over Miss Hong.'

'Or ending up like her.'

We let the conversation slip away from the edge of the gloom to our experiences in Korea in years gone by when things were in many ways startlingly different. She told me a story from a few years before I arrived. Then President Chun, Doo-hwan was an army general boosted into dictatorship by military coup, and who sat back in the reflected glow of a booming economy that he had nothing to do with creating. Like all dictators he was unable to resist painting his presidency in glowing colours, at times even literally. Rose told me of a grandly orchestrated occasion when he formally opened the massive re-development of the Han Riverbanks. Chun made an imperious boat trip up the river as if to claim credit for the feat of engineering as his very own, and it was, of course, live on television, cameras in helicopters hovering overhead.

The huge expanses of new riverside parkland had yet to grow vegetation, and the proud leader couldn't possibly preside over a river flanked by twin broad strips of brown mud. When the helicopters rose and the cameras panned out, the parkland on each river bank was a sea of lush green. Except it was a make-shift sea, mile upon mile of riverside submerged under millions of gallons of green-tinted water. While Chun's moment of glory was broadcast around the country, half the population of Seoul sneered into their *soju*. In Korea, then as now, things were often not quite the way they seemed.

We dissolved in escapist laughter and I lay back on the rock, head cushioned by my rucksack, closed my eyes and savoured a rare moment of contentment.

I can fall asleep anywhere, so it was no surprise when I popped out of slumber and looked at my watch. I had been out for maybe ten minutes. Pushing myself up onto one elbow, I saw Rose a few feet away, sitting cross-legged on the dusty ground, leaning against the trunk of a wiry tree, looking out to sea.

I went over and sat on my heels just out of her line of sight. It was a while before she turned to look at me. I spoke gently:

'Want to talk?'

'About what?'

'Well, you heard me out, and I was glad of it.'

'So now it's my turn?'

'Only if you want.'

'How do you know I have anything to tell?'

'Just a feeling.'

Emotion blurred her eyes. She swallowed it, and paused before answering.

'I came down here to escape from Seoul for a few days, too.'

'If you feel like talking about it – ' I left the sentence unfinished.

She forced a smile. 'Don't tell me – you're not running to any sort of timetable either. Compared to your mess, mine's nothing, but I still don't know which way is up.'

I sat down. She would tell me in her own time.

'Ten years ago, when I left to go to university in Canada, I was sick of Korea and tired of my parents' never-ending struggle in their funny little missionary world. I was a teenager, and I just didn't get it.

'So in Vancouver I put all that behind me. I went apeshit – from one extreme to the other. Shed my virginity even before the jet lag wore off, so drunk I have no idea who the lucky guy was. Got into the whole party scene and spent four years drinking and smoking and popping pills while I scraped a degree in Finance.'

'Just your run-of-the-mill student existence.'

'I suppose. Then, very first interview after graduation, I walked into a job with a downtown brokerage. Perfect, I thought. Not for me, the missionary life of sufferance and self-denial. Inside a year I was in the Dealing Room, making obscene amounts of money. Huge bonuses, expense accounts, club memberships – the whole grubby shebang. Ski weekends in Aspen, canary yellow Porsche Cabriolets – two of them; I wrote one off, out of my mind on tequila. A string of messy relationships. Partying almost non-stop, with a personal trainer to keep me fit enough to handle ten-hour days of screaming down telephone lines to New York and London and Hong Kong and Tokyo.

'I don't know how I managed it, but I lasted six years in that cesspit. I was never for a minute really happy, but in that screwed-up world, the illusion of contentedness is expressed in dollars, and I was making plenty of those.

'About six months ago, something snapped, I walked away, and two days later I was on a plane. I hadn't been back to Seoul in nearly ten years.'

'Knowing Vincent and Jemma, they welcomed you with open arms.'

'Not so much as one word about the prodigal offspring.'

'And that was six months ago?'

'After a few weeks I drifted back into doing little things with the church, until I was at it almost full-time. It's unpaid, but that doesn't matter. I saw a few morons come away from years in a broker's seat with nothing but credit card bills and a terminal coke habit, but I wasn't one of them.'

I sipped at a bottle of mineral water, wishing it was beer, while Rose leaned back against the tree, finger and thumb kneading the middle of her forehead.

'Compared to what you've – '

'Don't go wishing for problems to compete with mine.'

She sighed. 'I've enjoyed working for the church these past few months. Maybe it's what I needed after years steeped in materialist bullshit, but try as I might, I can't go along with the whole Christian thing any more. I can't worship God again any more than I can worship money.'

'I bet your parents could come to terms with that.'

'Maybe, but I've been going out with a lovely guy I met at the church, a missionary too, training to be ordained.'

Here we go, I thought.

'Last week he proposed to me.'

'And Vincent and Jemma love the sound of that, do they?'

'Oh yes.'

'So what are you going to do?'

'It's just that, well how the hell can I be in love with the guy?'

'What's his name?'

'Francis Kim. He was born in Korea, moved to Canada when he was a kid. He's a lovely guy but we hardly know each other so, almost overnight I'm in this old-fashioned dating situation with a guy who wants to marry me. Francis is so straight. He doesn't drink and if he's feeling really romantic he might hold my hand softly – but never without asking me first.'

'So?'

'Now I don't have a clue what way to turn. I'm in love with a guy who has hardly touched me. Maybe this is just another obsession to get me over the jadedness of the past few years.'

'Why not just drag Francis into the sack and fuck his brains out?'

She gave me a withering look of the sort that women reserve for creatures of the opposite gender.

'You just don't get it. It's not about sex. It is about having the guts to follow my heart instead of my fears.'

I had no answer to that.

'There's more. Francis wants to stay in Korea, work for the church, help his own people. And I don't know if I can handle the idea of being my Mum.'

We packed up the remains of the picnic and headed down in silence, my conscience nagging at me the whole way. Rose was in a situation where her instincts cried out at her to follow her heart. I had never entertained such a thought in my life. I always figured that a conscience was a bit like the human appendix. Everybody had one, but it was surplus to requirements.

She made me realise just how casually I had disregarded Jung-hwa, not only this week, but ever since I broke up with her and moved back to London. In ten years I had written her a couple of letters, letting the lack of responses offer me the easy way out – either she wasn't interested, or she didn't merit the effort in the first place.

Since getting back to Korea I had revelled once again in wild and wonderful times with her, but in the last couple of days she was never foremost in my thoughts.

Chapter Thirty

At the postage-stamp field overlooking the bay the farmer and his boy were gone, toil over for the day. Ankle-deep in soft soil and secured to a post by a length of golden-brown hand-made rope, the ox chewed slowly on a pile of brittle yellow straw. Next to the straw sat a shiny red plastic bucket full of water, as incongruous as a Ferrari in down-town Kabul.

Rose stopped just before the *yogwan* car park.

'I think we should get you out of this place.'

We. I liked that.

'You do?'

'The police are on the lookout for a single male. They will run a check on every *yogwan* in the country.'

She was right. One phone call and the local cops would have their very own potential murderer to visit.

'We can move into a *min-bak*.' She meant a Korean Bed & Breakfast, but without the breakfast, a rented room in a private home. 'A couple travelling together won't ring so many alarm bells.'

'You sure about this?' I raised both hands, palms out. 'Hands off, I promise.'

She laughed. 'They'd better be. Francis takes his Tae Kwon-do first degree black belt next month.'

I could probably kick the shit out of Francis with my hands in my pockets, but for once in my life that was never going to happen.

At the *yogwan* we went to our rooms to pack up. I was thinking about a quick shower when Rose banged on my door.

'Quick, switch on the TV.'

I flicked the television on and lifted the door latch. Rose pushed past me and changed the channel to a Korean news bulletin of a press conference already under way. While studio voices discussed the proceedings, the view swung around for the shot of themselves that media people love, the one that says 'look how many cameras are here; we *must be* important', before switching to a forest of logo-emblazoned microphones. Peering out from behind them, looking small but defiant, sat Naz.

Speaking through an interpreter, she dealt calmly with a barrage of questions and waited patiently whenever the shouts overlapped to become an impenetrable din. Beside her, squirming like he had soiled his pants, sat the man who yesterday told me to give myself up, Eric Bridgewater of the British Embassy.

Bobby must have called her at the studio when I went missing and, as usual, Naz had taken the bull by the horns and headed straight to the airport. No wonder I couldn't get through to her in London. With me being off the map and the story coming off the boil, the moment the Press picked up on a friend of Korea's Most Wanted arriving, they would have been after her like hungry dogs. It was typical of Naz that she saw how to put this to her – and my – advantage by putting a human face on the story.

'When was this?'

'It's live. From Seoul. She flew in today, and first thing she did was call a press conference. The woman's got balls.'

Onscreen Naz calmly announced that if anyone had any information that might help, to contact her at the Hyatt.

'Maybe this is my chance.'

She looked at me, confused.

'You wondered about the videotape, and how important it might be, and why Schwartz is so determined to get his hands on it. What if I get the tape to Naz, and let her find out?'

I switched on the purple phone and keyed in the number of Mr Cho's mobile. The connection went through instantly, and I listened to the electronic ring tone repeat itself over and over. Just when I was about to hang up, a bleep sounded, and I heard Mr Cho.

'Yoboseyo.'

'Mr Cho it's me.'

'I see.'

'Is this a good time to talk?'

'I will call you back.'

I disconnected, and within a minute the purple phone jingled its pop song ring tone.

'Hello?'

'OK, this telephone is better. Nobody can listen.'

Mr Cho the dark horse was playing cautious, and I was glad.

'Did you know that my friend Naz is in Seoul?'

'I saw her on television.'

'I need to ask you a favour.'

'No problem.'

'It could be a big problem.'

'Tell me about the favour.'

'That package I left with you. The police are looking for me, but they are also looking for the package, and other people are, too. Bad people. I might have put you and your family in danger.'

'Only I know where it is. Don't worry.'

Just like that. Don't worry.

'You are sure?'

'I said, don't worry.'

'I've been wondering why the other people are so serious about finding it. Now Naz is in Seoul, maybe she can look at the tape for me and get it to the British Embassy if it can help me.'

'You want me to give it to Naz?'

'Do you think you could get the package to her without anyone else knowing?'

'I can do that. Will I give her this telephone number?'

Rose and I finished packing and slipped out of the *yogwan* separately. Forty-five minutes later and after a brief stop at the tiny village post office to send letters to Seoul and London, we sat in a bus that rattled as the driver threw it around the twisted ribbon of hilly blacktop connecting Haekumgang to the rest of Geoje island and beyond. We had a short wait for a connecting bus to the mainland and soon after crossed the bridge over the narrow coastal strait. Rose made some enquiries of a chubby woman with the burnished copper tan of a farmworker.

'She says there's a coastal village a few miles outside Tongyeong, well-known for its seafood and full of *min-bak* rooms for rent. She'll tell us when to get off.'

'Great.' My mind was elsewhere, running through the events of the past hours. Earlier, I had been cheered by the thought that at last I was taking positive action, rather than being forced from one calamitous error to the next. I was delighted by the arrival of Naz in Seoul, but it had also made me ashamed. While I ran away and achieved next to nothing, she confronted my problems head-on. Now I had an opportunity to seek control by getting the videotape to her. Mr Cho could arrange that without raising any suspicions, no matter how closely anyone was watching Naz. '*What have you got to lose?*' was Rose's reaction. That was when it hit me.

'Oh fuck. Oh no.'

'What?'

'The videotape. I know Mr Cho can get it to Naz, but what then? What if Schwartz guesses that Naz has it? For all he knows, I asked Naz to come to Seoul for the tape.'

The alarm in Rose's expression was the confirmation I did not want.

'You think you've put Naz in danger?'

'After what happened to Miss Hong? What do you think?'

The farmer woman across the aisle spoke to Rose, and shouted something at the driver. The bus slowed.

'Tell them don't stop, that we've changed our minds and are going to Tongyeong.' The bus pulled to a halt in a fishing village that was little more than a row of single-storey cottages facing the shore. Rose called forward to the driver, who shrugged good-naturedly and pulled away.

In Tongyeong, we hurried to the inter-city bus terminal while I tried to raise Mr Cho on the mobile phone. The first three times I dialled, his number was engaged, and I started to panic that something had already gone wrong. On the fourth attempt, I got through:

'It's me again.'

'I will call you back.'

I thumbed the red button, and thirty seconds later, the purple phone rang again.

'It's about my friend in Seoul. Did you get that package to her yet?'

'It was difficult, but yes, she has it now.'

I looked at my watch. He had managed to get the videotape through an air-tight police cordon in under three hours. My fault for telling him it was urgent.

'I made a mistake. Maybe this puts her in danger. I have to come back.'

'OK.' He thought for a second. 'You remember the first time we met?'

I mulled that over for a moment. 'Yes.'

'Go there. Do you take the bus or train?'

'Bus.'

'Somebody will come to you.'

He gave me detailed instructions, and I warned him about the new hairstyle and that I might not be alone. Rose signalled that we would travel up together. I told Mr Cho to expect her.

'No problem.' He disconnected.

Mr Cho had done it again. I hadn't even asked for help, and now he was arranging a way into a city full of cops carrying my photograph. I had to get back in time to help protect Naz from Schwartz and Chang, and how I might do that was unimportant. What mattered was doing for Naz what she had always done for me.

Suwon is Seoul's unwanted bastard son, a satellite town less than an hour from the capital but tucked out of sight of the neighbours. Every big city has them, the urban clans of poor relations, underachievers barely beyond the horizon but best forgotten, tough market towns that cannot, or will not, hide their scars for anyone.

My first ever taste of Suwon was at a Tae Kwon-do tournament in the early 1990s. Much to the bemusement of the rest of the participants, a Canadian friend, Brian, was the only non-Korean contestant entered in the tournament. They stopped grinning when Brian wiped the floor with the biggest Korean in the building to take the heavyweight division title. Only afterwards, when he refused the opportunity to treat the judges to dinner and drinks, did they give the medal to the loser. It was an eye-opening show of small town thinking with a significant touch of racism thrown in for good measure.

As we left the hall, a lean track-suited Korean man took us aside. In English, Mr Cho introduced himself and apologised on behalf of the judges. We rode back to Seoul in a minibus full of fighters from Mr Cho's gym, several of them sporting new medals, and a friendship was formed that survived today.

Thanks to the manic efficiency of Korea's inter-city bus

network, it took less than five hours before the ancient city walls of Suwon swung into view. Rose and I had spent much of the trip in contemplative silence, and now she was smiling quietly to herself. I gave her a playful nudge.

'Have you made up your mind?'

'I think so. God knows I never loved any of the other men in my life, so why back off from Francis?'

'If you did, you'd forever wonder if you had made the wrong decision.'

'You might actually be learning.'

Not before time, I thought.

I saw them first, posters stuck hurriedly at odd angles on the stands next to every bus terminal bay, rough, two-colour things that spoke of rushed production. Two faces to a poster, one a clumsily-altered photograph and the other a pencil drawing. Mine – complete with short dark hair – and Rose's. I looked sideways. Every fleck of colour had fled Rose's face. I followed her gaze to the poster, to where her name was mis-spelled, twice. Underneath the pencil drawing it said 'Rosemarry Daley'.

She pulled hard at my sleeve.

'Over there. The toilets.' She dragged me across the hall.

When I came back out, head buried in my hat, Rose was waiting, her hair tied up and back with a red print bandana. She held a copy of a Korean newspaper.

'Remember the police reward the television and newspapers talked about?'

'You think somebody has tried to collect?'

'They know about your new look and they know about me. It must have been our German friend. In the restaurant in Haekumgang, I remember he watched the TV report with interest, even asked me to translate parts of it for him. If he put one and one together, my name was right there in the *yogwan* register.'

A main exit spat us onto a crowded street. The best thing would be to split up but whoever Mr Cho sent would be looking for two of us, so for now we had to hide behind a hat and a headscarf. His instructions were to exit the bus station and turn right. As we made the turn, I saw a policeman to our left. His gaze passed over us without pause, until he was interrupted by a woman. I recognised her immediately as a fellow-passenger on the bus from Tongyeong.

I found myself staring along her outstretched arm as she yelled into the cop's ear. The policeman thumbed the button on his radio and started towards us. I gripped Rose by the elbow.

The pavement was thick with pedestrians. I flicked a glance over my shoulder to see him close down on us as he shouted into his radio for support.

Rose looked the other way, and I followed her gaze to twenty yards ahead, where another policeman rounded the corner holding a radio to his ear. We were trapped.

Next to us, the side door of a van rolled back and several pairs of hands wrenched us off our feet. Tyres squealed even before the door slammed and the van leapt from the kerb, ran a red light and took a sharp turn, throwing us around like clothes in a dryer. After five or six more corners the van pulled to an abrupt halt, banging us against the bulkhead. The side door opened again, and two figures leapt out and split up. Fifteen seconds later, we were on the move, the two men back with us in the rear compartment, each holding a registration plate. They weren't so much as out of breath.

I spoke Korean to the nearest guy.

'Mr Cho sent you?'

'Yes.'

Rose looked at me with a puzzled expression on her face. 'Just who the hell *is* Mr Cho?'

'He owns nightclubs.'

She nodded, as if that explained a lot. It did.

Chapter Thirty-one

A few miles later we pulled over and Rose asked one of the Koreans what was happening. I got the gist of what he said, but Rose translated for me anyway:

'They're going to switch us to a different car before heading for Seoul.'

'That makes sense.'

'I've been thinking about how my face being on all the posters changes things.'

'I'm sorry about that. I never – '

'It's done already, but now I have to get on the phone to my folks and Francis, put their minds at ease, then put some distance between you and me.'

'Get out of Seoul and turn up in a day or two, on your own.'

'Right. Make a point of being seen arriving alone.'

'Thanks to the German guy, the police are still going to give you a rough ride.'

'Not if you get busy in the meantime. They have no actual proof that we were still together in Suwon. When I get back to Seoul, I stick to a story that we met up, but soon went our separate ways. If you can clear your name, I am not going to be in trouble for spending a day with you.'

The heightened crisis had brought about a stark change in her, and now I saw the cool professional who used to juggle millions of dollars of other people's money before the rest of us had breakfast. Rose pulled a writing pad and pen from her backpack, and while we exchanged phone numbers she explained to the driver what we needed to do. I sat by, meekly acquiescent while she took care of things.

I hoped that police alerts would still be based on the notion that we had to be somewhere near Geoje Island. Even if word of our near-capture at Suwon had already gone out, surely they wouldn't waste too many man hours on trains *leaving* the capital. We pulled up near a main branch station on the outskirts of the city.

'Just when you make up your mind about Francis, you have to leave town again.'

'I'll speak to him tonight. You should do the same.'

'Speak to Francis? Do you think he would like that?'

'Funny. Call Jung-hwa. You owe her that much.' She squeezed the breath out of me with a sisterly hug, then walked towards the station without looking back, shadowed discreetly by one of Mr Cho's men. I wondered if Francis knew just how lucky he was.

Rose was right. I had to speak to Jung-hwa, even if only to find out how deeply she was involved in all this.

The Korean slipped back into the car.

'Ga-seo,' he said. *She's gone.*

I sat low in the back seat as the driver weaved an indirect trail through sprawling suburbs, one watchful eye on his mirrors. Beside him, his partner kept eyes front, sweeping from one side of the road to the other, scanning parked cars and quiet side streets for any threat. Nightclubs in Korea operate on the fringes of organised crime, and the men Mr Cho had trusted to deliver me were professionals. To watch them at work was almost comforting. The chirrup of a phone broke into my thoughts, and the front seat passenger passed a mobile back to me.

'No problems?' *Mr Cho.*

'No, it's cool. Thanks, I mean thanks for everything – '

'We can talk later. My friends will bring you somewhere safe.'

'Thanks, Mr Cho.' I was speaking to myself. I tapped the shoulder of the guy in front and he palmed the mobile.

We pulled up in the gritty eastern district of Chong-nyangni, where buildings off the main drag were densely-packed and single-storeyed with sagging tiled roofs. My escorts pulled soft bags from the boot of the car and led me up the stairs of an ugly three-storey building that stood alone among the traditional houses of a back street. Before I saw a sign or heard the slap of instep on leather, the peculiar odour mix of dust and dried sweat told me all I needed to know. Mr Cho met us at the entrance to the gym wearing his Tae Kwon-do uniform. My escorts bowed deeply, twice. Once to Mr Cho, and once to the Korean flag on the far wall. The *dojang* had maybe twelve people stretching and kicking and punching at bags and at mir-rored reflections. My escorts pitched their holdalls onto a corner pile and plucked folded uniforms from a neat line of pegs under a line of windows that ran the lengths of two sides of the room. I kicked my shoes off and bowed to the flag before following Mr Cho into the gym.

'We will start soon,' he said. My participation in training was a given.

'Can I make a telephone call first?'

'Use the mobile phone on my desk.'

I backed out of the *dojang*, bowed to the flag, and turned into the small office with the wide window that looked out on the training area. The mobile was where Mr Cho said I would find it. I dialled the Hyatt switchboard, asked for Naz's room, and listened to the telephone ring out until a voicemail prompt asked me if I wanted to leave a message.

'Naz. It's me. I'm worried about you, so for goodness sakes keep your head down and watch out for yourself. I'll call back soon.' I hung up, and headed back to the gym, where Mr Cho waited.

'You have your *tobok*?'

My Tae Kwon-do uniform was in a bag at Seoul Station.

Mr Cho spoke quietly to a grey-haired man who was stretched out on the floor nearby. I winced when he leapt from full splits to upright in one move. He told me his name was Cheung, and while we shook hands he measured me up with a look before going along the pegs reading the labels on the inside collars of the uniforms. He passed me a folded *tobok*, holding it by the belt that was wrapped neatly around it.

'Ken-chun-ayo?' *Is that OK?* He meant the belt, which like the *tobok*, was crisp and new and white, a novice's.

I took the uniform with two hands and stole a furtive glimpse of Mr Cheung's belt, grey-black with off-white flashes at its tips that made him a fifth-degree black-belt. He was about forty-five years old, and he was one of the *students*. Most of the other belts in the room told similar tales of decades of devotion to the national martial art.

'That's fine, Mr Cheung.' In this kind of company, a novice's outfit was about right.

I stripped off and changed as quickly as I could, then found a quiet bit of floor to warm up, and absently began to worry how much of a showing-up I was about to experience at the hands and feet of enthusiasts who trained several times a week.

Martial arts movies and magazines are obsessed with the notion of higher spiritual planes achieved through selfless devotion to the art of hand-to-hand combat. If such planes exist, I never saw one. Just the same, I knew that it was possible during dedicated training for a mind to divert itself to a place far removed from a body being worked at full steam. I was well into the familiar torture of the two-hour training session before it occurred to me that Mr Cho was forcing me to go there, to a place where the most opaque of conundrums clarify.

Before the class started, Mr Cho told me this was one of Seoul's few remaining adult groups. Modern Tae Kwon-do, the Olympic sport, is a kid's game, and no amount of guile or experience can counter the whippet speed and instantaneous reactions of youth. Most adults were too busy working and raising families to keep up their training, but Mr Cho's classes still drew long-time students from all over town.

The training reminded me why, after more than fifteen years, I still made my way to a *dojang* as often as I could. The regular sweat sessions were part of a payback process, one that chipped away at the damage I did to myself from too much alcohol, long hours in the studio and binges of the lousy food that turns so many Westerners into lard buckets. The hedonist in me disregarded concerns over a plainly excessive lifestyle, but in turn, the pragmatist laughed in the hedonist's face, and quietly relished every moment spent at lung-stretching pace in the gym.

Fifteen minutes of careful warming down brought the training session to an end. Mr Cho went to the office to change while the rest of us did the informal locker-room thing at the line of pegs by the window. Mr Cheung and two others complimented me on my fighting skills, flattery that I talked down as modestly as possible. I felt like a house painter having his whitewash brushwork simultaneously admired by Rembrandt and Van Gogh.

I knocked on the office door and stepped into the room which, after the chilled neon of the *dojang*, felt cosy and dark. Mr Cho was talking on a telephone. I picked up his mobile and re-dialled Naz's room at the Hyatt, but got the same unanswered ringing sound followed by the invitation to leave a message. Mr Cho wrapped up his call.

'No answer from Naz,' I said. 'That's twice, two hours apart.'

'What about the mobile?'

'I don't understand.'

'*Your* mobile. You told me to give her that number. Are there any messages?'

I had completely forgotten about it. I dug it from my bag,

and as I thumbed the power switch, the Korean pop tune ring-tone came alive.

'Naz?'

Complete silence. Then:

'Alec, it's me.' *Naz. Thank fuck,* I thought. I mouthed her name to Mr Cho. He nodded.

'Where are you? I've been calling the hotel. Are you OK?'

From the purple earpiece came only roaring mechanical noise, increasing in volume.

'Naz? Are you there?' The roaring receded, then:

'She's here alright.'

Oh no.

'At a loss for words twice in one day, Brodie?'

I breathed deeply, tried to maintain some sort of control. Mr Cho looked on, concerned.

'I'll keep this simple Schwartz. You put so much as one finger on her, and I will hunt you down and bury you.'

'Brave words.'

'Brave nothing. I'll break bones you've never even heard of. Then I *will* bury you and let dehydration do the rest. If you think I am bluffing you are even more stupid than I thought.'

'*You* think about it. We have your ugly little friend, and we have the videotape. You have nothing. So save the movie hero bullshit threats for someone who's listening.'

I was straining to hear him. There was roaring in my ears again, part internal seething and part fresh onslaught of screaming mechanical noise from the earpiece. Schwartz waited until the background din receded, and then he told me exactly what to do.

Chapter Thirty-two

Mr Cho pulled a jar from a desk drawer, spooned instant coffee into two cups and filled them from a thermos jug that lived on a shelf behind his chair. He handed me a cup, and waited. The man had the patience of a saint. I cradled the burning cup in a two-handed grip close to my lips and talked through the steam that swirled from it.

'Schwartz has got Naz. I was right to worry about her, even if I was too late. I left her unprotected and vulnerable.'

'What does he want?'

'He wants me to surrender to the police, and to keep quiet about anything to do with K-N Group's new stock market deal.' I explained the GDR in detail. Mr Cho listened without interrupting, and spoke only when I finished.

'If you do what he wants, how can you be sure that will make Naz safe?'

'I can't. But I do know how serious Schwartz and his friends are about the GDR. The Group's survival depends on it. Their personal stakes must be in the many millions. They were somehow involved in what happened to Miss Hong, so how can I take a chance with Naz?'

It was about time I spared a thought for someone else, but even with the best of intentions, what could I achieve to make things better? I could do nothing for Naz from a police cell, so going to the authorities now, while the hunt for me was ongoing, was hardly an option. Worse, if word got to Chang and Schwartz that I was talking with the police, they would assume that I was spilling the beans on the GDR, something that in any case I had already done with the letters I posted this morning to the Press and to Whitehall. How the contents of those letters might affect Naz, I didn't even want to consider.

'There is another choice,' said Mr Cho, as if reading the despair on my face.

'What?'

'Find out where your friend is.'

'She could be anywhere.'

'Think about your conversation with Schwartz. What did you learn?'

'Apart from that he had Naz?'

'Did it sound like he was talking on a, how do you call it – ' he pointed to the office telephone on his desk. Unlike me, Mr Cho was still thinking straight.

'A landline? No, I think it sounded like a mobile.'

'Why? Could you hear something? Maybe they were in a car?'

I remembered the background din. 'No, not traffic noises. It was sometimes very quiet, just the sound of Schwartz's voice, then it quickly became very noisy, maybe like the sound of aircraft arriving.'

'An airport?'

'Hang on.' Of course. Why hadn't I thought of it earlier? I picked up the purple mobile and worked my way through the menu until a number came up. The last incoming caller, a mobile number – he had neglected to hide his caller ID. I dialled, and after a few seconds, I heard ringing.

'Yoboseyo.' *Yes.* I paused for a couple of seconds:

'Schwartz. It's me.' I had to keep him on the line. There was a pause as if he was taken aback by me calling, and that worked fine for me.

'What do you want now?'

I paused again, straining for anything at all, the smallest

clue. Did it sound as if he was speaking from within a large open space?

'Brodie?'

'I was thinking – ' Pause.

'Thinking what?' Still silence, but not just silence, something more than that. His voice, despite the tinny phone speaker, boomed like he was in a huge space, not out in the open but in a large indoor location. I might be on the right track – but my silence had gone on for too long.

'What do you – '

'What if I do as you ask?'

'What *if* you do?' *If only he'd keep talking.* I stayed silent, and he spoke again:

'I already told you. And don't think I'm going to go through it again in detail. What do you take me for? You're probably taping this.'

I wished I had thought of that.

'How do I know you'll do as you promised?' Still, there was an airy silence at his end, but could I hear something brewing in the distance? Was I imagining a steady drone, building up, getting closer?

'That is not the issue, Brodie, and you know it.' He talked more loudly. The background noise *was* approaching, and growing fast.

'What do you mean?'

'It's what happens if you don't do as I – ' He gave up as the roar exploded to a crescendo, drowning him out before it receded quicker than it had arrived. 'It's what will happen if you don't do as you're told that you should be concerned about.'

I had him. I knew that noise. It took an effort to keep the excitement out of my voice:

'I'll hand myself in tomorrow.'

'Not a chance. If I don't get a call from my police contact by midnight – ' He left the sentence unfinished and the line went dead. I put the mobile in my pocket.

'Mr Cho, you are a genius. I told you about the fake factory in the warehouse in Cholla-do? He's there. The warehouse is on the edge of a military airfield. The roar I heard was fighter jets making low-level passes.'

'Where is this warehouse?'

'North of Kwangju, in open country, with rice fields all around, only one or two kilometres from the main highway. I can find it.' I was getting ahead of myself. I looked at my watch, and my heart sank. Seven p.m. 'Schwartz only gave me until midnight to hand myself in to the police, and the warehouse is five or six hours' drive.'

'Drive?'

He reached for a telephone book.

Chapter Thirty-three

Seven of us wearing dark track suits with the name of Mr Cho's *dojang* on our backs approached the security checkpoint. This was the bit that worried me most, where an alert official might connect my face to the sketches and photographs on notice boards and newspapers all across the country. Never mind that I was using a Swiss passport that said the guy in the photo – who even looked a little like me – was Berndt Tischler. When I asked about it, Mr Cho just shook his head. Some things I didn't need to know.

We formed a ragged line for the X-ray machine and shoved our holdalls onto the rollers, Mr Cho first, with me close behind. As our bags disappeared into the machine, we shuffled forward casually.

Mr Cho walked through the detector frame. I glanced over my shoulder in time to see one of his students, the youngest one at the back of the line, stumble and go down hard. An airport gift shop bag burst against the polished floor, and eighteen shiny new golf balls flew off in eighteen different directions.

While every bystander within twenty yards watched four athletic men chase down bouncing golf balls I backed through the metal detector and past security guards whose smiles beamed everywhere except upon me. By the time the comic turn was over, Mr Cho and I were half way to the departure gate.

We took the nine p.m. to Kwangju, the last flight of the

day between the capital and the biggest city in the country's south-west, and an hour later, we piled aboard a black van outside the Kwangju terminal building. I looked at my watch. We had just under two hours before the midnight deadline Schwartz had set. We might still make it, but only if I guessed right – and only if they stayed where I thought they were.

A little over one hour later the van pulled up a hundred yards from the tall, windowless warehouse building which, surrounded by the impenetrable darkness of rice fields, stood out in the glare of floodlights fixed along its high roofline. Glimmers of cool fluorescence slipped out from beneath a concertinaed goods entrance. Four empty cars occupied lined parking spots a few metres away from the doorway. From a mile across country came the unbroken drone of highway traffic.

One of Mr Cho's men, the grey-haired Mr Cheung who had befriended me at the training session, slipped silently from the side door of the van, stripped off his track suit and turned it inside-out before he pulled it back on, white flashes and *dojang* lettering gone from view. As he merged with the darkness we waited in silence for what felt like a very long time. I scanned the gloom for any hint of Cheung's return but saw nothing until he scared me by slipping noiselessly into the van, his breathing calm and regular. He murmured a few words to Mr Cho, who turned to me.

'It's good. No security cameras and no guards outside.'

'But four cars could mean twelve or more people.'

'No problem.' The standard Mr Cho response to any challenge, no matter how daunting. Speaking softly, he outlined his plan. We got out of the van and reversed our track suits and removed our shoes. Carrying a t-shirt and a jerry can, one man crept forward. Stopping behind the car closest to the warehouse he pulled a screwdriver from his belt and gently eased it under the metallic flap that hid the petrol cap. The crack as the lock sheared was muffled by the t-shirt but in the still of the night, it made me jump. He stopped and we all strained for reaction from inside the building. There was none. He opened the jerry can, drenched the t-shirt in petrol and, using the screwdriver, stuffed one end of it into the fuel tank opening.

Six of us edged towards the warehouse. Above the doorway and about eight feet from the ground, protection from the weather took the form of a three-foot-wide concrete ledge that butted out from the warehouse wall. We waited while Mr Cheung put his ear to the metal door. He shook one hand at us, palm out, an urgent request for silence. A clanging sound came from inside the building, something hard and metallic being thrown down, followed by angry shouts coming closer. With nowhere to hide we made like statues, all watching Cheung, whose ear never left the door's surface. Seconds stretched to minutes, until at last he gave us a rolling hand movement. *Go.*

A pair of stocky athletes leaned into each other like a two-man rugby scrum, heads and arms interlocked while Mr Cho moved them into position. Another man quickly went down on all fours, and I stepped from his back onto the top of the two-man scrum and reached up to grasp the ledge. Two men climbed me like a ladder and secreted themselves face-down above the doorway. The entire move took less than five seconds, and was achieved in complete silence.

The two guys below lowered me to the ground, and we hurried back to the van, which we carefully pushed into place behind the car with the t-shirt poking from its bodywork.

So far everything had gone painstakingly slowly. Now, somebody hit the fast-forward button. The t-shirt came to life, fire glinting off paintwork, thick black smoke backlit by the glare of warehouse floodlights. The side door of the van lay wide open, a shoe jammed in its track. The fire starter jumped aboard. Four of us huddled by the open door like a parachute display team ready to leap. The car's petrol tank blew and the van shook, first from the nearby explosion and next from its engine firing up, revving hard.

At close range, the ferocity of the petrol fire was terrifying. Glass popped, explosive aftershocks rocked the entire car, and fresh blasts of flame shot skywards.

Beyond the fire and smoke a gap appeared at one end of the concertina door and three figures carrying what looked like lengths of pipe ran out and stopped, hands raised against the glare. Twin shadows floated to the ground behind them and one of the three turned straight into a front snap kick. A fresh explosion obscured them from view and when the flames receded, the other two opponents were down and out of the game. A dark-suited shoulder hit the concertina door hard, and our driver ground the accelerator pedal to the floor. As the fluorescent rectangle grew, the second point man gripped two groggy figures by the scruffs of their necks. He almost got them clear but van wheels hiccupped over two sets of shins as we thundered into the building, tyres wailing. Our driver brought the van to a squealing broadside halt that fired the four of us out the side door in a dead run.

Bare feet on cool concrete, we pulled up in a lop-sided V-formation, Mr Cho half a step in front, the two point men joining us from the doorway, one on either side. The van engine roared, rubber tracks smoking as it shrieked to a halt facing the door. Squaring up to us, eight Koreans with bad haircuts and blank, street thug expressions fanned out in front of the phoney factory building. A warehouse office door behind them opened and out poured four more. There was no sign of Naz.

Six against twelve was bad enough, but with every one of the twelve swinging an aluminium baseball bat, whichever way we looked at it, this was going to hurt.

They formed a loose arc, far enough apart to swing their

weapons, but close enough to make the line seem impregnable.

Two of them slouched forward. One offsider and an obvious alpha male who was so ugly it hurt just to look at him. About thirty-five, he stood maybe five foot eight, with a bald full-moon head and facial features like fungi on a log. A black hat baddy straight from Korean Central Casting, a troll without the hair, he didn't have an ounce of fat on him, and his unblinking black-brown eyes held not a trace of emotion. They didn't even blink when Mr Cho roared:

'CHOOM-BEE.' *READY.*

I feared for the innocents I had dragged into this, even if they were here for Mr Cho, a man they would follow into a burning house. By now I should be used to bringing grief upon the innocents around me. Miss Hong, Rose, Bobby's family and Naz. And Jung-hwa. Now Mr Cho and his student friends were dragged into life-threatening roles in my private nightmare. These middle-aged dads owed me nothing, yet they were squared up to hired thugs who would merrily decorate the warehouse with their brains.

If the alpha male gave a signal to his offsider, I failed to detect it. Leaping forward, the offsider flicked his bat high and brought it down in a deadly arc aimed at Mr Cho's neck. What happened next was like a dance move made murderous. Mr Cho glided under the strike and with a windmill sweep of one arm pinned the attacker's wrists under his left tricep. The attacker's momentum drove him forward and down, Mr Cho going with him, legs bending until everything went into reverse and he drove upwards, his right forearm locked under the other man's elbows. Through the offsider's screams I heard a sound like fenceposts shearing, and the baseball bat rattled off the floor. The thug's eyes turned opaque and he went rubbery at the knees even before Mr Cho folded him in two with a side kick that surely destroyed much of the man's rib cage.

Action erupted all around me. I sensed as much as saw other combatant pairs dance and strike with deadly effect. A glancing blow from a bat pitched one of our guys to the floor. The bat rose for a finishing strike until a flashing kick from Mr Cho changed the batsman's looks forever, splatter trails of blood and mucus flying. Mr Cho whipped around to see another goon lurch towards him. He drove the knife-edge of his foot into the side of the thug's knee. More screaming, and surely more work for the bone setters.

Meanwhile, the alpha male chose me for his own. He presented one shoulder and crept directly forwards, primed like a batsman at the plate. I fell into the classic Tae Kwon-do defensive stance, left leg leading, feet at ninety degrees, arms front and high, fists lightly clenched. I had a vacuous knot in my stomach and a ready stance honed over thousands of gym hours. Up against a thug with no fear waving a baseball bat, I didn't much like my chances.

I went for him at floor level, feet first, legs scissoring around his ankles, body twisting like a crocodile death roll. He fell onto one hip, and I was back on my feet, measuring up my next strike, when a bat came at me from nowhere and nicked the crown of my head, setting off bells and knocking me off balance. The guy swinging it turned away to face one of Mr Cho's men who swept in to my assistance.

I dipped a shoulder and turned the hit into a forward roll that threw me back to my feet. The gang leader's bat whispered through the air and rattled the floor behind me. I walloped both of his arms with a spinning kick that knocked the bat flying, and a quick feint sent the arms up. I half-spun again and drove my heel deep into his midriff, but the bastard was tough, and he surprised me with a round-house right to the kidneys that brought us into a clinch, his face only inches from mine. I tried to head butt him but he dipped forward, and the clash of skulls hurt me more than it did him, but it distracted him long enough for me to clamp my left hand hard between his legs and jerked downwards. He gasped in pain, his arms fell and I twisted my hips, put every ounce of body weight behind the heel of my right hand, and drove it upwards, clean through the end of his ugly nose. Bone and flesh and cartilage turned to bloody pulp in my hand and his eyes rolled into the back of his head. He was unconscious before he hit the floor, and I wished he wasn't. I wanted to wake the bastard up and do it to him all over again.

One of our team, the young one who'd done the airport stunt with the golf balls, was down, eyes open and un-blinking, a thin line of blood running from forehead gash to floor.

Mr Cho held a plot of ground that he had made his own, four broken bodies lying around him like litter. A writhing tangle crossed between us: Mr Cheung going hand-to-bat with two opponents. Before I could react Mr Cho picked one of them out with an axe kick to the face and battered the other in the kidneys with an elbow strike. The goon twisted in agony, and Mr Cheung put him down with a straight-arm to the throat.

Fast movement. Two men ran for the office door that four guys had come out of just minutes before.

'Mr Cho,' I pointed as I broke into a hobbling run, trying to ignore loud screams from various points in my body.

One guy fiddled with the door handle. The other faced up to me, bat high and ready. Naz had to be beyond that door, so there was no way these two were getting through it before I did. I was so pissed off that all I could see was the door. Mistake. A full swing of the bat took me high on the upper arm and bounced me sideways.

Numbing pain froze the arm long enough for me to fear for what came next, until Mr Cho arrived in mid-air with a flying front kick that caught the goon in the sternum. He fell straight back and his head rapped concrete with an eggshell crack. The second thug, face wide with panic, still struggled with the door. My friend and mentor flew at him, the thug side-stepped, and as Mr Cho blew the door open with both feet, he clothes-lined the other guy with a forearm to the side of the head. I followed Mr Cho in.

Naz leaned forward in a padded armchair, wrists and fingers bound with heavy tape, ankles taped tight on either side of a solid concrete block.

'Hi, Mr Cho.'

After a strained attempt at a smile, she turned to me and her gaze cooled.

'You took your fucking time, Brodie.'

Chapter Thirty-four

We were an hour into the trip to Seoul before Naz even looked at me.

'Schwartz left about an hour before you showed up. He said that whether or not he saw me again was up to you. I don't know what he was on about.'

I was getting good at summarising the huge GDR con game, how it was vital to the survival of the debt-ridden K-N Group, and how my threat to bail out of the scam cost Miss Hong her life.

'Schwartz gave me until midnight to hand myself in to the police and keep quiet about the GDR, or you were dead. Not in as many words, but that was the message.'

'How did you find me?'

'I was there a few days ago, shooting pictures of the fake factory. We could hardly hear ourselves think for the noise of fighter jets flying overhead. When I spoke to him tonight on the phone, the background noise was enough to tell me where you were.' I didn't tell her that I remained uncertain until the moment I set eyes on her, but typical Naz, she read it somewhere in my body language.

'Enough to take a chance on not handing yourself in before the deadline?'

'We did alright, didn't we?'

'Mr Cho and his friends did.'

Mr Cho was in the seat beside the driver, eyes front, face

intermittently bleached white by lights from oncoming vehicles. His expression gave nothing away.

The rear of the van was unfurnished. Six of us lay spread over the ribbed floor, backs to thin metal walls that buckled and flexed with the roar and rumble of passing traffic.

The warehouse gamble had been kind to us. Mr Cho of course looked unscathed, while the rest of us wore only a variety of scrapes and bruises. The young guy who was knocked out sat in the corner. He had a cut on his forehead and one eye swollen shut, but his moody silence spoke loudly of a dented pride hurting worst of all. He had put everything on the line the same as his friends had done, and I felt for him.

The Doppler-effect wail of a truck horn scared me from a shallow sleep busy with confused thoughts. I ached all over, especially around the shoulder that the last thug had caught with his bat, the same shoulder Naz was now using as a pillow. I tried to move my legs, but they stayed where they were, knees drawn up in front of me as if all lines of communication between brain and limbs were cut. I pushed at my thighs with the palms of my hands and waited for the agony of circulation regained. While excruciating pain tore through my leg muscles, I tried to recall the final sliver of the dream sequence that was interrupted by the wailing truck horn. Something to do with last night and how and why it happened. I had fallen asleep thinking how fortunate we were, which sparked another line of thought. Were we clever and lucky – or just plain lucky?

The threat to Naz – and to the rest of us when we got to her – was real enough, but the way things worked out owed more to the presence of Mr Cho and his men than even I had previously thought, because the set of circumstances that led us to Cholla Province left too many questions unanswered.

Why was Naz held so far out of town – and why was it so easy for me to work out her location? Schwartz had played me like a grifter, setting me up with sufficient clues to convince me I was being clever, when in truth he led me by the nose all the way to the warehouse. Even the timing of his call was probably calculated to let me hear military jets roaring overhead. I was duped.

The misplaced conviction that I had discovered something vital nullified my immediate threat to the GDR and forced me out of my unknown place of sanctuary and into a zone where Schwartz held control.

He even gave me enough time by throwing in an arbitrary midnight deadline. Why give me hours, when I could walk out of any building anywhere in Korea and inside five minutes turn myself over to the nearest policeman?

The unanswered questions did not end there. Why surround one small woman with a hardened squad of mercenaries? The conclusion was shockingly obvious. Naz was the bait and I was the target. I was *meant* to find Naz – and the goons were there to make sure we both disappeared. Mr Cho and his men were not the only reason we were safe. They were they only reason we were still *alive*.

There was mumbling in my ear, and Naz sat up and rubbed at her face. The pain surges in my legs at last receded to a dull ache, and I stretched them into a narrow gap between two prone track-suited figures.

'You alright?'

'Yeah. Sorry I was such a grouch.'

'I deserved it.'

'I know you did.' In the gloom, I saw her face rise in a half-smile.

I remembered. *The videotape.*

'Did Mr Cho get a videotape to you before Schwartz's boys picked you up?'

'Yes, but I didn't even get to see it because the camera battery was dead. Schwartz was delighted to get his hands on it.'

'I really messed up there. It was the tape that put you in danger, but I thought you could work out why it was so important.' I explained about fixing a video camera in my hotel room to film the fun with Miss Hong. Naz shook her head like a disbelieving mother.

'Boys and their toys.'

'I know. But this one could have been important, and I was banking on it helping me somehow.'

Mr Cho turned around to lean over the seat back. 'We can see it when we get back to Seoul.'

'What do you mean?'

'I knew it was important, so I copied the tape to DVD before I gave it to Naz.'

If I had the strength to raise my arms, I could have hugged him. 'Why didn't you tell me?'

He fired me a look of reproach. 'What was the purpose of the trip to Cholla?'

I thought about that for a second. He was right, of course. 'To protect Naz.'

The tape was important, but our priority was to make sure that Naz was safe. And now, thanks to Mr Cho and his friends, both were safe and well. I lifted the aching arm and wrapped it around her shoulders. She didn't resist.

It was gone four o'clock in the morning when the driver pulled into a quiet lane that backed onto a line of houses hiding behind high walls topped with broken glass. Mr Cho murmured to the driver who sounded the horn, three short beeps, irregularly spaced. The neighbours must have loved these visits. I followed his gaze to a video camera high on a post next to a heavy metal gate hung with gleaming tiaras of razor wire. The camera pivoted and swept the alley in both directions before the gate pulled aside with a low electronic hum.

I shook hands with the rest of the crew and thanked them

as profusely as my language skills allowed. They waved me away as if I was making a fuss over nothing. Mr Cho spoke quietly to his friends before the van drove off and left the three of us facing the open gates.

A door at the other side of a tidy courtyard opened. Mr Cho led us forward and shook the hand of a small man of about sixty. He wore an immaculately pressed yellow satin shirt and navy trousers with a beltline so swollen it looked in danger of letting go at any moment. Mr Cho made the introductions.

'Alec, Naz, this is Mr Ryu. Mr Ryu is my good friend. We are safe here.' Behind us, the gate hummed shut.

The house was decorated with no expense spared and zero taste applied. Gilded mirrors and reproduction European landscapes competed for space on flocked floral walls. Eye-wateringly ugly carpets changed from room to room, and a stuffed deer stood sentry in the hallway, red glass eyes sparkling in the flickering light from fake candles sprouting from candelabras that would have made Liberace blush.

All I wanted was to view the video. Mr Cho had another word with his friend, who led the way to a living room with the biggest home TV screen I ever saw.

I wanted to watch it alone but instead found myself with friends who had put everything on the line for me, and a stranger who had opened his home to the nation's most wanted man. Under the circumstances, it might have been churlish to ask them to leave the room. Mr Ryu pointed to a DVD player, and pushed a drinks trolley shaped like an antique globe to a strategic point within our reach. I poured a large single malt and hit the play button, deeply unsure about all this. Naz was bemused.

'All the way to Korea for my first ever bachelor porno party.'

What played out in front of us took place only days before yet might as well have been in another lifetime. On the second night Miss Hong came to my room, while she showered, I had set the little camera to record and clipped it to a curtain rod. The wide angle lens took in almost the entire room. In the bottom right the television flickered, mute. A king-sized bed dominated the left side of the frame and beyond that was the bathroom and the door to the corridor, safety chain engaged. Onscreen, I paced the floor until backlit steam followed Miss Hong from the bathroom. Her hair was clipped high and she wore only a thick white towel tied above her small breasts. She looked stunning.

Even played at double speed what happened next made for sordid viewing. In the past I had made these tapes for innocent fun, to be viewed with a partner by my side, inspiration for more of the same. Now I watched myself as I cavorted and giggled and had sex with an attractive young woman, and all I could think of was that beautiful body, mutilated and bloated, snagged on debris in the frigid waters of the Han River.

Naz sucked on a chilled white wine, face blank. Mr Cho and Mr Ryu said nothing, the clink of bottle neck on crystal the only intrusion in the silent porno flick that played out in front of us at double speed.

A welcome break appeared in the onscreen action. After a long session of sex broken up by periods spent lapping Scotch out of Miss Hong's belly button, I got up, visibly pissed, and weaved an unsteady path to the bathroom where I automatically closed the door behind me.

I thumbed the button that slowed the recording back to real time.

Miss Hong took two tall glasses from above the mini bar. She poured generous measures of whisky over ice and filled the glasses with Coca-Cola while her free hand rummaged in her clasp bag. In full view of the camera she cracked two capsules and quickly stirred their powdery contents into one of the drinks.

When I came out of the bathroom she was waiting, a drink to her lips, the other held out to me. The camera's microphone picked up the dialogue but I wasn't listening. I didn't have to. The memory of what happened next was sharpened by equal measures of regret and disbelief.

'What is this?'

'Whisky-coke.' She leaned forward and with one hand she clinked glasses. Her other hand dipped gently between my legs. How well I remembered soft fingertips cooled by chilled glass.

'Cheers.' She moved in to kiss me. I smelled the sex on her breath and the fine sheen of soap and sweat that coated her powdery-smooth skin. She ran her hot tongue around my mouth before pulling away and knocking back her drink. After waiting while I did the same she led me back to bed.

In the discomfort of Mr Ryu's ugly armchair, I leaned my head back and stared at the ceiling. The soundtrack led me through my last few minutes with Miss Hong, and which came back to me with shocking clarity. We tumbled around the room with renewed vigour, changing positions frequently, until at last we pulled apart. Miss Hong leaned back on the pillows and plucked the whisky bottle from the bedside cabinet, free hand pointing theatrically at her stomach. Three sheets to the wind I did what I always do when I'm drunk. I reached for more drink. I took the bottle and leaned forward to fill the yin yang recess in the middle of her beautiful flat tummy. Miss Hong giggled while she lounged back, her hair, moist with sweat, fanning out over soft down pillows.

That was when the frame in my memory froze.

I looked up to the big screen where the naked me wavered like a sapling in a breeze and collapsed face-first on top of Miss Hong's lovely legs. The bottle slipped from my fingers, whisky seeping across the rumpled bed linen. Miss Hong ignored it. She wriggled free and from her bag plucked a mobile phone, dialling as she walked to the bathroom, the cheeks of her beautiful backside jiggling seductively.

Onscreen I lay inert for several long minutes before she re-emerged from the bathroom wearing the same skimpy dress she had arrived in. Her hair was twisted in a towelling turban that she shook off and discarded on the floor next to the desk. Pulling the dryer from a drawer, she sat in front of the mirror and set to work on her hair. She broke off from the task only once to look at her watch, her movements relaxed and unhurried. I was well out of the game, shoulders sighing regularly.

Hair and make-up done she sat back in the chair, lit a cigarette and used the remote control to scan TV channels, settling for a Korean soap opera. She looked at her watch again. A knock at the door was so quiet that the microphone barely picked it up. She muted the television and with one last look of appraisal in the mirror, plucked her bag from the desktop and walked away from the camera.

The security chain rattled and the door swung wide. One figure, a little taller than Miss Hong in her three-inch heels, face obscured by her hair, spoke quietly in Korean. She responded, equally quietly, and pulled back to allow the newcomer into the room. He walked quickly to where I lay, and delivered a vicious hooking punch to my ribs. I had wondered about that bruise.

Ben Schwartz.

Miss Hong looked on like an acolyte desperate for a word of praise. Schwartz turned and kissed her full on the lips, and with an arm around one shoulder led her from the room. The door closed after them with a solid clunk. The video frame became a still-life save for the flickering screen in its bottom corner, where an overlit farming family argued in a rural courtyard, unnoticed by the naked foreigner face down on the bed.

Mr Cho rose from his seat and pointed at the screen.

I froze the picture and he strolled to the television, one finger extended. He tapped at the soap opera scene.

There, in the top left corner of the television picture, next to the broadcasting company logo, was the time. 03:45.

Chapter Thirty-five

As well as playing host to some of the world's most visually offensive home furnishings, Mr Ryu plainly had a soft spot for electronic gadgetry. When I wondered aloud how I could make multiple copies of the DVD, Mr Cho translated and Ryu bounced to his feet, fished a brick of blank disks from a drawer and opened black gloss cabinet doors inlaid with snakes' heads fashioned from abalone shell. Inside was a professional-quality digital dubbing deck.

Maybe Ryu had an ever-growing brood of beloved grandkids and spent his free time making home movies for all the family. Or possibly it was something to do with the giant rococo wall unit filled with European hardcore porn.

Mr Cho, Ryu and I worked like a team fuelled by occasional refills from the drinks globe, while Naz slept curled up on a puce green leather sofa.

Ryu produced a sheaf of padded brown envelopes ideally-suited to posting DVD cases to grandchildren, and we huddled together to work out where to send the copies. The first name was easy: Detective Kwok at the police station where he and the brother cops had done such a number on my kidneys. Numbers two and three both went to the British Embassy. Thinking that Bridgewater might try to bury it, I neglected to tell him in the accompanying note that another copy was already on his ambassador's desk.

Disks four, five and six went to the bureau chief at Reuters news agency and his opposite numbers at AP and the Korean news agency Yonhap. Seven and eight I addressed to the newsrooms at the two big Korean television networks, number nine went to the U.S. Embassy, and the tenth I saved for Korea's best-selling economic daily. All were accompanied by a lengthy explanatory print-out typed on Mr Ryu's desktop computer. I quickly discounted sending one to Nethers Hollands of the Due Diligence team, as he would find out soon enough just how surplus to requirements *he* was.

I thought we were finished, but Mr Cho had other ideas.

'Two more, for safety.'

'Who for?'

'Chang and Schwartz.'

'Give Schwartz the warning he needs to get out of town? No way. I want him locked up for what they did to Miss Hong.'

'Your video will mean big problems for Chang as well. He introduced you to Miss Hong, and Schwartz works for him. And he knows you will talk about the GDR. When he hears about the DVD he will fight back.'

'What can he do to me now?'

'Not you. Other people. Like Bobby's family and my family.'

Cue another reality check. I wanted to avoid scaring Chang and Schwartz into running, but maybe by showing my hand I could *force* them to disappear, and in doing so protect the people who had stood by me.

It took Mr Cho one telephone call to set everything up. In a couple of hours ten envelopes would arrive at a courier company in the city, to be delivered mid-morning at the latest. The other two DVDs would be waiting for Chang and Schwartz when they turned up at K-N Towers.

At breakfast time Mr Cho went home. My body screamed out for sleep, but first I had calls to make.

At the Embassy I put up with the usual phoney respect stuff from the same Korean woman with the Home Counties accent until finally Bridgewater came on the line.

'Bridgewater here.'

'I take it the Queen of Hearts at the front desk told you who this is?'

'Of course.'

'I want to know what you have done since the last time we spoke. I have sent the letters to Seoul and to London, both Whitehall and what used to be Fleet Street.'

'You are in no position to be making demands. Until you surrender to the authorities, there is nothing we can do for you.'

'Are you telling me you've done nothing since we talked?'

'We have done everything possible – '

'To save your own stupid heads from rolling when this one goes pear-shaped.'

'That sort of talk is not going to get us anywhere, Mr Brodie. So far as I can determine, your allegations are without basis.'

'Are you saying the GDR is completely above board?'

'Geoff Martinmass is a respected figure in the Seoul business community. I have discussed this matter with him, and I agree with his conclusion that you may be trying to divert attention away from the death of the prostitute.'

'So I'm guilty until proven otherwise, but Martinmass is in the clear.'

'If you surrender to the authorities, we will extend all reasonable consular assistance. While you remain a fugitive, there is little we can do.'

'Thank you for being so understanding. You're in for a long day. Keep a watch on the incoming mail, because what's coming to you is also going all over town, to the police and to the media.'

'What is?' At last, a hint of panic in his voice.

'Wait and see. And if I were you, I'd steer clear of dark alleyways for a while.'

My next call was to the Seoul office of Reuters News Agency. I brayed at the receptionist in my best haw-haw accent.

'Eric Bridgewater of the Embassy here, British Embassy. Connect me to Vincent Cray, please.'

'I am sorry, Mr Cray is in a meeting, may I – '

'Did you hear me? I am calling from the British Embassy.'

An electronic string quartet was foisted on me until:

'Eric. What's the problem?'

'I have to talk to you.' I used my own voice, which is about as far from Eric Bridgewater's as you could get.

'You are?' The man was quick.

'Alec Brodie.'

'Just one moment.' I made out the rustling of paper and urgent instructions muffled by a hand over the receiver.

'OK, go ahead.'

'Very soon you will receive a DVD that will clear me of involvement in the Miss Hong murder. Sorry it's not an exclusive, but you are the only media person to know of it ahead of time.'

'I appreciate that, but how will it prove anything?'

'The video puts a fresh suspect square in the picture, but that is not what I called about. There is an even bigger story here, and I am giving you an early heads-up.'

He had the practiced ear of the experienced media professional who knows the importance of keeping the other guy talking, knowing he could sort the facts from the bullshit later. I concentrated on how the GDR was about to embarrass all sorts of prominent people. To the newsman, embarrassment is the food of the Gods, and any story that brings shame upon big business or senior government – or both – is manna from heaven. He asked pointed questions about how the police hunt for me was related to the GDR, and I filled him in as best I could.

'I can't run this without some sort of corroboration.'

'To a man with your resources, confirming at least parts of what I've told you should be a piece of cake.'

He couldn't get off the phone quick enough. Maybe he suspected that the moment I heard the line go dead I would call Associated Press, which is exactly what I did.

I spent a couple of restless hours bobbing atop a waterbed under a fake Siberian tiger-skin blanket, its back feet clawing at the pillows, head hanging off the end of the bed like it was trying to eat the lemon coloured deep-pile carpet. I ached all over and couldn't keep my eyes open – but my mind raced out of control.

I pried myself from the tiger's clutches mid-morning. There was no sign of Naz, who had been steered to another bedroom just before daybreak, nor of Mr Ryu. In an eye-straining stainless steel kitchen, I stood in front of a refrigerator the size of a Tokyo hotel room, wolfed cold orange juice straight from the carton and fed the empty container into the raggedy maw of a waste bin on the run from a Star Wars set.

I confronted an Italian coffee maker as complex as an airliner flight deck for all of ten seconds before filling a kettle and making do with instant that I eventually located inside a life-size ceramic soccer ball.

Eleven o'clock. With luck, most of the DVDs would have been delivered and viewed by now. Wondering how long it would take for the ripples they created to show up, I called Bobby Purves at his office.

'Can we meet?'

'Where and when?'

'*Halmoni's* tooth, the observation floor? Forty-five minutes?'

'OK.'

Halmoni's, or Grandma's tooth, was the local nickname for a monster office building that sprouted from a residential district on Youido island. Clad in shimmering gold-toned glass and surrounded by off-white apartment buildings, the tower stuck out like a Grandmother's solitary gold tooth. An insurance company HQ and famous for being the tallest skyscraper in Asia when it was completed in 1985, it was informally known as the 'sixty-three' building after its number of floors, never mind that three of them were below ground. At the top of the skyscraper, an entire floor served as an indoor observation deck.

Even mid-morning on a weekday, the observation deck was busy with out-of-town visitors who pointed out landmarks and lined up to have their photographs taken. I was looking through a coin-operated telescope at mountains to the north of the city when Bobby arrived.

'Anything unusual happening in the Market today, Bobby?'

'I might've known you would be in on this.'

'In on what?'

'Don't even try to play dumb. The Market's in a freefall set off by rumours that K-N Group is about to be stomped on by the government for irregularities over the GDR. There's talk of police investigations and arrest warrants, and the wire services are rushing out updates at ten-minute intervals. Trading in K-N stocks was suspended after they plummeted by twenty-five percent in half an hour.'

Yessss. 'Just your average day at the office then?'

'K-N's public relations department is playing possum. Not one word of damage control coming out to refute the rumours, which at a time like this is corporate suicide. No sign of Schwartz anywhere.'

'So I've done it.'

'I've saved the best 'til last – wait, what d'you mean you've done it?'

'You first.'

'There's talk that K-N's private jet took off from Incheon about an hour ago, three crew members and two passengers on board, and a flight plan filed for Tokyo. Apparently Chang and his missus were the passengers.'

The shit had truly hit the fan.

'So how did you do it?' Bobby smiled as he spoke, looking forward to the explanation.

I told him about Naz being snatched from her hotel by Schwartz's goons, and how Mr Cho and his students had helped me rescue her the night before. I went on to explain about the video camera and the duplicate DVDs, how I helped the Press link what was in the film clip to what had been going on at K-N, and how Schwartz and Chang had received copies of the video before anyone else.

'You certainly know how to piss on someone's parade. If Chang is on that jet and Schwartz isn't manning the battlements, maybe they're both on the run.'

'What about Martinmass?'

Silence.

'Bobby?'

'He might be in the clear.'

'How the fuck – '

'You're not going to believe it.'

'I already don't believe it.'

'I spoke to a mate who works with him at the bank.'

'And?'

'Martinmass is in the office as usual, his faced fixed with a cocky leer. Staff have strict instructions to counter all enquiries, police included, with a clear 'no comment'. All calls from London head office to be patched straight through to Martinmass.'

'I don't get it. The bastard should be bricking himself. Maybe he's done a deal with the authorities, immunity in return for testimony against the others. But there was no time to set that up, and even if he had, right now he'd be sweating bullets in an interrogation room, not swanning around his office playing Mr Happy.'

'You got one bit right.'

'What?'

'He's got immunity.'

'How?'

'*Diplomatic immunity.*'

'You're shitting me.'

'I wish I was.'

'He's a banker, not a bloody diplomat.'

'I'd forgotten all about it. About eighteen months ago, Martinmass was appointed Consul of some banana republic tax haven in the Caribbean.'

I shook my head in disbelief.

'He and his bank had done a lot of business with the government there, and they wanted representation in Seoul without spending any money, a free way to attract dodgy money to their offshore banking industry. A secretary at his bank doles out a couple of dozen visas a year, and Martinmass gets to call himself a diplomat. He and his old lady even made the news when they went to the Blue House to present his credentials to the President.'

'And that gives him diplomatic immunity?'

'I don't know how he swung it either, but I do remember talk of him retiring there in the next couple of years.'

'No wonder he's been sailing so close to the wind.' I thought about it for a moment. 'I'm guessing he'll be celebrating tonight at the Nashville.'

Chapter Thirty-six

I found Naz sitting in Mr Ryu's kitchen nursing a large mug of freshly-brewed coffee from the flight-deck machine.

'Ever see a machine so flash? Where did you get to?'

'I filled Bobby in on what has been happening.'

She pushed a mug of black-brown mix across the counter. I explained what Bobby had told me and outlined our plan for the evening. Soon after, coffee or no coffee, fatigue closed in on me and I went to lie down with the Siberian tiger.

When I finally resurfaced, the K-N story was at the top of the six o'clock news. Stock market unrest, handwritten signs stuck to K-N office doors and nervy-looking staff clustered in corridors at K-N Towers. An interview with a white shirt at Incheon Airport was intercut with grainy security camera footage of two figures scurrying aboard a private jet, steps folding up behind them and wheels rolling, even before the aircraft's door was fully closed.

It was an easy link to the Brodie and Schwartz show. *Ongoing investigations change tack due to new video evidence just in.* Soft, freeze-frame images taken from the duplicate DVD: Brodie in bed with Miss Hong, body parts not very carefully frosted out; Miss Hong leaving the room with another man, his face much more carefully obscured; lastly, a full-face corporate portrait of Schwartz. K-N public relations supremo sought in connection with the death of Miss Hong, as well as for alleged trading irregularities that led to the collapse in K-N stock prices early today. British photographer no longer a suspect in the death of Miss Hong, though police remain anxious to talk with him.

Alec Brodie and dignity never did go together, but this time I had excelled myself. From murder suspect to friendly witness in the space of a few hours – and all it took was to bare my bits on national television.

The three of us huddled in the near-darkness of the dingy alley while Bobby spoke into his mobile. He broke the connection.

'I was right. If it's dark or a weekend, Jerzy McTague is in there. He's on his way out.'

A metallic clatter rattled the doorway and light fanned out to briefly flood the alley as a stout figure squeezed through the emergency exit and gently closed it behind him.

He was an overweight little guy with the corned-beef complexion of the committed drinker and the unkempt look of a middle-aged divorcee. He nodded to me and to Naz, and turned to Bobby:

'I don't know about this, man.' The accent was American, Southern states. He looked deadly serious.

'Don't worry about it Jerzy, we'll – '

'What if y'all are here with somethin' innocent or honourable in mind?' His red face broke up in a grin and he turned to me when I answered:

'No danger of that.'

'Fuckin'-ay, man. I heard what his people done to little Min-tae. So you do whatcha havta do, and make sure you give the asshole one for me.'

'That's a promise.'

'He's surrounded by the usual buncha flunkies. Talkin'

loud about how the Caribbean beckons. Been drinking litres of draught for a couple hours. S'only a matter of time before he has to go drain the snake.'

We thanked him and he slipped back indoors, leaving the emergency exit off the latch. Through the crack between the door and the jamb, I had a clear view of the entrance to the Nashville's toilets.

'How the hell did he know about Min-tae?'

'There's not much Jerzy McTague *doesn't* know,' said Bobby. 'He's career CIA.'

'A wee fat drunk for a spy. Talk about perfect cover.'

'A bit more realistic than Pierce bloody Brosnan,' said Naz.

Traffic in the corridor was steady, and it was only minutes before we saw the big frame of Geoff Martinmass push his way through the toilet door.

He soon came back out, head down, watching his step the way drunks do. The temptation was just too great. I nipped through the emergency exit and snatched at the wig, which came away with a sticky rasping sound that took me by surprise. A big hand flew to his pink scalp and he turned to find me in the corridor, dead bird in hand.

'You little prick.' He stood six inches taller and out-weighed me by at least ninety pounds, most of it muscle, and I was alone. I tapped twice on the emergency exit and in blew Bobby, arms outstretched, grabbing for the big guy's chest. Seconds later, Martinmass was picking himself up in the alley.

He got to his feet, a leer on his face. Two of us, and he still fancied his chances.

'I get it,' he said.

No he didn't.

'You try to destroy me, but you can't do it, not on your own or together, not even when you fly your Paki bitch in to do your dirty work for you.'

He inched forward, fists clenched.

'Are you sorry bastards really going to take me?' He had contempt in his eyes and clouds of stale beer on his breath.

'No.' I backed off a half-pace. 'We're not.'

Uncertainty flickered across his eyes.

'She is.'

Naz exploded from the shadows and buried a steel toe-capped boot in his crotch. He went down like he had been hit by a train, and she wasted no time laying into him, talking to him between wild swings of her feet.

'That,' *Whump*. 'Is for Miss Hong, and so is this.' *Whump*. 'That,' *Whump*. 'Is for what you did to Min-tae, you ugly piece of shit. 'And *this*,' *Whump*. 'Is for calling me,' *Whump*. 'A Paki.' *Whump*. 'Bitch.'

'Don't forget our promise.' I angled my head at the door. Naz's grin was raging on adrenaline.

'This one's by special request.' *Whump*. She backed off a pace and went in for more. Her boots re-broke his nose and destroyed his front teeth and opened ugly gashes in his cheek and forehead, but I felt no pity. When she was done, Martinmass was unconscious, his face like raw meat, Naz's boots covered in blood.

In my hand was the forgotten wig. I flipped it at Naz, who plucked it from the air and stooped to finger it into what was left of his mouth.

The emergency door creaked open, and the three of us darted for shadows.

'Geoff?' The voice was loose with beer. 'Are you there, Geoff?' *Eric Bridgewater*. His head slipped out in a crack of light and I hit the bottom of the door with my foot, wedging his ears in a wood sandwich. He squealed like a teenage girl.

I reached in to grab a fistful of tie. The prat wore a tie to the Nashville. I launched him against a pile of dusty beer crates as Naz and Bobby slipped around the corner.

'What did I tell you about dark alleys?'

I was going to hit him, but as he stood shaking with fear and nailed to the filthy alley, he wet himself. It was time to go.

Still buzzing, we flagged a taxi heading south. Fifteen minutes later saw us in the living room of Bobby's apartment across the river. Myong-hee rushed around playing hostess, pretending she didn't want any help from Naz. Elder son Min-hong played computer games in a nearby bedroom, and Min-tae sat astride my tired legs and tickled me without mercy, wiry fingers unerringly exploring every point on my body that hurt most. Naz brought over bulky glasses and Bobby and I each took a long pull at the cold beer.

'Hell, that was good.' He wasn't talking about the beer. I could see him re-playing the alley scene in his head. 'I'm just sorry I didn't do it myself, get the boot in for the little guy.' Meanwhile, the little guy was pounding at my sore shoulder with meaty fists not much smaller than his Dad's.

'Don't talk daft,' I said. 'It was dodgy enough you just *being* there.'

Naz backed me up: 'Martinmass got a bit of what's coming to him. That's all that matters.'

We drank to that, and Myong-hee nodded in agreement. Her husband was just back from gambling with his livelihood and his freedom, but as that was for Min-tae, it was alright by her. I couldn't argue with that, even if Min-tae chose that precise moment to burrow a forefinger into a kidney still reeling from the phone book session. I hid a wince and turned to Bobby.

'Bring me up to date on the business front.'

His big face lit up.

'For the K-N Group investor, the day started out terribly, but it soon fell away. Rumours all over town made the money men run for cover, and they soon started dumping anything connected to the Group. Before long, panic set in and K-N stocks were offloaded at any price. Group sub-sidiary companies, Korean Banks they owe money to – which is all of them – and Managed Funds that were warm to the GDR, they all took a beating.' He paused to re-fill his glass and pour a long draught of beer down his neck. 'Confidence in the whole Market started to dive, so people did what they always do – they ditched shares and bought gold. The index plummeted, gold went through the roof and the Korean *won* fell like a boulder down a well. It's meltdown, and everyone, but *everyone*, is setting the blame at K-N's doorstep.'

'I've never heard you string that many words together before.'

'It's the excitement.' He took three long paces into the open-plan kitchen and grabbed two fresh bottles from the refrigerator. 'I'm not myself right now.'

'Was Chang on that jet this morning?' said Naz.

'Looks like it.' Bobby flicked the tops off the beers. 'Heads are rolling already. The chief of security at the airport has resigned and the Minister of Transportation has offered to do the same, never mind that Chang got out before an arrest warrant was even written up. It's always the way here, ritual blood-letting, high-profile sacrificial lambs stepping up to pay the price for things they had nothing to do with. When this is all forgotten, the same guys will be quietly rewarded with bigger jobs.'

'Any word on Schwartz?'

'Nothing. The bastard's disappeared. What is Jung-hwa saying?'

I tried to hide in my beer.

'Don't tell me you haven't called her?'

'What am I going to say? *'I'm really sorry I put the murder squad onto your husband'*?'

'When it comes to women, you never fail to disappoint.'

'I'll call her tomorrow when I have a better idea what's happening.' I could do without this. Jung-hwa had popped into my thoughts throughout the day, but I still hadn't picked up the phone. I pushed my empty glass at Bobby. 'I have to go.'

'What's the hurry?'

'I have a date.'

Chapter Thirty-seven

Viewed from a window seat in a tea house on the first floor of a crumbling city centre block, a little corner of night-time Seoul spread out in front of me like a drunken ant farm.

Jong-gak district in the centre of the capital sits shadowed by tall glass towers lining broad city avenues. Behind the modern towers smaller blocks from the sixties and seventies host hundreds of little businesses that exist to feed and refresh the tens of thousands of office workers who converge on downtown daily.

The old city's main east-west axis of Chong-ro lay fifty yards away and choked with buses and taxis, horns blaring incessantly. The aggression and competitiveness innate to the Korean psyche turns city streets into barging, horn-blaring never-ending confrontational chicken sessions. In front of me a narrower lane that ran parallel to the main drag was just as clogged with pedestrian life, almost as raucous but infinitely less threatening than the neighbouring motorised chaos. Restaurants of every stripe lined the thoroughfare, from wood-and-vinyl *pojang-macha* handcarts to exclusive upmarket Japanese establishments, windows curtained and air-conditioners humming. The lane shone with coloured signs advertising bars, small stores, fried chicken joints, bars, donut shops, coffee shops, bars, barber shops and more bars. Koreans like their bars, and it is not for nothing that they are known as *the Irish of Asia*.

Pairs of office girls hurried towards bus stop or subway station with arms entwined, shoulders rubbing and faces close enough to touch as they giggled their way homewards. Male colleagues more seriously intent on making the most of what was left of the evening drew meandering trails from restaurant to bar to *pojang-macha*. A gap in the buildings framed a grid-fenced enclosure where men faced automatic pitching machines that spat baseballs at frightening speeds. The metallic ding of bat on ball drew cheers from friends huddled behind fences. I watched them for a few seconds before I looked away, memories and bruises from men with baseball bats all too fresh.

In an odd shaped expanse of open ground between the tea shop and Chong-ro loomed a symbol of the city's ancient origins. The Po-shin Gak Pavilion was a classic gathering of sweeping tiled rooflines propped upon towering red pillars that housed a massive bronze bell rung only at Lunar New Year.

I looked up as Detective Kwok took the seat across from me and sent the waitress scurrying for another glass of ginseng tea. From beside the ashtray he plucked a matchbox with the name of the tea shop on it and lit a cigarette. He leaned back in the chair and stared, anger and uncertainty bubbling near the surface. When he spoke, smoke billowed from his mouth.

'My seniors are very unhappy that I have not brought you in for questioning.'

'The same seniors sent my picture around the country with me labelled a sex-murderer. Now when I solve the case for them they're pissed off? To hell with them.'

'You are right.' Kwok leaned back in his chair, and his slim features wrinkled in what might have been amusement. 'Off the record, I thank you for the DVD.'

I sipped at the ginseng tea. Bitter but sweet, like what Kwok was swallowing right now. He spoke again:

'I have just come from Yonsei University Hospital.

It seems your banker friend Martinmass had an unfortunate accident.'

My attempt to suppress a smile almost certainly failed.

'An ambulance was called to Itaewon. He was found in an alley, very badly beaten. He claimed he had too much to drink and fell over – several times, it would seem.'

Whatever he had in mind I would soon find out.

'His jaw was broken in four places, most of his front teeth were gone – and he has bootprints all over his face.' He changed tack with practiced abruptness. 'When did you last see Martinmass?'

'I didn't touch him.' It was the answer to a different question, but it was the truth. Kwok shook his head, and went on:

'We were looking for him, so when the Itaewon station informed me that he was on his way to Yonsei Hospital, I stopped in to speak to him. He was not very cooperative.'

'I hear he is protected from prosecution.'

'He *was*.' Emphasis on the second word. 'Not any more.'

Yessss. Kwok saw my delight, and played to his audience:

'His Caribbean employers are in the final stages of negotiations with one of the Korean *Chaebols* to build a harbour and casino complex to attract giant cruise liners out of Miami. Such visits will create hundreds of permanent jobs that are much-needed on the island. The project's funding is from a collaboration of Korean banks underwritten by my government. It took one ministerial-level telephone call to have his immunity revoked, and I assure you he will be charged with very serious financial crimes. Did you know that a few years ago, he gambled heavily on dot-com start-ups and lost everything?'

I didn't know that but it explained the desperation to keep his share of the GDR profits. Kwok's investigative powers were proving to be a surprise.

'What about Miss Hong?'

'After I saw the DVD, we went back to the Hyatt security camera footage. Schwartz slipped in through an entrance by the swimming pool and later appeared briefly in an elevator that stopped at your floor. He and Miss Hong were observed in the car park getting into a Hyundai registered to K-N Group.'

'What does that tell you about our scene with the telephone books?'

'So far as I and my colleagues are concerned, that never happened, though you are, of course, welcome to try and prove otherwise. In any case, I only did what I thought was necessary.'

'Or what you were told to do.'

The amusement evaporated and I pressed on:

'Somebody in your department has been keeping Chang informed all along.'

'If there is a problem in my office I will deal with it.'

It was as near as I could expect to an admission of culpability. It never happened but whoever did it, Kwok would take care of it in his own way. He looked grim. I didn't envy anyone on his watch who was guilty of leaking information to K-N.

'I sent copies of the video to the British Embassy as well as the media.'

'I know. Eric Bridgewater called my superiors. There is to be a press conference tomorrow at noon in the British Council Building.'

'Nice of him to tell me.' I wasn't thinking straight. Bridgewater had no way of contacting me. 'And Rose Daly?'

'Her involvement in this matter is over. We no longer wish to talk to her.'

Kwok took a final long drag at his cigarette before grinding it to shreds in the ashtray.

'Before you ask,' he said, smoke trailing from the corners of his mouth, 'According to his office, President Chang is in

South America seeking urgent medical attention. My friends at Immigration believe he is presently in Tokyo and in perfect health. It is not unusual in this kind of situation.'

I understood. Chang wasn't the first business leader to disappear overseas pleading a mystery illness that coincided with his company hitting the skids.

'Any word on Schwartz?'

'We are doing our best, but it is difficult. We discovered that he has a second passport, an Irish one. A significant number of Americans do, it seems.'

Kwok sipped at the tea, his dark eyes wandering the room. Primary-coloured embroideries and monotone watercolours fought for crowded wallspace. Next to the entrance, an *ajimah* in acrylic pink hovered cross-legged behind a cash desk, proprietorial antennae on high alert. The old dame could spot a cop the second he crossed her threshold, and the possibility of any kind of ruckus had her visibly on edge.

'Immigration are watching for him and searching their records but, so far, nothing. Where are you staying?' Another abrupt change of tack. He pulled a fresh cigarette from his top pocket and lit it.

'With a friend.'

'Not at the Hyatt?'

'You know the answer to that. Thanks to Schwartz and company, I owe the Hyatt too much money already.'

'I need an address. For my superiors.'

'Do what I would do.'

'What is that?'

'Make one up.'

I left him staring into space through a cloud of cigarette smoke. One thing continued to bug me. I still had no idea why Schwartz had chosen to involve me in all this.

Talk about running the gauntlet. To get to the British Embassy I first had to get past the British Council Building where the press conference was to be held at noon. The narrow pavement was crowded with journalists and camera crews. I directed my taxi driver to go past them, all the way to the heavy Embassy gates. The moment the cab stopped I threw money at the driver and jumped out and spoke urgently at the Korean security man in the Embassy gatehouse:

'My name is Brodie and I have an appointment with the ambassador.' I looked over my shoulder to see a mob of TV cameramen, soundmen with boom mikes and journalists with tape recorders swarm towards me. Not so much a well-oiled Press machine as a careering cloud of hornets.

'These people are going to block your entrance.'

The gatehouse guard raised one eye from the papers in front of him, shifted his gaze to take in the approaching horde, and triggered the electronic lock release. I slid around the gate, slammed it shut behind me and set off up the short driveway. The pack wailed through the gates, desperate for an image or a sound bite before the press conference got under way. If these were only the journalists covering the street, the main event was going to be a three-ring circus.

The heavy glass door hissed closed behind me and a figure from the wings leapt out with one arm extended.

'So glad that you are able to be here. We are very eager to put your case to the media, to do everything we can to clear your name.'

Eric Bridgewater, cool as you like. I surprised him with an enthusiastic embrace of his dead-fish handshake.

'I *do* hope you've changed your underwear, Eric.'

'Derek Howell, Ambassador,' said a tall red-headed man in an expensive suit. He had a moustache that looked like caterpillars kissing, his handshake was businesslike, and his eyes looked through me as if I was not there.

'*So* glad that justice is being done, at last. Been doing

everything we can here, you know. From day one my people have exerted every available channel of influence.'

I wondered how many bare-faced lies the man could build into one short statement. We both knew my letters and the DVD had put a ferret down his trousers, and that this was all about damage control. He went on:

'Sorry to say that I am unable to attend the press conference, but Eric will take the chair on the Embassy's behalf. If there's anything you need, simply ask.' He shook my hand again and disappeared. The grubby world of sex industry murder victims and corporate crime involving friends of the Embassy were not within the chosen domain of Her Majesty's envoy to Seoul.

Detective Kwok and four uniformed cops joined us as Bridgewater ushered me out the door.

'It would be better to say nothing to this lot.' As he spoke, the compound gate swung wide and the media swarm fell into step in front of us, slowing our progress, shouting all at once.

I blocked out their questions and smiled towards TV camera lenses, looking every viewer in the eye. Nothing to hide, was my message. A stills photographer got under the heels of a TV cameraman and they tumbled backwards, expensive equipment crashing to the ground. Our escorts swerved us around them like sheep around a gatepost, and I glanced down to see the cameraman trying to film us while lying on his back. Squashed on the ground below him the stills photographer looked indignant.

Inside the building, Kwok leaned close to speak quietly in my ear.

'I would like you to meet someone, a good friend, my alumni.' I remembered *alumni*, the odd '*Konglish*' term for a graduate of the same university. In Korea, ties between old university mates are unbelievably strong.

'Who is he?'

'*She* is the editor of *TWIK!* Magazine. Very powerful in my country.' I knew the magazine, a splashy weekly that specialised in investigative reportage and controversial exposés. Gaudy but well put-together, it was hugely successful.

'She has an offer for you.' He looked pleased with himself and pulled me into a side room. A Korean woman of about thirty-five with spiky grey hair and wearing a blue-black pinstripe suit slouched against one wall, an unlit cigarette dangling precariously from a bright red slash of a mouth. Liza Minnelli in *Cabaret*. Several copies of *TWIK!* sat on the table in front of her. Kwok cut in:

'Hurry, we have very little time. This is Miss Choy of *This Week Inside Korea!* Magazine. She wants to buy your story.'

This was so Korean. The lead investigator in a murder case helping the former prime suspect peddle his story to a rag edited by his *alumni*. Not long after I first arrived in Seoul, I was busted for teaching English while on a tourist visa. Before I left the Immigration office with a deportation order in my passport, the official who put it there fixed me up with a new job to come back to. At the language school of his *alumni*.

It took me three minutes to cut a deal with Miss Choy. All Hyatt expenses for myself and Naz for as long as we remained in Korea, plus twenty million *won* in cash. About twelve thousand pounds. Miss Choy shook on the deal without bothering to take the unlit cigarette from her mouth. She hardly spoke a word. My kind of journalist.

Kwok opened the door for Miss Choy. I closed it behind her.

'Thank you for this, Detective.'

'The situation was unfortunate, and I knew Miss Choy could help.'

'Thank you anyway.'

He nodded in understanding as we shook hands. In another life, perhaps we could have been friends.

I didn't enjoy the press conference, twenty minutes of probing direct questions met by circuitous half-truths for responses.

Bridgewater used it to make up lies about how concerned the Embassy was for the good name of one of its citizens and its deep sadness at the tragic death of Miss Hong, a young lady in the prime of her life.

Kwok used it to deflect attention from his department's inability to conduct an effective investigation without direct assistance from its primary suspect.

I used it to stare intently into cameras and announce that I bore no grudges, and to assure Koreans that this was an *international* problem, with heavy foreign involvement, and that much of the assistance I received had come from Koreans whom I was very proud to call my friends. Next, I made certain that every television station in the land broadcast the fact that Rosemary Daly's reported involvement was a police error, and that she was no longer wanted for questioning. Eyes glinting at having been set up on nationwide television, Kwok graciously confirmed that Rose was in the clear.

As Bridgewater curtly brought the conference to a close, a pretty girl waving the microphone of a local radio station broke with a question:

'What will you do now?'

I looked straight into the phalanx of cameras:

'I think I will go out for a quiet drink. With a good friend of mine.'

As Kwok's uniforms led us out of the hall, I cadged Bridgewater's mobile phone, dipped into the room where earlier I had met Miss Choy – and dialled Jung-hwa's mobile.

'Hello?'

'Were you watching television?'

'Of course.'

'What about a drink?'

'OK.'

'Nine o'clock, King Club?'

'Alright.' A dial tone buzzed in my ear.

At least she was still talking to me.

Chapter Thirty-eight

The alcohol-fuelled sex bazaar that was Itaewon fifteen years ago might be mostly a thing of the past, but at least the King Club still clung doggedly on, its darkened barn buzzing with beautiful women tipping back cocktails, defiantly smoking cigarettes and jiggling animatedly on the crowded dance floor.

If Seoul's deluxe hotel nightclubs were the capital's Penthouse pick-up joints, crawling with high-end whores and their expense-account clientele, the King Club was the city's sub-basement fuckjoint. Teeming with local girls, underpaid American GIs and the usual collection of sundry foreigners.

Not much had changed since I last savoured its appeal. Pillars remained topped with ghastly fake bronze mouldings that always made me think of the Third Reich. The sixty-foot bar that stretched the length of one wall was lined with Western men. One loner in a Harley t-shirt, Stars & Stripes headscarf and wrap-around mirror sunglasses picked his way through knots of drinkers to an empty stool and waved to catch a barman's attention. Atop his perch he sucked a beer straight from the bottle, and watched the moving scene in mirrors behind the serving staff. Or maybe he was checking out his new t-shirt and watching himself drink beer. Whatever was going through his little mind the sunglasses that hid half of his face never left the mirror. There was always one.

Less than thirty yards from where we sat, a four-storey building occupied the site of the Cowboy Club into which, in another lifetime, I pursued Jung-hwa, and Bobby Purves spent months hanging around Myong-hee's DJ booth until at last she agreed to go out with him. I thought of tangled threads and how, all these years later, here we were again, threads stubbornly intertwined.

Bobby sat bunched up against the table, one big paw enveloping his wife's tiny hand. With her other hand Myong-hee traced patterns in the hairs of Bobby's forearm. Maybe if things had been different, I thought. Jung-hwa had yet to arrive but my arm lay draped over the back of the chair next to me, holding a place for her. Even after everything that had happened in the past few hours, I remained stiff with tension, as scared as I was excited by the thought of seeing her again. Thanks to me, her husband was ruined and on the run, but what now for us? The re-ignition of past joys was a revelation to me, and I had to wonder, did Jung-hwa feel the same way? Could there be more to the attraction than the purely physical? I was as confused as ever. I rubbed fatigue from my face and looked around the busy club.

Through narrow aisles between packed tables, gum-clacking waitresses in handkerchief-sized skirts and broad-brush make-up strutted, loaded trays pointed at the nicotine-burnished ceiling. Only a fool crossed a King Club waitress, and no fool was big enough to ever do it twice. I remembered watching one of them, five feet nothing in her high heels and a hundred pounds soaking wet, reduce a table and chairs to rubble in a forty-five-second frenzy of violence. It took the club's Sumo-sized bouncer to snatch her out of the mayhem and away from three blood-ied male victims. She dusted herself down, picked up her tray and went back to work, revelling in respectful smiles beamed her way by colleagues.

At the far end of the club, the small dance floor swarmed

with pretty things in revealing outfits and gangly army boys in tight jeans and t-shirts with the sleeves cut back to show off their tattoos. *Death Before Dishonor* and bleeding daggers protruding from skull eye sockets were as popular as ever. Perhaps bad taste was congenital.

Tina Turner roared *Simply the Best* through wardrobe-sized speakers, and, occupying a corner of the dance floor, Naz gyrated in a space of her own making.

Ballsy Tina gave way to syrupy Elton John, and Naz picked her way through the throng until she stood beside us. She wiped beaded sweat from her brow with both hands, drew them across the ass of her jeans, and flopped into her seat.

Across the room Jung-hwa walked in, head high, scanning the tables. I stood and raised a hand in welcome, catching her attention almost immediately. A glow came to life in her eyes, but a second later it was gone, lancing my shaky confidence in an instant of dawning realisation. I had done it again.

What a fucking fool. When I called her after the press conference, we hardly exchanged ten words. I asked her to join me, and she naturally thought I meant just the two of us. The King Club was no cosy romantic rendezvous, but it was our kind of place and we could kick back and celebrate, together but alone. Or so she thought. Now she knew differently.

Damage control time. I ushered her into the seat but before I could say a word, another figure forced a space where there was none, between Jung-hwa and Naz. The loner I had seen at the bar, the Stars & Stripes headscarf gone, sunglasses pushed to the top of his head.

'Alright if I join you?' It was not like we had a choice.

A few simple changes had swept away the preppy MBA look. His thick dark hair was reduced to a shadowy military outline, and he wore jeans and a black Harley-Davidson t-shirt. In this part of town and at this time of night, even without the headscarf, he was just another military face in a crowd full of foreigners.

Jung-hwa looked at her husband in disbelief.

'Why are you here, Ben?'

'Brodie destroyed the biggest deal of my life, but no way he's taking you, too.' His hand closed over Jung-hwa's elbow. She flinched but the hand remained, fingertips pushing white petals in her arm.

'Good idea, Ben,' I said. 'Kidnap her. That will win her back. You might want to try some violence, too, prove how much you love her.'

'Save it for someone who gives a shit what you think. We belong together.'

'Sure you do. That's why you had to follow me to find her.'

He let go of Jung-hwa, and spun to grab hold of Naz. Something glinted in the club lights and in that instant I knew we were in real trouble. A wicked clasp knife, its fat stainless blade, four inches long, curving to a tip as threatening as any surgeon's scalpel.

'Since when were you a knife man?' I stopped. *Since Miss Hong. Probably with the same blade.* He raised his eyebrows at me, amused. Jung-hwa looked back at him, repulsed.

'What are you *doing?*'

'He knows I couldn't hurt you.' He wrenched at Naz's arm. 'But this bitch?'

I had to divert his attention before he did something we would all regret.

'Did killing Miss Hong give you a taste for this?'

His face twisted in what looked like delight.

'What do you expect – a public confession?'

'Ben?' Jung-hwa again. 'What is he talking about?'

'Forget it. It doesn't matter now.'

'Did *you* kill the prostitute?' Under the flickering club lights, her face was deathly pale. Talk about denial. The media was full of reports about Schwartz being wanted for questioning over Miss Hong's death, and still she wouldn't connect the dots. Schwartz spoke to me:

'You should have got what happened to Miss Hong, the moment we were finished with you.'

'It was a set-up from day one, wasn't it?' I tried to gauge my chances of getting to him before he could use the knife. Slim to none. 'Right from when I got the call in London, *come to Seoul, Alec, President Chang wants you.*'

He snorted. 'I told them how easy it would be. You were the perfect patsy, and we played you like a goddamn drum.' Head flashing sideways, he glared at Bobby, and snatched hard at Naz, pulling her closer, digging the curve of the knife into the folds of her blouse.

'Move another inch and you get to see exactly how sharp this blade is.' *Sharp enough to dismember poor Miss Hong.* I understood completely, and hoped that Bobby would, too.

Bobby moved back in his chair, one big arm extended in front of Myong-hee. Not a soul looked our way. Just another busy cluster in a bustling club full of crowded tables. Any attempt to move on Schwartz could be deadly for Naz, and any effort to draw attention to him would surely have the same effect.

His face had a manic sheen to it, like he hadn't slept for days and was running on something a lot stronger than caffeine. His eyeballs glinted like polished ceramic, the pupils dilated. The bastard was high on speed.

Myong-hee looked terrified. Bobby and Naz shared a look of pure fury that mirrored my own. Jung-hwa's momentary smile from only seconds ago was no more than a memory. I spoke quickly:

'Congratulations, I was your patsy. But you didn't need to bring me all the way from England. Anyone could have done my job.'

'You were perfect. You're not only bankrupt, you're a moral bankrupt – you'll do anything for money. We needed new pictures, we wanted your North Korea photographs to sucker the Due Diligence clowns. We stood to make tens of millions, until you fucked it all up.'

What hurt most was that he was right.

'And ruining me in the process was part of the attraction.'

The manic grin regained its strength, and he glanced at Jung-hwa before answering.

'Let's call that our little bonus.'

'Our'. Surely not.

'Isn't that right, Jung?' he said.

Silence.

I looked at her. 'You were a part of this?'

'Not all of it,' said Jung-hwa, no shame in her lovely eyes as she stared me down.

'What does that mean?'

'I wanted you to come back to Korea. I wanted to hurt you for what you did to me. Ben's plan helped me do that.'

I stared in disbelief. She went on:

'You never understood, did you? Ten years ago I was almost thirty years old, and suddenly after five years my foreigner boyfriend was gone. In Korea that left me with no chance to marry. Too old, and after years with a foreigner – '

Anger gave me my voice back.

'So you decided to set me up for murder.'

Jung-hwa shook her head.

'I didn't know about Miss Hong. And don't you remember? I *helped* you, I told you to get out of Seoul. The rest was up to *him*.' She flicked a hand at her husband. The smug look on his face faltered.

'You see my situation ten years ago? I *had to* get married before it was too late, and look,' Her thumb jerked sideways. 'I married this *asshole*. You wonder why I am angry?' She pushed her small handbag under one arm and stood. Schwartz looked confused, but his grip on Naz held, the knife edge hard against her side.

'What about us?' I looked Jung-hwa in the eyes. 'What was that all about? Why did you come to my room in the middle of the night?'

A glimmer of what might have been joy crossed her face, and then it was gone. Schwartz was nailed to the edge of Naz's chair, hanging on every word.

'For a while I forgot I hated you. I wanted you again.'

'And you got me.' I forced a triumphal leer at Schwartz. He recoiled like he'd been slapped. I pressed on:

'It's true, *Ben*. I was only in town a couple of days before we were fucking like rabbits.' A lone bead of sweat swelled from under the sunglasses on the top of his head and ran, un-noticed, into one eye. He didn't blink, said nothing, but remained seated, trembling. Beside him, Naz looked fit to explode, knife or no knife.

'Just like old times, wasn't it, Alec?' said Jung-hwa. 'Did you think it was so wonderful, maybe I could forgive you for leaving me?'

The look on my face gave me away. I had hoped for precisely that.

Schwartz shook his head and spluttered aloud. She ignored him.

'Even after I helped you get out of Seoul, what happened next? Nothing. Not a word from you. And tonight, you invite me out, and I find you drinking with your friends. But why should I be surprised, Alec? What were you going to say to me tonight? Thanks for the great sex, but it's time for me to disappear again?

'Or maybe you hadn't made up your mind. Were you still thinking about taking me with you?'

She read me like a book. Even now, I didn't have a clue.

'I know it's too late, but really, I'm so – '

'Shut up.' Her face was an expressionless mask. 'You're not in control any more. You haven't been in control since you came back to Korea. I didn't come here tonight to make you happy.' She patted the clasp bag under one arm and glanced at Schwartz, still forcibly sharing Naz's chair, knife slicing a gash in her blouse.

Jung-hwa's gaze flickered back and forth between us, lover and husband, husband and lover.

'Fuck you. Fuck both of you.' She turned on her heel, then stopped, turned back, and looked at me through tear-smudged eyes:

'When you ran away, I was *pregnant.*' She swivelled and marched towards the exit, shouldering aside people twice her size. I felt like throwing up. Pregnant? How could I not have known?

'JUNG!'

Schwartz's scream coincided precisely with an abrupt break in the booming music. Heads all around us turned, but not Jung-hwa's. She held course for the exit, no falter in her stride. Tears already running down his cheeks, Schwartz raised both hands in the air, one still gripping the knife. This was Bobby's cue. He up-ended the table, drinks and all, and threw it at him.

Schwartz fell flat on his back taking Naz with him. He writhed and swung the knife in deadly, random slashes, any one of which could kill Naz. I plucked a spinning bottle from the floor and launched it at his head. It exploded next to his face, drawing blood, but still the knife swung in lethal arcs. Bobby reached down, gripped Naz by both wrists, and heaved her out of range of the slashing blade. Still on his back, squinting through a mask of streaming blood, Schwartz slashed out. I watched the tip of the blade slice through my trouser leg like a razor through paper.

All around us was the cacophony of mass panic as people scrambled away before, almost as one, they turned back to form a chaotic human ringside, still squealing with fear yet barely out of range of the flashing knife. A drunk westerner tumbled to the ground and through an upturned table leg, snapping it clean off. With one hand I heaved him up by the trouser belt and threw him aside with strength fed only by adrenalin. With the other hand, I picked up the broken table leg.

Schwartz kicked himself out from under the table and sprang to his feet, eyes burning like spotlights. With a full, two-handed blow I brought the table leg down on the arm that held the knife. Schwartz's forearm snapped like a breadstick, and with a dull thud the fat blade quivered in the underside of the upturned table. Above it, his arm hung like a bird's broken wing, yet his expression revealed no pain. Instead his eyes darted back and forth between me and the knife, measuring the distances and the options. He lunged downwards with his good hand.

In my mind's eye I watched basement beatings and near-drownings and thugs manhandling Naz and a tearful Min-tae with ugly red letters scrawled on his puffy little chest. And newspaper headlines and frenzied press conferences and wanted posters and Jung-hwa striding towards the King Club door. And Miss Hong, mutilated and naked, sightless almond eyes open to the chilled murk of the Han River.

I swung the table leg into his face hard enough to knock him off his feet. A red mist of blood and tooth shards sprayed from his mouth, spraying rainbows in the club lights and making the front row of rubber-neckers recoil. Then three hundred pounds of Sumo-man the bouncer hit Schwartz in a belly-flop dive that squashed him flat as a fossil.

I held the table leg in a grip that tied knots in my arms. Club lights gleamed in the dark pool of blood that grew around my foot. I twisted and craned my neck to look over the crowd, searching. *There*. Still with her back to us, Jung-hwa paused at the exit. I raised a hand and silently begged her to look around. Her shoulders swivelled and my heart stuttered. A chorus of oohs announced the arrival of four

American Military Policemen barrelling through the doorway, batons drawn, eyes wide, scouring the crowd for the 'GI' with the knife.

Beyond them Jung-hwa's slim frame merged into the neon-tinged night. She didn't look back.

Chapter Thirty-nine

Schwartz lay in a foetal curl, hands cuffed tight behind him, spectacularly broken wrist and all. So much blood frothed from his nose and mouth that he looked like he had stopped a runaway motorcycle with his face, yet he and I were the only victims of a few seconds of flailing violence that could have turned out so much worse. Blood from the neat slice in my calf flowed through slashed trouser fabric and seeped into my shoe so steadily that it squelched with every shift of weight.

As Myong-hee whispered urgently in my ear, paramedics sat me down and bandaged my leg painfully tight before trying to usher me towards a waiting ambulance. I knew the wound would never close without stitches, but I had been the centre of attention for long enough. When I raised my chin in the direction of the Gents' toilet, the nearest Military Policeman shrugged and I hobbled out of the limelight, one shoe laying a sticky red trail behind me.

I used to joke about spending so much money in the King Club that I should have shares in it, but right now the only proprietary interest I could draw upon was the insider knowledge born of a long-term drunk. One night I got so plastered that while searching for toilets visited a hundred times before, I staggered through an unmarked door and down a long corridor to a musty stairwell that spat me into a grotty alley adjoining Hooker Hill. Now, with a limp instead of a stagger, the same route took me onto a hillside full of milling clubbers and predatory hookers touting their services with only a hint more circumspection than I recalled from all those years ago.

I hoped that the relative darkness of the street would hide the bloody trouser leg, but failed to take into account shimmering neon and beaming bar façades that lit up the street almost as bright as day and drew me curious stares and pantomime elbow nudges. At the corner of Hooker Hill where Bobby and I once met a would-be Cavalryman with a felt hat clasped gently to his chest and a roadmap of childhood scars on his close-cropped head, the same pharmacy remained open, its utilitarian decor virtually unchanged. Someone had made a *lot* of money from all those years of late-night sales of rubbers and antibiotics to generations of hookers and their johns.

Across from the pharmacy, temporary food stalls stood in spots occupied nightly for decades, still dealing up the same local favourites as when I first spotted Jung-hwa attacking a bowl of fat noodles. A few metres uphill, an ugly four-storey structure clad in pink tiles stood where the ramshackle Cowboy Club used to buzz to records spun by Bobby's future wife Myong-hee.

Plus a change, plus c'est la même chose.

I needed a drink, preferably somewhere not too peaceful.

The Blues Room was only about one-third full, but Junior Kim and his band played to the sparse crowd as if in front of a packed Hollywood Bowl. As I walked past mostly empty tables and chairs to the same alcove I occupied with Jung-hwa only a few days before, they wrapped up *Honky Tonk Woman* with a jangling percussive bang before taking it w-a-y down to segue neatly into the 1920s classic *I'm Sitting on Top of the World*.

A blues anthem exists to suit every emotional condition, I thought – and this wasn't it.

I flopped into the alcove seat and sent a waitress scurrying for beer. When she returned I rebuffed her friendly offer to pour it for me. Only after she left did I regret being so abrupt with her. It wasn't her fault that I had fucked up again.

Jung-hwa was pregnant when I left Korea ten years ago, something I never heard even a murmur of until tonight. Would knowing then have changed anything? No matter what the answer to that might be, the time for such thoughts was long gone. Myong-hee's urgent whispers in the King Club had made that clear.

'You didn't know she was pregnant?'

'Of course I fucking didn't.'

'We didn't see her again for a long time after you went away.'

That did not surprise me. Never mind that by local standards Jung-hwa was rebellious in the extreme, Korea's conservative family traditions run deep, and the desire – even the *need* to marry and have children is a given. When I bailed out on her she was nearly thirty, almost an old maid by local standards. I remembered now that her parents were forcing her to attend 'introductions' – uncomfortable, contrived coffee shop sit-downs with suitors, two sets of parents hovering in the background assessing every aspect of their kids' suitability in what was a brutally practical exercise. Before they reached the meeting stage, candidates on both sides of the table were vetted according to family social standing, education, job and income; only after that were they brought together at a coffee shop to see if they 'clicked'. This callously pragmatic match-making system was alien to me back then, yet I knew it still went on.

Even then, a regimented society's old-fashioned customs led to crises that called for modern solutions. Every man's right to a virgin bride was so fundamental that surgical procedures to repair long-gone hymens were common-place, and stories were legion of sexually experienced brides having to fake wedding night trepidation in the clutches of fumbling virgin grooms.

I felt for the Korean men who turned up to coffee shop meetings in search of a chaste, virginal bride-to-be, eyes downcast, and found themselves across a table from Jung-hwa. We laughed about it later, but I remember being more sorry for the would-be grooms, and hardly giving any thought to the feelings of Jung-hwa.

Back in the King Club, I had asked Myong-hee the big question:

'What about the baby?'

She answered with the familiar hand-flapping motion that swept downwards from below her waistline. My heart sank.

'She had an abortion?'

'That's what I heard. She got very sick afterwards, then not much later she started going out with Ben and they got married very quickly. But she couldn't get pregnant, and I heard that Ben was angry about that.'

I thought I could now see how I ended up here and how Miss Hong ended up dead. Jung-hwa's words and actions – oh christ, the *actions* – flagged a miserable marriage, and Schwartz's hatred of me from day one was obvious. *'You'll do anything for money,'* he told me, and how right he was. The GDR gave him the chance to inflict upon me not only embarrassment but bankruptcy by luring me all the way from London for an illusory dream assignment.

He played me like a drum, right up until I bucked a lifelong trend and stood up for myself. I threatened to expose their fraud, and that was enough to cost Miss Hong her life. Never mind that the threat was empty, the danger it posed to the GDR was so real and the stakes so high that they forced Schwartz's hand. Now I had to live with the consequences.

I finished the beer and waved for a fresh one. The thought that this could be another long night flashed through my mind just as the door to the club flew open and two drunk Westerners stumbled through, laughing uncontrollably. In front of them came a startled Jung-hwa, in mid-leap from the glee that followed her. One or both of the bookish-looking drunks had groped her from behind.

I left the alcove at a hobbling run, except the straight line between me and the cluster at the door went by way of several tables and a couple of dozen chairs, some of them occupied. Empty chairs bounced aside, tables tipped and drinks spilled, customers yelped, their attention divided between the drama at the door and the new one that involved them and the lumbering idiot with one trouser leg soaked in blood. My mind was reeling. Did I misread Jung-hwa's anger at the bloody fracas that unfolded in front of her at the King Club and was she really here looking for me?

As if in a silent movie played to the band's spirited version of *Sweet Home Alabama,* Jung-hwa squared up to the two men, who waved contempt at her, much too drunk to be wary, too fired up on alcohol and testosterone to understand how far over the mark they had stepped. Such thoughts would normally be reserved for after the onset of tomorrow's hangover, but right now Jung-hwa had other ideas. She back-handed the leading drunk across the face, opening a gash on his cheekbone from the chunky ring she wore on her index finger. The fool tapped at the gash, looked at fingertips freshly smeared with his own blood, and raised the hand to slap her. Before it moved, the slim figure of The World's Most Low-Key Bouncer morphed from the shadows of his doorside lair and in a single fluid motion took the hand in a martial arts grip, spun the drunk around until he barged face-first into his friend – and fired them back out they way they had just arrived. Through intermittent gaps between wildly swinging doors, flickering violence played out like freeze frame snapshots as the two drunks' evening came to a painful close. This all played out to the tune of Junior Kim and the band drawing their song to a close.

Jung-hwa turned around to see me frozen in place, fists raised in the Tae Kwon-do ready stance, leading leg soaked in blood. One glance told me everything I needed to know, answered every question buzzing through my mind. It was a look filled with a rank mixture of surprise and rank derision. Whatever she was doing here, she certainly hadn't come looking for *me*.

For the second time in the space of an hour, she spun away from me and headed for the exit, leaving me speechless.

Onstage, Junior Kim peeled off a wailing pentatonic progression on his Fender before his band launched into the opening lines from the great Bobby Bland hit from the sixties, *I Pity the Fool*.

My waitress took me into her care, and like a kindly nurse leading a geriatric patient across the wide ward, sat me back down in the blood-smeared alcove. This time I let her pour my beer.